REA...
Love is...
Foreve... is Tricky

Love Is Simple;
Forever Is Tricky

CAS SIGERS

URBAN BOOKS

http://www.urbanbooks.net

This is a work of fiction. Any references or similarities to actual events, real people, living or dead, or to real locales are intended to give the novel a sense of reality. Any similarity in other names, characters, places, and incidents is entirely coincidental.

URBAN SOUL is published by

Urban Books
1199 Straight Path
West Babylon, NY 11704

ISBN-13: 978-1-59983-035-3
ISBN-10: 1-59983-035-3

First Printing: January 2008

10 9 8 7 6 5 4 3 2 1

Printed in the United States of America

PROLOGUE

Last year this time, I was living in Virginia, thinking it might be my last Christmas. If only I could take all sixteen pills I was holding in my hand, my misery would be over. Battling a stint in an alcoholic clinic, I was struggling to put the pieces of my life back together. I had lost contact with all my friends, and my ex-boyfriend was just coming out of a coma from a car accident I witnessed first hand.

However, this Chistmas I am now a mother and in a relationship with a man who adores me. I'm truly happy for the first time in seven years. It's taken a lot of work and trust, and more faith than I thought I possessed. It's amazing how one year can change a lifetime. Here's the one that changed mine.

1

Inside an empty two-bedroom condominium on the third floor of the Riverfront, the smell of freshly painted walls breezes through. In the bedroom are two large boxes—one marked MEMORIES and the other marked JUNK. The brand-new silver-and-black appliances are luminous; not a single fingerprint is in the place. Suddenly, the cracked door flings open and two burly men in gray jumpsuits march in, carrying a cozy, modern rust-colored love seat. With a yellow notepad in my hand, I follow closely behind, direct the gentlemen as to where to place the sofa, and check off my diagram as the men bring in each piece of furniture. One bar and stools, one chair, a television stand, one armoire and one bed later, I finally collapse face forward across the bare mattress, prop my chin on the edge of the bed frame and peer around the bedroom.

"Time to get it together," I whisper to myself.

There was a terrible accident three years ago that changed my life. It left my ex-boyfriend Omar Kirkland slightly paralyzed, sentenced his brother Tracy to two months of defensive driving school, and finally jerked me from my denial. I was an alcoholic spiraling out of control. I immediately left Omar in New York, and checked into a clinic in Richmond, Virginia.

Omar felt I deserted him in his time of need. He hated me for it and still does to this day.

"Time to get it together," I whisper, louder, while staring at the textured ceiling. Yet, an hour passes before I actually move from this spot on the bed and begin to unpack, a rather short process for I only have ten items of clothing to hang in the closet. Unintentionally, yet gratefully, I lost forty-eight pounds, bringing my five-foot seven-inch frame from a plump 189 pounds to a svelte 141.

"Mental note: I must go shopping this week."

Fumbling through the huge cardboard construction, I pull out several miscellaneous items from the box marked JUNK. A couple of books, an unfinished cross-stitch project, a cell phone and some old VHS tapes are amongst the stuff to be thrown out. Moving to the box marked MEMORIES, I softly lay my head against its corner and cradle the cardboard like a lover. I dig into the memory box, pull out a few candles, some jewelry and a photo album. Wrapped in a blanket, I flip through the pages, chuckling and laughing at all of the silly pictures I've managed to collect over the years. I place the books back into the box and push the box into the spare bed-room closet.

"I need a bookshelf," I murmur, looking around the room. I also need a floor rug, shower curtain, comforter, lamps, mirror, plants, alarm clock, coffeemaker and a blender."

I trot back into the bedroom, grab my hat, shades and purse. After sliding into my flip-flops, I leave for three hours, then return with four large bags. Immediately, I drop the bags in the kitchen and rush to the bathroom. Sitting on the cold toilet, I stare at my feet.

"Oh, my God, I need a pedicure."

I've never been one for things like manicures or pedicures, but in the past year, I've made many changes—one adjust-ment being a desire for feminine grooming.

"Caring for your body starts within, but we should never

neglect our outside for it's what we see every day, and if we don't see a beautiful reflection, it's very easy to feel ugly," my counselor at the clinic said.

Chuckling, I take the largest bag, from Macy's, and dump it on the bed. Quickly, I strip down to my underwear and try on each item. Prancing back and forth, I walk from the bedroom to the living room and back to the bedroom. Lastly, I try on a fitted maroon wrap dress.

"This is it!" I yell. Turning my rear to face the mirror and stretching my body around to see, I check out my reflection from behind. "This is definitely it." Ten minutes later, I'm enjoying my hot shower. With Prince playing in the background, I get ready to go out.

I haven't been out in years and haven't seen my friends since before the accident. So tonight everyone will be surprised at the new and improved Gwendolyn Pharr.

At 10:00 P.M., the cabdriver lets me out at the corner of Bragg and Tenth.

"Ole Skool," I whisper, and with a confident nod, I slowly walk up to the huge bouncer standing at the door. Shyly, I tap him on his side. Without looking at me, he responds. "The line starts back there."

Shocked that he didn't even turn to acknowledge me, I raise my voice and sass.

"Moo Moo, don't point me to the back of the line."

Suddenly, the six-four, 242-pound male whips around and cuddles me like a newborn.

"Gwen!" he calls out. He picks me up and twirls me around. Steadily, I hold my dress down; his rapid turns are exposing my booty cheeks.

"We have missed you. We missed you so much," he says, placing his enormous face against my tiny cheek.

"I have missed you guys too."

"No one told me you were coming . . . wow! You look so . . . little," he comments.

"Thank you. I wanted to surprise everyone. Who's here?"

"The normal gang. We got a new bartender, though."

"What happened to Ralph?"

"Arrested. Possession."

"Oh no! He should have known better. We all tried to tell him."

Nodding, Moo Moo agrees. "Go on in," he says, lifting the rope for me to pass under. "I think Rome is in the back."

I give him a quick hug and walk into the club. The atmosphere is lighter than it was a couple of years ago. The sconces have been replaced with track lighting and the dance floor has lighting along its edge.

"I bet that was Lia's idea," I say with a chuckle. "I wonder where she is."

Lia McNair is my only female friend. She is part of the gang that Moo Moo spoke about earlier. She is footloose and fancy-free and her life always embodies chaos. She is a bit insecure, and though she's very pretty with a petite frame, Lia needs constant validation. I find that most women are like this, which is why I only have one female friend. Lia works for an advertising company. It pays a great salary and Lia spends most of it shopping. And, if she is not in the malls, she is out on dates. Hardly ever spending an evening alone, she keeps a steady, but always has a couple of candidates on the side.

I continue to canvass the crowd in search of familiar faces, noticing a few regulars and speaking to a few of the new waitresses. Suddenly, I hear a familiar voice over by the pool tables. I look over and see Rome leaning over to take a shot. Rome is my dearest male friend. We've had a couple of romantic encounters, but he's one of those guys you don't try and tie down. It would be a big waste of time.

Slowly, I walk toward the table, but halt when I see a long-legged young woman come up behind Rome. As she distracts

Rome, he misses his shot. While stroking his back with her right hand, she wraps her left fingers around his pool stick and slowly slides her hands up and down his pole. Rome gives her a suggestive look as she rubs her leg against his and slowly saunters away. She glances over her shoulder and winks as he watches her walk toward the back lounge area.

"Groupies," I whisper.

I quickly walk through the crowd and stand at the end of the table where he just made his shot.

Startled, Rome rushes over, grabs me by my waist and hoists me in the air. He nearly falls off balance with excitement.

"When did you get here?"

"Yesterday."

Rome places me down by the chair and rubs his hand across my face.

Staring intently, he speaks. "You look amazing." Smiling from ear to ear, I pose, turning right and left, and pose again.

"It's me, in the flesh."

Rome hugs me one more time, yet I nudge him off, taunting. "I see the old dog is still up to his tricks."

Rome moves in close to my ear and whispers, "Woof!"

Chuckling, I move a step back and sit in the chair.

"I missed you," I say.

"I missed you more. C'mon, let's go to the office. We can't talk out here."

Quickly, he unlocks the door and rushes in. After moving the stack of papers from the desk seat, he leans against the desk corner.

"What in the hell happened to this place?" I ask, looking at scattered papers everywhere. "Who's been doing the books?"

"Lia."

"Lia!" I shout. "Lia can't balance her own checkbook, I know she can't run this place."

"She's good at keeping the money straight—she's just not good at organizing."

"I got her e-mails updating me on the club's status, but I had no idea she was doing the accounting."

I hop up and immediately begin going through the paperwork. Moving one pile, I place it on top of the file cabinet and begin looking through the set of papers in front of me. Rome attempts to remove the papers from my hand and make me relax.

"Stop it! You just got here. Relax!"

"There's no time to relax, look at this place. Did you file taxes this year? Where are the returns from last year?"

"Be still," he says, grabbing both of my arms and placing them by my side.

Rome moves close to me and stares into my eyes.

"Are you all right?"

I slowly nod my head while peering at him.

"I need to hear an answer," he comments.

"I'm fine."

"Are you sure?"

Removing my hands from within his, I take a step back. "I said I'm fine. I know I've been gone and I appreciate you letting me be a silent partner for the last three years but I'm back now."

Rome hops onto the desk and motions for me to come closer.

"Your eyes say something is wrong."

I look away while answering. "This place just holds so many memories. It's hard, you know. But I'll be okay."

"I wasn't sure you were coming back."

"At times, I wasn't sure, but I helped build this place. I had to come back. This is our place, right? Our dream to own a successful nightclub," I ramble while walking through the office. Then I pick up a picture of Omar, Rome and me.

"The Three Stooges." I smile and then take a brief pause before asking, "Have you talked to him?"

"Once, right after he came out of the coma. He didn't want

to talk, said he was still mad about that old bullshit we got into before he moved to New York. You talked to him?"

"I tried, but he wouldn't take my calls. He said I abandoned him in his time of need and that he never wanted to talk to me again."

"Damn. I can't believe I haven't seen you in three years."

"I didn't plan on being gone this long, I just didn't know how to deal with everything. I needed that time I spent in Virginia."

Slowly rubbing my shoulders, he responds. "If it's too soon, it's okay. Maybe the club isn't the place for you to be."

Whipping around, I angrily ask, "Why would you say that, Rome?"

"I . . . mean, with everything . . . you know."

"Know what?"

"The drinking. This isn't the best place for someone with . . . with a . . . well, someone who stopped drinking."

Defiantly, I step back and retort, "I don't have a drinking problem . . . not anymore. I was in the program for a year. I stayed in Virginia because of my depression, which I got from being in the program. But this club is a part of my life, and I wanted to come back." Sadly, I pause and look up at Rome before continuing. "You don't want me working here?" I softly question.

"Of course I do," Rome states. "I just want you to be happy."

"Then let's end this conversation."

Raising his hands in the air to indicate defeat, Rome moves closer.

"Fine, let's start a new conversation. You are looking incredible in that little dress and I love your hair. You look like a new Gwen." He flirts.

Ignoring his flirtatious remarks, I place a stack of papers between our bodies.

"How about you help me clean up this office. I don't see how either one of you can get any work done here."

Rome tries to move the papers away and tickles my sides. Giggling, I move behind the desk so that he can't get to me. Playfully, he chases me around the desk until there is a knock on the door. Suddenly, we both stop. Abruptly, there is another knock. From outside the door, a soft, girly voice hollers, "Open this door, Rome."

"What do you want, Lia?" he calls out.

I quickly motion for him not to inform Lia that I'm in the room.

"Look, I don't care what or who you are doing. Open this door, my hands are full."

"Wait a minute," Rome says, laughing quietly.

"Open it now," Lia yells while kicking the bottom of the door.

"Didn't he say wait a minute?" I shout in a disguised voice.

Agitated, Lia hollers back. "Oh no, ma'am, you don't talk to me like that." She continues to yell through the door while searching for her keys. "Rome, whoever that is, you might want to set her straight before I get in there."

"Bitch, I ain't scared of you," I yell while chuckling underneath my breath.

Lia finally gets the door open. "I got your bitch," she says, swinging her purse in the air and holding food in her other hand.

"Oh yeah," I say, coming from behind the door. Lia spins around, charged and ready to aim, but to her amazement, she sees me. Frantically, Lia jumps up and down and into my arms. She drops the bags of food on the floor.

"Oh, my God! Oh, my God! It's you!" Lia screams, holding me tight around the neck. "I missed you, Gwenie. I missed you!"

"I should let you two catch up," Rome says while picking his food up from the floor.

"The food. I'm sorry."

"It's okay, finish hugging your friend. I got it."

Rome places the food on the desk, kisses me on the cheek and leaves us to catch up. Lia leads me to the chair, sits down and pulls up a stool.

"You lost so much weight. You look really good!" she says.

"Well, did I look that bad before?"

"No. But now, you look almost as good as me."

Lia stands up and shimmies her full-C cups while gyrating her hips from side to side. I laugh, lean over and push her back into her seat. Giggling, she sits and oddly stares.

"What?" I ask.

Lia places her hand against my face and continues to gawk.

"Stop staring at me."

"I'm sorry, I just can't get over it. The last time I saw you in the clinic, you didn't look so good. The doctors said that you had gotten a hold of some pills and that you overdosed. I didn't know what to think," Lia sadly expresses.

"I never wanted to kill myself, but the therapy and the counseling groups got to me. I kept blaming myself for the accident, and Omar was still in the coma at that time. I thought he was going to die."

"I know," she softly consoles.

"To stop drinking was one thing, but to deal with the reality was just too much. I just wanted to escape."

"So you've officially stopped drinking?" Lia asks with a smile.

"Two years, six months and two weeks," I proudly testify.

"Good. I'm going to stop drinking too," Lia comments.

I look on with doubt.

"I am. Friends have to support each other. If you aren't drinking, I am not drinking."

"That means no drinking, period—not just around me."

Lia pauses and scratches her temple, then responds. "Cool. No drinking, period." She extends her hand and gives me a firm shake.

"I missed you, girl."

"I missed you too," says Lia. "Where are you staying?"

"I got an apartment at the Riverfront."

"Very nice. I must come see it this weekend."

I stand and give Lia a long hug. Lia, smiling, pulls me toward the door.

"Where are we going? I have to clean up, I can't leave this mess here," I comment.

"Please, this looks good. You should have seen it last week. Besides, you just got here, let's have some fun before you start working."

Sighing, I follow Lia out of the office and into the lounge area.

"I want you to meet my friend," she says as we walk up to a tall, handsome, bald gentleman. "This is my best friend, Gwen. Gwen, this is Rob."

The man takes my hand and kisses it.

"My pleasure." He speaks in a baritone voice.

"Same," I respond.

I pull Lia to the side. "Is this your man?"

"No, we've gone out a couple of times. We haven't had sex or anything."

"Good."

"But we might do it tonight." Lia winks.

I shake my head with strong disagreement. "What about—" I ask before being interrupted by Rob.

"Excuse me. Lia, I'll be over here when you're ready. Nice to meet you, Gwen."

"Yeah, you too," I quickly reply.

Lia softly covers my mouth with her hand. "Shh! I'll tell you all about it later. Right now, my date is waiting." Lia and I hug again. "I'm so glad you are back. Call me in the morning. We have to do lunch tomorrow."

Before her sentence is complete, Lia is whisking her way through the crowd to meet her date. Standing in the center of the dance floor, I begin rolling with laughter. True, I haven't seen my best friend in almost three years and yet she ditches me for a date. I wouldn't expect anything else from Lia McNair.

After a few minutes, I find Rome flirting with the young woman from the pool table. Strutting over to him, I rudely interrupt their conversation.

"Excuse me. Rome, I'm out."

"Okay, but I don't have your numbers."

"I don't have a phone yet. I'm staying at the Riverfront. I'm getting a cell tomorrow." Rome moves away from the woman and pulls a card from his back pocket.

"Here's my cell. Call me tomorrow so that we can go to lunch."

"I'm going to lunch with Lia."

"Just call me," he says.

Rome leans over and kisses my cheek.

"Oh, I forgot. I don't have a car either. I took a cab here."

Laughing, Rome walks closer to me and responds. "Are you trying to borrow my car?"

"That would be nice. You still have Macy, right? I could get Lia to bring me over tomorrow."

"Are you crazy? I preserve Macy for car shows. Here. Take the BMW. I'll drive the pickup. Your license is straight, right?"

"Yes, Rome," I say grudgingly.

"It's parked around back. I'll have Rashelle take me home—"

"Who's Rashelle?" I interrupt.

"My girl right there." Rome motions.

I look over his shoulder and make a funny face.

"You sure," I ask, batting my eyes.

"I'm sure that was your plan all along," he comments.

I smile, suggesting he's exactly right.

"Get home safe," Rome says, kissing my forehead.

"Thanks," I say before trotting away.

I go to the back, click the alarm on the key chain and a

silver BMW 525 lights up. I dance over to the car, get in and crank it up. Immediately, I have to turn down Jay-Z blasting through the speaker system.

"Damn, Rome, are you deaf?" I say to the speaker system. About fifteen minutes later, I hear a phone ringing in the car. Searching the seat and the floor, I realize the ringing is coming from the cubby between the seats. I open the top and retrieve the phone. Upon checking the caller ID, I see that it is the number from the club. Quickly, I answer.

"Are you home?" Rome asks.

"I just pulled up, stay on the phone with me while I go in."

I get out of the car, lock the door and walk into the elevator. Of course the phone cuts off. Once I walk in my door, Rome is calling me again.

"Is everything okay? Do I need to come over there?"

"No, I'm fine. I'm home now. I'll call you tomorrow."

"Call me if you need anything," he states.

"I will. Thanks."

"Good night," he says before hanging up.

I remove my clothing and put on a nightgown. Grabbing my blanket from the bed, I walk into the living room, check the locks on the front door and lie down on the sofa. At first, I'm unable to fall asleep. Then I rise and put on the Prince CD from earlier, and before long, Prince and the New Power Generation are singing me to sleep. Slowly, I drift off and don't awaken until ten o'clock the next morning when Rome's cell phone starts ringing. Disquieting my rest, I pop up, nearly falling off the couch. Still wrapped in the blanket, I hop over to the bar where I left the phone. Thinking it's Rome, I answer, "Hey, babe."

"Who is this?" says the island-accented female.

"I'm sorry. This is Gwen."

"Who?"

"I—I'm a friend of Rome's. He let me borrow his cell phone."

"Well, this is Frieda, I'm also a friend. I guess you are the reason why he stood me up last night. Tell him, don't bother calling me again," she says with a hint of anger.

I don't try to explain. After seconds of silence, the young lady hangs up. Wrapped in the cover, I hop back to the sofa and call Rome, but he doesn't answer. Lying back down, I try to remember Lia's cell phone number. However, after two wrong numbers, I scroll down Rome's phone Rolodex to find the number for Lia. She is the first number in his recent call list. Lia answers on the first ring.

"Yes, dear Rome, what do you want?"

"It's me, Lia," I respond.

"Hey, what are you and Rome doing?"

"Nothing. I have his phone. Are we still going to lunch, 'cause I need to go get a phone today. Where are you, anyway?"

"Don't worry about where I am," Lia responds.

"I take it you are somewhere you aren't supposed to be. Come pick me up."

"From where?"

"Home. I'm on the third floor, 302," I reply.

"Yeah, yeah. The Riverfront, right?"

"Right. What time?" I ask.

"One."

"Good. See you then."

I hang up, walk into the kitchen and stare into the empty fridge.

"I'm hungry. I don't want to wait until one to eat."

I put on music, walk into the bedroom and begin to prepare my day. Flipping my hands between the hangers, I pull out a pair of black pants and a melon-colored fitted T-shirt. Holding the outfit up, I walk to the mirror.

"This is cute," I state.

Laying the clothing on my bed, I grab a pair of panties and a bra and look at all four items. This is normal routine for me; everything must be examined and strategically planned. Once

I lost weight, I discovered all the cute-colored panties that come in small sizes. Since then, my underwear must not only match each other, but also match the outfit. Lastly, I place a pair of black strappy shoes by the bed. Pausing, I look at the shoes, then at my feet.

"A pedicure, I still need a pedicure." Sighing, I replace the open-toe pair with black mules. "This is better," I respond aloud.

I step into the steamy, hot shower, and moments later, I am refreshed. I walk downstairs to grab a bagel from the cafe, one block down the street, before I will head to my therapist. It's my second appointment. I believe it's helping.

I eat my cinnamon raisin bagel and chase it with a black coffee while sitting at a table in front of the cafe.

"I can't believe I actually like this stuff," I say to the pigeon sitting on my table.

The pigeon tilts its head sideways as if he understands, and I, in turn, tilt my head as if I understand his morning issue. I then laugh quietly underneath my breath and finish my drink. Coffee drinking is a new habit for me; I only took it up after I stopped drinking alcohol. It started as a gradual tendency; however, it is now part of my everyday routine. My day doesn't start until I've had a cup of black coffee. Taking in a deep breath, I let out a cough. My system needs time to readjust to Detroit's dirt particles. I continue to clear my throat, and the cell rings. This time, I check the caller ID before answering. It is Rome.

"Yes, dear."

"I saw you called. Whatcha need?"

"Who says I need anything, I could have called to see what you were doing."

"I just got up."

"Are we still going to lunch?" he asks.

"No, I told you. We are going to dinner. I'm having lunch with Lia."

"Fine."

"Oh, Frieda called," I tell him.

"She left a message?" he asks.

"Yep. She said never bother calling her again. You stood her up last night."

"Oh yeah, I forgot. I'll send her flowers and a gift. She'll be all right by the weekend."

"You are pitiful. Where do you find these dumb-ass women?"

"They aren't dumb. They just love what I give them. Don't act like you forgot."

I purposely avoid his snide comment. "I don't know about dinner out. Let's do something at your house."

"You want me to cook?" he asks with skepticism.

"Of course not. I'll go shopping and come over to your place and cook."

"Oh, that sounds like a plan. You need money?"

"No, I'm cool," I state.

"You sure. How are you getting money?"

"Don't worry about that. I'll let you know when I need something. By the way, I need to use your car for a while. I have some money saved, but I don't want to buy a new car with it."

"I may need my car."

"C'mon, Rome. You have a truck and the Mustang."

"I told you, I only put Macy in car shows. I don't drive her on these raggedy Detroit streets."

"Please, I'll pay you," I comment.

"We'll talk over dinner."

"Cool. See you tonight."

"Tonight," he concurs.

I toss my trash in the can, nod *bye* to the pigeon and walk across the street. Before I can completely cross, the phone rings again. This time, I answer it immediately, thinking it is Rome, and keep walking.

"Yes."

"Who's this?" says the male.

"Who's this?" I say.

"This is Lucas."

"This is Gwen."

"The infamous Gwen? I've heard so much about you."

"Who are you again?" I ask.

"This is Lucas. I'm one of Rome's boys."

"I know all of his boys. How come I don't know you?"

"I just moved here a year ago. You were away."

"Oh," I say, pausing.

"So when will we meet?" Lucas asks.

"I don't know. I'm sure I'll see you at the club."

"Yeah, I'll be there later this week," Lucas comments.

"I'll look for you," I respond.

"Bet."

"I'll tell Rome you called," I say, and hang up.

I enter my therapist's office.

Meanwhile, Lia is on the other side of town at her home, desperately trying to get her date to leave. It was so late when she finally left the club that she invited him to stay. Originally, she had plans to sleep with him. However, last night, he got so comfortable that he removed his socks. When she took a good look at his feet, she decided sex with this man was never going to happen. Lia McNair is exceedingly picky. Sure, smelly underarms, bad breath and bad manners are normal social turnoffs. Yet, Lia will dump a *GQ* model if he happens to have chapped lips in the dead of winter. She feels that if she takes the time to always look perfect, then her dates should too. Ridiculous defense, yet it is one of the foibles that makes her Lia.

She walks into her kitchen and sees her date drinking apple juice. He gulps while he drinks, another major disgust. "Listen, I have an early lunch. I really have to get out of here."

"Oh, okay. Well, I have to go, anyway. Can I see you later tonight?" he asks, trying to grab her waist.

Lia squirms her way from within his arms.

"You know what, I think I am busy tonight, and I know I am busy tomorrow night. I can call you, though." Pausing his flirtations, Rob looks at Lia. "What's wrong?"

Lia walks into the dining area and sighs. "Nothing. I just don't want to lead you on."

"What are you talking about? We are dating, getting to know each other. We haven't even done anything yet."

"Exactly. And if we keep seeing each other every day, then it may lead to more of a commitment than I actually want. I just don't have time for anything serious."

"I am not asking for anything serious. Just the other day, you said you wanted to start seeing more of me. Even last night, you were hinting around like you wanted to be intimate, and then you just flipped the script and went to bed. What is wrong with you?" Rob asks, flustered.

With a disgruntled face, Lia folds her arms, turns to him and responds. "It's your feet. I can't stand your feet."

"My feet?" he asks.

"Yes, they're scaly and bumpy. You have two warts and your toenails are out of control. I don't mind the hair on top of the foot—that can be waxed—but your heels look like gravel. I can only imagine how they feel," Lia says, shivering her shoulders as if she is trying to envision.

Dumbfounded, Rob looks at her expression with disbelief.

"I'm sorry. They turn me off."

"My feet turn you off?" Rob asks, still in doubt.

"Yes," Lia says dramatically, before turning away from him.

Rob walks out of the kitchen, grabs his shirt from the couch and places it on. Lia remains silent as he passes her. He puts on his shoes and heads for the door.

"They told me you were crazy and I told them you were too fine to be crazy. I guess I was wrong."

Lia quickly questions, "Who are *they*?"

LIA
Session One

I met Lia Oshun McNair when I worked for Shefland & Associates. Lia worked for our sister company. I was over specialty liquors and my client was doing a huge print campaign. Lia was in sales. Her job was to nego- tiate ad prices. She and I met over lunch and, honestly, it wasn't instant chemistry. I thought she was strange. Not in a quirky, cute way, but in a "single white female" way, the urban version. She just had a crazy stare in her eyes as she complimented me on everything from my hair to my shoes. I now realize that it's just the way she tries to make friends. I believe all of her compliments are sincere. She simply overdoes it. Lia seeks out all of the good and delivers it in the first fifteen minutes of conversation. People read it as fake, or crazy, like I did.

Anyway, because of the great deal Lia negotiated, our client decided to do a series of three different layouts. We came up with several hot concepts. I remember the ads were in black and white, but the liquor bottle was red and gold. Lia kept calling me to say how much she loved the ads and that she hoped we could work together more. When she found out that I was doing something at Detroit Nights, she mentioned Rome. They were friends. I saw her a couple of nights at the club, and she took me home one night when I was drunk. I was supposed to be there working, but I was drinking, and she never said anything to my superiors. I thanked her over lunch, and after that, we started going to lunch on the regular.

In no time, her infectious, childlike spirit took hold. Lia is the epitome of spontaneity, a trait I wasn't born with and couldn't understand. I'm a planner. She would meet someone on Wednesday, and rendezvous with them by the weekend. Her life seemed like fiction. I didn't get the whole bisexual thing, but as long as she wasn't hitting on me, I didn't care. Ironically, the more she talked about sex, the closer we became. I was not that active, but her exploits often mirrored my drinking escapades. I didn't make an excuse for my overconsumption and she didn't make one for her outre sexual behavior. We both knew that our behavior was risky, but we needed it. It's how we coped with everything. I asked her once if she ever felt like a slut, like her partners thought of her as just a piece of meat. By this time, we were close and I felt she would give me an honest answer. She told me that most times she didn't feel anything. She said that each time she lay with someone, she would secretly hope that this would be the one who made her actually feel an ounce of passion. In a later conversation, she made quick mention that her first sexual experience was with her mother's boyfriend. She was thirteen at the time and they secretly had an affair for three years. Yet, I don't know if "affair" was Lia's code for molestation or if she actually welcomed it. That's the thing with Lia—you never know what she's thinking. It's something about her eyes. But she's the most giving, sincere person you ever want to meet. As selfish as she is, she's the type of person that would sacrifice her life for a stranger in need, like a walking double standard. Always in good spirits, Lia has a dirty joke for every occasion. She could be a part-time truck driver and perfectly fit in. I fell in love with her candor. I envy it and all of her dramatics. I was never one to vent, rant or cause a scene, but Lia could and would at the drop of a hat. She said she desired my serenity. So we hung out more, just to soak up some of what we each lacked. I saw her frankness as someone with courage, and she looked at my calmness as a person of control. Funny, we had neither. I wasn't in control and she wasn't brave and we both knew it. Yet, we constantly applauded each other for

*strengths we didn't have and that's because we em-
pathized with the other's vulnerability, and to flat out
speak truth and say "yeah, we're both screwed up" would
only make things worse. I know it sounds dysfunctional,
but isn't dysfunction the basis of all lasting friendships?
If two people are perfect and never truly need the other
for anything, time normally separates them. But that
won't happen with us. The lies we say to each other's face
hearten us to actually face the truth. Not many people get
that, but she does, and that's why she's my friend.*

Session Done

The morning passes quickly, and before I can finish pro-
gramming all of my cable channels, Lia is downstairs ringing
my buzzer. I go down to meet her.

Lia hops into her silver SLK 280 and she bobs back and
forth to the 808 bass. Her convertible's stereo is blaring.

"You still listen to hip-hop? Don't you think you are a little
old for that, Lia?"

"Nope. I like hip-hop. You need to relax."

"I am relaxed," I say, rolling my neck around and lying
back in the seat.

With my peripherals, I see Lia dancing about in her seat.
As we approach a light, it turns yellow. Lia speeds up to go
through the light just as I yell.

"Lia! Stop!"

Lia slams on the brakes and the car slides through the
intersection.

"What?" Lia says as she snaps around.

"The light was red."

"It was yellow, not red," Lia says with much agitation. "Do
not yell like that. I thought something was wrong."

Extremely petulant, I look out the window in silence.

"I'm sorry," Lia apologizes.

I'm still quiet.

"You can't yell like that, it makes me nervous. I'm a very careful driver."

I slowly turn to her and respond. "I just . . . I get edgy at times. I didn't mean to scare you."

Lia leans over and rubs my leg. "I know," she says softly.

The remainder of the ride is quiet until Lia pulls up into the parking lot of my favorite Italian restaurant.

"Yeah, this place is still here," I say, clapping my hands like a child.

Lia and I walk in and enjoy a very delectable lunch. Although I can tell Lia wants to discuss my treatment, she doesn't bring it up. She doesn't know how I will respond and she wants it to be a peaceful lunch. Therefore, we simply eat our food and smile a lot. I occasionally ask Lia about her stable of dates.

Afterward, we go to Bed Bath & Beyond for towels, sheets, and various household necessities. Then we head to Verizon to purchase a phone. This worrisome cellular ordeal almost takes as long as our dining process. I call and give out my new number, and then Lia and I get back to the apartment. Lia is tired and ready to return home, or so this is what she tells me. In reality, she decides to go visiting.

Back in her car, reaching in her purse, she pulls out her cell and dials her friend. "What are you doing?" Lia immediately asks.

"Trying to get some rest, I had a late evening," says her friend.

"Well, I'm coming over," Lia responds.

"No . . . I'm tired."

"Too late, I'm pulling up to your building right now."

Seconds later, Lia pulls in front of a three-story brick building with a dark green awning. She walks in and greets the doorman with a pleasant kiss.

"*Hola,* Senor Gomez."

"*Hola,* Senorita Lia," he responds.

She whisks past the desk, gets on the elevator and goes to 222. Lia impatiently knocks on the door. A minute later, a tall young woman answers. She poses with her right elbow against the frame and her left hand on her hip. Lia looks her up and down.

"May I help you?" she asks.

Lia, quiet, folds her arms and stares at the woman, who wears a sports bra and jogging pants.

"What do you want?" she questions again.

Indignantly, Lia responds, "Your man."

The young woman slams the door in Lia's face. Lia furiously bangs on the door while yelling. "Open this door. I'm going to kick it down if you don't open it."

Seconds later, the young woman opens the door again. This time, she wears boy-cut panties to complement the black sports bra. With a furtive smile, she poses the same question. "May I help you?"

Lia begins to grin as she takes a step closer to the woman, whose name is Jasmine.

"Of course you can," Lia responds.

Lia leans in and kisses Jasmine's neck. Jasmine places her hand around Lia's back, pulls her into the apartment and closes the door behind them. Lia lovingly looks upon Jasmine. As Jasmine strips her underwear off, Lia gazes at her from head to toe.

"Now, that's what I call perfection," Lia says softly.

Jasmine slowly walks over to Lia, stands her up, removes her shirt and caresses her hands against Lia's body. Although last night was a disappointment for Lia, this afternoon delight never disenchants. For six years, Lia and Jasmine have had an on-again, off-again relationship. And although they are currently off, today they decide to get it on. Two twenty-two Flint Street could tell stories that would make a sailor blush, and today is just another day in its journal.

* * *

As for 302 Riverfront, the only tossing and turning it will see is my horrible sleep patterns, due to my incessant nightmares. This afternoon is no different. I sleep for twelve minutes before they start. Ever since the accident, I rarely make it through a night's sleep. I often dream about Omar and the accident, but this afternoon, I dream that I'm watching a dogfight in a neighborhood alley. Suddenly, the dogs brutally turn against the spectators and begin to rip their skin from the bones. I watch in fear just as a dog leaps to my face and pulls me to the ground. As my dreaming continues, I violently kick and moan until I've removed all of the covering from my bed. Abruptly, I wake up, dazed, and look around the room.

"No, no, no," I moan. "I'm tired and I want to sleep." I walk into the bathroom, open the medicine cabinet, turn all of the items to face forward and remove the Tylenol PM. Taking two pills, I grab a blanket and lie down on the couch.

"Let's see what's on television."

Flipping through the channels, I land on a talk show and quickly fall back asleep. Three hours pass before I awaken. This time, my sleep interruption is due to the incessant ringing of my cell phone. Moaning, I roll off the couch and crawl over to my purse that sits by the door.

"Hello."

"What are you doing?" asks Rome.

"Sleeping."

"Wake up. I'm hungry. What time are you coming over?"

I look around the room for the time, but soon realize I have no clock.

"What time is it?" I ask.

"Six-thirty," Rome answers.

"I slept longer than I planned. I'll go to the grocery store and be at your house before eight."

Sighing, Rome doesn't respond.

"Do not eat before I get there. It will spoil what I'm cooking," I tell him.

"But I'm hungry," Rome says, gobbling food in his mouth.

"Stop eating that Twinkie," I say accusingly.

"What are you talking about?" he responds innocently.

"The Twinkie in your mouth. I hear you chewing."

"Fine. Hurry up and get over here. How did you know?"

"I know you," I say before ending the conversation. By 7:45 P.M., I'm pulling into Rome's driveway. He helps me with the bags and I immediately begin cooking.

"I really miss this," says Rome.

"What? None of your numerous women cook for you?"

"Not really. A few of them have occasionally, but most of the time, I eat out."

"Well, you should take better care of your body."

"You're back now, so I'll let you start on that." He responds with a wink, which I ignore while looking the other way.

"I finished school while you were gone. Finally got that video and film degree," Rome continues.

"I am very proud of you. I really didn't think you would finish school."

"I told you I was, and remember those young cats that used to perform at the club on Saturday, In Tune?"

I nod.

"Well, they got a record deal, and asked me to do their video. I've done eight videos since, and the budgets keep getting bigger. I really like doing this."

"You have had fifteen careers since I've known you. You've never been able to commit to one thing . . . or one woman for that matter."

Rome laughs as he walks into the kitchen to peruse my proposed menu.

"Well, you've known me way over twenty years, so I don't think that's fair," he responds.

"First you were a catalogue model, and then I remember when you rebelled against being a pretty boy and wanted to become a boxer. We all thought you were crazy, but when you wanted to be a stuntman, the insanity was confirmed. So I figured film school was just another whim."

"Ha! I fooled you."

Smiling, I retort, "You truly did."

"Did I tell you how much I like your new hair?" he says, running his hands through the back of the short flip.

"Thanks. I've never had short hair before. I think it works," I say, tossing my head back and forth.

With a flirtatious grin, Rome comments, "It sure works for me."

Hiding my giggle, I finish the chicken and place it on top of the noodles and vegetables.

"Let's eat. Make yourself useful and grab a plate."

During dinner, Rome and I catch up on the drama at the club. I make sure to give him his cell as he gives me the 411 on everyone from Moo Moo catching his wife with another man to Ralph's arrest. I laugh hysterically while trying to chew my food.

"There is something different about you," states Rome.

"What are you saying? I'm the same old Gwen, just a few pounds lighter."

"No, there is something more womanly about you. It's not just your hair or the weight, it's something else."

"I'm wearing lip gloss," I respond.

"No, it's nothing you have on. I've seen you in lip gloss. It's that you are glowing."

Shyly, I look away from the table.

"I'm serious. You look beautiful."

"Please, Rome, your lines don't work on me. They never did."

Laughing, Rome takes a sip of the cider and comments, "Oh, but I do remember a time when they did work."

"Oh please! If you are talking about our little one-night stand years ago, that doesn't count. I was drunk."

"You weren't that drunk."

"Yes, I was. Besides, I don't even remember it."

With an intent look in his eyes, Rome retorts, "I do."

I rise and remove my plate from the table just as the door-bell rings.

"Answer the door and get your mind out of the gutter," I reply.

Rome walks to the door, opens it and Andre Sean walks in, talking loudly on his cell phone. I see Andre and hide my body behind the open pantry door. Andre walks in the house and immediately goes into the kitchen. As soon as he steps in front of the fridge, he sees me. Losing control, Andre drops the phone, screams my name and rushes to give me a hug.

"Gwendolyn!" he yells.

"Andre!"

We hug in the kitchen for close to thirty seconds. As the embrace breaks, Andre stares at me.

"You're back. I can't believe it. Why didn't you call?"

Shrugging my shoulders, I make a quirky face and answer, "I was."

Andre steps back and takes another look at me.

"You look amazing."

"Told you," Rome adds to me.

"Well, damn. I must have really looked like a fat mess before."

Laughing, Andre pulls me into the living room, just before grabbing his phone from the floor.

"I gotta call Tonia back."

He dials the number and immediately speaks.

"Babe, you will never guess who I am talking to."

Quickly, he hands me the phone. I briefly speak to Tonia, Andre's wife, before handing him the phone again. He finishes his conversation and gives me his full attention.

"So how are you?"

"I'm fine. Just getting adjusted to everything again."

"You staying here with Rome?"

"No. I have my own spot, 302 Riverfront."

"Oh, that's nice. You and I have got to get together."

"Okay," I reply.

"How about tomorrow? We can go to the park."

"I will call you. How is Zora?" I ask.

"She's in school now," Andre responds.

"I can't believe it."

Rome cuts in the middle of the conversation.

"Okay, this is my evening with Gwen. Why are you here, Andre?"

"Oh, I came to bring you this." He hands him two back-stage passes to the Roc-A-Fella tour rolling through town next week.

"I spoke to my boy at the label about you doing the official after party."

With a loud clap, Rome excitedly grips Andre by the shoulder. "Good looking out!" he elates.

Andre stands and walks toward the door.

"All right. See ya, Dre."

"Love ya, girl."

"Love you too."

Andre throws up his fist and walks out. Rome, still grinning, sits down beside me and places his arm around my shoulder.

"Dinner was lovely."

"Good. 'Cause the dishes are on you."

"No problem. What should we do now?" he asks.

I shift in my seat, rise and walk over to his DVD collection. Moving the discs around, I see a stack of videotapes.

"Do you still have the club opening on tape?"

"I do," Rome states as he rises to pick out the video. "You wanna see it?"

"Yeah, I think so."

Rome disconnects the DVD player and hooks up the VCR.

He pops in the tape and takes a seat next to me. Laughter immediately fills the room as we watch the tape roll.

"Look at Lia and Jasmine," I say. "Are they still messing around?"

"Who knows?" Rome comments.

"Look at Omar's shirt," I screech. "I hated that shirt."

"I liked it," Rome replies.

"You should. You bought it for him. It was horrible."

Mirth continues between us as we watch several old-school artists perform on the stage.

"I still don't understand why we had Christopher Williams come and sing."

"What! This is Ole Skool. He was the man back in the day," Rome comments as he stands to perform one of Christopher's old songs.

I pull on his arm in an attempt to get him to stop.

"'Sit your five-dollar ass down before I make change,'" I quote from the infamous *New Jack City*.

Somewhere close to the end of the tape, the amusement dulls; Rome quiets down and grows serious.

"I miss Omar," he states.

"It's a shame you two couldn't get it together."

"He was the one that thought I took his shares of the club. It was business," Rome defends.

"Whatever," I say.

I walk into the kitchen. After staring into the pantry, I notice four boxes of Hostess Twinkies. Smirking, I grab a pack and lean over his counter. I offer him the second Twinkie and walk back into the living room. By this time, the tape has run to the end.

"You've got to look at the tape from this party I promoted in Chicago last year. It was crazy," he says, boasting.

Smiling, I stretch across the couch. Suddenly, a picture of Omar and me interrupts the static on the videotape. Apparently, the evening's events were recorded over old footage.

Rome watches as Omar counts the money by the bar and drinks a beer. I step into the picture, dancing and singing to Omar. It is obvious I had a little too much to drink.

"It was a beautiful night, baby," I say.

"It was," he replies.

I reach behind him and hold him tight. Omar shrugs me off while he counts the money.

"How much money did we make?"

"Don't know yet," he says, still counting.

I try to remove the money from his hand and place my body in his arms. This time, he pushes me away forcefully.

"I'm working, Gwen."

"Everyone is gone. Rome is out back emptying the trash—give me a little kiss." I cozy up to him once more.

Omar, perturbed, gives me a quick peck on the cheek. As I lean in for a bigger kiss, he pushes me away again. I playfully snatch the money from his hand, laugh and toss it on the bar. Omar aggressively grabs me by the arm and snatches me up so that my feet dangle off the floor. He looks me in the eye and sternly speaks.

"Don't you ever snatch anything from my hand again."

"I was p-playing," I stammer.

With my feet still dangling in the air, I am tossed down on the ground by Omar.

"Pick up the money!"

I quickly pick up the money and stand, while Omar snatches it from my hand. Instantly, I smack him on the right side of his face. "Fuck you and your money!" I challenge.

Omar smacks me in the face, nearly spinning my body around, and we begin to tussle.

The tension in Rome's home is grave. I rise from the couch and rush to stop the tape. Biting my bottom lip, I slowly turn and face Rome. In disbelief of what he just witnessed, he sits on the couch with his mouth wide open. Not knowing what to say, I walk toward the door and grab my purse. Still silent, Rome quickly rises and scuttles behind me. By the time I reach the door, he has his hand on my shoulder, but I don't turn around when I speak. "I have to go."

"Please don't," Rome responds.

Rome places his hand on the door as I attempt to open it. I pull on the doorknob, but am still too embarrassed to face my friend.

"Please, Rome. Let me go!" I beg.

Gently, he lifts his hand from the door and I walk out down the walkway to the car.

"Call me," he calls out.

I hop in the car and drive off, leaving Rome standing on the doorstep, watching. As soon as I get home, I throw down my purse. Panting heavily, I pace back and forth. Suddenly, I crash down on the sofa and stare at the black television screen.

"Damn you, Omar," I scream, tossing my throw pillow at the screen. Though I try to block my thoughts, my mind is saying, "This is a perfect night to drink."

Instead, I take two Tylenols, lie down and listen to music in the dark.

Everyone knew my relationship with Omar wasn't perfect, but no one ever witnessed our fights. My dark complexion hides bruises. However, the look on Rome's face tonight was one of pity, and I feel stupid. I haven't wanted a drink in a while, but right now, I would love a glass of wine, nothing too hard, but something to calm me. These Tylenols are not working. You would think the urge to drink would leave after thirty months of being dry, but it's not that easy. I drank for fifteen years. It was almost as common as eating. Some habits are hell to break. I have an appointment in the morning. I have a feeling I know what we're going to talk about.

DRINKING
Session Two

I first started drinking when I was sixteen. My parents were divorced and I lived with my father during the school year. Though my mom got custody during holidays and summer months, I only spent two summers and one Christmas with her. My father worked crazy hours and I pretty much raised myself after my mom left. I spent lots of time in the street. I wasn't a bad kid, but I did my share of stealing and drinking. Anyway, my mother drank alcohol like it was orange juice. At first, it was social, but by the time I was ten, her drinking became an everyday habit. But she never called it a habit, for the word "habit" comes with underlying tendencies of addiction. She called it "relaxation." Therefore, every night around seven-thirty, Mom would settle down and pour herself a nice glass of relaxation. Stressful days, she would start relaxing after work. It was no big deal. Therefore, once I became a teenager and acquired a little freedom, I, too, decided I could use a little relaxation. Yet, as a teen, relaxing was the very last thing I thought about. I would drink in order to let loose and have fun with my friends. I was never one for big crowds or loud noise. I was an introvert, even as a teen, but my friends—they loved to party. They enjoyed it so much that I believed that there was something wrong with me for not finding pleasure in it. But when I drank a little, the atmosphere, no matter how rowdy, became a lot more pleasurable. With warm liquor running through my veins, I no longer felt uptight or uncomfortable. Why I normally felt uptight and uncomfortable is another long story, so I'll save it for another session. I didn't think we would have money for school, so I planned to go to a junior college in the neighborhood. However, my aunt

*saved up enough money for my first year and she and my
dad helped me throughout. I got a scholarship, but I had
to keep a 2.7 GPA, so I thought I would have to stop
drinking to keep my grades up. But, by my sophomore
year, drinking was a part of my normal routine. I would
go to class Monday through Thursday, and after my last
class on Thursday, I would hit the bar. Since I only had
two classes on Friday, I didn't mind the buzz from Thursday night. Normally, I completely regained my sober
state by 2:00 P.M. on Friday, just in time to take a nap
and awake around six at night. I would do my lab work
between 7:00 and 8:00, eat between 8:00 and 9:00, and
then hit the streets between 10:30 and 11:00 P.M. I did
this for three consecutive years. I even got a job as a
bartender during my junior and senior years. Amazingly, I graduated. I was a fifth-year senior, but still
graduated, nonetheless.*

*After school, I no longer had to wait until the week-
end to drink. I was finally free to drink whenever I chose.
Of course, there was the issue of working nine to five,
and luckily, I was able to use my marketing major at my
first job. I was a junior marketing executive at Shefland
& Associates, the Detroit branch. And guess what, they
put me in the department that handles specialty liquors
and champagnes. This was perfect. It didn't pay but
$30,000, which is not much in Detroit, but I didn't grow
up with much money, so to me this was good. Plus, I was
always receiving a free bottle here and a free bottle
there. No longer did I have to pay for this thing that I
loved so much. Furthermore, I was expected to immerse
myself in the merchandise. There was a board in our
office that read KNOW YOUR PRODUCT. What better way to
know your product than to ingest it? Finally, I had an
excuse; I drank because I got paid to do it. And the more
I drank the expensive stuff, the more elite my taste buds*

became. However, the job pressure was high and the position was very competitive. I finally understood what my mother was talking about when she said, "A little relaxation takes the edge off the day." I no longer used alcohol as a tool to wind up; I used it as a tool to wind down. It helped me sleep, and, thus, wine and alcohol became my nightly prescription.

Our company was sponsoring an annual event held at Detroit Nights, one of the largest nightspots in the city at the time. Romulus Sutton was the club manager and event coordinator. Ironically, he and I are from the same neighborhood in New York, but when his mother left, she remarried into a rich Detroit family and we simply lost touch. I figured he didn't have much use for his old friends. I heard he was still in Detroit, but I didn't know how to find him. I was so surprised to see him at our first event-planning meeting. Though it had been over a decade, we surprisingly connected like it had only been ten days. After the event was over, we hung out at least once a week. Rome was doing very well for himself, managing one club and making plans to purchase his own. A few years later, I was ready to leave corporate America because I was sick and tired of the backstabbing. My job may have paid me to drink, but they didn't pay me enough to lie, and I was ready to relinquish my nine to five and never look back. Romulus was looking for someone to do marketing at the new club he was opening. Of course, he hired me on the spot. Even though it paid a little less than my corporate job, my hours were flexible, the atmosphere was laid-back and, most important, I still had access to free "relaxation."

Session Done

2

My second week back, I am into the full routine at the club. It is late Friday, three in the morning to be exact, and Club Ole Skool is dim. Only a few employees still remain inside. I'm alone in the main dance area. With my right arm propped on the edge of the bar, I wipe the surface with my other. I hear a knock on the side door. Knowing it's Rome, who just took out a bag of trash, I pretend not to hear it. He knocks again. I still don't answer. Finally, Rome walks around to the front of the club and knocks on the glass doors. I look up and see him, laugh, then saunter my way to the front. I walk to the door and speak through the glass.

"We're closed."

"Gwendolyn. Open this damn door."

I laugh and unlock the door. Rome rushes in and lifts me.

"You heard me out there knocking," he says, carrying me to the bar.

"Rome, put me down."

Rome places me on the edge of the bar and quickly removes my shoes.

"Rome, give me my shoes. I can't walk barefoot on this nasty floor."

Rome walks to the other side of the room, holding my

shoes. "Not until you say that you heard me knocking," he comments.

"What?"

"You heard me," Rome continues.

At first, I'm silent, then I realize that Rome is not going to give me back my shoes and that I'm going to be trapped on the edge of the bar until I give in.

"Okay. I heard you. I was playing. Now give me my shoes."

Rome slowly walks back to the bar with my shoes. He hands me the right shoe and holds the left over my head. "Say you're sorry." I look at Rome in silence, and he pretends to toss my left shoe across the room.

"Okay, okay. I'm sorry. Just give me my shoes so that we can get out of here."

Rome finally places both shoes back onto my feet and helps me down from the bar.

"We're done here. We can go," Rome says.

"I just want to check one more thing in the office, but you can go if you like," I respond.

"No. I'm not leaving you here. We are leaving together."

"And they say chivalry is dead," I mock.

"Stop playing tough, like you don't need people. Everyone needs something from someone," Rome states.

"Is that so?" I ask as I walk around the back of the bar to grab some water. "Well, then, what is it that you need?"

Rome leans over the bar and grabs my water. He takes a swig and answers, "Love."

For a second, I am silent; then I burst into laughter while pointing my finger at him.

With a smirk on his face, Rome responds, "And that is exactly why I don't tell you shit."

"Romulus Sutton, I have known you for a very long time and that LL—'I need love'—rap is not going to work on me."

Rome follows me to the back office while speaking. "I am

serious, Gwen. I am tired. I have had my fun. I am sick of the dating, flirting, chasing and the—"

"The sex?" I interrupt. "Are you actually saying that you are tired of the sex?"

Rome pauses.

"See, I knew it. You don't want real love," I continue.

Rome places his hands on top of my paperwork and replies, "For your information, I am tired of the meaningless sex. And I don't mind committing for the right woman."

With him staring into my eyes, I rise from my desk and grab my purse while speaking. "It's time to go."

"Why, am I getting to you?"

"No. I'm done with my work and it's time to go."

Rome steps in front of me. "Seriously, Gwen. I think that it's time that I settle down."

Silently, I lean against the file cabinet and listen to Rome. "You and I are great friends. Don't you think we would make a great couple?" he adds.

I simply stare at Rome without commenting.

"Don't you hear me talking to you?" he asks.

"I hear you. And I've heard this before. You were talking about settling down five years ago. At that time, I think you were seeing Jada. Things went real well for you two until you met Talisha and you knew she was the one—that is, until you met Rhonda. But she definitely wasn't the one, so when Talisha wouldn't take you back, you went on a pussy spree for what . . . four, five months. Who knows how many right women have come along since I've been gone?"

Rome moves from the door to the desk and places one foot up on the corner. He pauses before commenting. "You may not believe this, but I did love Jada and Talisha. It was just bad timing. Rhonda, well . . . she was . . . you know I have a thing for brown girls with green eyes. Anyway, they were like runners-up. I am ready to commit now. I'm ready to be in love, but I just want to make sure it's right."

I look up at Rome, who is now staring intensely at me. With a slow-motion blink, I reply, "Sometimes you don't know, until it's gone. Then what do you do?"

Smirking, Rome responds, "Well, damn, Gwen. You don't have to be so real about it."

"It's true."

"Well, how about this truth. You know how long I've been feeling you. I think you first went out with Omar just to make me angry."

"No, I didn't!" I exclaim.

"Then why wouldn't you date me?"

"We have known each other forever, Rome."

"And—"

"And you're a ho!" I respond.

"C'mon, Omar had his faults too."

"He did," I answer, looking away.

The mood softens, but the tension builds.

"I knew a little, but I didn't really know. You know . . . about the fights," Rome whispers as he lines up with my pupils.

"We were alcoholics. Let's just say it wasn't the healthiest relationship."

"So why did you stay in it?"

"I don't know." I sigh. "He just loved me so much. . . . He wasn't going anywhere. It was secure." I run my hands through my short hair, intentionally sidestepping the conversation. "I miss my hair."

Rome lightly kisses my forehead and replies, "I love it. It shows off your face."

"Times like now, I want to hide it."

As I cover my face, Rome places his chest over me. I can feel his heartbeat against my shoulder. Quickly and quietly, I move to the side and away from the cabinet. He abruptly changes the mood.

"Fine. I'm a ho. But I wouldn't be one, if women didn't make it so easy."

"Oh, my God, are you saying it's our fault? Do you have no self-control?" I ask.

Chuckling, Rome easily responds. "Nope. I'm a man. We do everything from buying clothing, to smelling good, to working out, just to get the coochie."

"So you probably wouldn't bathe if it weren't for the fact that you might not get laid?" I add.

After a quick pause, Rome responds with a jolt of laughter. "Probably not."

Shaking my head, I head for the door. "You are so pathetic. I'm going home."

Rome hits the lights and follows while talking. "I'm trying to get better. The whole thing with Omar was a big wake-up call—no day is guaranteed. There are things I want to do before I die, like have a family, a wife and a few kids."

"It took Omar to nearly die, before you realized you weren't going to live forever?" I shake my head in disbelief.

"I'm serious, Gwen. I'm changing. I need someone like you to keep me in line. Someone to smack me down when I think about messing up."

I get to the back door, quickly turn and frown at Rome.

"I'm sorry, I didn't mean it like that," he says before taking me by the hand to slowly dance. Softly, he begins to hum.

I play along and dance for a second before commenting.

"Stop it, Rome. I'm leaving."

"C'mon, baby, for old times' sake. We already did it one time."

"Get away from me," I say.

"Fine. I'll leave you alone." He walks away.

With a quirky expression, I glance at the silhouette of his broad back cascading off the dim golden hues. For a split second, I forget about Rome's lewd behavior and lose myself in his beautiful smile. My harshness melts as I try to explain my situation.

"It's not that I don't want you. . . . It's just that you are like chocolate. You're not good for me."

Rome slowly moves closer to me. With his arms folded, he tilts his head to one side. As if he were Medusa, I avoid looking him directly in the eyes, for if I do, I am sure to stiffen and crumble into tiny pieces. Rome leans in and whispers, "A little chocolate never hurt anyone."

Slowly, I back toward the exit.

"Good-bye, Rome," I say, walking out the door and to the car.

Rome rushes to catch me. He goes to his truck. I get in the car and adjust the mirror so that I can see Rome sitting in his truck parked directly behind me. Smiling, he waves. Quickly, I readjust the mirror, crank up and pull off. Rome lingers in my mind the entire ride home, and I find myself trying to hide the smiles that creep over my lips whenever I recall his cocky sense of humor. To blur my thoughts, I turn up the music and sing loudly to The O'Jays.

As soon as I step in my apartment door, I strip off layers of clothing and head to the shower. I let the cool water pool down my chest. Flashing images of Rome have me a little heated, so I stay in a few moments in an attempt to remove all of his traces. Wrapping my body in an oversized fluffy light blue towel, I stretch out on the bed.

"Now what?" I whisper.

Since my late teens, I have been a night owl. Something about nighttime and what it brings out in people has always intrigued me.

Placing on my robe, I rise from the bed and stroll into the living area to see what late-night videos are rolling on the tube. However, not before sticking my head in the fridge to search for something to drink. I jump as the door buzzer startles me. Slowly, I press the button and hold still until Rome's loud vocals burst through the speaker.

"Gwen, what are you doing?"

I stay quiet and still hold the button down.

"I know you are listening. Buzz me in," he yells.

"No, Rome, what do you want?"

"I need something out of the trunk of my car," he says.

"You are lying. I'm not letting you in."

"For real, let me in," he pleads.

I release the buzzer and lean against the door frame. I know Rome has respect for me as a friend, but I also know what kind of man Rome is. He's the type that doesn't make 4:00 A.M. house calls for friendly conversation, and I haven't felt a man's touch in a couple of years. I don't trust myself. Pausing a moment longer, I take a deep sigh and finally press the button to give Rome a final answer. "Rome! Rome!" I call out.

Rome doesn't answer; therefore I call his name again, and still, no answer.

"Oh well, I guess he gave up," I say softly, with a hint of disappointment. Strolling back into the kitchen, I think, *Damn, he gave up pretty quickly.*

Suddenly, my thoughts are interrupted by a soft knock at the door. I stop in my tracks and let out a small chuckle. Moseying to the door, I call out, "You think you're slick."

On the other side, Rome says nothing. I peer out of the peephole, stare into Rome's eyeball, then place my ear to the door. "You know I shouldn't let you in," I comment.

Rome still says nothing.

"Rome! You hear me?"

I glance out of the peephole once more. This time, Rome stands a few feet away from the door. His praying hands are clasped together in front of his face. He bats his large lashes as he silently begs from the hallway. I press my cheek against the wooden groove. Apprehensively, my heart pounds as I place my hand on the brass lock. After unlocking the door, I strut back to the living area, with the door remaining shut.

"It's open," I call out.

Very slowly, Rome opens the door and stands in the frame. "What's with all of the dramatics?" he says.

I don't even turn around to acknowledge his presence. Instead, I sit on the couch and continue watching television. He walks over and stands directly over me.

"You don't want to talk with me? Good, I like you better when you're quiet."

"Your car keys are on the counter. Get what you need and go home," I respond.

With my nerves boiling inside, I go into the kitchen. I get a banana Popsicle out of the freezer, unwrap it and crunch on the tip. Rome quickly follows. I can feel his warm breath on my neck as I blow out cool air from my frozen banana treat.

"You're so rude. You didn't offer me any Popsicle," he says.

With my body wedged between his chest and the silver fridge, I take another large bite from the top and turn to Rome.

"I'm sorry, want some?"

Nodding slowly, Rome reaches in and places his full, open lips over my mouth. With his tongue dancing around mine, he gets a mushy mouthful. As he withdraws his lips, he grins and states, "Tastes good."

"You are so nasty," I reply.

Rome takes the Popsicle from me and engulfs the remainder, licking the stick clean. He tosses the wooden stick in the sink and lifts me up into his arms in one swift motion.

"Rome, I don't think this—"

He suddenly interrupts my speech with another ardent kiss. In an instant, I am disrobed and lying in bed wrapped within Rome's biceps. I would be lying to say I allowed Rome into my bedroom due to my sexual drought. Rome is extremely sexy to me, always has been, but I have no desire to be in a relationship with a man I can't trust.

"Stop thinking so hard," Rome whispers, staring at my pensive expression.

"Thinking is what I do—"

He interrupts me with another passionate kiss. I sit up and push Rome off my body.

"I can't do this. You have to get up."

"Damn it, Gwen. Stop playing games with me."

"Me?"

I jump from the bed while wrapping my body within the sheets. "You're the one playing. Coming over here late pretending like you wanna be with me—"

"Pretending? I do want to be with you," Rome admits.

"For how long, Rome, for tonight? I'm just not up to this whole one-night stand thing."

"But we can do it more than one night and things will still be cool between us. I know that. We have that kind of friendship, and it could lead to more . . . you never know," Rome says, trying to pull me back into bed.

"No, stop it."

I jerk my arm from him.

"Then why did you even let me in here? And why were you flirting with me all night?" he asks.

I toss the sheets on Rome's head, roll my eyes and walk into the living room. He falls back onto the bed, sighs and closes his eyes. I lay on the living-room couch and turn on the stereo. Within minutes, I'm fast asleep. One and a half hours later, I pop up and rush into the bedroom to find Rome asleep.

I playfully slap Rome on the chest and speak. "Get up, Rome, it's almost six. I want at least two more hours of sleep. Lia is coming before noon. You need to get out of here."

Rome, pretending to be asleep, rolls over. Since he refused to get up I get into the shower. I suddenly feel a cool breeze overhead as Rome opens the door.

"Can I join?" he asks.

"Rome, don't come in here messing with me," I plead.

With a chuckle, he says. "I just want to take a shower."

He then steps in the shower as I try to get out. He grabs my waist and turns me toward him. As he pulls my body into his, I cross my legs and arms. He kisses my neck.

"Just go with it," he whispers.

Rome presses my wet body against the white cool tile and softly moves inside me. I whimper softly, but don't fight him. With warm water beating down on his back, Rome slightly lifts me from the tub floor. As I wrap my legs around his back, he steps from the shower and rushes to the bed. I hold on tight. With our wet bodies and hands interlocked, we continue to make love for about a half hour. Moments afterward, Rome is sound asleep. Slamming my face down on the pillow, I speak softly to myself.

"Why, Gwen, why? You know this is a big mistake. Make Rome leave your house right now." I repeat the sentence, tossing my face right and left onto the pillow. After a few more twists and turns, I eventually calm down and fall asleep.

Two and a half hours later, a buzzing alarm goes off. I lean over and hit snooze. Exactly five minutes later, the alarm sounds once again. Once more, I depress the snooze button. Five more minutes pass and the buzzes start over.

"Gwen, stop hitting the snooze and get up," states Rome in a grouchy stupor.

"Okay, okay," I respond.

I look at Rome curled up within my covers. "You gotta get out of here," I state, tapping on his head.

Rome opens his eyes and squints. "What time is it?"

"Time for you to get up and go!" I say while pulling the covers from his body.

Rome rolls over on top of my stomach.

"Stop being cute. For real, you have to go," I say, pushing him away.

Rome rolls back over and out of bed. Rubbing his eyes, he makes his way toward the bathroom. I ogle his mocha brown tattooed skin as he struts across the floor.

"Where's your underwear?" I ask.

"You know I've been sleeping naked since I was seventeen."

"No, I didn't. Put some clothes on. There's an extra toothbrush in the top drawer," I mention.

Rome nods and closes the door behind him. I rise and go to the closet to pull out my clothing. Moments later, Rome, still naked, walks up behind me and wraps his arms around my waist. Kissing my neck, Rome whispers. "You really turn me on."

Pressing his hips into my behind, he hardens. Rome takes my hand and places it at the head of his shaft.

"See what I mean," he says.

I turn around and glance down at his erection.

"Stop playing," I respond.

"Does this look like I'm playing?"

I keep my lips closed as Rome moves closer to my face. "Stop, I haven't brushed my teeth," I finally state.

"I don't care. That's how much you turn me on." Rome chuckles.

I ease my way from around Rome and step out of the closet. He tugs at my shirt as I try to get away.

"Stop it. You have to get dressed. Lia will be here in a—" The ringing doorbell interrupts me. "What! I know that's not Lia. Shit!"

I rush around the room, grabbing Rome's clothing. I run into the bathroom, grab the Lysol and spray the bedroom.

"What are you doing?" Rome asks.

"Getting rid of the evidence. C'mon, you gotta get your stuff and go."

"Go where?" he whispers.

I frantically run around the bedroom while grabbing Rome's shoes and socks. I toss them into the living room. Grabbing the pillow and comforter, I throw them on the sofa. Rome rushes to put on his jeans.

"Get out here. Hurry up." Sniffing like a hound, I ask, "Does it smell like sex?"

Rome looks on in disbelief as I rush to the door.

"Damn, girl, were you sleeping? I've been out here ringing the bell forever," says Lia.

"How did you get up here?"

"Oh, this cute guy was leaving as I was coming in. He held the door open for me. Hi, Rome. Why are you here?" Lia asks.

"I was hanging out with Gwen last night and decided to crash here," he responds.

"Oh." Lia walks into the bedroom with me. She continues to ask questions. "Why aren't you dressed? I told you I would be here by nine."

"I'm tired, Lia. I didn't get home from the club until after three. Could you be sweet and run across the street to get me some juice?"

I walk into the bathroom and Lia walks into the kitchen and opens the fridge.

"You already have juice," she comments before pouring herself and me a cup.

Lia places my glass on the counter and walks over to the couch.

"So what are you two doing this morning?" Rome asks.

"Going to pick up Andre's birthday gift," Lia responds. "It's a Rottweiler puppy. I met this guy at the club who breeds them. He said he would give me a good deal. I set everything up. All we have to do is pay and pick out the puppy."

"Good, then you can put my name on the gift too," Rome notes.

"What? No, go get your own gift," Lia responds.

"I was going to get him a dog, but you guys already have that covered."

"No, you weren't. You forgot it was his bithday and you're just trying to be cheap. You cannot put your name on our gift."

"Fine, forget you," Rome says as he pokes Lia on the forehead.

"Forget you," she says, also poking his forehead.

Playfully, Rome and Lia begin tussling on the couch. Tickles and giggles soon follow.

Clearing my throat, I walk in. "Rome, why are you still here? I thought you were gone."

"What's the rush? I thought maybe you two wanted some breakfast. My treat."

"No, we don't have time," I quickly respond.

"Hold up, girl. Don't pass up a free breakfast so fast," Lia replies.

"I'm not hungry," I say.

"But I am," retorts Lia.

"Damn, Lia, you had two dates last night. Didn't you eat?"

Smirking, Lia sticks out her tongue and flicks it up and down suggesting sexual overtones. "Don't ask what you don't want to know," she answers.

"Oh, my God, you are the nastiest."

Lia laughs as she rises from the couch.

"Speaking of the nasty, we could all skip breakfast and have a little dessert," Rome says as he grabs us both by the waist and winks.

"Oooh, interesting," remarks Lia.

"Take your ass home, Romulus. I swear, I have the most distasteful friends," I say, walking to the sink to rinse my glass.

Rome laughs. "I'm only joking."

"Yeah, right," I call out.

He opens the door and leans his head against the edge.

"Call me later. I probably won't be at the club tomorrow night. I have a busy week."

I follow Lia to her convertible Mercedes and the two of us head to the dog breeder to pick up the Rottweiler.

"You mind if I turn on the radio?" I ask.

"Go ahead," she says.

I flip through the programmed channels until I land upon one with smooth R & B. Five minutes into the ride, Lia initiates small talk.

"So, don't you think Rome has one of the best asses you've ever seen?"

I nearly choke on my water. Finally, I give a stuttering response. "Why, why . . . would you say that? How would I know?"

"Did you not see him this morning in those jeans?"

"I did, but it's Rome. I don't look at him in that way," I remark.

"Well, you should. He's fine. Just admit it."

"Okay, Rome is fine. There, you happy? Why don't you go out with him?"

"Not my type, he's way too needy. If anything, you should hook up with Rome. You've known him forever," she adds.

"Rome and I are friends."

"That's how the best relationships start."

"I don't think so, Lia. Rome and Omar were close friends."

"So, Omar is not here. You have to move on, Gwen. How long has it been since you've been with a man?"

I bite my bottom lip and avoid the question. "Rome is a handful, Lia. I know him very well. He talks about commitment, but he doesn't even know what that means."

"Yeah, you do have to watch the women. He dated some crazy girl last year—"

I quickly interrupt. "I thought you said, you two didn't go out."

"Ha-ha. Seriously, when they broke up, she started stalking him. She was a gorgeous model, very striking. All I remember is that she had a funny name. Who's the Little Mermaid?"

"Ariel?" I suggest.

"That's it. We talked about having a threesome with her,

but between her and Rome's height, I thought I would get lost in all of their stature. Plus, if I'm in a threesome, I have to be the dominant female."

I laugh at Lia's carefree expressions as we pull over to the curb.

"I think this is it. What does that address say?" she asks.

"Can't you read it?"

"No, my shades aren't prescription," she says.

"You still haven't gotten contacts?"

"No, I can't stand anything going near or in my eye. It freaks me out, you know that."

I step from the car. "This is it, 2260 Doorman, right?"

"Right. Good, let's go get this dog, and it better be in a cage or we're leaving it here, taking this four hundred dollars and going to the sale at Bloomingdale's."

Throughout the day and into the night, I can't get my night with Rome off my mind. Man, it was good. I can pretend all I want, but I know why he has women chasing him. Rome is fine and he's very charismatic. However, we have a deep history, and I know what kind of man he is. I see what he does to women and I vowed I would never be one of them. I care deeply for him and there is an attraction, but I would be setting myself up for a big disappointment by allowing more. I tried to explain it to my therapist, but she said it was fear. Maybe she's right. He's the one that could really hurt me, and that's a pain I don't care to deal with.

ROME
Session Three

When people ask me about Romulus Sutton, I always tell them that we have a special relationship. I'm not sure why I use the word "special," our relationship is un-defined. We met when we were seven. Rome was my first everything—my first crush, my first fight, my first kiss and my first . . . first. We're both from the same borough in New York, the Bronx. We grew up in the same apartment building. I lived in 10A, he lived in 12F. Our mothers gambled together in Atlantic City and shopped together in Manhattan. We had no choice but to be friends, which is something I didn't have too many of. I was a chubby kid. I got picked on, but Rome always stood up for me. He even got into a few fights on my behalf, but then he kept rubbing my nose in it, so I had to fight him in order to shut him up. However, his mother remarried and moved to Detroit our eighth grade year. I was thirteen. He tried to convince her to let him stay with me, but Rose, my mom, had just left and Dad said it wasn't a good idea. We promised to keep in touch, and we did for two years, but eventually I stopped writing and calling. By my senior year in high school, we had lost contact completely. I had stopped speaking to my mom, so I had no way of getting in touch with his family.

I moved to Detroit twelve years ago, and amazingly, I was still a virgin. Not that I wasn't into men, I just didn't want to get caught up in some meaningless relationship. I saw this happening to many of my girlfriends. They would sleep with the guy, start to like him and then create this happy "he could be the one," relationship. All the while, though, the guy was simply trying to get laid. Not to mention, the girls who got pregnant usually dropped out of school. I just didn't want to go through that drama. Next thing I know, four and a half college years pass and I am still tight as the day I was born. However, the month I moved here, I ran into Rome at a function my company gave at Detroit Nights, one of the hottest spots in the city. Rome was the manager at that time and I have to admit, once we were reunited, having sex with him was definitely one of the first things that popped into my head. Yet, we had to work together, and

I didn't want to mix business with pleasure. Besides, he was my childhood friend, and I wasn't even sure he looked at me like that. So we worked on this marketing project for five months. But the night before Detroit Nights' big gala, he and I were having drinks to celebrate the completion of the project. He smiled, I laughed, we reminisced. Before our bottle of champagne was empty, we're having sex on his living-room floor. I didn't even give it a second thought. We were good friends, so perhaps this swayed my decision. Or maybe it was because I had waited long enough. Either way, we did it, and it was wonderful. Unfortunately, after I sobered up, I realized that Rome was in no way ready to be in a relationship. He was a handsome club manager in his twenties—a profile that attracted woman after woman after woman, and he salaciously enjoyed his lifestyle. So we continued to be friends and acted as if the night never existed. The interesting thing is, it worked. We maintained a close friendship, and though we flirted with each other here and there, we rarely talked about that one evening.

After I started working with him, our relationship grew closer. We saw each other every day and my affinity for him—to my dismay—grew. Though I despised his roguish ways, part of me longed to be the woman who could make him change. Of course I never shared this— I just laughed at the silly women who actually made attempts at this impossible endeavor. I spent many nights at his home, and he spent many nights at mine, but I never allowed myself to sleep with him again. When I saw some of the skanks he actually took home, it was a lot easier to refrain. My father always told me, "To love someone is to accept them as they are." Rome was a womanizer, and I understood that. I knew he had at least ten more years of running around, and when he talked about traveling and promoting, I knew this would only heighten his whoring potential. Three years after I moved here, Rome's old friend Omar asked me on a date and I gladly accepted. Before long, he became my drinking buddy and eventually my lover. We kept the romance from Rome for several months, until Lia accidentally exposed us. Part of me didn't want Rome to know. Not that I was ashamed, I just didn't want him to stop flirting with me. Of course, once he knew, our relationship became much more platonic. I would catch him glancing at me from across the club, but he no longer made sexual advances. I think he was happy for me, not knowing my relationship with Omar was a bundle of codependent violence. Though two alcoholics have plenty in common, this doesn't mean they are good for each other. I would only drink wine or champagne in social environments. Unfortunately, I worked in a social environment, and when Rome and Omar opened Ole Skool, I found it hard to turn down a glass of wine. I would tell Omar that I shouldn't drink as much, but he never tried to help me stop. Not that it was his responsibility and it's not like I did much to help him quit. Rome, however, would occasionally hint about my excessive drinking. One night we were standing at the bar, amazed at the crowd of people gathered on a Thursday. This unusual evening, I was not drinking. Then out of the blue, Rome asked me if I was happy in my relationship. I told him yes and he replied with a quiet smirk. Then a few seconds later, he kissed my cheek and said. "Gwendolyn, you are so beautiful and when you're sober, your beauty lights up the room."

That was the most wonderful thing anyone had ever said to me. Of course I never forgot that evening.

Session Done

3

Weekends at the club are always jumping. The club's total capacity is 1,200 people, and on a warm fall Saturday night, like tonight, the place packs in at least 95 percent. Tonight the club is wall-to-wall with partygoers of all social and economic backgrounds. Ole Skool is one of the only clubs in Detroit that welcomes blue-collar, white-collar and no-collar clients to mix and mingle together into the wee hours of the morning. I sift my way through the dense crowd while hacking and coughing on the malodorous mixture of designer perfumes, designer impostors and overworked sweat glands. As I work my way in and out of the moving arms and legs, I accidentally bump into the back of a tall man. Unbeknownst to me, the man is Tracy, Omar's baby brother. I've always held a soft spot for Tracy—he is like the brother I never had. He even lived with me for a few months while Omar and I were on a relationship break. I convinced him to go back and get his GED, which he did. I was hoping he would go to trade school, but he got caught up in some quick-money scheme and ended up doing two years for fraud. I always expected more from him. Ashamed of disappointing me, he decided to wean his contact.

"Gwen?" he asks, turning to acknowledge the elbow in his lower back.

"Tracy?" I say with a twinkling smile.

"Damn! I can't believe it's you. I haven't seen you since, well . . . the accident," he somberly comments.

"I know."

Tracy leads me out of the congestion and over to the side of the front bar. The lean, six-foot five-inch young man hovers over me to block out the noise of the club.

"You look good," he states.

"So do you. So, are you visiting?" I question.

"No, I'm back in the D now."

"Since when?" I ask.

"About a year ago. Last time I talked with Lia, you were in Virginia. When did you get back?"

"A little over a month ago. You taking care of yourself, Trace?"

"I am. How are you doing?"

"Decent," I respond.

"You look better than decent."

"Well, then, I'm sensational. How's that?" I remark.

Spinning around to check me out, Tracy grins. "I would say that's about right. I really like your new look."

"I'm not too little. It's weird. Omar always liked girls with a little meat on their bones."

Tracy looks over my shoulders, peeps at my butt and then responds, "You left the meat in the right places." With a quick gasp, I chuckle. Tracy bobs to the music for a second, while the conversation withers.

"Where's your crew?" Tracy asks, scanning the crowd.

"Around here, somewhere," I reply with a sincere smile. Tracy takes my hand within his.

"Let's dance," he says.

"It's too crowded."

"Not up there," he says, pointing to the roped-off stage.

"We can't go up there, that's the stage," I say.

"And?"

I hesitate while looking around the dance floor.

"This is your club," states Tracy. "Who's gonna say something to you?"

With a quirky expression, I wrinkle my lips and answer, "C'mon, let's go."

I follow behind Tracy and we walk to the stage area. He unlocks one rope from its stand and escorts me to the stage. Immediately others try to follow, but he quickly closes the ropes off behind us. Of course, with the two of us dancing alone center stage, the crowd begins to gaze.

"People are staring at us," I say.

"So let them stare."

I attempt to block out the gaping eyes and enjoy my dance with Tracy. At first, it is awkward, but by the third song, I'm moving like we are the only two people in the club. I could have danced for another four or five songs—had it not been for Lia crashing the dance party.

"Gwen!"

Finally, after yelling intensely over the loud music, Lia ducks underneath the rope and forcefully taps me on the shoulders.

"What are you doing?"

"I'm dancing," I say, swiftly moving around my partner.

"Well, I need you to come with me," Lia states while pulling on my shirt.

"What do you want?"

"I want you," she whines.

Tracy leans over and speaks to me. "Listen, I understand if you have to go."

He reaches in his back pocket and hands me a card. "Call me, this is my cell phone."

I take his card and wrap my arms around Tracy's waist. "It was so good to see you. I'll call, I promise."

Before I can complete my sentence, Lia is whisking me off
the stage, through the crowd and into the back. Although Lia
stands several inches shorter than me, she is commanding her
way through the crowd at a swift pace. Once we get to the
back room, she walks over to the VIP section where Rome,
Andre and a few others are waiting.

"Everyone was waiting for you before we toast for Andre's
birthday."

"Please tell me that was not the emergency?" I say.

"Yes, we were waiting and the champagne was getting
flat," she says.

Frowning, I walk with Lia over to the section to greet the
others.

"Happy Birthday, Andre!" I lift my imaginary glass.

"Here," says Lia, shoving a glass into my hand.

"What's this?" I ask.

"It's cranberry juice, I know you don't drink."

I take the glass from Lia and lift it to join the toast.

"May you have another blessed thirty years," Rome says as
he turns up his glass.

While laughing and cheering, everyone walks around to
give Andre hugs and kisses. From the other side of the table,
I smile and blow a kiss to Andre. "Your gift is in the office,"
I yell through the noise.

"I love you," Andre yells.

"Love you more," I call back, just before whispering to Lia,
"Who is that heifer hugging on Andre? Where's Tonia?"

"I don't know that girl."

"So who are those two Hispanic look-alikes sitting with
her, and why is the skinny one rubbing on Rome's head?"

Lia and I stand to the side of the table and listen to the girls
speak Spanish to each other.

"Me gusta la música. ¿Te gusta?"

"Sí, sí, la música es muy bueno."

Rome rises and offers his seat.

"I'm fine right here," I say, standing close to the table. Quickly, Lucas stands and introduces himself to me.

"Gwen, we finally meet. I'm Lucas."

With my focus still pitched toward Rome, I speak. "Yes, great to meet you too."

"Please have a seat," Lucas offers.

"That's okay, I have work to do," I comment.

I stay and listen to the women continuing to chat in their native tongue. Lia walks around the table to refill her glass.

"I thought you stopped drinking in support of me?" I ask her.

"Oh yeah, that's going to take some time," Lia says as she places the last drop of wine into her glass. "I'm gonna stop, though, I promise."

Rome and Lucas continue to laugh and flirt with the senoritas, until finally I have heard enough. I can speak a foreign language too and therefore I will.

"Allons-nous lui donner le chien avant ou après la célébration?" I say to Lia in French, asking if we should give Andre the gift before or after the celebration.

After releasing a tiny chuckle, Lia answers. *"Absolument après. Je veux voir son expression."* Lia winks and turns up her glass of wine. Yes, it's petty, but my point is made.

"You are so rude," Rome comments.

"Qui moi?" I state, delivering a tiny wave before walking back to the office.

As soon as I get into the office and close the door, I begin pacing and talking. "What in the hell is going on and why is it upsetting me? Who were those women and why were Andre and Rome all over them? I would expect this from Rome, but Andre is still married."

I continue to pace as I rub my hands though my soft curls, which are turning into soft waves due to the heat.

My pacing is halted when I hear three consecutive knocks

followed by seven syncopated knocks to the rhythm of "Another One Bites the Dust."

"I'm busy, Rome," I call out, recognizing his infamous knock.

In spite of my comment, he quickly opens the door. "You don't look busy. I have to talk with you."

I cut my eye in his direction, but I stay silent as Rome comments. "Those women are friends of Lucas's. They're nice and we're just having fun."

"So?" I quickly deliver.

"So what is wrong with you?" he asks.

I walk around the corner of the desk and take a seat. With my elbows propped up on the accounting books, I look up at Rome, frown and complain. "I don't understand why they don't speak English, 'cause I know they know how."

"What?" Rome asks with confusion.

"You know what, never mind," I say.

Rome walks over to the desk and kneels. "Are you all right?"

With my hand slightly covering my face, I irritably reply, "I am fine, Rome."

"I don't want to upset you and it's obvious you're pissed about something. If you don't want to see me with other women, just say so."

With an indignant expression, I stare at Rome. "You are so arrogant. I don't care about you dating other women. I don't want to date you. I already told you that." Rome is quiet as he stares at me.

"Why are you looking at me?" I ask.

Rome shakes his head and stands. Walking toward the door, he glumly responds, "You know what, Gwen, I really enjoyed the other night, and I think there might be something between us. Something we should pursue."

I give a sharp reply. "There is absolutely nothing for us to pursue."

"Oh, I see. Well, I'll be out there. Join us if you can get your attitude together." Rome quickly leaves the office and walks back into the club to wrap up Andre's birthday party.

Frustrated with my behavior, I follow him out of the office, walk up front and search the crowd for Tracy. Just as I'm about to give up, I spot him walking toward the front door. I rush through the crowd and call his name. He turns, but can't see me approaching due to the dim lights and dense crowd. Therefore, he continues to exit. I follow, and as soon as I step from within the club and take a breath of fresh night air, I call his name again. This time, Tracy turns and sees me furiously waving my arms in the air. Grinning, he switches direction and walks toward me.

"Where are you staying?" I ask.

"At my boy's house."

Taking a deep breath, I reply, "Are you sure you're staying out of trouble?"

Tracy displays a crooked smile.

"I know what that look means," I comment.

"I'm good. I promise you. We can talk this week and catch up. Call me tomorrow," Tracy adds.

"I will."

Once again, I wrap my arms around Tracy's waist and tightly clutch.

"I missed you," Tracy says as he leans over and kisses my forehead.

"Same here."

Tracy and I release from the hug and wave good-bye. I step back into the club, and before I get two feet in the door, I'm greeted by Rome.

"Was that—"

"Yes. That was," I respond.

"What does he want? You shouldn't be hanging out with him."

I stop and stare Rome in the face before responding, "Why? Huh, Rome? Why is this any of your business?"

"'Cause I'm your friend."

"And Tracy is my brother."

"No, Tracy is Omar's brother," he remarks.

With an attitude, I place my hands on my hips and look away.

"He stays in trouble. Gwen, look at me."

I slowly turn my head toward Rome.

"Look, I don't know why it's so weird between us, but as your friend, I care about you."

I slightly part my lips and murmur, "I know, but Tracy is my friend, and I'm not going to stop hanging with him 'cause you don't approve."

Rome walks back in the club as I watch Tracy walk across the parking lot. I laugh as he sways his rangy body side to side. Tracy sees another brother by his truck and Tracy reaches in his back pocket and hands the guy a tiny bag. This was a common sight I saw growing up in my neighborhood, where drugs were prevalent. Of course I disapprove of Tracy's behavior and habits, but there's so much more to him than the drug-dealing thug people see. He has the biggest heart and he is brilliant. He's read hundreds of books on politics, money, history and religion. He always says he's going to make money and buy back the land the black people used to own in Detroit.

"The revolutionary drug dealer," I mutter with a giggle.

I walk into the office, grab my portfolio and place some paperwork inside. I clean the desk and prepare to go home.

Over the next hour, the hundred or so party people dwindle to eight; the manager, two bartenders, two dishwashers, one bar back, one bouncer and one drunk in the corner asleep. The bouncer Moo Moo calls a taxi for the drunk and the others close the doors on another night at Ole Skool.

At 302 Riverfront, I am sprawled in the middle of the floor on top of stacks of purchase orders placed over the last six months. With my huge calculator by my left hand, I rapidly peck away at numbers.

"Why did we order so many boxes of straws and matches?" I mumble to myself.

Finally, after rolling around in the paper clutter, I rise and walk to the kitchen. My mind is running everywhere. Seeing Tracy tonight really made me think about Omar. If I am not thinking about Omar, I'm thinking about Rome. If I'm not thinking about Rome, I'm thinking about the club. If I'm not thinking about the club, I'm thinking about drinking. And when I think about drinking, it takes me back to Omar, and the chain begins again. Frustrated, I stack the paperwork in the corner, stroll to the bathroom and run warm water in the oval-shaped tub. As I run my fingertips through the water, an overwhelming urge to talk with Omar fills my chest. Suddenly, the heaviness develops into tears that fill the corner of my eyes. Quickly, I reach for the tissue near the sink, turn off the water and sit on the floor with my back against the cold porcelain. In light pink boy shorts, I crouch in the corner of my bathroom with my body rolled into a fetal position. Although only four tears actually fall down my cheek, I mourn my old relationship for at least an hour. Slowly, I turn and look at the fizzled-out bubbles scattered in the cool bathwater. I lean over, lift the silver-plated nozzle and empty the water from the tub. Using the sink to pull my body from the floor, I rise. After brushing my teeth, I slowly walk into the bedroom, pull back the sheets and slide my body within the covers.

4

Close to seven on Wednesday morning, my body springs up like a toasted Pop-Tart. Gasping for that first morning air, I take short quick breaths as my eyes focus on the colors and shapes around the room. Quickly, I hop out of bed and head for the bathroom. However, when I get there, I'm light-headed, almost dizzy. I have to sit on the floor before I can actually use the bathroom. I lean over and turn on the bath valve. I sprinkle my face with cold water.

Giggling to myself, I comment aloud, "This is too famil-iar." Many hungover mornings, I would sit on the bathroom floor, sprinkling my face with cold water. Some mornings, I would completely immerse my head in a tub of cold water.

"I must have jumped up too soon." I giggle.

As a youth, I remember springing up hastily from bed some mornings, which would often cause dizziness. My father would say that I left my soul in bed and that it took a second for it to catch up with me. Of course now I understand blood circulation. However, I still take a second before rais-ing from bed in the morning just so my soul isn't left behind.

Upon looking at the clock, I realize that it is still very early. I lie back down in the bed, hoping to sleep until at least nine. But after an additional twenty or so minutes of tossing and turning, I know that my morning has started and I might as well rise and start with it. I grab the cordless phone and check the dial tone. Finally, it is working. The phone company came out last week to install the lines, yet the outside wiring had trouble. I started not to get a landline, but it still seems weird to only have a cell, so I changed my mind. I rapidly dial New York.

"What's up, old man?" I say to my dad.

I grin as I hear my father stretching on the other end of the phone.

"I can't believe you are still asleep. What time are you going to work?"

"I'm off today," he responds.

"What? You're never off on Thursday. That's the start of the weekend."

"This is Wednesday, Gwendolyn."

"Damn, my body calendar is off-kilter," I say.

"Well, would you like me to send you a paper calendar? You know we have plenty of them at the mortuary."

"Ugh. No thanks," I comment.

My father lets out another sigh from stretching and continues to converse with me. "So, are you calling from your home phone?"

"Yes, my number should have come up on the caller ID."

"Things haven't changed that much. You know I don't have caller ID. Let me get a pen and jot down your number," he says.

"You have to have caller ID, phones come with the ID built in."

"Not my phone. Now, what's your number?"

I give my father the number and he repeats it twice to assure it's correct.

"So how's business?" I ask.

"Good. You know business always picks up during a recession. I don't know if people are dying of poverty or depression. Maybe, it's both. Oh, you remember Mrs. Casterhall?" he asks.

"Recession, Dad? Never mind. What happened to Mrs. Casterhall?"

"Her granddaughter died. Got hit by a delivery truck. Saddest shit you ever want to see," he tells me.

"Oh no."

"Yeah, we had to do a lot of work on her. Her head was damn near detached from her body."

"Really?" I say with morbid curiosity.

"Yep. She was only twelve. That was some really sad shit." He groans.

"Wow. I know Mrs. Casterhall is devastated. Wasn't she raising her?"

"Yep, from birth. Her daughter is still running behind that no-good boyfriend. She almost didn't make it to her own daughter's funeral," Dad responds.

"That's a shame."

"Yep. Saddest shit you ever want to see."

I chuckle silently at my father's repetitive tendency. "Well, Dad, go back to sleep. I just wanted to hear your voice and give you my number. I'll call you later this week."

"Okay, are you doing all right? You need anything? Your bills paid? How's your money?"

"I'm doing fine, Daddy. I don't need anything—my bills are paid and my money is okay. I love you."

"Love you too, baby girl. Bye."

I hang up the phone.

"My day has officially started."

While brushing my teeth, I get the urge to go jogging. Therefore, as soon as I spit and gargle, I slide on my sweatpants, a sweatshirt and sneakers. In close to ten minutes, I'm grabbing my keys and my silver iPod and leaving the house. I used to run track in high school, but since then, I hadn't thought about running. Then my counselor at the sanatorium recommended that I get outside daily and get fresh air. The first couple of weeks, I would sit underneath a big elm tree and read or sleep, but sometime during this fresh-air period, other patients would attempt to strike up conversation. I absolutely despise making conversation with strangers, especially when I am going through hard times, so the exchange was never pleasant. Running was a way to get fresh air and be alone. Not many of the other patients ran and those who did usually wanted to be alone as well, so jogging became customary. Now that the weather is warming up, I want to keep it up as a routine. This morning, I jog about three miles—two and a half miles south and one mile east toward the coffee shop. By the time I get to the shop, I have worked up an appetite.

"I think I want a blueberry muffin to go with my coffee," I say to the cashier. I pay for my coffee, walk outside and pull two chairs from underneath the table. I sit in one and place my legs on the other. Leaning over, I stretch out the back of my thigh muscles, and when I lift up, a familiar face is standing over me.

"Rome," I state with a startled look upon my face.

"Gwendolyn, what a surprise."

Though I'm happy to see Rome, I pretend as if I could care less. However, I can't help but smile when he leans over to give me a hug.

"You following me?" I say, trying to be coy.

"Not this time," he responds.

"I didn't think you ever got up this early. Have a seat," I comment, removing my legs from the chair.

With an odd expression, Rome stammers, "Well, I'm k-kind of with . . . someone."

Just then, another familiar face eagerly trots up beside Rome and interrupts him.

"Sorry, babe, I had to take that phone call. Oh, hi," states the young woman, noticing me.

I try to give a pleasant smile, which comes out as an indistinct grin. Quickly, Rome interjects to avoid more awkwardness.

"You remember Lola from Andre's party. Lola, this is Gwen."

Lola immediately extends her arms to give me a comforting hug. I am drawn into the embrace, but I purposely keep my arms down by my sides.

Lola enthusiastically speaks with a heavy accent. "I've heard so much about you. We didn't talk that night, 'cause I could tell you were busy. My sisters and I love the club. I'm sure we will see you there again. Our brother José, that's Rosita's twin, just got hired in the kitchen. You will love him. The girls and I get together every other week for movie night. You should join us."

Amazed at the speed of her vernacular, I sit and stare at Lola's moving lips. With my skewed grin even more distorted, I finally let out a retort. "Yeah, okay."

"Great. I'm going in for my morning java. *¿Café, Papi?*" she says to Rome.

"I'll come in a moment," he replies.

Lola smiles and walks into the coffee shop. With an accusatory, intimidating stare, I face Rome. He bites his bottom lip and looks the other way. After a few seconds, he turns back to see me still gawking. Eventually, he defensively speaks. "Go ahead and say it, Gwen."

I say nothing, but continue to stare. This is a technique I use to get my friends to let down their pretenses and ultimately come clean. Rome succumbs to the pressure.

"Look, you are not going to make me feel bad. She's a nice girl with a good head on her shoulders." I, still silent, turn to finish my coffee. Rome continues. "Why haven't I talked to you in a week? You come in the club during the day and leave every night before we open. What's that about? If you have a problem with me, you should say it. Stop being immature."

Finally, I respond. "I can do my job during the day without interruptions. You haven't talked to me 'cause you haven't called. I have no problem with you, Rome—you are my dearest friend."

I rise and toss my garbage in the trash, smile and kiss Rome on the cheek.

"Enjoy the rest of your morning, Papi," I comment with a wink, then place my earplugs back inside my ears.

I jog down the street, leaving a bewildered Rome standing in front of the coffee shop. Of course I don't turn back to even see if he is still watching me jog away. Confidently, I know he is. I pick up my pace and make it home within ten minutes. I go straight to the shower, turn on the lukewarm water, strip, and wash away the sweat, frustration and confusion.

"I am not going to let him get to me," I repeatedly say aloud.

As I dry my body, my voice level grows, and before I realize it, I've made an entire song out of this one phrase. I walk into the living room, pass the phone, stop, stare at the receiver and keep walking. Then, quickly changing my direction, I turn, go back to the phone and grab the receiver from the base. Opening the tiny drawer on my nightstand, I pull out the blue-and-yellow business card with Tracy's phone number. He answers on the second ring.

"Hi, Tracy, this is Gwen."

"What's up, love? I thought you would have called earlier?"

"Sorry, I was working through some things, but I do want to see you."

"I'll be there tomorrow. The Riverfront, right?"

"302. What time?"

"Is seven good?" he asks.

"Good."

"You cooking? You know I love your lasagna," Tracy suggests.

"Is that a hint?"

"A little."

Snickering, I stretch out across my bed and wrap up our conversation.

With utterly no plans for the day, I attempt to busy myself by

cleaning up my home. However, I'm a compulsive cleaner—
my home stays immaculate. So, after fifteen minutes, everything is back in place and I sit in the living room, twiddling my
thumbs, and looking out the window for a bit of excitement.
The club paperwork is caught up, the kitchen is fully stocked,
the clothes are washed and I just finished exercising. I have absolutely nothing to do.

"How depressing," I state aloud.

The day passes slowly as I watch television, cook pasta and
watch more television. Looking at my nightstand, I'm reminded of my doctor's words: "Writing is therapeutic."

Dr. Felizia Bourceau, my psychiatric counselor, constantly
encourages me to write daily in my journal, but I normally
use the journal pages as a grocery list. However, I pull out my
journal today and attempt to do some writing, but nothing
comes out. I stare at the blank page for almost thirty minutes.

"I have to cope with the past during my sessions. I don't
like writing," I say to the blank journal page before I toss it
back into the drawer.

My phone doesn't ring all day, and close to 5:00 P.M., I
decide to leave the house and head to the mall. I walk into the
lingerie store and buy $150 worth of fancy undergarments. I
get home and fold them nicely in the drawer, another pathetic
moment. Who knows when I will get to parade around in
these silky undergarments? Though it's great to buy nice
things for yourself, it's better when you get to show them off.
Grabbing a book from the stack by the window, I retire to the
bedroom and read until nightfall. Unfortunately, the next
morning starts just as slow. I stay in bed half the day and read
until Lia calls around 2:00 P.M.

"What are you doing and why haven't I seen you in a few
days?" Lia asks as soon as I pick up the receiver.

"I don't know. Where have you been?" I ask.

"Where have you been?" Lia repeats.

"I asked first," I say with the tone of a child.

She laughs, which starts me laughing, and soon we are both giggling like teenagers.

"I missed you, Gwen."

"Well, you need to act like it and stop ditching me for all those damn dates," I voice.

"Fine, let's get together tonight."

"I have plans tonight," I huff with a hint of snootiness.

"With who? Rome?"

"No," I respond.

"Who?" Lia continues to ask.

"Tracy," I utter.

Lia is silent and I'm forced to question her.

"What? You have nothing to say?"

"No," Lia remarks.

"You sure?" I ask.

"Yep. I mean. You know I like Tracy but . . . well, he might have climbed up the ladder from street hustling, but I'm sure he's still gambling. Tracy is a sweetheart, but he's a thug. Let's not forget how he hid that stuff in your house that time and those guys broke in and crashed your place, and I'm not even going to mention the accident."

"For someone with nothing to say, you sure have said plenty, and I don't want to talk about the accident."

"Fine—he's still trouble."

"Look, Tracy has always treated me with nothing but respect. He is like my little brother."

"I don't know why you always stick up for him," Lia says.

"I owe him. You wouldn't understand."

"Make me understand," she retorts.

"Look, you don't just throw people away because they have faults, Lia. Deep down, Tracy is a good man and we are having dinner tonight."

"Fine. Whatever. But you don't owe him anything."

"Is that all, Mother Lia?" I smirk.

"That's all."

"I'll see you this week. I promise," I assure.

Lia and I hang up and I walk into the kitchen to prepare dinner.

Five minutes to seven, I remove my lasagna from the oven, toss the salad and set two plates on the small, square table for two. Once everything is prepared, I look at the clock. It is 7:20 P.M. Knowing Tracy is never on time for anything, I decide to give him a couple of minutes before calling. I turn on the tube and quickly become engrossed in some reality show. Before I know it, fifteen more minutes have passed, and I still haven't heard from Tracy. It's close to eight o'clock and I'm hungry, so I give him a call, but get no answer. Finally, around 8:15 P.M., I fix myself a nice portion of lasagna and sit down in front of the tube. Another thirty minutes pass, and my buzzer rings. I press the button and speak.

"I'm sorry I'm late," Tracy immediately apologizes.

"Yeah, yeah."

"I'm downstairs," he blares over the speaker.

I buzz him up. Within minutes, Tracy is knocking on my door. I walk over, look through the peephole and stare at Tracy's profile. As soon as I open the door, Tracy briskly walks in while speaking. "Where's your bathroom?" I point to the bedroom and he rushes past.

"Where have you been?" I call out.

Tracy doesn't answer. Instead, he closes the bathroom door. I quietly sit on the couch until he makes his appearance into the living area. As soon as he steps in, I notice a huge purple bruise on his left cheek and a cut just above his right eye.

"What happened to you?" I ask.

"I got in a fight. Can't you tell?"

"No, I just assumed you were wearing purple blush. Hell yeah, I can tell," I mock.

"Please, Gwen, don't say it. It wasn't my fault, this time. I promise."

Calmly, I speak. "Are you hungry?"

With a nod, Tracy leans against the bedroom door frame.

"Well, you have to heat up your own food. The lasagna is in the fridge."

Tracy slowly walks into the kitchen to fix his plate as I silently watch TV.

"There's salad in the fridge," I comment.

"This is cool."

I watch as Tracy wolfs down a huge portion of lasagna. There is no time for conversation because his plate is wiped clean within minutes. When he rises to wash his plate, I also stand and go to the bedroom. I return seconds later with a pillow, a sheet and a blanket.

"Here," I say, tossing the items to him.

"I'm not crashing," he says.

"I know you need a place to stay," I say.

Tracy proudly turns away. I walk up to him and place my hand around his waist. I pull his lean frame away from the wall and pull him toward the couch.

"Things aren't cool where you are. I sense it. I would feel better if you stayed with me . . . at least tonight."

Tracy looks down at me before placing his head within the palms of his hands.

"I need the company," I add.

With a small grunt underneath his breath, Tracy once again looks at me. I smile while gesturing toward the couch. Sluggishly, Tracy takes a seat.

"Only tonight," he states.

"That's fine, but I will give you my extra key just in case. You wanna watch a movie?" I ask.

Tracy and I sit on the couch and watch a straight-to-video independent thriller. My head is gently placed in his lap, and Tracy softly strokes my temples.

"It's good to see ya, Gwen."

"Yeah, it's good to have an old friend here. I've been through a lot these past couple of years."

"You've been through a lot? I don't even want to talk about what I've been through."

"I know. It just feels good to have you here," I comment softly.

Before the movie ends, I fall asleep. Next thing I remember is Tracy grabbing my arms.

"O', stop it. Fuck you. Stop it!" I yell, still halfway asleep.

"Gwen, stop! You're asleep!"

I slowly come from my stupor and lay helpless in Tracy's arms. "What?"

"You were having a nightmare," he tells me.

I look away and then back at Tracy. "I'm sorry," I whisper.

Tracy rushes from the room and comes back quickly with a glass of water.

"Can you get me the Tylenol PM from the cabinet?"

Tracy quickly retrieves the medicine and I take it with the water.

"I have nightmares a lot."

"I wonder why," Tracy asks.

I lay back down on my pillow and stare at the ceiling.

ABUSE
Session Four

I don't know why anyone ever stays in abusive situations. I can't answer that one question, and I was in one for over four years. And it's not like it was good in the beginning. It was bad from the start. The crazy thing is, he was my friend first, so I knew about his erratic behavior, and dated him, anyway. I have a problem with trying to fix people. Part of me thought that Omar just needed love. I actually thought that if I cared about him, he wouldn't have to be so hateful and mean. But he was mad at the world—mad at his mom for cheating, mad at his dad for killing his mom and mad at God for making him witness the whole thing. He was only eleven when it happened. Though he was amazingly gentle most times, when he got mad, he was the Devil reincarnated. I would do things to make him mad just to see how far I could push him. I wanted him to realize what he was doing. I never wanted him to hit me. I thought that one day he would actually take a look at himself and see that he was fucked up. He never did, though. He didn't think he had a problem. He thought we had a good relationship. For a while, I did too. In all honesty, we loved each other; we just didn't figure that "respect" was part of the word "love." In fact, I assumed the more you could affect someone emotionally, the stronger the love was. Crazy, right?

I vividly remember our first fight. We were drinking and he started talking about how this fine woman asked him out on a date. I asked him what made her fine and he started talking about her eyes and her breasts. I got so jealous. He said, "That's why you can't tell bitches shit, 'cause they can't take it." I don't know if I was angry with him and the other woman, or if I was angry about the word "bitch," but either way, I reached across the couch and slapped him in the face. He waited a second, then slapped me back just as hard. It would have ended there, but I'm not the type to let anyone have the last word. So when I stood up, I kicked him in the leg. He snapped, grabbed my leg and dragged me across the room. From that point, the harder we loved, the harder we fought.

For the first two years, I didn't even care. It became part of our relationship. I didn't see it as abuse. Hell, when I was a child, my next-door neighbors used to fight every Sunday, like clockwork. My mom and I used to sit on the couch and listen. She would say, "Boy, they must

*really love each other." On the opposite spectrum, my
mom and dad never fought. They hardly talked. Plus, she
left him for another man when I was twelve. My old
neighbors are still together and probably still fighting. I
compared Omar and myself to them. I knew he would
never leave me and he took care of me. He understood
when I wanted to talk and when I wanted to be alone. He
didn't care that I was overweight. He thought I was
beautiful. He would say it all the time. And we waited
close to a year before we ever had sex, so I knew what
we had was real. I had other men try to get with me.
They thought I was easy because I was a heavy girl,
thinking my insecurities would lead to an easy lay. They
never called me beautiful. If our relationship was perfect 80 percent of the time, I could overlook the other 20
because every relationship has its ups and downs.*

*But then one morning, I was watching television and
Omar was still asleep. Some FBI program came on and
they were on a manhunt for some guy who killed his
wife. They were interviewing some of her friends and
each of them talked about how abusive he was and how
she used to hide it. This prompted me to wake up Omar.
I went into the bedroom, rolled him over and leaned on
his stomach. He slowly opened his eyes and smiled,
thinking I was in the mood. "Would you ever kill me?" I
asked looking him directly in his eyes. He wiped the
corner of his right eye and slowly responded. "I don't
think so, I mean . . . unless you did something crazy?" I
sat for another four seconds, then quietly got up and
went back into the other room. From that moment, I no
longer took our highly spirited relationship as normal.
I went above and beyond not to provoke him, but each
time we got drunk, which was at least twice a week, we
argued and fought.*

Anyway, I was still determined to make us work. Part

of me wanted to leave, but part of me would never walk out on him. I saw what that did to my father. A great part of him died when my mom left and he was never the same. I could never do that to someone I loved, and I truly loved Omar. I loved the fact that he loved me with all my faults. I loved the fact that I knew he would never leave me. There's something so comforting about knowing that another person needs you as much as you need him. But I got tired, the relationship was draining, so slowly I started to detach myself from him. It wasn't intentional—I just didn't have that same "love conquers all" feeling anymore. It was obvious to him that things were different and he started accusing me of cheating. The more I denied it, the more we argued. The fights were more violent and I seriously considered leaving. Still, I didn't. He didn't have anyone. No mom, no dad, only one brother, who was in and out of lockup. I wanted us to work. I really did. Excluding the abuse, we made a really good couple. So I suggested we stop drinking, but that only lasted a couple of months. When we began to drink again, we drank more. I figured this was my life. I knew Omar was going to propose and I could never say no. It would devastate him. Plus, part of me thought if I turned him down, things would really get out of hand. So I decided when that day came, I would say yes, under one condition that we never fight again. Funny . . . I actually thought that ultimatum would work.

Session Done

5

Over the next few weeks, I totally immerse myself in getting the club up to par. Every morning, I wake up at eight, go jogging, eat breakfast and arrive at the club by 10:30 A.M. I normally stay until 5:00 P.M., go home and relax. Compared to my life three years ago, this is quite boring. However, I am finding comfort in the routine. I finally see the pieces of my life coming back together. This morning, I wake up a little earlier, six o'clock to be exact. Still nauseous from the night before, I head toward the bathroom to find something for my upset stomach. Unfortunately, there is nothing in the house. I take a shower and decide to go jogging, but before I can leave the house, my buzzer is ringing. Wondering who could be ringing my door before seven in the morning, I slowly walk to the door.

"Hello," I say, pressing the button.

"Gwen, it's me," says Lia.

I buzz her up and unlock the door. As soon as Lia steps in, she drapes her thin arms around my neck and bawls. Not sure of the circumstances, I simply hold her until she quiets.

"Come, sit down," I urge.

Lia walks to the couch and slouches against the pillow.

"My life is over. My life is over," she wails.

I rush to the bathroom to retrieve a box of tissues. When I return, Lia hands me a letter. I read the letter quietly:

Dear Ms. McNair,
    This letter is to inform you that one of your partner(s)
that you engaged in contact with has tested positive with
the HIV virus. Partner(s) can be defined as anyone with
whom you've shared body fluid contact. . . .

I stop reading. I can feel Lia's watering eyes ogling me. I don't want to look, 'cause as soon as we make eye contact, I am going to also break down. I continue to stare at the letter, as if I'm still reading. Finally, Lia places her hand across the paper and comments.

"I don't know what to do, Gwen."

Without facing her, I place my hand atop my friend's and reply, "You have to take the test."

Lia takes the paper, rises and walks to the kitchen. She rips the paper in half and then in fours.

"I don't want to."

I finally focus on her and respond, "You have to. This is not a joke."

Lia ignores me, opens the fridge and pours a glass of juice.

"Want some juice?" she asks, but I don't respond.

Then Lia casually walks back into the living room and turns on the television, as if the morning's events had not transpired.

"What in the hell is wrong with you?" I ask.

Drinking her juice, Lia turns toward me and smiles. "Nothing. I have just decided that I am not going to the stupid doctor just so he could tell me that I'm HIV positive."

"Lia, listen to yourself. You've never had an HIV test?"

Lia, still watching television, shakes her head. I remove the remote from her hand and cut off the television.

"Lia, I know you don't take a lot of things in life serious,

but this is something you can't ignore. I can't believe someone like you has never—"

"What do you mean someone like me?" Lia says, offended.

"I mean . . . it doesn't matter. I just can't believe you have
never had a test," I remark.

"Have you?" Lia asks.

"I believe they tested me once when I was in the hospital,
but no, not voluntarily."

"So why are you judging me? If I have it, which I don't,
then I'll get sick and die, but I'll be happy until then. I am not
going to find out and worry myself into an early grave."

"You sound so stupid!"

Lia forcefully walks to the kitchen and slams the glass
down on the counter. "I'm leaving. I don't know why I came
over here. You are always insulting me."

"What? I am not insulting you. I am telling you the truth.
You came over here because I am the only one who tells you
the truth. I am not going to kiss your ass or let you believe
that your behavior is okay. You are promiscuous. You need to
go get your ass tested."

I walk over to Lia and lightly tap her on the head, as if I'm
knocking sense into her brain. I take Lia by the shoulders and
tell her, "This is your life, Lia. Stop messing around and get
it together."

Lia vehemently jerks away from me. She slams the door as
she exits. After moments of silent meditation, I retreat to the
bathroom to prepare for my morning jog. At work today, all
I can think about is Lia. In our twelve years of friendship,
we've never argued. Although I disapprove of Lia's wanton
lifestyle, it's normally done in a joking manner. This morning
was not the time to joke.

As soon as I step through the door at the club, José, who's
stocking in the freezer, tells me about a plumbing problem in
the men's restroom. Then Martin, one of the bar backs, mentions that our main vodka distributor is no longer carrying our

most popular brand. Before I can get back to the office, at least
two more problems pop up. I can tell this day is going to be
hectic. As soon as I sit down in the office, José comes to get me.

"There's a guy out here to see you."

"Who is it?" I ask.

"He didn't say. He just asked if you were here."

Slowly, I walk toward the main part of the club. Suddenly,
I see an image of a man before me. My movement, my breath
and even my heart stops. The man is Omar.

I haven't spoken with him since the night of the car accident. The last time I asked about Omar, I was told he wanted
to kill me. Though I believe he was figuratively speaking, I
envision him pulling a gun and shooting me in the head instantly. My body becomes so rigid that I begin to tremble.

"You okay, Gwen?"

I nod slowly, but remain silent. Omar continues to approach, and my heart rate speeds. I don't know why he is
here. Now we stand face-to-face, and I can't bear to look him
in the eyes. I lower my head and stare into his chest.

"I haven't seen you in three years and all you can do is look
at the floor," Omar says as he takes my chin and raises it
toward his face.

I stare without a blink, and then say, "I have to pee." I turn
and quickly run to the restroom. I nervously stand against the
locked door. Ten minutes pass and I'm still confined within
the bathroom walls, until a startling knock pounds the door.

"Gwen, are you okay? I need to talk to you," says a calm
Omar from the other side.

Slowly, I open the door and walk out to face him.

Omar takes me by the hand and sits down at the bar.

"I can't believe you're here," I state while continuing to
stare as if he were a ghost. "You said you never wanted to see
me again."

"Did I tell you that?" he asks.

"No, your aunt told me that when I called to check on you.

Then I made Tracy tell me what you said about me when you came out of your coma."

"What did he say?"

"He said that you said, and I quote, 'I don't ever want to see that bitch again. Tell her not to come see me or I'll fucking strangle her ass to death.'"

"I didn't . . . ," he says, trying to interrupt. I give him a doubtful smirk. "Okay, I was pissed. You left me, Gwen. You didn't even call until five months after the accident."

"I know," I state while glancing across the room. "I'm sorry. How's your arm feel?"

"I'm paralyzed. I have no feeling from here to here," he says, pointing from his shoulder to waist. "It's only on the right side."

"I'm sorry." I feel the need to apologize again.

"No, please. It's not your fault. I'm good. I'm happy to be alive and I got my life together. I just can't drive a stick, but it's a good thing I was left-handed."

"Oh, you want something to drink?" I say, rising. "Beer?"

"No, I don't drink anymore. I'm sober. I've been in AA, and I've been dry for a year, eight months."

"Two years, seven months and one week now."

"It's a process," he comments.

"So how about two juices on the rocks?" I pour a cranberry, apple mixture and slide the glass across the bar. I lean over and smile at Omar.

"Yeah, well, I figured I could stay mad at you for the rest of my life or forgive you and start over," he says.

"How long have you been back in Detroit?"

"A year, but I've been living in Warren," Omar answers.

"I can't believe Tracy didn't mention it," I say.

I asked him not to," he says. "I needed some time."

"Have you seen Rome, Lia, anyone?"

"You know I don't talk to Rome." Omar says.

"I can't believe you're still mad at him about this club?"

"He went behind my back and bought my shares," Omar starts up.

"You didn't want the club anymore. You should forgive him. It was a misunderstanding," I say, defending Rome.

"Look, I really wanted to leave my old life behind, start over. I figured if you weren't here, there was no reason for me to be here. But since you're back . . . ," he hints.

I give a slight smile and then continue to look away. Omar breaks the silence with a soft caress upon my neck. His touch makes me quiver.

"Sorry, my hands are cold," he says.

"They always are," I reply.

"Cold hands, warm heart, they say." Omar takes my hand and places it over his heart. "I forgive you for leaving."

I look at him and see the sincere, warm Omar I once knew. Riddled with guilt, I move closer to embrace him. I wrap my arms around his body.

"I've missed that smile," he says as I bashfully giggle. "I'm also missing about half of you. Where is the rest of your body? You're so thin."

"You think I'm thin? Not too thin, right?"

"You know I like my girls thick, but you look good, really good."

I walk around the front of the bar, stand beside Omar, look him square in the eye and say, "I have thought about you a lot. I'm glad you're well." I finally embrace him without fear and release a deep sigh.

"So we should go to lunch, dinner or something."

"I would like that," I answer.

"Well, I have a doctor's appointment. I just came here to see you. Take my numbers down."

I quickly grab a pen and jot his numbers down on a napkin.

"I should be in the city more often. I put a bid on Frank's old spot, thinking of making it into a sports bar."

"That would be good. I'll call you."

We hug again, and he leaves. I watch him stroll out of the bar. Still stunned, I am motionless minutes after he has disappeared. I knew I would see him again, but after two years passed, I thought, *Maybe not.* Sometimes when people break up, they part for good. Problem is, we never really broke up. I simply left after the accident, while he was in his coma. It was immature, but it's how I handle things—I run. But now that he is back, something tells me I'm not going to be able to keep running. Plus, he looked really good, and if he's sober, who knows? I wish I could call Lia, but I'm sure she's still upset about our morning. Therefore, I will keep this visit quiet, have dinner with O and see what happens.

That evening, around seven, I called Omar. I don't know if it was boredom, but I invited him over. We had a great evening. It was just like old times, but without the liquor. It was so good, that we make plans for the next night, and the next and the next. I didn't realize how much I missed him. Yes, there were reasons why I left, but this Omar is different. He's not violent and he's not an alcoholic. Timing makes a big difference. Though I haven't told anyone, I'm hanging with Omar again—it could be something there. We are starting with a clean slate . . . well, almost. There is one secret about the accident that I haven't shared with him. Something in my gut says be honest, but I'm not willing to risk it, not even with my therapist. Sometimes there are things that you simply have to take to your grave.

THE ACCIDENT
Session Five

I was in New York celebrating Omar's new job at Sony. He was drinking, so was I, and this was pretty much a normal evening for us. When I was leaving the restroom, Omar walked through the club and around toward the back. As he made his way through the crowd, he spotted me standing by the restroom, talking to a guy. The

*man leaned in and whispered in my ear. I giggled, and
Omar recognized my flirtatious, nervous laughter. His
temper started to rise, but he stayed positioned for a few
seconds and continued to watch me. Smiling, I took a
step closer to the man and brushed my hand against his
arm. Omar assumed we were flirting.*

*With flared nostrils, he stared into my eyes and spoke.
"Are you sleeping with that nigga?"*

*I simply lowered my head and let out a low moan.
Omar grabbed my chin so tight my teeth dug into my
jaw. He then slammed his fist against the wall right next
to my face. His knuckles were so close, they braised
against my cheek.*

*Slow and deliberate, I finally responded to him. "I am
not cheating on you. Now get your hand off the door. I'm
going home."*

*Omar kept his hand positioned above me, cornering
me between his body and the door.*

*"I said, move, Omar!" I shouted while shoving him in
the chest. I left the club and went to the bar down the
street. I just needed to calm down. An hour later when I
came back to the club, I couldn't find Omar. I sent him
a text, but I got no response. When I ran into Tracy, he
said that Omar left about fifteen minutes ago. We went
out back and still saw his black Yukon in the parking lot,
and Omar was in the backseat passed out. I cranked up
the truck as Tracy tried to convince me to move to the
passenger seat. However, he'd been smoking weed and
I'd been drinking, and I felt like I should drive. The first
few minutes of the ride were quiet. I thought Tracy was
asleep until he spoke.*

*"Omar is going to propose tonight. He has the ring in
his pocket." I didn't respond.*

*I ran through a string of yellow lights and made great
timing to the other side of town. About four blocks from*

the house, we crossed the intersection just as the light turned yellow. Of course, I sped up in order to get through the intersection before it turned red. However, the light turned red just as the front bumper hit the crosswalk. With music blaring, I leaned my head back and let out a tune. As soon as I looked forward again, I realized that we were going through another intersection—this time, the light was red. As the brakes were slammed, the back end of the truck swerved, but didn't stop. I quickly looked to the right and saw bright lights heading straight toward us. Another car was passing through the intersection. Quickly, we swerved and kept going, but the truck slammed into a telephone pole. The force sent Omar's body through the window and into the intersection. Still vital, I began to hyperventilate. Panicked, I opened the door and fell into the shattered pieces of glass. Tracy's body was pinned in the truck between the dashboard and the front seat. He was motionless. On all fours, I looked over at my boyfriend's body. My mouth gaped as if a horrific scream was being let loose from within, but there was no sound. Light-headed and petrified, I attempted to stand, but stumbled. I looked at Omar's mangled body lying in the street and then focused on the streetlight dimly illuminating the tragic scene. Then I noticed another sparkle by my left hand. I reached forward and picked up the extremely bright piece of glass and realized it was the ring. I let out a faint whimper that resembled the sound of O. Just then, I heard Tracy moan. My weak body caved, then flattened onto the street, and then suddenly, everything went black.

Session Done

By the following Monday, Lia finally comes around. She comes to the club and sheepishly asks Moo Moo to come get me from the office.

"Lia's outside, she wants to come in," he says, peeping his head in the door.

"And?"

"She's at the bar bugging me. She said you two had a fight and she knows you're mad. You know Lia, she keeps going on and on. She's been drinking."

I look at the clock. "It's one o'clock in the afternoon, and Lia's drunk?"

Moo Moo nods his head and exits the office. After a few deep breaths, I rise and go to the bar area. Before I can get close, Lia jumps up and runs to meet me.

"Gwenie! I'm sorry. Please don't be mad at me."

Lia falls into my chest, but I quickly stand her up and keep walking toward the bar.

"This is ridiculous, for real," I tell her.

I walk behind the bar and grab a bottle of water.

"Come here, Lia."

Lia slowly swaggers to the bar and sits.

"What is your problem? Why are you drinking?" I ask.

"You know why," she comments.

I lean on the bar and pull Lia's body closer. "We are going to take the test this afternoon. You will be fine."

"And what if I'm not fine?" Lia mumbles.

While tightly holding Lia's hand, I whisper, "You will be."

Lia slumps over the bar and begins to breathe heavily, as if she is having an asthma attack.

"What is wrong with you?" I ask.

"I'm praying," she answers.

"Like that?"

"If I breathe like this, God will think it's an emergency and really listen."

I take Lia's arm and lift her from the bar.

"We're going now."

I walk back to the office and grab my things. Rushing back to the front, I lift Lia from her seat and the two of us leave the club. Carrying her to the car like a helpless child, I open the car door and push Lia in. Twenty minutes later, we are pulling up to the walk-in health clinic. I get out of the car and begin walking toward the door, but soon realize that Lia is not following.

Standing in front of the car, I yell, "Get your ass out here!"

Moping, Lia sluggishly opens the door and minces toward me. Taking her by the arm, I rush her into the clinic. We walk to the counter and I do all of the talking for my comatose friend.

"She's here to take a test for HIV."

The receptionist gives me a set of papers attached to a clipboard. "Here," she says, handing the papers to Lia.

"Take one too," Lia whimpers.

Highly agitated, I push Lia toward the chairs to fill out the papers. As Lia is writing, I glance at all the women in the clinic. Not one of them looks sick.

"What if they are all positive?" I say underneath my breath. Then I look over at Lia, who is flipping through the sets of paperwork. "What if we are all positive?" I whisper.

Suddenly, I hop up and briskly walk over to the desk and retrieve a set of paperwork for myself. As I return, Lia musters up a crooked smile.

"Thanks, Gwen."

I nod and the two of us fill out our future-determining formalities.

"Look right here."

"What? Where?" I ask as Lia points to section four of the fifth page.

"It says to list the number of your sexual partners."

"So," I say.

"Do you think they mean in the last year?"

"No, I think they mean total."

"What!" Lia yelps. She leans in and whispers, "I don't know how many people I have slept with. Is that bad?"

"It's not good," I respond.

"Well, do you know?" Lia asks.

"Yeah."

"How many?"

"None of your business," I reply.

"No need to be ashamed."

"I'm not. I just don't want to embarrass you. Once you hear my little number, you're the one who's gonna be ashamed."

Lia moves away and frowns. After staring at the paper for seconds, she says, "I'll just make up a number. How does forty-two sound?"

"Like a lot. You're only thirty-one. Your number should never be more than your age."

"Really?" Lia says with wide, concerned eyes.

I simply look at Lia with a sober expression.

"Okay, I'll flip the numbers, make it twenty-four."

Lia writes "twenty-four" on her paper, finishes the remaining questions and turns the clipboard in. I quickly finish and we both wait to be called. After moments of silence, the nurse calls her to the back.

"Lia McNair."

Nervous, Lia walks to the back. I'm called in a few minutes later. Afterward, we retreat back to the hallway and wait to be called into another room, where we each will meet with a counselor as our tests are run. In the hallway, at least a half-dozen other silent young women sit staring at each other from the corners of their eyes. They pretend to hide their curious peeps within the office periodicals. Finally, Lia is called into the room, and three minutes later, I am called into another. Though I tread quietly into the pale room, I am sure that my test is negative. Lia, unsure of her results, goes into the room, loud and garrulous.

"I really don't want to hear some lecture about my promiscuous behavior. Just tell me my results and what kind of medicines I will have to take, if I have to take them forever and how much is all of this going to cost," Lia says.

Her counselor looks up from her desk and smiles. "Well, Ms. McNair, no one said you were promiscuous. We are not here to judge, we are here to assist you with a better quality of health care."

"Please, from the time the lady gave me that ream of papers to fill out, I have been judged."

"Maybe you are judging yourself. Just have a seat. My name is Carol Cox, call me Carol," says her counselor. Carol scans over the paperwork.

"Can I smoke in here?" Lia asks nervously.

"This is a medical facility, of course not."

"Well, can you hurry? I have to get back to work."

"Ms. McNair, you are not HIV positive."

"Oh, thank God!" Lia shouts.

"At least, not this time. You can be positive and it not show in your system for years. With someone as sexually active as you, you should come in once a year for testing."

"But I've only had twenty-four partners," Lia comments.

"And you're only thirty-one," Carol says, flipping through the paperwork. "It says here you started having sex at the age of twenty-two. This means you have had twenty-four partners within nine years. That's an average of two and one-half different partners each year."

"Oh, well, see I lied. I started having sex at thirteen. So that makes my average much better, right?" Lia says innocently.

Carol sighs and continues looking over the papers. "And it says here that you have had unprotected sex, but this is the first time you have ever been tested. What prompted this visit?" Lia is quiet as she asks again. "Ms. McNair, what prompted this visit?"

"I got a letter. Someone I had sex with is positive."

"I see," Carol says as she writes on her paperwork. "I will need to see you back here for another test in about seven months. We just need to make sure you are not carrying the virus. And please, no more unprotected sex. It's not safe."

"I know. I use protection ninety-nine percent of the time," Lia states.

Carol closes her folder and looks squarely at Lia. "I would suggest you make a list of all your partners. I know this may be difficult, but if you see the names and numbers on a sheet of paper, it's a wake-up call. It may make you think twice before having unprotected sex again. I know you have to hurry, but we have counselors here if you ever want to make appointments to talk."

"Counselors, like psychiatrists? You think I'm crazy?" Lia asks.

"No, but sometimes it helps just to share . . . to talk about why we do the things that we do."

Lia walks to the door. "I have to go. Thanks."

Carol nods and Lia leaves the office. She waits in the lobby for me. About fifteen minutes later, I walk into the lobby.

"'Bout time. Let's go," she says to me.

Lia grabs my arm and the two of us walk to the car. I reach in my purse and hand Lia the keys.

"You drive."

"But you drove here. Why can't you drive?" she asks.

"'Cause I don't want to. Take me home."

"But my car is at the club," Lia gripes.

"Fine, take me to the club."

Lia frowns and gets behind the steering wheel. Within the first moments of driving, Lia shouts out, "I'm negative. You were right. Everything is fine. I'm fine and you're fine. We're all fine. I'm so glad you made me come. I feel much better. They think I should see a head doctor. What do you think?"

"I can recommend mine."

"You're seeing a doctor?" Lia questions.

"Yes, Lia, and there's nothing wrong with it," I firmly state.

I am silent the remainder of the ride and Lia is so wrapped up within her own joy, she doesn't ask my problem until we are pulling into the parking lot.

"Why are you so quiet? You okay?"

"I'm fine," I say, stepping from the car.

I walk around the front and take the keys from Lia. Lia gives me a hug as I step back in the car.

"You going home?" she asks.

I nod, close the door and roll down the window. Peeping in the window, Lia bends over and speaks. "Well, I'm going into the club. If I see Rome, want me to tell him anything?"

I sigh and respond, almost out of breath. "Tell him my test was positive." I drive off, leaving Lia standing shocked in the parking lot.

6

Under the influence of sleep aids, I'm out the rest of the day and don't awake until close to two the next morning. I look over at the clock, slowly get out of bed, waltz into the living room and turn on the television. Flipping through eighteen channels, I finally land on a Danielle Steel movie on Lifetime and stay up until 4:00 A.M. watching the sappy love mystery. Afterward, I walk back into the bedroom and lie down in bed. Ten minutes later, my phone rings.

"What the hell?" I whisper. "Oh God, I hope no one's dead."

My childhood memories of living with a mortician associate early-morning phone calls with the news of death.

I fumble for the phone and quickly answer. "Hello, what's wrong?"

"Gwen, where have you been? I've been calling you for a day."

"Lia, is everything okay?" I respond.

"No. I'm coming over there. Why did you leave me like that? And why haven't you answered your phone?" Lia yells.

"Lia, it's four in the morning," I calmly state.

"I don't care. You're positive . . . I can't believe it. You haven't slept but with, what, four men? Are you okay?"

"Lia, I'm pregnant."

The line is quiet. I place the phone on my pillow and put it on speaker.

"Lia?"

"You are pregnant. When? How? Who?" she asks.

"Not right now, Lia. I gotta figure some stuff out."

"I'm coming over there."

"I'm not letting you in," I respond.

"But why?"

"'Cause you're too much right now, I just don't have the energy for it. I love you, though. I'll call you later, promise."

Lia softly sighs on the phone.

"I promise. Bye," I repeat.

I reach over, click the phone and fall back onto the bed. After twenty minutes of staring at the ceiling, I sit up in the bed.

"Damn, now I'm wide-awake."

I go to the kitchen and get a Popsicle from the freezer. Leaning over the bar, I stare at the phone. Slowly, I lean over and dial Andre.

"Dre, I gotta talk to you. Can I come over?"

Forty minutes later, I am stretched out on the floor of Andre's living room, with a fluffy chenille pillow covering my face.

"You can't hide from this. You and Rome are adults. You can't decide to abort this child and not tell him."

"First of all, I haven't decided exactly what I am going to do. Secondly, you know Rome. Everything excites him at first. Then once the excitement is over and the responsibility kicks in, he's over it. This is not something he can just get over."

"He won't—this is a child," Andre comments.

"Rome is a child," I retort.

"You slept with him."

"Oh, don't remind me," I say, clutching my stomach.

I roll over on the floor, kicking and screaming, as the Rottweiler puppy rushes over to lick my feet.

"Why is this happening to me?"

Andre laughs. "This is life, Gwen. People get pregnant all the time."

"I've never been pregnant. Then again, I was on the pill for years."

"Maybe you should have stayed on."

"No vanity meds in the clinic."

"Vanity meds?" he questions.

"Pills that aren't necessary for living. Can I have some water?"

Andre goes to the kitchen and brings me a Dasani water. I look at the bottle and frown.

"What's wrong now?" Andre questions.

"I like Evian," I complain.

He shakes his head. "You will make a great mother, Gwen, a picky one, but a great one."

"I won't do this alone."

"You won't have to. I keep telling you that Rome will step up," he says.

I face Andre and respond to his encouragement. "With Rome, it will be like raising two children. This is my decision. I just needed to talk to someone."

After a loud, noisy exhale, I walk to the door. Andre follows behind. We walk arm in arm toward the car. With Andre's arms wrapped around my waist, he gives me a tight embrace.

"Love ya, girl."

I kiss him on the cheek, close to the corner of his lips.

"Thank you, baby. Tell Tonia I'm sorry if I woke her."

"Have a little faith in my boy. I gotta go out of town for a gig, but promise me you won't do anything till I get back," he requests.

I give a warped grin, roll the window up and drive off. Andre tosses his hand up as I pull away from the parking lot.

I stop by Rome's house on my way home. I sit across the street outside his home for minutes before deciding to get out.

I get halfway across the street, then suddenly retreat back to the car while whispering to myself. "It's almost six A.M. Rome is sleeping. I should call first."

I pull out my cell and dial Rome's number. Of course he doesn't answer, so I get back in the car and try the number again, but don't leave a message. Laying my seat back, I decide to wait another fifteen minutes before trying once more. Fatigue, however, creeps through my troubled mind and I quickly fall asleep. When I awaken, it is after seven. Startled, I jump up, wipe my face and look at the beaming sun. Suddenly, Rome's door opens, and he and a young woman step out. He stands on the doorstep and kisses her neck while groping her ass. I quickly close the car door, crouch in my seat and watch.

"Who is she? I thought he was with ole Spanish girl," I whisper.

Rome, in his loose jeans and a shabby wife-beater, walks the petite beauty to her car parked down the street. He leans over and gives her one more kiss before closing her door. He rushes back to the house and goes in. With my mouth agape, I sit in the car and watch the girl drive past and out of sight. Debating whether or not to go in, I sit in the car and stare at Rome's front door. Nearly twenty minutes pass and I decide to finally get out and tell Rome. I pull down the mirror and check my face. When I flip the visor up, I see Lola pulling up to Rome's house.

"I don't believe it."

Lola walks from her car and rings Rome's doorbell. Within seconds, a refreshed Rome comes to the door, wearing a black robe. He smiles and pulls Lola into the house.

"That son of a bitch," I murmur as I watch his door close.

Now more stunned than before, I crank up the car and drive away.

"'Have a little faith in my boy,'" I mock. "Your boy is a ho.

That's what he is, and I will not mess up my life by adding a whorish baby daddy to it." I sigh continuously.

Late afternoon, Lia comes by the club looking for me.

"Gwen, where are you? Who are you messing with? You better call me . . . today. My best friend is pregnant, and I don't even know what guy she's seeing? This does not sound like best-friend behavior. Call me!" Lia closes her phone, turns around and sees Rome behind her. With an intent stare, he folds his arms.

"What?" Lia innocently questions.

Without saying a word, Rome bites his bottom lip and briskly walks toward the rear exit. Lia follows behind.

"Rome, wait. Rome, did you hear what I was talking about?" Rome leaves Lia blabbering in the parking lot.

To get away, I go to Virginia for a week. This way, I don't have to face Omar or deal with Rome. However, I return Monday to Detroit the following week with the intention to abort the child Rome and I conceived. I call Lia and ask her to meet me at the clinic on Thursday, at 9:00 A.M.

"But I—" Lia tries to explain.

"No 'buts,' can you meet me or not?"

"Yes. But there is a 'but,' please listen," Lia begs.

I put the phone on speaker, place it on my desk and begin unpacking as Lia delivers Rome's defense. Like an attorney, she scrambles to state her client's case strongly. Unbeknownst to Lia, I have walked out of the room to get a Popsicle from the freezer. When I return, Lia is still talking.

Finally, I respond to her. "So I think eight might be better."

"Have you been listening to me?" she asks.

"Yeah, yeah," I reply. "We agree to disagree. Are you meeting me or what?"

Finally, after realizing that she has lost the case, Lia agrees. "I'll meet you at eight."

I hang up, grab my iPod and a towel, and go for my morning exercise. Though my morning runs are usually peaceful, today's jog was just the opposite. I couldn't get Rome or this child off my mind.

I know I'm doing the right thing, I continuously think. *I'm doing what's best.* I turn up the volume on my music to drown my thoughts and run an additional mile just to prove my thoughts can't get the best of me.

After an hour and a half of running, I slowly walk back down the corridor of my building, stick the key in the door and see Tracy sitting in my living room.

"I keep forgetting you have the key," I say, slightly startled.

Tracy rushes over, picks me up and spins me around.

"When did you get back?" he asks.

"Last night, and please stop spinning me. It's going to make me sick."

Tracy gently places me on the ground and smiles.

"Why are you so happy?" I ask.

"Lets go talk over breakfast, my treat," Tracy proposes.

"Sounds like a plan. Let me shower first."

I rush into my room and hop in the shower. Moments later, Tracy and I are having brunch downtown at a quaint cafe.

"Atlanta is a really good opportunity," Tracy explains to me.

"But you just got a good job here, working in marketing, that's what you want to do. You don't need to move to Atlanta," I comment.

"But I'll be part owner at the club. I'll have three nights to promote on my own."

"Why don't you talk to Rome about promoting some nights at Ole Skool?"

"Rome ain't gon' let me do shit at Ole Skool. You know that," he says.

"I'll talk to him."

"I don't need you to talk to him—I'm moving to Atlanta. Just be happy for me."

"I am. But you don't really know these guys and I don't want you going down there getting in trouble."

"I'm a big boy. Take that back, I'm a grown man. I'll be okay. You'll be proud of me."

"I'm already proud of you. So when are you leaving?" I ask.

"This weekend."

"No, that's too soon. Do you have a place to live? I have a good friend there. Call her before you go, she'll help you."

I quickly grab my cell phone and scroll to find the number of my friend.

"Her name is Kendra."

Tracy covers my hand and closes the cell phone. "I have to do this on my own."

I look up at Tracy. He gives me a nod of assurance. After hesitating, I smile.

"So what's up with you and Omar?" He grins, which of course makes me grin. "I know you two have been kicking it."

"Don't worry about me and Omar. You worry about you."

We finish our food and head back to the house. By the time we return, Tracy has fully convinced me about his move. I become so enthralled in his new venture that for a moment I forget about my own problems. That is, until I step off the elevator and run smack into a very angry Rome. Without hesitation, he begins the attack. "What the fuck is wrong with you?" Immediately, Tracy steps in to defend me. "Move, Tracy, this has nothing to do with you," Rome demands.

"If you're talking to Gwen like that, it has everything to do with me," Tracy retorts.

Tracy moves toward Rome as he steps toward me. The two men connect by the biceps.

"I don't want to hurt you, Rome," he says.

"Nigga, please, you couldn't hurt me."

The grip between Tracy and Rome gets tighter and is

heightened by a slight shoving motion. Hurriedly, I reach in between the two heated men.

"Stop it, you two. I mean it." I raise my voice.

Though the intense stare increases, the shoving stops and the bicep grip slightly loosens.

"Tracy, I need to speak with Rome. Can you excuse us for a minute?" I ask.

"Yeah, I'll be back to get my stuff," he utters hesitantly. He looks at Rome and slowly turns toward the elevator. "Call me if you need me. I'll be down the block." Tracy continues to stare until the elevator doors close.

I push Rome into my home, and as soon as the door closes, he begins pacing and huffing.

"Now that you've caused a big scene, you have nothing to say to me?" I question.

"Oh, I have plenty to say to you—I'm preparing my words so that I don't hurt your feelings."

"I'm a big girl, Rome. The sooner you talk, the quicker we can be done."

I take a seat on the couch and stare at the blank television set. As a way to not get emotional, I place my mind elsewhere. I will listen to Rome, but I'm sure not to give much weight to what he is about to say."

"Why didn't you tell me you were pregnant?"

"Because I don't want this child and I knew you would try to change my mind."

Rome stays positioned by the door as he makes his statement. He looks in my direction, but places his focus above my head while I stare at the black screen.

"How do you know? I may want you to have an abortion. There is a reason why I am a thirty-four-year-old man without any children. It's real arrogant of you to assume I want you to have my child."

"Well, since it's come to this, do you want me to have this child?" I ask.

"I don't want you to have an abortion."

"See, I knew it," I reply.

"Gwen, this is about you not even considering me. When did it get so difficult to talk to me? We used to talk all the time."

"No, you talked all the time, I just listened. I've always been a private person and I don't ask permission or consult others when making personal decisions."

"Look at me, Gwen," Rome states.

Rome walks to the couch and stands in front of me. Now looking at his stomach, I continue to pierce through him. He kneels to my eye level, forcing me to face him. His approach then softens.

"Why didn't you tell me?"

This time, I am silent. Though still angry, I am defenseless when I look into his eyes. It worsens when he touches me, which is just what he does. Leaning over, he scoots closer, almost in between my legs, and places his hands on my thighs. I try to turn my head away, but he lightly nudges my chin forward.

Again, he asks, "Why did you keep this from me?"

Finally, after a few slow blinks, I answer him. "Because this child would ultimately tie me to you forever and I don't want that."

"So you don't plan on being my friend forever?"

"You know what I mean."

"No, I don't," responds Rome.

"I don't want either of us to feel obligated to be with one another because of this baby."

The room is silent as we turn in opposite directions. Finally, Rome rises and walks into the kitchen. He grabs a bottle of water from the refrigerator.

"Want one?"

I shake my head. Rome grabs another bottle, anyway, and brings it to me.

"Stop being so angry, you know you're thirsty," he says.

I take the water and place it in my lap. Rome takes a seat on the couch.

"So you don't want me in your life?" he asks.

"I didn't say that. I said I don't want to be tied to you because of this child. If I want to be with you, it should be by choice."

"You chose to have sex with me."

"And that was stupid. We had no business doing it. Now look at this mess."

"Don't have the abortion," he persists.

I look at him, smirk and walk into the bedroom, but Rome quickly follows.

"Don't do this, Rome. You are not responsible enough to have a child. Hell, you are a child."

"What?" he snaps.

I whip around and charge in his direction, ultimately backing him into a corner.

"How can I trust you to be there for me and this child when you are too busy running around town chasing every round ass that passes your way? I don't want to be a single mom. I want to be in a stable relationship with the father of my child. I want to be married to a good man. I don't want the father of my child or my husband to be a whore. And that is what you are."

With his mouth open and shoulders hunched, Rome stands in the corner of the bedroom. Shocked, he replies, "How can you say that about me?"

I raise one eyebrow and peer at him from underneath my brows. Quietly, I walk into the bathroom and shut the door.

Rome calls from across the room, "I am hurt."

Upon opening the door, I respond, "Yeah, I hear the truth does that."

"Okay, Gwendolyn, you win. You've insulted me and confessed that you would rather take a life than be tied to mine. I'm fucked up. I admit it. But I want to have this child . . . our child.

You can't take that away from me, simply because I like to fuck women. I'm a good man, a cheating man, but a good man."

"That makes no sense," I state.

"Yes, it does. I'm kind. I'm funny. I'm smart. I'm diligent. I'm driven. I'm sincere. I'm honest. Oh, and you know I'll make pretty babies," he says, laughing and lightly tapping my stomach.

"This is not funny. See, that's exactly why I didn't tell you."

"I'll be there for you, Gwen. Shit, let's have a family, let's do this."

"You are not ready."

"This child just made me ready, and I'm happy about it. I'll change. You'll see."

"I don't believe you. A leopard doesn't change its spots," I state.

"I'm not a leopard, I'm a man. Men change, especially when we have a good reason. Gwen, you've known me all my life. I would never leave you hanging. I'm not that guy."

I look at him and plop back down on the couch. Slowly, Rome continues his conversation. "Let's have this baby. Let's be together. Please don't do this."

"I don't know," I murmur.

Rome walks toward the door and leans against the wall.

"If you decide to abort this child, you will not use me as an excuse. If you go to that clinic, it's because you don't want to deal with becoming a mother. And you will have to deal with that. I can sit here and talk to you until I'm blue in the face and it won't matter because you're so damn stubborn." Rome opens the door and continues. "I'm here if you need me. Let me know what you're going to do, beforehand." Rome leaves.

Staring into space, I sit on the couch for minutes before rising to get a banana Popsicle from the freezer. Just as I take the first bite, there's a knock on the door. I shuffle over and look out of the peephole, but I see nothing but a chubby thumb.

"Who is it?" I ask.

"Open up."

"Identify yourself."

"Gwen, you know it's me. Open up this door, girl."

I open the door, and before I can step from the door frame, Rome has me in his arms. He locks his lips around mine and literally takes my breath away. I gasp for air when I release. Rome continues to hold me in his arms as he looks into my eyes.

"We can do this," he says confidently.

I am silent as I give a look resembling a ten-year-old child's demeanor after being lost at a park. Nonplussed, almost in tears, and unsure about my future, I simply nod. Rome lightly places his forehead against mine and pecks my lips.

"We can do this," he reiterates with a whisper.

I close my eyes and embrace my close friend, who is now the father of my unborn child. The hug lasts for close to a minute, and then I realize I'm dripping banana ice juice on his shirt.

"Oh, I'm making a mess," I comment.

Quickly, Rome turns and tries to reach around to see the back of his shirt.

"Let me get it," I say, rushing into the kitchen to get a towel. I place the remainder of the Popsicle in the sink and dampen a cloth. Tenderly, I wipe the back of his shirt.

"See, you're already getting into the nurturing role," he says.

I immediately stop wiping his shirt and toss the rag on his shoulder. I sit on the couch and Rome quickly moves to my side. He rubs my belly.

"Stop it. You're going to make me vomit." I laugh, slightly pushing him off the couch.

Rome kneels and takes my hand. As he looks into my eyes, I look away.

"Gwen, look at me."

I slowly face Rome as he bats his large light brown eyes my way.

"Promise you'll give me a chance," he pleads.

I cut through his endearing look and give him a cold stare. Holding up my right index finger, I silently mouth the word "one."

Rome gives a smirk and responds, "One is all I need." He takes my finger and kisses the tip. "I'll call you tomorrow."

I watch him disappear. My fear won't allow me to tell Rome that I would love to make a relationship with him work. I used to be able to say anything to him, but now my feelings hold a certain vulnerability—one that hadn't been there before. I have always been an expert when it comes to facades; I'm superb at masking my emotions. In fact, Rome is the only person in my entire life that has been able to unveil any of my superficial veneers. He loves to call me out. Unfortunately, this time, he's the one person I must fool, and I pray I'm not making a big mistake by trusting him. Also, what am I going to do about Omar? Things are really starting to jell between us. He's going to lose it when he finds out I'm pregnant with Rome's child.

7

Early Thursday morning, Lia bangs on my door.

"Gwen! Are you in there?"

"I'm coming, I'm coming," I yell through the room just before opening the door.

"Did you forget about our little appointment this morning?" she asks, pointing at my belly.

Gasping, I respond, "I'm sorry, I forgot to tell you."

"I've been waiting at the clinic for an hour. I thought I had the wrong time, and then I thought I had the wrong day. I didn't want to leave, 'cause I thought you would show up and be alone. What happened? Why are you still here? Are you . . . did you change . . . did you change your mind?"

I shrug my shoulders nonchalantly and waltz back into the bedroom. Lia hastily follows, buzzing with a barrage of questions. "So, are you keeping the baby? When did you decide? Why didn't you tell me? Did you tell Rome?"

I plop onto the bed and place the pillow over my head. Lia leans across the pillow. I wiggle to remove Lia from atop my face.

"Get off me," I muffle through the down fluffiness. Laughing, Lia rolls over beside me and lightly rubs my belly.

"Are we having a baby?" Lia asks in her best gushy baby-talk voice.

"If you're going to talk like that for the next nine months, we can go to the clinic right now and get this over with," I say.

"Don't talk like that." With a loud, quick scream, Lia sits up and speaks into my stomach. "She didn't mean it, Baby Pharr."

"Seriously, Lia, don't do that," I reply while covering my stomach.

I rise and sit on the edge of the bed. Staring at my stomach, I whisper, "I don't know about this, Lia. I'm . . . I'm scared." I finally admit the truth.

"Scared of what?" Lia asks.

"Scared that this whole thing is a bad idea. Scared that I might not know what to do. Scared that Rome is going to mess up. Scared that I'm going to mess up. Scared that we're going to mess up this baby. I don't think I'm ready."

"Yes, you are. You're going to be a magnificent mother, and I'm going to be one of the flyest godmothers ever known to man."

I chuckle as Lia embraces me. I begin to gasp uncontrollably.

"What's wrong? What's going on?" Lia questions.

I forcefully point to my drawer and she quickly scrambles through my nightstand. "What, what?" she asks.

I join in the search and retrieve my inhaler. I inhale a quick intake of air.

"Since when did you have asthma?"

I place the inhaler down. "I had it when I was younger and it mysteriously appeared again last year." I take in one more gasp of air before rising. Lia follows me into the kitchen, continuing with an onslaught of questions. "Did Rome change your mind? When did you talk to him? Have you told your dad? What's he going to say?"

"Lia, please!" I snap. "Stop asking me a million questions.

Rome and I talked. He really wants to have this baby. I haven't told my dad. I'm making an appointment with the doctor next week. As of now, we're having a baby. If you keep asking me questions, you will not be one of the flyest god-mothers ever known to man, 'cause I will not make you god-mother. Now let's go eat—your treat."

"Fine. Get dressed," she responds.

An hour later, we are eating sub sandwiches at my favorite hoagie spot in town. The entire time we eat, Lia has a starry-eyed, goofy expression on her face. She is doing everything in her power to keep from asking me a million questions about the baby.

"I know it's killing you, I can tell," I state. "How about this, you write the questions down and spread them out over time—this way, you still get your answers without getting on my nerves," I offer.

Lia wrinkles her face and shakes her head. "That won't work. The questions come too fast. Just let me ask one an hour."

"How about one a day?" I counter.

"How about five a day?"

After a slight pause, I agree. "Five a day . . . okay."

"Good. So, do you want a girl or a boy?" she starts.

"Hold it. You've already asked your five for today. Remember the fourteen questions you asked at the house? You aren't allowed any more questions until Sunday." I laugh.

"But—"

Just then, my phone rings. It's Omar. I've been avoiding his calls for a couple of days. Now that I've decided to keep the baby, I know I have to face him soon. But right now is not the time. I let the voice mail pick up.

Late that night, Tracy comes by to pick up the gift I purchased for his new Atlanta job. It's a leather attaché case. Tracy grabs the gift, gives me a quick peck on the cheek and leaves. I do hope he is careful. He's that one friend that I constantly worry about. However, he's an adult, and if he's not concerned about himself, then I have to let it go.

At six weeks I finally make peace with the pregnancy. I haven't told Omar yet, and we are still spending time together. I enjoy his company. I just don't know if he's going to want to still go out with me once I tell him. And though Rome says he wants to be in a relationship, he hasn't cut off ties with Lola. Not that I can talk, but I'm not the one trying to make us into one happy family. He even told Moo Moo we would soon be moving in together. But has he mentioned a thing to me? Absolutely not. This is the immaturity I'm talking about. I am determined not to stress over the issue, but as weeks pass, my anxiety builds and it's obvious I'm irritated. Finally, Rome approaches me with the situation. He pulls me from the desk and forces me to take a break. With my head hanging low and my feet dragging, I scuffle down the block with him. Acting like a kid, I refuse to say anything as he continually asks me what is the problem.

"Gwendolyn, I'm not going to beg you to talk to me. I know there is something wrong. Act like an adult and discuss it."

I peer up from stirring my tea, sigh and then bite into my sweet roll. Rome takes the roll from my hand and places it underneath his napkin. He then speaks to me. "I'm not going through eight more months of this. How do you expect me to be with you if you can't communicate with me?"

At last, I speak. "How do you expect me to be with you if you're still fucking other women?"

Rome is quiet.

"You wanted me to talk. I'm talking."

"I'm not sleeping with anyone else. If you are talking about Lola, yeah, I've seen her a couple of times. But we are just friends," Rome states.

"Friends? I don't buy it."

"I'm not asking you to buy it. I'm telling you it's the truth. I don't have to lie to you. I told you I was going to make this work and I meant it. Now, you calm your ass down, stop acting like a child and communicate with me."

I push away from the table and attempt to leave the bakery, but Rome lightly grabs my wrists when I rise. With his teeth clenched, he whispers, "Sit down, Gwendolyn, do not embarrass me. We are talking."

I look at him and cut my eyes toward my wrists. Rome loosens his grip. "Please, I'm trying to talk," he begs.

Slowly, I take my seat again. With an intent look, I murmur, "Give me my roll."

Rome slides the cinnamon treat across the table. "I'm doing right by you. I had to explain the situation to Lola. We went to lunch right after—two days after that, I gave her some of the things she had at the house. She has gone her way. I've gone mine. Baby, I promise I'm doing right." Rome reaches across the table and places both his hands on top of mine. "I will make this work."

I take a deep breath and kiss the top of Rome's right hand. "I'm trying, Rome," I whisper.

"I know you are, baby. Promise, you'll talk to me."

I nod and give a bashful smile. I guess I should tell him that I've been seeing Omar, but that would make the whole Lola situation seem of little importance. So I'll have to wait until later.

Two more weeks pass and I don't tell Omar that I'm eight weeks pregnant, but I do admit that I'm going though some issues and that I want us to chill for a minute. Of course he asked the normal questions, but the one that stuck out the most was the one concerning his handicap. He thinks that I might not want to be with him because of his paralysis. If only he knew that is far from the truth. I'm actually torn. Omar is stable, reliable and trustworthy, but Rome . . . . Somehow he is quickly working his way into that small crevice of my heart that I rarely allow men into. I've always loved him as a friend, but carrying his child has opened up a new consciousness. I see him with new eyes. I still don't trust him, but I am seeing what a great father he will be. I'm still not moving into his place, though he constantly tries to persuade me. Not that I am opposed to "shacking up," but I fear that quickly giving up my independence is a big mistake. To my dismay, I still drive his car. He insists I can keep it, but I refuse to accept it as a gift. Lia thinks I'm crazy, but I have to do things my way.

Close to two in the morning, I wake up from a bad dream. I stare at the pillow, wondering if Rome is asleep. This baby already has me going through changes, I'm going to wake him up and let him know. However, there is no answer. At first, it doesn't bother me, but then I start to wonder why he isn't picking up. I wait ten minutes more and call again—the same outcome, no answer. Now, as much as I hate it, I can't sleep. I'm sure that he is asleep, but where is he sleeping? These thoughts continue to flash, until I'm so flustered that I place my clothes on and pace the living room. I try to call him again. Ultimately, after four unanswered calls, I find myself pulling up in front of his house.

"This is crazy," I admit. "Am I this woman?" Nervously at his door, I rock from side to side. At last, I knock—lightly, at first, then with a force.

"Who the hell is it?" Rome yells.

A little frightened, I timidly reply, "Rome, it's me Gwen."

Quickly, he swings open the door. I step in and place my head on his shoulder. Immediately, Rome thinks there's a problem. There is no way I can admit I came across town to make sure he was alone, so I went with his assumption.

"I was having nightmares. I got scared and I couldn't sleep."

"Why didn't you call me? I would have come over."

"I did. You didn't answer. I thought something might be wrong, you know how I worry."

Rome wraps his biceps around me, his seemingly distraught girlfriend, and holds tight. I feel metal on my back.

"What's that?" I ask, pulling from his grasp.

"Sorry. It's three A.M. and you were banging on the door like crazy. I wanted to be prepared," he says, placing the handgun on the coffee table.

"Let's go to bed," he says.

Rome and I retire to the bedroom, and with his arms around me, I sleep peacefully through the night.

On the way to the club the next morning, my dad gives me a call. Our conversation is brief, for he is preparing for a funeral. He asks about my health, promises to visit and delivers a request that I'm not prepared to hear.

"Call your mom, Gwen."

I am silent as I await a reason for this appeal, but he doesn't give one. Instead, we stay on the phone in silence. I open up the dark club and walk into the office. Finally, he speaks. "I love you, baby girl. Good-bye." He hangs up, and for the next hour, I sit at my desk and ponder my dad's comment. The silence is driving me mad, so I turn on some music, hoping that the music and the large stack of paperwork will busy my mind for the rest of the day. However, by noon, the music has simply become the background to my thoughts and the stack of work has only been skimmed. I call Lia.

"I need a distraction. Whatcha doing? Let's go shopping."

"I'll be there in an hour," Lia responds.

Happily, I hang up, rush through my work and look forward to spending an afternoon with my friend. I know with Lia's nonstop blabbering, my thoughts won't be able to form, and this is just what I need.

The minutes are ticking by slowly, and Lia should be here now. My pensive thoughts have now become anxious habits.

From the tapping pencil to the clicking heel on the bottom of the chair, my nervous energy is starting to mimic someone with withdrawals. When I go to the restroom, I hear someone coming in the door.

"Finally, my distraction is here." I rush from the office and into the main club area. When I get close to the dance floor area, I see Omar approaching.

"I've missed you," he says, scooping me around my waist.

"You smell good," I respond with a big whiff.

"Let's go away this weekend."

"I can't," I immediately reply.

I can't go away with him. I can't be intimate with him while I'm carrying Rome's child. Suddenly, I get nervous and my stomach starts to flip-flop.

"You okay? You don't look that good. I think you've been working too hard. Let's just get away, not that far. How about Rosewood Pointe?"

"I do love the lake," I remark. "But we need to talk. I don't want things to move too fast. I have some decisions I have to make."

Omar pulls back and looks me in the eye. "You seeing someone?" he asks.

Before I can answer, Lia comes bouncing through the doors with high-pitched whining. "Why the hell aren't you answering your phone? I wanted you to—" She abruptly stops midsentence. Lia gazes at Omar, turns to me and then back to Omar.

"Can you believe it?" I say, breaking the awkward moment.

Lia rapidly shakes her head before replying, "How are you?"

"I'm good, Lia. How are you?" he answers.

Lia walks to him and rubs his face and chest as if she can't believe he's real. "I'm so shocked. You know I tried to call you."

"I know. I didn't want to talk to anyone. But I'm back now."

"For how long?" she asks.

Omar gazes at me, then responds. "We'll see. Excuse me." He goes to the restroom.

Before he gets a few feet away, Lia is feverishly whispering to me.

"What is he doing here? Are you okay? What did he say?" I couldn't answer her fast enough. "What did he mean by 'we'll see'? He still wants you?" She continues to whisper.

"Lia, I've been kicking it with him for a while. I didn't want anyone to know."

Lia smacks me on the arm, leaving a sting. We hear the toilet flush. "We'll talk later," I comment. We gather our composure and politely smile as Omar exits.

"I know you were talking about me, it's okay. You have the rest of the afternoon to wonder what's on my mind. Gwen, I have to go take care of some business. Call me tonight, okay?"

"Okay."

He softly kisses my cheek. "Bye, Lia."

As if we've just witnessed an apparition from a parallel universe, we gape into space. Suddenly, Lia shouts.

"The baby? Does he know about Baby Pharr?"

"No."

"Aren't you concerned? You should be concerned," Lia rambles.

"Do you know he almost died in the accident?" I comment in an eerie monotone.

"That was three years ago."

"He probably won't ever get feeling back in his arm."

"He's going to be pissed once he finds out you're pregnant. He came back for you, not you and some man's baby. Excuse me, not just some man, but his friend's baby."

"Rome was my friend first and he and Omar don't even speak anymore. But I can't think about that right now."

"I can't believe you didn't tell me about Omar. Shame on you." Lia smacks my arm again.

"Will you stop? That hurts," I command.

"Good. Now let's go shopping."

"Oh, I don't feel like shopping anymore," I comment.

"What! But I have on my shopping shoes, see!" Lia points to her sneakers.

"So what, you have on Pumas," I state.

"I only wear sneakers when I'm going shopping."

"Oh, so I guess we have to go now," I mock. "What if we go to the movies? Can they be movie sneakers?"

"I could do a movie. Grab your stuff."

I rush to the back, get my purse and phone.

By nightfall, I am on pins and needles. I haven't called Omar and I don't want to. I also know I can't run from him. So after an hour of looking at his phone number, I dial his digits. He answers on the first ring.

"Hi, Omar."

"So you miss me too," he states. "I got used to seeing you almost every day, and now it's like you're avoiding me."

"What's up, O?"

"Nothing much, looks like I might get that spot I was telling you about."

"Good," I state.

"Can I tell you something?"

"Of course."

"I was going to propose to you the night of the accident."

I am silent. There is no way I can tell him that I knew and yet I still left and moved to Virginia.

"I want to start over, for real. None of this 'kicking it' thing. Let's try this again."

"Things are different, Omar," I state.

"Now that we're sober, we should be better," he says.

"All I'm saying is that you can't just come back and expect to jump back into the scheme like nothing has happened. I'm enjoying your company—let's just chill and leave it at that."

"So you are seeing someone?"

"No, not really."

"Are you sure this is not because of my arm? Because I can show you that the paralysis is not below the waist." We both laugh and again I'm silent.

"Look, I have dealt with this. I know what I am capable of and what I'm not. I don't want to deal with sympathetic looks and pity. I'm taking one day at a time and I want to take those days with you," he continues.

My phone clicks, so I put him on hold.

"Whatcha doing?" Rome asks.

"Talking to Omar," I say candidly.

"Omar? When did you start talking to him?"

"I will call you back."

"No. I need to talk to you."

"I'll call you back," I say.

"I want to see you, I'm coming over," he says.

"Not tonight, Rome. The day has worn me out. I want to be alone."

"Fine, call me when you get off." I hang up and click back over.

"Who was that?" Omar asks.

"Nosey, none of your business."

"Excuse me," he says.

"O, I'm tired. I'll talk to you later this week. I have to go to bed."

"Okay, babe. You sure you're okay?"

"I am. I'm just not feeling my best. I promise I will call, though." I hang up.

After a steamy, hot shower, I slide into bed. Though my mind is racing, I immediately fall asleep. I think therapy is actually helping, because amazingly, I rest through the night without a single interruption and don't awake until my phone rings at 9:35 A.M. Groggy and hazy, I roll over and look at the phone, but don't answer it. I scroll through the caller ID, wipe my eyes and focus on the number, but don't recognize it.

Therefore, I toss the phone down and go to the bathroom to start my day. An hour later, while eating breakfast, the phone rings again. This time, I catch it on ring number two.

"Hello."

"You feeling okay this morning?" Rome asks. "You didn't call me back last night."

"I'm feeling fine, Rome, and you?"

"I'm good," he says. "You talk to Omar anymore?"

"Is that why you called? Please don't start bugging me about O."

"How long have you been talking to him? When you moved back, you said you hadn't spoken to him since the accident."

"He called me about two months ago. We've been talking since. I've even seen him a couple of times." Rome is silent. "He's sober. I'm sober. We've been through a lot. We both had much to forgive each other for."

"He came back to get you?" Rome asks. This time, I am silent. "Do you want him back?" Rome asks.

"Hold on," I say before answering my call-waiting.

"Hello," I answer.

"What's up, girl? You talk to Omar anymore?" Lia asks on the other line.

"Damn, between you and Rome, I don't have time to talk to anyone. I have to call you back—he's on the other line," I tell her.

"Fine. Call me as soon as you hang up." I click back over.

"Okay, I'm back. What were you saying?"

"You know what I was saying. Do you want to be with him?" he reiterates.

As I hesitate to answer, my phone clicks once more.

"Damn it, hold on. I'm sure it's Lia again." I click the phone for a second time.

"Yes, what now?" I say, slightly irritated.

"Hi, Gwendolyn," says the woman.

"Hi. Who's this?" I quickly ask.

"Well, you know you've been a terrible mother when your only child forgets your voice."

As though my mouth is wired shut, my face tenses and muscles in my neck bulge as I try to answer, but can't.

My mother continues. "Gwendolyn, don't you have anything to say? How have you been?" she asks.

Finally, I respond. "I'm fine. I was going to call, but I'm on the phone right now. Can I call you back?"

With uncertainty, she responds. "Um . . . yeah. Do you have the number?"

"It's on the caller ID. Can I reach you at this number?" I ask.

"Yes."

"Okay." I quickly hang up and immediately the phone rings. I pick it up.

"I'm sorry, Rome. . . . Rome, you there?"

"Yeah, you had me on hold long enough. Who was that? Omar?"

"You will not believe who that was. It was my mom," I answer.

"When was the last time you spoke with her?" Rome asks.

"Sometime last year," I respond.

"Does she know about the baby?"

"Probably. I'm sure Dad told her."

"So she's on the other line, I'll let you go."

"I told her I would call her back."

Rome is silent.

"Rome, did you hear me?" I ask.

"Yeah. Go ahead and call her back. I'll see you later today. You coming in the club?"

"Maybe tonight. I don't know yet. But we don't have to get off the phone—"

"Yeah, we do. Go call your mother. I'll hit you later." Rome hangs up, leaving me startled as I listen to the dial tone. I hang up, get another bowl of cereal and flip on the television.

Two hours pass as I watch an old black-and-white movie on AMC. At the film's end, I busy myself with a load of clothing and some light housecleaning. Finally, when there is no more work, I realize that I can't put off calling my mother any longer. I pick up the phone and dial my dad, but there is no answer. I hang up, take several deep breaths and scroll through the ID to call my mom. After three rings, she picks up.

"Hello," answers Rose Pharr Oliver. There is silence on my line as she speaks again. "Hello," she says louder.

"Um . . . hi," I say quietly.

"Gwendolyn, I thought for sure I was going to be the one to call back. How are you?" she kindly asks.

"I'm fine, and you?" I respond.

"I'm surviving. Besides the constant growth of gray hairs, I'm good."

"Well, if all you have is gray hair to complain about, then I would say you were better than good," I comment before a few more seconds of silence.

"How have you been?" she asks once more.

"You've already asked me that. I told you I was fine. I'm surprised to hear from you. I mean, are you calling for some reason?" I question.

"Yes. I needed to hear from my daughter. We should talk more often."

"You think?" I ask.

"Don't you?" she says.

"Not really. We don't have much to say—look at this conversation."

"Gwendolyn, I worry about you," Rose says abruptly.

"Well, that's funny. What are you concerned about? I'm fine."

Another moment of silence falls over the line. This one lasts close to a minute.

"You don't have to pretend as if you don't know. I know you know," I comment.

"Know what?" she says innocently.

"You are not a good liar."

"I know this, which is why I don't lie anymore. I was never good at it. I really don't know what you are talking about," she says.

"Have you not talked to Dad?"

"I spoke to him to get your number."

"Why did you want my number?" I ask.

"I miss you, child. Aren't you listening to me? Is it a crime to miss my daughter? I haven't spoken to you in a year and a half." Rose takes a brief pause before continuing. "I woke up the other night and you were on my mind, which happens often. But usually I think, you don't want to talk to me, so I don't call. The last thing I want to do is bother you. But that particular night, I had the feeling that you needed me, so I called and got your number. I just wanted to let you know that I'm here, just in case."

"Needed you? Wow, I haven't needed you in a long time."

"Yeah, well. I still wanted to talk to you, but, I guess, I don't have anything to say. So maybe if you think of something, you'll call me? You have my number. This is my cell. It's usually on." Rose delivers a big sigh at the end of the sentence, followed by a low hum.

I hear ice tumbling in a glass, so I inquire, "What are you drinking, a White Russian?"

"Cream upsets my stomach. Black Russian is my drink of choice now," she says.

"I guess some things do change."

"Well, they say black is the new white," she jests.

"Does your Caucasian husband know that?"

Rose quietly smirks and follows it with a low growl.

"Well, I don't drink anymore," I admit, abruptly ending Rose's low rumbles.

"Oh, that's good, baby. That's real good. It's hell on your liver, I can tell you that."

After a quiet moment, I comment, "So you really don't know?"

"Know what?"

I sneer, then respond, "I'm pregnant."

Rose gasps, nearly choking on her coffee liqueur and vodka combo. "Get outta here. You're having a baby? How far along are you? I can't believe Marvin didn't tell me. Were you not going to tell me?"

"I would have . . . eventually," I confess.

"I know I am a loser in your eyes, but please don't say you hate me that much." Rose lets out a few more loud sighs, then says, "I'm going to be a grandmother."

"Yes, Rose, you are," I say very calmly.

"Wow . . . um, congratulations."

"Thanks."

"Who is the father? Is it serious? Are you getting married? Dear God, are you already married?"

"No. You would know if I were. The father . . . well, you know him. It's Romulus Sutton."

"Patricia's baby boy? Does she know? Oh my, I haven't talked to her in years. I knew you two were still friends, but I had no idea you were seeing one another. Well, this is good news. I should visit," Rose says in one big breath.

"Not right now. Things are still wishy-washy and I have too much going on to deal with you too."

"Deal with me," Rose says, obviously offended.

"That didn't come out right. It's just bad timing. Maybe in a few months."

"Well, we're about to go on vacation, so I guess a few months will be better for both of us," says Rose, attempting to save face.

"I'll call you, though, I promise." I sound as though I am parting from a new summer-camp friend.

"I would like that," Rose faintly replies, as if she knows that that call may never come. Then after two more sighs and one groan, she continues. "Okay, well, it was good to hear your voice. You sound good and um . . . congratulations again."

"Thanks. I have to go," I quickly comment.

"Call me."

"I will," I whisper before releasing the call. The disconnection between Rose and me is palpable. I stare at the phone, desperately trying to shake the torture I just endured. While releasing a loud grumble, I shake my shoulders uncontrollably, as though I am releasing a demon. Unfortunately, this wicked time capsule is buried far too deep to gyrate loose. Thank God I have a therapy appointment in the morning.

ROSE
Session Six

I used to joke and tell my friends that my mom's name is the reason tulips are my favorite flower, but I'm not sure if it's truly a joke. I've only said this aloud once before, but I really wish we had a normal mother-daughter relationship. But wishes do not make reality. Honestly, my mom and dad should have never married. To this day, I'm not sure why they did. My dad is the most giving, nurturing man I've ever known, and maybe some tiny part of her needed that. Her real dad was never around, and with my dad being a little older, it gave her a sense of fostering. Of course, this is only my speculation.

Our family was normal for the most part. My dad did the cooking and my mom did the cleaning. My dad did my hair because my mom couldn't braid. Though on occasion, she would give me ponytails. I felt like a big girl on ponytail days. We did things together as a family—went to Coney Island a few times and to Niagara Falls once. My mom and I didn't spend that much fun time together, though; she was always busy doing stuff. Oh, but she did teach me how to play cards when I was nine. We used to play every Sunday after church. Dad always had a funeral on Sunday, so we would go home, eat what he cooked the night before and play tonk and gin rummy, which was my favorite.

However, it seemed that not a lot of black people died in the Bronx between 1978 and 1980, and my dad almost sold the lot that the business was on. I was only four but my mom used to talk about all of the things we were going to do once he sold the land. But he never did. He couldn't. He wasn't going to be the generation that ended the family business, which had been in that building, at that address, since the 1940s. Plus, that's all he knew how to do. I would hear him confess often and frankly that he didn't want to learn anything else. When they fussed . . . well, she fussed, Dad used to sit and ignore her, and she would say, "You're so complacent, Marvin, you are so complacent." I didn't know what that meant, but I liked the way she said "complacent." She would emphasize the p and stretch out the "pla" syllable. I would mimic her— that's what daughters do, I guess. From ages ten to twelve, everything, from my dolls to my food, was complacent. But after the age of twelve, I never used the word again. I still don't till this day.

In 1986, one month after my twelfth birthday, a Sunday, my mom went to Atlantic City, and that Friday, she left us. Just like that. She vanished like those people in horror movies. She told me that she was going on vacation. I remembered wanting to go, but she said it was a vacation for grown folks. She hugged me extra tight and I didn't see her for another two years. My dad tried to make excuses for her.

He said that she was sick and had to go get help. But I soon found out that help came in the form of a very wealthy restaurateur named Jack Oliver. They got married when I was fourteen, and my mom had the nerve to ask me if I wanted to be a part of the wedding. I hadn't seen her since she abandoned us and she wanted to know if I cared to be in her freaking wedding. Finally, I started to believe my dad. She was sick—sick in the head. But you know what, I went. I didn't participate, but I was in attendance. I wanted to see my mom and I wanted to see what she left us for. When I saw the big house, the exotic flowers and the fancy clothes, I understood why she left. This is where she belonged. She was never the wife of a mortician; she just played the role for as long as she could bear it. I wasn't completely mad at her for leaving. I was mostly mad 'cause she married my dad in the first place. My mom was from Canada, but moved to Manhattan in her twenties. All three of her stepfathers were well-off. She had no business marrying a mortician from the Bronx. It was a bad decision. When she saw him after church one Sunday, she should have kept on walking. Rose wanted to make my dad into some other guy that he wasn't. She used to say, "Your father would be wonderful, only if . . ." I guess it was the "only if" that made her drink and eventually made her leave.

I was supposed to stay with her in the summers, but she was often out of the country. So when she returned, it was time for me to go back to school. She, Jack and I went to Acapulco once, but the sight of them kissing made me violently ill. My mom disliked public affection, or so she used to say. But now, everything was different— she was a stranger and our relationship became more distant. She missed my high-school graduation by a few hours. Her flight was delayed. But to make up for it, I got a new car, and everyone on the block was jealous. I fed into the hype for a minute, but it was a poor substitute for my mom's presence. So many times I wanted to call her, but I didn't know what to say. The good thing is that my dad and I grew closer, but he never remarried—the business became his second wife. He started aging faster, and my mother was getting younger. I hated that. It's like she stole life from him to rejuvenate herself.

She and Jack came to my college graduation, but by then, I was over her. I went from not choosing to be around her to not liking her altogether. My dad now smoked because of her. I was fat because of her. I was insecure because of her. I drank because of her. I blamed her for everything. It was easy, she wasn't around to defend herself. She never was the maternal type. She never had any other kids and she rarely talked to the one she did have. I always wondered why she didn't just keep walking that afternoon when she saw my dad leaving the church parking lot. Why did she marry him? Why did she have me? I guess we were just a phase—the first two chapters on disillusionment in her book of dreams. I'm not mad at her, not anymore. I just don't see her as my mother. Is that bad? She's more like an acquaintance, someone I used to kick it with. And though I'm not angry, I vowed never to be like her.

One good note—because of her, I don't make hasty decisions, and I always follow through because it's irresponsible to bail out on people. This is why I still stress over bailing on Omar. I still feel I should have sacrificed and been there for him. But anyway, I got my devotion from my dad. His dedication to commitment is infectious. I can't believe I'm admitting it, but I still pray that a little of that would have rubbed off on Rose. Then maybe, who knows, things may have been different.

Session Done

8

At twelve weeks along, I surprisingly have a little pouch. It looks more like a very big dinner instead of a fetus, but nonetheless it excites Rome. He comes into the office today and wants to draw an outline of my belly against the wall. At first, I deny him, but finally I give in. Once I see the belly outline, I display a slight bit of joy.

With my shirt down, I push my stomach out so that it protrudes at least five more inches. "Imagine when I get this big," I say with a giggle. Rome rubs my tummy as I snuggle my head onto his shoulder. Just then, Omar knocks on the partially cracked door and walks in. He views Rome and me in our embrace, with his hand on my somewhat swollen belly. Immediately, we part. I briskly walk to my desk and fumble through the papers. Quickly, Rome breaks into conversation.

"O, man, what's up?" Rome moves to greet Omar, but Omar doesn't immediately respond favorably. "How are you doing? Long time, why didn't you call me?" Rome continues.

With his hands by his side, Omar looks at me. I purposely make no eye contact.

"Yo, man, what's up?" Rome repeats.

Finally, Omar speaks. "You tell me, brother. What is up?"

"Not much, just trying to keep everything going here. It's

good to see you." Rome tries to embrace Omar, but he stays positioned by the door. "You look good."

"Thanks, man. So . . . what were you and Gwen doing?"

"Huh?" Rome responds with a blank look.

Omar places a smile on his face and walks over to my desk. I recognize this expression. It's the "calm before the storm" smile. When he would start to get upset, Omar would get a nervous grin. It's crooked and only bares his teeth on the left side. I shift my position away from the desk toward the bathroom.

"Man, you know me and Gwen. We were just playing around."

Omar eyes me as I nervously move around the office. "Yeah, I almost forgot how close you two used to be." He gives Rome a blank stare, then motions toward me. "You ready to go to lunch? We have so much to talk about."

I have completely forgotten about my lunch date with Omar.

"I don't know. I do have a lot to do."

"C'mon, girl," Omar says. He reaches for my hand. "You gotta eat. Just one hour, please."

I look at Rome anxiously.

"Why don't we all go to lunch?" Rome suggests.

Omar hesitates, bites his bottom lip and responds. "No offense, man, but I really want to talk to Gwen alone."

"It's cool. We can go, but I can't be gone all afternoon. I do have work to do," I state.

"Great. Let me use the restroom and I'm ready."

As soon as the door closes, I rush over to Rome. "I'm going to tell him at lunch," I whisper.

"No, we should tell him together."

"No, Rome. He is my ex-boyfriend. I owe him the explanation, not you."

"And what if he gets mad at you?"

"That's why I'm going to tell him in a public place," I explain in an undertone.

"Tell me what?" Omar says, walking from the restroom.

I whip around and ask, "Did you flush? 'Cause I didn't hear a flush."

"No, I just needed to wash some guck from the car off my hands."

"Oh." I smile and grasp for something else to say.

"Tell me what?" Omar reiterates.

I exhale and look at Rome. I know that Omar is going to persist to get an answer the entire lunch until I reveal what Rome and I were discussing, so I figure there's no better time than the present. I walk over to Omar and take him by the hand. I look him in the eyes and speak. "I'm pregnant, O. I wanted to tell you over lunch, but there you have it."

He continues to hold my hand, but his gaze turns cold. So frigid is his look that a chill comes over the room. I slowly loosen my grip and back away from Omar. I position myself against the wall by the chalk drawing. A very stiff Omar looks at me and glances down at my belly. He doesn't move his head, but his eyes travel up and down my body.

"I'm sorry . . . . I mean, I'm not sorry. But you've been gone, and you didn't want to see me, ever." I am rambling.

Omar holds his head down and smirks. After a few deep breaths, he lifts his chin. "So, can we still go to lunch?"

I purse my lips and respond, "I guess. You okay?"

"I'm fine. I have no reason to be upset. I wish you'd said something earlier, but hey—"

"Okay, where do you want to eat?" I walk by Rome as I grab my purse from the file cabinet. Rome makes eye contact to make sure I am okay.

"Rome, I'll see you later," I say.

Omar nods to Rome, but says nothing. He then angles my body toward him and delivers an unimpassioned gaze.

"You're pregnant . . . wow . . . you're having a baby." I give several consecutive nods as I move toward the door. However, Omar isn't budging. "Who?"

"Huh?"

"Who? Whose child are you having?"

Rome shifts from the file cabinets to an erect position by the desk chair. I let out a loud, nervous chortle. The more I try to talk, the louder the mirth becomes. The chuckles quickly evolve into gasps. I desperately reach inside my purse for my inhaler. Both men rush to my side.

"You okay, babe?" they say in unison.

Rapidly, I nod and suck in air. With Rome to my right and Omar to my left, both men take me by the shoulder and attempt to comfort me.

"I'm okay, I'm okay," I manage to whisper in between inhales.

Omar steps back as I take a seat.

"When did your asthma start back?" Rome asks.

"Last year."

"When did you have asthma?" Omar asks.

"When she was a little girl," Rome answers, kneeling by my side. He places one hand on my stomach and the other on my back. With a gentle circular motion, he rubs around my navel. "Are you sure you're okay? Maybe you should go home and lie down. Want me to come with you?"

With my panting calmed, I breathe quietly. I tilt my head to the side and slowly bat my eyes at Rome. He slowly moves his hand from my back to the back of my head. Softly, he tangles his fingers within the curls at the nape of my neck. His other hand lies still on my stomach. Omar stands to the side and witnesses the connection between us. Though he stands less than a few inches apart, he surely feels miles away.

"Oh shit," Omar observes.

The remark jars me from Rome's embrace. I straighten up and face Omar. His stare is more intent and I'm positive that he now knows Rome is the father.

"I can explain—" I comment before Rome interrupts.

"Look, man, we should talk. You know how I feel about Gwen."

Omar squints, attempting to form the right words, but nothing comes out of his gaped mouth. Rome rises and pushes my seat back so that he and Omar are face-to-face.

"Look, man, I know we haven't been cool for a while, though I've apologized several times. But I love Gwen, and I have for a long time. I know you're not going to understand this, but she and I are together now, and I'm the father."

With the tension as thick and funky as old cheese, I don't know how to cut into the conversation. Rolling my chair, I continue to push my way back into the corner. Omar is motionless and silent.

"I'm not going to apologize, you're just going to have to deal with it. I just hope you—"

Before Rome can finish his sentence, Omar gives him a left hook, nearly knocking the wind from his pipes. The blow sends Rome to the other end of the desk, but he grabs the corner, uses it for momentum and counters with a swing. He makes contact just below Omar's jaw.

"Stop it!" I yell. I get in between the men, but to no avail. They continue to roll around on the desk, punching each other silly. I run from the office to find Moo Moo. Screaming through the halls, I nearly trip rounding the corner as I enter the main room. "Moo Moo! Damn it, where are you?" I finally find him in the stockroom unpacking cases of hot wings. With earphones obstructing his tympanic membrane, Moo Moo can only hear Nas's latest masterpiece. I snatch the cords and replace his music with even louder noise. "Omar and Rome are fighting!" As quick as a 240-pound bouncer can run, he rushes back to the office. By now, the men have wrestled their way to the floor and Rome has Omar pinned between the bookshelf and file cabinet. In my highest pitch, I scream for the men to stop. But with one hand, Moo Moo bends down and lifts Rome from atop Omar—and just like that, the fight is over.

"You two are upsetting Gwen. She said stop!" Moo Moo says in a sluggish, deep voice.

He holds Omar at bay with his right arm and places Rome on the floor a few steps away. Moo Moo is like a brick wall between the two men. Between his height and girth, they can barely see one another. Puffing out bursts of air, Omar walks to the bathroom and slams the door. I immediately hit Rome in the chest.

"What's wrong with you? Punching him like that! He can barely move."

"Me! Did you see him hit me? Fuck that, I'm supposed to let him hit me 'cause he's handicapped?" Rome's voice grows louder as he obnoxiously addresses Omar through the door. "Fuck him and his handicap!"

Omar whips the door open and quickly approaches. "What did you say?"

"You heard me," Rome banters.

Moo Moo physically removes Omar from the room.

"Nigga, put me down," Omar bellows as he is being carried away.

"You can't ever come back in this club again!" Rome yells.

"Fuck you!" Omar shouts from the hallway.

Rome kicks the desk chair across the room. "Damn it!" As I step to him, he moves away. "Did you just defend him? He hit me first."

"I know he hit you, but he was angry. I told you to let me tell him. But no—"

"That nigga tried to dislocate my jaw," Rome says, moving his jaw side to side.

"You still should have pushed him away, not hit him. You could have ended it if you wanted."

"I'm not going to let a man sucker punch me like that—I don't care if he has no arms."

I look at him and smirk, which soon turns to a full grin and then tiny chuckles quietly seep out. An inquisitive look befalls Rome's face. "I'd like to see a man with no arms punch you," I comment.

Rome can't help but laugh. "You know what I mean." Rome pokes out his bottom lip and mutters, "He hit me first."

I comfort Rome. In baby talk, I cuddle him into my breasts. "I'm sorry, baby. I didn't mean to take his side. You okay? Let me see your cheek."

"It's my jaw," he says, giving in to my coddling.

"Oh, let me see your jaw."

"It hurts," he whimpers. Men are such big babies.

I cover his jaw with tiny pecks, leaving a trail of mauve lipstick stains. "We should go. You hungry? Let's go eat." I usher Rome from the office to the main room. We meet Moo Moo at the bar.

"What was that about?" he asks.

Rome keeps walking, but I answer him. "We told O about the baby. He flipped. We're going to eat."

"You coming back?" Moo Moo asks.

I nod. Moo Moo goes back to the stockroom and I rush to catch up with Rome.

The next week is very peaceful. Though I peer around every corner before turning and watch my back throughout the day, Omar doesn't surface. I did call him to apologize for not coming clean sooner, but he didn't answer. Therefore, I continue to practice my "what if I run into Omar speech"—just in case—but luckily, I don't have to use it. No surprise calls from my mom, no Omar and Lia only calls twice. I am ecstatic about my well-deserved days of peace. Seven days pass and I don't even realize that it has been a week since the infamous fight.

Early Tuesday morning when I walk into the club, the office phone is already ringing. I rush to answer it.

"Hello, Ole Skool."

"I'm looking for a Gwendolyn Pharr."

"This is she."

"This is Madeline Wright. I'm a nurse at Northside Hospital in Atlanta, Georgia. I'm calling about Tracy Kirkland. You were his next-of-kin contact and I wanted to inform you that he was shot and is in critical condition."

"Oh, my God!" I nearly miss my seat as my body loses the strength to stand. I hold on to the corner of the desk for support. "What? When did this happen?"

"Last night, around two in the morning."

"Oh God! How critical is he? He is going to live, isn't he?"

"Well, we have to operate to remove the two bullets. We won't be able to operate until we stabilize his blood pressure. But luckily, the bullets aren't against any vital parts. Though one bullet is relatively close to the spine, the doctors feel secure they can remove it during the surgery without any chance of paralysis."

"Okay, okay. I'll be there tomorrow. What's the hospital address? What's your name again?" I grab paper and pen and quickly jot down the information. As soon as she hangs up, I get online to purchase a ticket. "Shit, I gotta call Omar."

Hesitantly, I dial his number, but he doesn't answer. I dial two more times, but still there is no answer. I hang up and begin to book my ticket when my cell phone rings. It's Omar.

"Where are you? Why didn't you pick up the phone?"

"What do you want?" he asks.

"Tracy is in the hospital. He was shot. They say his condition is critical. He's all by himself, I'm booking my flight right now."

"Book mine too. When are we leaving?"

"Tomorrow morning good?" I ask.

"Yep. Call me back and let me know the details. I'll give you cash for the ticket."

"Fine. I'll call you back." I hang up and book a flight leaving Wednesday at 8:00 A.M.

The rest of the day, my nerves are rattled. I continuously call the hospital to check the status of Tracy, but it remains unchanged. Rome is prepping for a video shoot, so he doesn't come by the club. I neglect to tell him about Tracy. However, when I do decide to place the call, I'm a bit apprehensive. Rome is going to object to the Atlanta trip, he'll be even more wary about me going with Omar. Therefore, I prepare myself for his argument. However, he doesn't answer the phone, so I'm off the hook. He may not check his messages until the morning. "Rome, there's been an emergency. Tracy is in the hospital. I'm leaving in the morning for Atlanta. I'll be back in a few days. You can reach me on my cell. Oh, I'm going to bed early tonight, so if I don't answer, I'm asleep." I hang up and plop on my bed. Knowing it's going to be difficult to relax, I take a bath to calm my nerves, and then climb underneath my sheets.

Omar and I arrive in Atlanta by ten the next morning and make it to the hospital before eleven. Because the flight was almost full, we didn't sit next to each other. Therefore, the cab ride was the first time we actually communicated. Omar only said four words: "Thanks for calling me."

We say nothing else until we are walking into Tracy's room. I rush by his bed, grab his arm and hold it close to my chest. He lies with his eyes closed. His room is sterile white. His sheets are folded and pin tucked tightly underneath the mattress. I lean over, caress his face and then glance up at Omar, who is standing by the closet door. He stares motionlessly at Tracy.

Omar stares at the numerous tubes feeding in and out of his brother's nose and hand. "I don't like to see you like this. You have to get better, okay? You're all I got and . . ." Omar begins to get emotional.

"I'm better already. Ain't no gunshots gon' bring me down," Tracy mutters with his mouth partially closed.

I speak in a consoling tone. "You know you're coming back to Detroit after you get out."

Ignoring my comment, Tracy states, "I'm glad you two are here together—"

"Oh, we aren't together," Omar interrupts. "We just came here to check on you."

"We came here together, that's what he means," I irritably respond.

Thankfully, Tracy doesn't notice the tension as he reaches for both our hands. "I'm glad you're here."

Suddenly, both Omar and I realize the importance of our presence.

That night, I return Rome's four unanswered phone calls. Though he is livid, I assure him that I'm okay and that it's important for me to be here for Tracy. Rome doesn't like my bond with Tracy. You see, I don't have many sounding boards, but I found one in Tracy. None of my friends were there during the many late-night sessions Tracy used to have with me over a glass of scotch. We talked about the absence of our mothers, insecurities and addictions. We have much in common. We both would rather run than confront the truth. Sure, Tracy gets in his share of trouble, but he has a heart of gold and I see that. If he needs me, I will be here, and no one is going to convince me otherwise.

Tracy's surgery is a success. He is stabilized and the doctors look to release him in four days. I decide to stay until Tracy gets out and back on his feet. I wait on him hand and foot. Unsurprisingly, this pampering comes with mothering advice, which he doesn't like. But during the weekend, I get the scoop on what really happened and why my lil' brother ended up in the hospital with two gunshots to the chest. Apparently, it had something to do with the Cubans his partner Jason borrowed the money from. When they came to collect, Jason was out of town and an altercation developed. Luckily, a bartender was still there, heard the shots and found

Tracy in the back parking lot. The whole incident leaves me utterly disturbed. I insist that Tracy move back to Detroit, but it falls on deaf ears. He is going to stick this venture out. The day I leave, I try again, but his mind is made up.

Omar is opening up a sports bar about five miles from Ole Skool. Though it's not a nightclub, Rome feels it's direct competition, and he is enraged. He asks me to hire someone to do some extra marketing and he wants space in the office, which is already too small. Lia is having her bathroom remodeled and she wants to stay with me for a week. Finally, Rome is hired to do his largest video job, so he's a little stressed. And who does everyone call? Me. Lia moves in and is already driving me mad. The first night, she wants to stay up, bake cookies and watch old movies. The second night, she wants to go bowling. The third night, she wants to double-date with Rome and me. By the fourth night, I am exhausted. I come home and go to bed before Lia can get there. However, when Lia hits the door, she rushes to my room, wakes me up and insists that we go out dancing. This night, Lia gets a pleasant cursing.

"Go by your damn self. I'm tired, Lia. Can't you be still and quiet at least one night? I'm pregnant. I'm not going out dancing."

"You don't look pregnant, not really," Lia says, lifting my nightshirt.

"Girl, put my shirt down. I'm not going. Don't you have some other friends to bug?" I ask.

Lia releases my shirt, sits on the edge of the bed and lowers her head. She is quiet, which is rare, so I know something is wrong. Slowly, I prop my upper body onto my elbows and nudge Lia with my knee. Lia turns, with a piteous look, and replies, "No . . . no, I don't."

"No what?" I ask.

"No, I don't have any other friends to bug. I don't have any other friends, period," she solemnly says.

I completely lift my upper body and lean against the headboard. "You have friends."

"No, I don't," Lia sulks.

"Why would you say that? Rome is your friend. Jasmine is your friend. And what about that other girl you hang with sometimes? What's her name? Langley?"

"Rome is my friend, so I have one other friend, but he's got you, so we don't hang out anymore. Jasmine is my lover, ex-lover, so she doesn't count. Langley is my shopping partner—she's not my friend. She's someone who appreciates a good designer sale as much as I do. That's hard to find. Other than you and Rome, I don't have any true friends." Lia walks into the other room.

I follow behind her. Lia is a drama princess and I know this better than most, but the more I think about this, the more I realize that it just might be true. However, having two good friends is one more than most have, so it's not as bad as she makes it seem. I walk into the kitchen and grab a banana Popsicle from the freezer. "Want one?" I offer. Lia silently nods.

I take a seat next to my gloomy friend. "You don't bug me, not all the time. You're just so active that it's overwhelming. You know me. I'm mellower than you. I have to take you in doses, small doses. But I still love you," I admit.

"I know you love me, Gwenie. I'm sorry. I try to do all this stuff when we're together because I don't see you that often. And when the baby comes, you really won't have time to hang out with me."

"But we didn't hang out all the time when I was with Omar."

"Yeah, but Jas and I were together then. I'm one of those people," she says.

"What people?" I question.

"Those people that always need to be with someone. I'm

needy. I can't help it. That's probably why I don't have that many friends, you think?"

"No. Some people just don't make friends as easily as others. But you're a great person," I tell her.

"Yeah, I guess. But I'm not like you. . . . People flock to you. Hell, half the time you don't even want them to like you, but they do. I want people to like me. I work at it."

"Maybe that's the problem. You shouldn't work at it. People will either like you or they won't. Don't try so hard. People sense that and then they think something is wrong with you. Just be you."

Lia takes the remainder of my Popsicle and removes the frozen yellow ice from the stick. She crunches it with her teeth. "I guess," she finally responds.

"This is not an after-school special. Is this some sad little ploy, so that you can get me to agree to go out?" I say.

"No. I don't care if you go out or not. I'm just glad we're sitting here chilling." Just then, Lia's phone rings and she answers. "This is Lia." She's briefly quiet, then lets out a surreptitious chuckle. "I'll call you." Lia hangs up the phone.

"Who was that?" Lia doesn't answer as I persist. "You're the needy friend, and I'm the nosey one. Who was that?"

"It was Jas," she responds.

"She's in town?" I ask.

Lia nods and then looks across the room.

"What's up with you two?"

"She's my girl. I love Jasmine. But . . ."

"But what?" I continue to pry.

"I don't know why we still hook up. It's not like it's going anywhere. I mean, we're not getting married. Even if it were legal, I wouldn't marry her. I can't spend the rest of my life with a woman," Lia says.

"Married? When did you start believing in marriage? And you could spend the rest of your life with a woman, if you wanted to. Where is all of this going?"

"I don't know. It's just ever since I got that letter, I've been thinking. I do love sex, but what has it gotten me? Who's going to take care of me when I get old? Maybe I should have a family."

I place my hand on Lia's forehead. "Are you sick? Hell, are you Lia?" I laugh as Lia slaps my hand away.

"These are just some thoughts. Don't get carried away," she says.

"No, it's cool. You are getting older, right? I guess it's just a natural progression."

"I guess," Lia says while rising to grab her purse.

"Where are you going?" I ask.

"You know where I'm going," Lia responds.

"But what about all that you just said?"

"That was the future. This is tonight. And tonight, I just want to be held," she replies.

"Held? Okay, well, you better take your ass to Jasmine, 'cause ain't no holding going on at 302 Riverfront."

With a huge smile, Lia leans over and kisses my cheek. "I love you, my friend," she says.

"You better," I respond.

"Can I have a Popsicle for the road?" Lia says, going toward the kitchen. "Damn, Gwen, you got five boxes of Pops up here."

"I know what's in my freezer, and it's only two banana ones left. You can't have those. Get another flavor."

"Fine. I'm taking orange. I'll call you before I come tomorrow." Lia leaves.

I flip on the television and curl up on the couch. However, after five minutes, I call Rome. "Hell, I want someone to hold me, too." I mumble to myself before he answers.

"What are you doing?"

"Looking over these résumés. I need to find an animator," he answers.

"For the video?" I ask.

"Yeah, we're mixing mediums. The treatment is hot. Why don't you come down to Miami next week? I'll be there three days prepping before we shoot. We'll have time to hang out."

"I just got back and I have my eighteen-week checkup next week. It's the first time we might be able to determine the sex of the baby," I tell him.

"No, you can't go without me. Wait until I get back."

"I can't. How about this, I won't find out the sex until my next visit."

"You'll cheat—you'll find out and not tell me. Then you'll act like you didn't know," he says.

"No, I won't, I promise."

"Why don't you move your appointment?" he requests.

"Look, go do your job. You better get used to this. You aren't going to be here for everything. Trust me, I'll wait. But why don't you put that work down and come over here."

"Well, well, you don't invite me over often," Rome comments.

"Yes, I do."

"No, I invite myself over," he counters.

"Well, I'm inviting you over tonight. And I don't want to hear no for an answer."

"You won't hear that from me. I'll be over within the hour. I still got some drawers over there?"

"Yeah, you still got drawers over here," I say, mocking him.

"Cool, see you in a minute." Rome hangs up, leaving a big smile upon my face.

I pop up from the couch and walk over to the kitchen. Grabbing my favorite teapot from the cabinet, I fill it with water and fumble through my box of herbal teas.

About forty minutes later, Rome is knocking on my door. Unlike most nights, I have set the mood. With candles burning, soft jazz music playing, I'm dressed in a sexy black nightgown. I open the door, wearing a stealthy grin. Rome steps in, looks around the room and gently lifts me into his arms. He says nothing, only carries me to the bedroom and lays me down. He slowly lifts my nightgown and kisses my skin.

"You smell like cocoa butter," he says.

"Yeah, I put it all over."

"All over?" he asks in a curious sexual tone.

I immediately get his underlying probing. "Yes, all over," I emphasize.

Rome moves his kisses from my navel to the tip of my vagina. I spend the next few hours with an arched back and curled toes as I gasp and whimper soft screams. Throughout the night and early the next morning, Rome and I make love and it is more than wonderful. It is so good, that I come over to his house the next night for seconds. Surprisingly, it's better than the night before. Always being a little reluctant to experiment, I normally stick to what I know when it comes to sex. However, I blame my adventurous sexual behavior on the pregnancy and try all kinds of new tricks. Rome is very receptive. We have sex five more times before he boards the plane. Needless to say, I send my man off to Miami smiling from ear to ear. That's right, my man, we finally decide to give the relationship a try. It may seem a little fast, but then again, maybe it's been happening all the while, and I'm just noticing.

The second night Rome is in Miami, Omar has the official grand-opening party for Comatose, his sports bar. He calls the club to invite Lia and me. Of course, I don't want to go, but he says it wouldn't be the same without me there. I listen to his imploring, and agree to come, but only for a few minutes. Lia thinks I'm crazy, but goes along for the ride and fusses the entire trip.

"Why are we going?"

"This is important to him and I want to show him that I can still be his friend."

"He's your ex. You don't have to support his dreams."

"I know, but look, we have to get along. He is going to be here, right up the street. So the easier I make this transition in our relationship, the easier it will be for everyone," I tell her.

"What transition? You left him. Now you are with Rome, carrying his child. The transition is you switching from one guy to another. It's best if you simply leave the ex alone," she warns.

Just then, Rome calls my cell phone. "It's like he knows when I'm talking about Omar." I quickly pick up. "Hey, baby, how's Miami?"

"Good and hot. What's up with you? I tried you at home, you at the club?" he asks.

"No, I'm out with Lia."

"Oh yeah, where are you going?"

I clear my throat to stall. "Hold on, baby." I quickly mute the cell phone. "He wants to know where we're going," I whisper to Lia.

"You better tell him something, and don't forget, Detroit may be a big city, but it's still a small world."

I hit the button and continue to talk. "Sorry about that. Yeah, I wanted some ice cream, so we went for dessert. Now we're just riding around. I don't know what we'll get into," I say.

Rome is silent for a second; then he finally responds. "Well, be safe. Tell Lia hello. Your doctor's appointment is in the morning, right?"

"Yeah, Lia is going with me."

"Don't—"

"I'm not going to find out the sex of the baby," I interrupt.

Lia snatches the phone away. "I'm going to find out, and then I'm going to tell you both when you get back."

I seize my cellular. "Don't listen to her. I'll talk to you tomorrow."

"Okay, bye . . . love you," he says.

At first, I hesitate. The first time Rome told me he loved me, we were teenagers and he was leaving for Detroit. We've said we love each other throughout our relationship, but this time his "I love you" sounded different. It was the tone. I do love him, but I'm not in love. I don't think.

"Gwen, you still there?" Rome asks.

"I love you too," I say quickly before hanging up.

Lia teases me. "Oooh, are we at the 'I love you' phase already?"

"Hush up, and let's go, say congrats and get out before anyone notices us." We park and walk into the grand-opening celebration.

Not five minutes into the club, Lia runs into at least three acquaintances. I see a few people I recognize, but luckily they don't see me. However, I soon lose Lia within the crowd of people. While looking for the bathroom, I run into Moo Moo.

"What are you doing here?" I ask.

"What are you doing here?" he replies.

"I was invited."

"So was I. Look, I know Rome and Omar have their beef, but I like Omar. I wanted to show my support."

"All I know is I better not see you working over here," I tell him.

"Never."

"Have you seen Lia? I'm ready to go."

Just then, Omar walks up and taps me on the shoulder.

"I didn't think you would come," he says.

"I wanted to show you my support. I'm not staying, I just wanted to say congratulations. I'm very proud of you."

Omar looks at me and extends his arm around my waist. "I'm sorry, I haven't been talking to you."

"It's fine. I understand."

We finally embrace. The entire time in Atlanta, Omar didn't say three words to me and he didn't touch me. As much as I understand his anger, I really want us to be friends. I still care for him a lot. I know it sounds like I want to have my cake and eat it too, and maybe I do. Perhaps it's my problem with never wanting to disappoint people. Either way, we continue to embrace, until Moo Moo breaks the hug.

"Omar man, congratulations. And I'm so sorry about the other day." He sticks out his hand as a peace offering.

"You were just doing your job. It's forgotten. No bad thoughts tonight, only good ones. It's a celebration!" Omar yells. "Let's go get something to drink." He grabs my hand and leads me to the bar. Begrudgingly, I tag along, searching the room for Lia.

"Orange-pineapple juice on the rocks. Make it two, but add Sprite to one," I say.

The bartender serves up two juices, and Omar and I lean against the bar and look at the crowd.

"This is a really nice place."

"Yeah, I got a great deal on it," he answers.

"How did you do everything so fast? This place used to be a dump."

"I've got a good team."

I sip quietly on my juice and continue to look at the crowd.

"I'm going to see if Tracy will come back and help me run the place," Omar says.

I turn to him and speak loudly through the music. "That would be good. He doesn't need to be in Atlanta. He's in over his head."

Omar moves closer to me. Though he says nothing, our arms graze slightly against each other. The hairs on the back of my neck rise. Seconds later, Lia appears from nowhere.

"There you are, I've been looking for you. Hi, Omar, love your place."

"You ready? I think it's time for us to leave," I say.

As Lia is about to speak, Omar cuts in. "You can't go yet. I have something to show you."

"But we really should be going," I reiterate.

"After this." Omar takes me by the hand and pulls me toward the back. I grab Lia's hand and the three of us move swiftly through the crowd to the back lounge. As we walk, I notice the signs painted above the different nooks within the bar. There's TRACY'S CURVE, a two-bench alcove with a flat-screen TV and a popcorn machine. There's CAROL'S CREVICE, named for his deceased mother. That section has a jukebox with nothing but old Motown songs. Finally, we walk into POP'S CORNER. This is the small game room. It contains Ping-Pong, air hockey and Foosball tables. Omar pulls me into the room.

"Each section is named after my loved—"

"I got that."

"My mom used to play Smokey Robinson and The Miracles and dance around the room. Tracy can't go to a sporting event without eating popcorn, and—"

"I love arcade games," I add.

Lia still holds my hand as I stand in the center of my dedication and watch the adults play with the fervor of children. I see Moo Moo's gargantuan arms maneuver the wooden knobs on the Foosball table. Lia breaks loose to go watch.

In awe, I murmur, "I can't believe you named this room after me."

With the same shudder in his voice, Omar says, "I can't believe you're having Rome's child."

Instantaneously, we rotate toward each other and make direct eye contact. Still holding hands, we silently stare at each other for close to a minute. In a room of twenty or more people, we stick out as we stand underneath the orange-and-blue lamps hanging from the ceiling. Moo Moo notices Omar and me and nudges Lia.

"What's up with them? Everything okay?"

"She's shocked. He named the room after her."

"What?" he says, confused.

"Pop's corner. Gwen is Pop."

"Oh yeah, I forgot he calls her that. Why?" Moo Moo asks.

"'Cause she's addicted to Popsicles," she says.

"Oh, so that's why there's a minifridge with free Popsicles against the wall," he informs her.

"Really? Where?" Lia rushes to the back wall with excitement.

I finally remove my fingers from within Omar's grip. "I gotta go." I scuttle over to Lia, grab her arm and quickly exit the club. Omar stands in the same spot and watches me leave. As soon as we exit, my breathing intensifies.

"Where's your asthma? I mean your inhaler," Lia asks.

I point to the car as we dash across the parking lot.

"Here, calm down." Lia rubs the cold treat across my lips. I smack the Popsicle away and it falls to the pavement.

"What the hell . . . my Popsicle," Lia squeals as she scurries along.

We get to the car and I grab my inhaler from the backseat.

"Why did you leave it in the car?" Lia asks.

I take a few short puffs before answering. "I didn't think I would need it. We were supposed to be in and out, not stay there for an hour."

I sit in the passenger seat with the door open and hang my head down in between my legs. Lia softly rubs the top of my crown.

"You okay?" she asks as I slowly nod. "What did he say to you?"

"Nothing. He just acted like everything was cool, but that's what he always does, acts as if nothing is wrong. He was never a man of contrition, even when we argued. He used to wake up the next morning, like it was all good. Tonight was the same way.

"He said he couldn't believe I was having Rome's baby."

"Duh? Of course he can't."

"It wasn't what he said, it was how he said it. His expression was staid, but the tone was disquieting. I can't truly describe it. It was scary."

"We should go home. You ready?" Lia asks.

I place my legs in the car and close the door. Lia gets in and we drive off. As soon as we get on the road, my phone beeps. I have a message from Rome.

"He knows we were at the bar," states Lia.

"No, how could he? He just wants to make sure I made it home okay."

"Fine, call him. But I'm telling you, he knows, so don't lie if he asks you. You know he knew the opening was tonight. Everyone in Detroit was in there. Someone saw you, called him and now he's going to see if you're going to lie." Lia breaks down the whole conversation.

I peer at her, then slowly dial Rome's number. Before I get to the last digit, I hang up. "I'll call him from the house."

Lia was right. Rome immediately asks my whereabouts.

"I'm home," I say with confidence.

"I know that, but where were you?"

I pause, but then answer calmly. I am sure not to raise my voice or tone, as to denote any worry or concern. "We went to the opening of Comatose. We were already out and Lia wanted to congratulate Omar."

"Did you know you were going when we talked earlier?"

"Not really. We thought about it, but weren't sure. Anyway, I stayed for a minute; then we came home."

"Yeah? Well, I heard you and Omar were holding hands. I heard you looked real . . . together, as in a couple."

"Well, you heard wrong. I was there, I saw him, had a juice, then left. Ask Lia."

"I don't want to ask Lia shit. What happened when you went to Atlanta? You tried to act like Omar wasn't there, but I knew he was. Tracy is his brother."

"I never said he wasn't there," I answer.

"I know and I never asked. I wanted to see if you would tell me, and you didn't. Now I get a call that you and Omar are at his spot holding hands, giggling and shit. What's up, Gwen? Is there something else you're not telling me?"

"You don't believe me?"

"I want to, but . . . ," says Rome.

"I want to be with you, and only you. I'm just now adjusting to being pregnant. Omar is upset that I'm with you and having this child. I don't know how to deal with that. I want to be his friend, but I don't want to give him mixed signals and I don't want you to be mad."

"I won't be mad if you don't lie. I need you to be honest. Do you still love him?"

I say nothing. Rome rapidly asks two more times. Finally, I respond with a loud, forced whisper. "Yes, yes. But I don't want to be with him. I can't help that I still care. That's not just going to go away."

"I'll talk to you later, Gwen."

"Rome?"

"I'll talk to you later, bye." Rome disconnects.

"Damn it!" I scream.

Lia hurries into the bedroom. "What happened?"

"He thinks I want to be with Omar."

"I knew it. Now we gotta figure out what bitch called him."

"How do you know it was a girl?" Gwen asks.

"This has 'bitch' written all over it. It's somebody trying to get with him and thought this would be the perfect opportunity to get on his good side."

"My head hurts." I walk into the bathroom, go into the medicine cabinet and grab a bottle of Tylenol, along with my anxiety pills. "I'm out of Tylenol. Could you please go to the store for me?" I ask nicely.

"No, and you can't mix those, anyway," Lia quickly says. "And you shouldn't be taking these. You're pregnant."

"Lia, I'm grown. I want the Tylenol now and these later. Besides, these are herbal," I say, holding the little white-and-green bottle. "I can't believe he doesn't trust me."

"You know why, right? He's a man. He knows what he would do and he thinks you may do the same. Rome knows that Omar wants you."

"But I'm carrying his child."

"The child you didn't want, and you have been talking to Omar. You went to see him. I hate to say it, but it looks like you still want to be with him. And you know what? You're always taking aspirin. That's not good. Just go to sleep."

Pulling the pillow over my face, I moan and grunt into the cloth. Eventually, Lia lies down next to me. She softly rubs my shoulders and soon falls asleep. I turn on my back and stare. For close to twenty minutes, I count the tiny starburst designs plastered on the ceiling. I softly rub the temples of my delicate friend. She awakens and looks at me.

"You okay?" Lia asks. I nod. She reaches for my hand and closes her eyes again. "I'm here if you need me, just let me know."

I quietly chuckle. It's funny how the most fragile always want to protect. I lay in bed until Lia is completely asleep; then I sneak in the other room and call Omar. I can't help it. I want to tell him again how proud I am of him. I don't know why I can't let go. Trust me, it's my biggest hurdle in therapy. I am trying, though. I can't string O along, and I don't want to. I just know we can make a great friendship work and we all can be one big happy family.

"Am I living in Disney World?" I whisper before leaving a message. "Hey, O, I just want to tell you how proud I am of you. I know starting over is not easy, but you are doing it—"

The phone clicks. It's Omar. I answer the other line.

"I was just leaving you a message," I say.

"What was it, sweetheart?"

I still get warm tingles when he speaks to me. I have got to get it together. I know he's not the one for me, but I can't help how I feel.

OMAR
Session Seven

When I first met Omar, there was an instant connection. I never told him this, but he reminded me so much of my father. My father didn't drink a bit and Omar drank like a fish, but the other similarities were uncanny. Marvin always has this lost look in his eyes, as if he's waiting to be rescued, and so does Omar. Instantly, I wanted to take care of him. Our friendship was kismet. He was a mess and I fell for him—hook, line and sinker. Men with baggage are my specialty. After all, I mended my father after my mother left. I am a pro. I could have put Humpty Dumpty together again, had he called. But when I met Omar I was going through my own mess, so our troubles simply worked together for our demise. Yet, our dysfunction came disguised as love and eventually it fooled us both. I didn't want to live without my O. He understood me, when no one else did. He knew I drank to let loose and he accepted my lame-ass excuses. Sometimes that's all you want, even if it's not good for you. Codependency aside, I fell in love with Omar's heart. It is as large as Asia. If he loves someone, he would risk his life to save her. Tracy is the same way—I guess it runs in their family. But Omar adores me and there is nothing that man wouldn't do for me. Issues or not, what girl wouldn't fall for that? When I am around him, I am all he sees. Never did I ever worry about him leaving me for another, which is a huge part of my attraction to him. I've always been one for safety. I don't like risks, and since love is a big one, why not go for the safest route possible? I always knew Omar would place my heart *first and foremost. Plus, he needed me. I know some people say they want their mates to complement them, not complete them, but I'm not one of those people. I am looking for someone to make me whole and I'm not ashamed to admit it. These are my issues, and he fit within my set of complexities.*

Relationships are about a good fit, and we had that. It's kind of sick in a way, because I sometimes see him as my child—my child that I can't abandon. It damn near killed me to leave him after the accident. But my plans were to get myself together so that I could come back and take care of him. When he no longer wanted to see me, I had to respect his decision. But I was devastated. However, now that he is back and he still wants me, I feel obligated to him. If the shoe were on the other foot, he would be there for me. Hell, he probably wouldn't have ever left. But things are different now. I realize what we had is not the love I want to experience, at least not forever. And, honestly, I'm not sure if we can ever have a healthy relationship. But in that same breath, I don't want to live without him. My bond with him is still strong. His honor to commitment is incredible and it's something I've always revered. It takes priority over all of his flaws. Is it enough? I don't know, but I can't throw the baby away with the bathwater. Especially when I am the only one the baby has.

Session Done

9

Rome is fourteen hundred miles away, and at three in the morning, he sits in his lavish hotel room going over the head-shots from the audition. Today he looked at a minimum of sixty multicultural beauties who came to audition for the latest garage band to hit the top of the *Billboard* charts. Head-shots are scattered throughout the room, his location papers are on the floor and he is stressed. I know he probably doesn't want to hear from me, but I have to call him.

Before he can say hello, I speak. "I love you."

"I know," he whispers.

We sit on the phone, quietly listening to each other's breathing.

"It's late. Why are you still awake?" Rome eventually asks.

"I couldn't sleep without speaking to you. Rome, I really do want this to work."

"It's working," he says. "Go to sleep. I'll call you in the morning."

He places the phone down, grabs his warm beer and takes a swig. Just as he finishes, there is a knock on his door. Slowly, he approaches and peeps through the hole, but sees no one.

"Who is it? Mitch, is that you?" he calls out, thinking it is the video AD, but there's no answer. Rome looks through the peephole once more. This time, he sees a young woman. He recognizes the face, but can't match a name. Slowly, he opens the door. A young woman steps halfway in.

"Whoa! Hold the hell up!"

"Romulus, you treat me like a stranger."

"Ariel?"

"You come to my city and don't even call. I should be offended." She brings the other half of her body into the suite.

"What are you doing here?"

"I saw you at the audition today, but there were so many girls and I got tired of waiting. But then as I was leaving, I saw you come from the room. You walked down the hall to go to the restroom. I couldn't believe it was you." Ariel continues to walk farther into the room and takes a seat on the chair by the bar.

"You gotta go."

"Why? I haven't seen you in a year. Not since the New Year's Eve party you had the week before the new year, remember that?"

"Yeah, I was going to be out of town for New Year's Eve, but I still wanted to party. Of course I remember."

"You know what I remember? The way you fucked me that night. No one has ever been able to put it down like that since. So how have you been?"

Rome treads slowly over to the couch. He begins gathering his paperwork and placing it in neat piles. "I've been good. How's Miami treating you?"

"Better than Detroit. The warm weather is better for my skin and the market is better for my career."

"Good. Why don't you leave me your number and I'll call you. I'll be here for a week," he says.

"Why don't you come over here and sit next to me and stop acting all scared."

Rome delivers an anxious but macho titter. "Ain't nobody

scared of you. I have work to do. Besides, your chair is suited for one." He continues to rifle through the papers to busy his sordid thoughts.

Ariel waltzes over to the couch, moves the paperwork out of the way and sits on his lap. "So I'll come to you. Or would you rather I come *for* you?" she whispers in his ear. She utters a soft moan. She sucks on the tip of his earlobe. Immediately, he jumps up.

"I can't. You have to go." He takes her by the wrists and pulls her to the door. She steps in front of him and blocks the exit.

"What's wrong? Have you forgotten what I . . . what we . . . how we make each other feel?"

"No, I'm with someone now."

Ariel looks around the room. "Is she here?"

"No, but—"

Ariel interrupts him with a passionate kiss. He fights her for a second, but then succumbs. While kissing, she removes her blouse, exposing her perfectly round, bare C-cup breasts. Rome pushes away. "Ariel . . . for real, you can't stay."

"Fine, I'll go, I will, after . . ." She kisses him again, and this time, she unsnaps his pants. While stroking him with her hands, she slides his pants off his waist. Rome makes a poor attempt to ward her off. His brain is sending signals to make him stop, but the blood flow to his larger head is slowing down to replace the flow to his other one, now exposed and in the hands of his ex-lover. Ariel goes from wrapping her tongue around his lips to wrapping her lips around his erection. Rome braces himself against the wall for support. Within moments, he has Ariel on the floor. Their sex is not gentle as he tightly wraps her long hair around his hand and clinches it to a fist. He tosses her head, to and fro, with her body pinned beneath him. They hit the edge of the coffee table and scatter the stacks of papers. From the floor, they move to the couch, and from the couch, they move to the counter.

Ariel is a screamer, so Rome takes cloth and jams it into her mouth. She bites down on the rag and subsides her screams to strident grunts. Twenty minutes later, Rome is in the shower and Ariel is gone. Rome scrubs away his transgressions and lets the warm water pour from his crown down his well-sculpted body. He steps from the shower and stretches his dampened body out onto the bed. The guilt is mounting, and sleep is nowhere to be found, so Rome rises, grabs another beer from the minifridge and gathers up his paperwork.

"It's going to be a long week," he mumbles to himself.

When we arrive at my ob-gyn's, they immediately bring me to the back. I strip, lie on the table and Dr. Shira Pagota begins her checkup. With Lia anxiously sitting outside the door, I ask questions and discuss concerns about the pregnancy. Finally, she wheels the ultrasound machine over to the table and invites Lia to come in. Lia rushes to the table and grabs my hand.

The doctor points to the screen and speaks. "Everything seems to be okay. But hold up." Dr. Pagota takes the cold stethoscope and again places it to my belly. She moves it up and down and then to the side. She leaves it on the side and lets out a tiny giggle.

"What? Is everything okay?" I ask.

"Everything is fine, Ms. Pharr." She removes the earplugs and smiles at me.

"Let me show you something." I close my eyes.

"I don't want to see the sex, I have to wait until the baby's father is back in town," I quickly say.

"No, I have something else to show you. You can't tell the sex right now, because of the way the babies are facing."

My eyes pop wide open. "Why did you say 'babies,' as in plural?"

"That's what I want to show you." I tune in close to the

medical screen. My heart is racing. "See right here, this is the head of baby number one, here is the arm and the legs. But see right here." Lia and I move closer. "There is another leg peeping out from the baby's back."

"Are you sure that's a leg? Maybe it's a growth, an extra arm or something. Maybe it's a tail."

"No, see the tiny foot. It's a leg. So I went back to listen because I've only heard one heartbeat at your appointments. Amazingly, the babies' heartbeats are almost in sync. Your second baby is directly behind the other. I can only hear the heartbeat difference from the side. Here, take a listen." Dr. Pagota places the stethoscope in my ears. I listen intently.

"I wanna hear!" Lia is excited. She removes the earpieces from me and jams them into her ears. "Yep! I can hear it."

I snatch the stethoscope from Lia. "You don't hear anything, stop getting excited."

"Ms. Pharr, you are having twins," says the doctor.

I am speechless. Lia is euphoric. "We are having two babies, one for you and one for me!"

"Now, the baby in front is lying on its back and I think . . . yeah, I can tell you the sex of baby number one. But can't even see baby number two, at least not today."

"I want to know," Lia shouts.

The doctor looks at me. "We'll wait until the next appointment," I state.

"Okay. Well, that should be in four weeks—unless you experience some pain or trouble before then. You can get dressed." The doctor shuts off the machine and I rise to get dressed. Still in shock, I say nothing to Lia until we are in the parking lot.

Lia is keyed up. She cannot contain her jittering and wiggles as she walks. However, I am the opposite, walking at a snails' pace.

Once in the car, I finally speak. "Lia, don't start with those questions and a whole bunch of talking. I have to process this information first."

Lia nods, quietly biting her lip. She turns on the music and drives off.

Amazingly, Lia is silent the entire twenty-minute ride back to the club. I am so startled, that I grant Lia permission to talk before returning back to work.

"Thank you for being with me, and thanks for the quiet time. Go ahead and say what you have to say."

Lia takes my hand and kisses it. "I love you, and this is a good thing, I promise."

I give an apprehensive smile. "You coming in?"

"No, I have to go to work."

"Talk to you later."

Lia leaves and I slowly trot back into the club. Before I can get into the office, Rome calls my cell. He wants to know the sex of the baby. I insist I don't know and I don't tell him about the twins, because he's on the video set. I will wait and tell him when I pick him up from the airport.

On Friday, I have an early dinner with Andre. Tonia took Zora to see their grandmother this weekend, so Andre is a free man. He's taking advantage of every moment. We eat at Suchan's Japanese Steak House and have dessert at a quaint coffeehouse on the east side of town. Over coffee, I almost spill the beans about the twins, but quickly cover, and Andre is none the wiser. Unfortunately, he is miserable at his new job, and spends most of our meal complaining about working as a mortgage broker at Fort Street Capital, instead of doing his music. I'm not able to get many words in at all.

Saturday afternoon, I pick Rome up from the airport. Eager to see my man, I am there fifteen minutes early. I even stop by a store to pick up a card. I'm letting my guard down a little and deciding to give him a sample of what's on my mind. This is a big step, and though I'm a little nervous about it, I know this is necessary for our relationship. I tell him I miss him, but he barely responds. In truth, he hardly says three words on the ride home. I figure I would wait and tell him about the babies when we get to his house. However, when we get there, he grabs his bags and gets out.

"I'm going to get some rest."

"You sure you don't have a little energy, not even for me," I say flirtatiously, winking.

"I'm sure." Rome leans over and kisses me on the cheek. "Thanks for picking me up, I'll call you later."

"But I need to talk. . . ."

He shuts the door and walks into his home. Taken aback, I sit in the car and watch him mope as he walks up the stairs and closes the door.

"Well, damn," I mutter to myself.

Later that evening, Andre and Lucas play pool downstairs in Rome's lounge room, while Rome prepares nachos.

"Man, hurry up, the game is about to start."

Rome rushes downstairs with a huge plate and three bowls. He has nachos and cheese with peppers and onions piled ten inches high. The guys dive in just at tip-off. Immediately, they want to hear all of the details from the shoot. Each is living somewhat vicariously through Rome. They want him to leave out nothing, especially the part about the video girls. However, Rome doesn't say much. He watches the first half in silence, and barely roots when his team scores. During halftime, Andre discerns something is wrong. He asks Rome several times, phrasing his concern with different questions. Finally, Rome sighs, slouches back in his La-Z-Boy and gives Andre a blank stare.

"What? You've been sulking all night."

"I saw Gwen today."

"So that's a good thing, right? Ya'll have a fight?"

"No . . . I saw Ariel in Miami," Rome confesses.

"And . . . ," Andre comments. But before he can get the next word out of his mouth, he already knows. "You didn't?"

Rome simply lowers his head.

"Damn, man, what happened?" Andre asks.

"Ariel happened. Man, you know her. First of all, she's fine as hell. Secondly, 'no' is not in her vocabulary."

"Can I meet Ariel? Does she have a sister?" Lucas comments, but Rome is not in the mood for jokes.

"Man, she came over at three A.M. or so, wearing this little-ass shirt and one of those flouncy skirts?"

"Flouncy?" Andre questions.

"Yeah, those tiny skirts that don't fit, they just flare out. Anyway, you bend over and everything is exposed. And she didn't have on nothing, man."

"So what happened?"

"What you think happened, nigga? He hit that shit. What else was he supposed to do?" Lucas offers.

"I was supposed to ask her to leave, and I did. But she started going down and it was all over. I feel bad. I was really trying to do right. And I didn't want to . . . but, damn, it was Ariel."

Both men lean in like young schoolboys on the playground listening to their friend tell his story about his first time. Their eyes are ablaze and their mouths are salivating.

"Ariel is a freak. I don't know how else to put it. She's out there and the shit is so good. Not that Gwen is bad, but I get excited just thinking about Ariel's shit. Only problem is, her ass is crazy."

Lucas nods and comments, "The crazy ones always have the best stuff."

All three men sit and ponder that statement as they stare into space reminiscing about their crude pasts.

"Dre, you gotta believe me, I really wanted to walk away.

But she got that comeback . . . and I came back two more times before leaving," Rome continues.

"Say it ain't so."

"Did you fuck her the whole time you were there?" asks Lucas.

"No, just the three nights. After that, I changed rooms and registered under another name," says Rome.

"So she doesn't have any of your numbers? 'Cause wasn't she the one following you around Detroit?"

"Yep."

"Well, you better hope she doesn't have your info, or her ass might be up here and that would not be cool. Hell, she could just pop up," Dre adds.

"Damn, I really thought I was ready for a relationship."

"Trust me, man, you're never ready, it just happens and you deal with it. Men don't have that relationship button that they can turn on and off," admits Andre.

"Yeah, I guess, but I do love Gwen and I wouldn't do anything to hurt her, not on purpose. She gave me a card today. Gwen never gives cards, she even wrote something in it." Rome's voice is filled with regret.

Both men can understand his situation, but have no suggestions to offer. They all quietly turn and finish watching the second half of the play-off game.

The next morning, Rome flies to New York to meet the editors and spends two days there going over footage. He and I play phone tag for close to forty-eight hours. Mostly, due to Rome truly not wanting to speak—and luckily, I have been busy at the club—I don't have time to wonder why he's acting strange. Unfortunately, I haven't had time to tell him about the twins.

The next week at Ole Skool is busy, I spend late hours at the club planning this big party with all the ole-school DJ's from the 1980s. Already confirmed is DJ Wiz, from Kid 'N Play, D-Nice, DJ Kool Herc and Spinderella. Late Wednesday night, Rome gets back in town and comes by the office. Lia and I are in the office doing more play than work. We've turned up the music and are having our own 1980s party.

"Well, if it isn't Gwen and the Get Fresh Crew," he says, walking into the room.

Yes, I'm happy to see him, but I'm a little upset that I haven't had any time to speak to him. Therefore, I give him a wave from across the room.

"I missed you," he says.

I smack my lips and respond, "Whatever. I haven't seen you since I picked you up from the airport four days ago."

"I'm sorry, baby, I've been a little stressed. How can I make it up to you?"

"You've done enough already."

"What have I done now?" Rome asks.

I point to my stomach. "You knocked me up."

"I know." He pulls me into his broad chest, but I, pretending to be upset, push him away. Rome takes to my joking and also turns away pretending to be distressed.

"With twins," I add.

Rome takes two steps and then suddenly halts his stride. He snaps around and peers at my stomach. I stand, giving attitude, arms akimbo.

"Twins?"

I nod, just as Lia exclaims in the background. "Twins! We're having twins!"

Rome's mouth flies open. He lifts me and twirls me around. With a huge smile, I lean my head back and enjoy my human merry-go-round.

"Oh, my God! When did you know . . . The appointment? Why are you just telling me? Are they okay? Did you see pictures?"

"Damn, you're worse than Lia. I wanted to tell you in

person, but you've been so busy, I'm just now getting to tell you."

Rome cuddles me, softly kisses my cheek, lips and neck. He gets on his knees, gently rubs my stomach and then lays his face against my protruding skin. Leaning over, I kiss the top of his bald crown. As Lia watches our affection from across the room, a rare flash hits her—this moment has nothing to do with her. So she gracefully exits the room, leaving the two expecting parents to savor this precious time.

Over the next three weeks, Rome and I do nothing but shop. Though the sex of one baby is apparent at the next appointment, we decide to wait until both sexes are revealed. But this doesn't stop us from spending money. Though I spend most of my nights with Rome, I decide to keep my place, at least until after the babies are born. The babies are increasing my vulnerability and each day my affinity for Rome grows more and more. I'm desperately trying to hold on to what little control I have, but my feelings are beginning to overwhelm me. I am in a new emotional place, and not sure if I like it.

Lia is also moving to a new position, one of responsibility. She finally decides to write down the names of her sexual partners. She knows in order to deal with her future, she must return to the past. She walks into the office and tosses two pieces of notebook paper onto my desk.

"What's this?" I ask.

"My sordid past."

I take the papers and read the names, first silently and then aloud. "This is your sex list? Oh, my God."

"There are twenty-four lines on each side, which means I have slept with over ninety-six people in my life. I tried to write them in order so I could remember them all. I am now officially a whore."

I continue reading the names.

"Did you hear me? I said I was a whore."

"I heard you. Normally, I wouldn't agree, but it's hard to argue with the facts."

Lia slams her face down onto the desk. She whimpers into the wood. "It's surprising I'm not positive. What have I been thinking?"

I console my friend, pull up a chair and softly rub the back of Lia's head. "Lia, you are a free spirit."

"Is that the new word for 'whore'?" she whimpers.

"No. The one thing I admire about you is that you do what you want, no matter what people think. You have enjoyed your thirty-one years on this earth. I can't say the same. I would love to have some of your spontaneous energy." I take the additional paper sitting atop Lia's purse.

"Is there more?" I say in disbelief while Lia shamefully walks to the restroom. I read the last eighteen names. "What? You slept with Rome?"

Lia rushes from the bathroom and snatches the paper from me. "I can explain."

"When did you sleep with him? I thought you guys never did it."

"I never said that. I said we didn't date."

"So when did you sleep with him, 'cause his name is second to last?"

Lia looks at the paper before answering. "I slept with him about a month before you moved back."

"When did you stop sleeping with him?"

"We only did it once," Lia owns up.

I give a stern look of disbelief.

"Twice, we only did it twice. I promise. It was the same week. We were drinking and it just happened. I swear."

"So in six months, you've only slept with one other person?" I ask.

"No, I've been with two old loves since, but I didn't do repeats on the paper. I've only slept with one new person since Rome."

I rove around the office. "Back when I was saying you two should hook up, why didn't you say something?"

"I didn't want you to know. I thought you and he should get together and I knew that if you knew we did it, you probably wouldn't want to hook up with him."

I take a seat at my desk and flip through Lia's list.

"What are you doing?" Lia questions.

"Just looking to see who else is on here."

My eyes widen and squint as I go through names. "You slept with him?" I ask, pointing to number 63. Lia comes to the desk to look and then nods with disappointment. "Wow, her too. I didn't even know she liked women."

"She didn't either," comments Lia.

I hand the papers to her.

"I'm so sorry, I didn't tell you about Rome. We agreed it was a mistake, one that no one needed to know about."

"I don't know why I'm so surprised," I state.

Lia takes the papers in shame and sits down at her desk. She can feel the awkwardness.

"Are you okay?" I ask.

"I'm fine. Are you okay?"

"I will be," I say.

"Good. I'll talk with you later. Don't stay here too late."

Lia leaves the office, grabs a cigarette and lights up. However, I briskly walk toward the door. "I'm not mad that you slept with him," I explain. "I'm mad that you didn't tell me once you found out I was pregnant. I should know if my best friend has slept with the father of my child."

Lia's eyes sparkle. "I'm your best friend?"

I snap my fingers and speak loudly. "Stay focused on my anger. This isn't about you."

"Sorry." Lia carefully listens.

"Have you slept with him, since I've been back?"

"No," Lia answers. "And we used condoms."

I pause and then mumble, "I can't believe you two."

I look into my friend's innocent eyes. At times, Lia looks like a child. And even though her acts are very mature, there is a very adolescent manner about her character that makes it hard to stay angry with her.

"Please forgive me?" she pleads.

I sigh and speak. "Fine."

Lia extends her arms, but my lukewarm expression turns cold.

"Not yet," I say.

Lia quickly retreats. "Let me know when you're ready."

"I should be ready tomorrow, maybe the day after," I say curtly, before turning to leave. "And stop smoking those damn cigarettes."

She gives a quirky smile, folds her list and places it in her purse. She takes one last puff and puts the cigarette out. Just then, a young woman walks down the hallway. Both Lia and I turn our attention to her. However, Lia waves and keeps walking.

She approaches me and speaks. "I talked to Rome and he told me to come by."

"Is it about the marketing position?" I ask.

She nods and we walk into the office. She actually has good ideas, and since she came with Rome's recommendation, I hire Marie on the spot. If Rome wants to continue these special events once a month, we need someone to handle the marketing duties. She can't work full-time, but can come in three days a week, which is perfect. Afterward, we sit and talk about the babies and unisex names. She seems nice and I welcome the help.

That night when I come home, Rome has a romantic dinner cooked. I can smell the aroma outside the door, but I have no idea of the feast. I glance at the table and see a beautiful salad with red- and green-leaf lettuce, carrots and walnuts tossed in an olive oil dressing. I try to peep into the kitchen as I sniff the entrée. Rome keeps me at bay and he moves me to the bedroom.

Folding my arms, I flare my nostrils and berate him. "I know about your little fling!"

Rome nearly drops the entrée as he pulls it from the oven. Nervously, he positions himself against the counter.

"What . . . what are you talking about?" he stutters.

"Don't play innocent."

Thinking I know about Ariel, Rome looks away as he tries to figure out how I could know. He figures his best move is to say nothing, so he lowers his head and remains silent.

"Oh, now you can't look at me?" I ask.

"Gwen, I'm sorry," he says with his head still down.

I walk to him and raise his chin to look me in the eyes.

"You should have told me that you slept with Lia," I say.

"Lia?" Rome questions.

"Yes, Lia. Don't play, I know she called and told you that I knew."

It takes him a minute to gather his composure. After a few nervous chuckles, he regains his poise. "Yeah, she told me. I was hoping you weren't still upset."

"Is that what this dinner is about?"

"No. I wanted to do something nice for my girl. I'm not thinking about Lia, and you shouldn't be either. That was a long time ago.

"Six months ago."

"Six months is a long time and it was only once."

"Once?" I question.

"Twice, damn. Baby, I don't want her. I want you. Now go wash your hands and change clothing so we can eat." Rome kisses me.

Once again, I sniff the aroma, and like an anxious child, I waltz away.

Rome wipes the sweat from his brow and finishes the

dinner. Minutes later, I return and sit at the table. Rome brings over the main course of lamb in a savory rosemary-and-mint sauce, served with creamy spinach and red potatoes. I am blown away.

"You didn't cook this. Who cooked this?"

"What? What are you talking about?"

"See, now I know you didn't. You're stuttering. Who cooked this?"

"Can I not do something nice for my lady? I did all of this for you."

Rome sits down and blesses the table. I take one bite of the tender lamb. "Oh hell, nah!"

"What's wrong?"

"This is so good. I don't care who cooked it. But I know you didn't."

"Just eat," he says.

We sit and enjoy our meal, with Teddy Pendergrass crooning in the background.

"You know I worked too hard to stay this size, just to get big again. I don't care if I am carrying twins, I can't eat like this all the time," I say while reaching for more potatoes.

Rome stares at me from across the table, then rises and walks over to me. He pulls me from my seat and gives me a tender kiss. Afterward, we embrace and stare into each other's eyes. "I wanted to wait, but I can't," Rome says while reaching into his pocket. He pulls out a little navy satin pouch and hands it to me. I take the pouch and feel the circular metal. Quickly, I pull out a ring. It has a diamond in the center with sapphires on each side.

"Let's get married, Gwen. I want you to be my wife."

Stunned, I say nothing but continue to stare into the stones. Immediately, my mind flashes to the ring I recalled seeing on the street the night of the accident. My jaw springs open to speak, but no sounds leave my mouth. After three attempts to talk, a very vague word comes out. It sounds like I am learning how to pronounce the letter *h*. Rome leans in as his mind tries to comprehend what I'm saying. None of the responses he could imagine start with that letter, so he is thrown.

"What's that?" he asks.

I look at the ring and kiss it. "It's so beautiful. You know I love sapphires." That's all I say. I turn, sit and begin to eat my food again.

"Gwen?"

I look back at Rome as he waits for a response. He suddenly realizes by my expression that I am not about to give him one, so he goes back to his seat. After a few bites, he slams his fork down.

"I need to know if you want to marry me."

"I'm not sure," I admit.

"So that means what?"

"That means I have to think about it."

Rome mopes through the rest of his dinner. He clears his side of the table and plops down on the couch. When I finish, I sit next to him. I glance at the ring, which I have purposely placed on my right ring finger. With my head in his lap, we watch television.

After one episode of *Law & Order,* I ask, "Why now?"

"Why now what?" he asks with a hint of agitation.

"Why propose now?"

"'Cause I want to marry you *now.* I love you *now.* You are carrying my twins *now.* I've been waiting for someone like you and you're here *now.*" Rome is sure to emphasize each "now" as he continues to speak. "We are great friends *now.* It makes sense *now.* You should be my wife *now.*"

Trying to jest, I say, "I sense a bit of urgency in your voice. It's like you're the one who got knocked up."

Rome looks down at me and walks into the kitchen to clean.

"You want my help?" I suggest.

"No. You relax."

I do just that. Lying on the couch, I watch another episode of the syndicated law show. Not many words are spoken the remainder of the evening. My mind completely perplexed, I can't think straight. Rome, with a slightly bruised ego, doesn't know whether to ask me to stay or leave. I finally retire to the bed and ask Rome to come cuddle. Still hurt by my nonchalant attitude toward his proposal, he decides to stay on the couch for a while. An hour after I am asleep, Rome crawls into bed. His body heat awakens me. I drape my arm around his chest as I spoon behind him. I rub my hand across his shoulder and down his arm. I can see the dim sparkle from the distant light shining through my window. My mind is telling me that this could be a mistake, but my heart is saying this is everything I want and more. I always choose mind over heart. Life makes sense that way. The heart is blind and this is why those who follow it end up lost.

"Did you want to marry me because of the babies?" I ask softly.

"I want to marry you because you are my best friend. I think we have a fighting chance at making it. It's not perfect, but if we love each other, that should count for something, right? And yes, I want my children to grow up with a family. One that is together."

I wait a few minutes, taking in his answer.

"Oh God, I can't believe this," I whisper.

"Believe what?" Rome says with his back still turned.

"I can't believe I'm going to marry you."

Slowly, he turns around. I look at my man, my fiancé.

"You're going to marry me?"

"I guess," I say, pretending to display mild enthusiasm. "I mean, I have known you almost all my life, and I always wanted to marry my best friend, so . . . yes, I will marry you."

Rome takes me into his arms and covers my face with kisses. He removes the ring from my right hand and places it on my left. He passionately kisses me. Rome slowly removes my shirt and caresses my nipples with his lips. As he moves on top of my body, he slides inside me. I close my eyes. My lips move, but no words release.

"God, please let this be the right thing. Please let this be the right thing." My next thought is Omar. I should be excited about my new life, but I'm still wrapped in my old one. How am I going to tell Omar that I am preparing to marry Rome? I lie in bed and ponder this for close to an hour. Why is it so hard to let go?

10

The news of the engagement spreads quickly. Patricia, Rome's mom, wants to plan an engagement party, and she is not taking no for an answer. Though no wedding date is planned, it doesn't stop everyone from asking. I am totally beleaguered. I could care less about a party. These days, all I want is for my food to stay down. I avoided morning sickness during my first trimester, but this month it's kicking my ass.

It's been two weeks and I haven't spoken with Omar since the engagement. I have to talk to him today. My pregnancy is very obvious, and when we see each other, Omar is taken aback when he sees my belly development. He puts on a smile, but I can tell by his twitching grin that it's false. I turn my ring to the inside when I see him approach.

He gives me a hug and brings me a treat, a Bomb Pop.

"I love these," I say with a huge smile.

"I know. The ice-cream truck was at the park entrance."

I immediately tear into my icy delight. Omar takes a seat next to me on the bench. There's an array of Chinese food spread out to share.

"May I?" he asks, extending his hand toward my stomach. I timorously nod as he caresses.

"I'm having twins."

Omar's mouth drops open. He gazes at my tummy and speaks. "I was a twin."

"What? You never told me that."

"I didn't talk about it. My twin died when we were two months . . . SIDS."

"Damn, I'm sorry," I say.

"Nah, it's cool. I just . . ." Omar pauses and redirects his comments. "I . . . I'm happy for you."

I continue to lick. I'm already down to the white part.

"How's the bar? I've driven by a couple of nights and the lot was packed."

"Business is good." He alters the conversation. "You look great. Things must be going well."

"They are. What makes you say that?" I ask.

"Your nails," he responds.

I look down at my hands, and then fold them into fists, remembering my ring.

"Your nails are growing. When things are crazy, you bite them. When you're happy, you paint them."

With a silly expression, I simply nod as Omar digs into his Chinese food. He struggles with his chopsticks. I notice his trouble.

"I'm left-handed, but you know I eat with my right hand. I haven't had Chinese takeout since the accident." He continues to place the rice in between the sticks, but it never makes it to his mouth.

I finish my Bomb Pop and help him out. I take the box from him and feed him. After a few bites, he takes the box away from me. "You shouldn't—"

"But," I interrupt.

"But nothing. I have to do things on my own." Omar takes the box and turns it up to his mouth. A big clump of rice misses his mouth and hits his shirt. I let out a loud chortle.

"I miss your laughter," he states.

I immediately stop. He is sitting too close, and I am too comfortable. So I nervously slide away.

"Rome asked me to marry him," I blurt out.

Omar leans back onto the bench and responds, "I know."

"What?"

"The city is small. People like to talk. I think I got about three phone calls that week. It's like when folks die, everyone always wants to be the first to bring the bad news. Not saying that this is bad news."

"Oh. I wanted to tell you before you found out," I comment.

Omar reaches across and takes me by the hand. He stares at the kids on the other side of the field. "I told you I was going to propose to you the night of the accident."

I quietly gaze into space. I don't speak. Two eerie minutes of silence pass as he continues to hold my hand.

"Think we would have been happy?" Omar asks.

"I think we would have slowly killed each other," I respond.

"Maybe. How could something so good be so bad?"

"No one knows, that's why they write songs about it." I face him. "Be honest, we weren't good for each other. You know that."

"Things would have been different this time around."

He releases my hand and leans in so that our foreheads almost touch. "I'm so sorry. I was a mess and I'm so, so very sorry." He glances down at me and says, "Congratulations."

Omar walks away and I watch until he disappears over the hill. I continue to sit on the bench and gaze at the green field. I ponder his question. How could something so good be so bad? More important, how could I miss something that wasn't good for me?

"I guess it's the same way people miss chocolate when they go on a diet," I whisper aloud. Quickly, I look around to make sure no one catches me answering my own question. "I did the right thing. I did the right thing."

* * *

That Friday, the club is packed to capacity. "Ole-School Night" is a success. Unfortunately, Rome doesn't make it to the club. He's out of town shooting this weekend. I'm used to it now, he's gone most every weekend. I was hoping that he could see how great Marie was working out, but he hasn't been around much since she started working. There was a time that nothing went on in this club without him knowing about it, but now he is clueless as to what is going on. I practically run everything. I don't know how I am going to do this once the babies are born.

On Saturday, all I want to do is sleep, and so I do. I reschedule lunch with Patricia for Sunday and spend the day in bed. Finally, I am starting to feel the weight of the Pharr babies and it's becoming more difficult for me to go all day without wanting to nap. However, on Sunday, there is no time for resting. The sex of the children is still unknown, and Patricia is not happy about it. It's the first item up for discussion during Sunday's brunch.

"How are people going to buy gifts if they don't know what the sexes are?"

"I thought we were here to discuss the engagement party, not the baby shower. Are we combining parties?" I say with excitement. "This would be good. Two parties for the headache of one."

Patricia sits back and sips her mimosa. "Well, the guest list for the engagement party is different from the baby shower. I'm not sure if we could do that."

"May I speak candidly?" I ask. "I don't want to be a bitch about this, but these twins are starting to wear me out. The weather is only going to get hotter and I'm not going to be in the party mood four months from now. Let's just have one party. It would be best for us all."

Patricia defers. "I do want to make my new daughter-in-law happy. One party it is. We'll do the baby shower an hour before the engagement party."

I give her a hug. "Thank you, Patricia." The rest of the brunch is a breeze.

Later that day, I talk with Tracy and things seem to be doing better for him. He is almost healed and he and his partner are working out their issues, plus he mentions the possibility of coming home to work for Omar. I tell him about the twins and he promises to come visit before I give birth. Though he sounds good, I have my doubts. Tracy wouldn't tell me if things weren't going well. He would simply pretend that they were, so I rarely know if he's okay. I want to visit him, but with the pregnancy and pending parties, there's no time. Right now, my concern is planning this birth, and the great thing is that Patricia is going to be a big help. Thank God she's cool and laid-back, because my nerves couldn't handle a nervous grandmother-to-be.

Sunday evening is spent catching up on phone calls. I call my aunt and my dad, give them an update and cook a wonderful meal. Close to midnight, I get the urge to call my mom. I fight it for about thirty minutes, and then give in. I dial the digits and suddenly hang up. Pacing the floor, I click the phone and begin to dial again. This time, I let it ring one time before hanging up. I toss the phone on the bed and walk into the bathroom and stare at my face in the mirror.

"My nose is getting bigger," I say while inspecting my face. Just then, the phone rings. I trot back into the bedroom and answer.

Damn caller ID. "Hi, Rose, what's up?" I answer.

"Why did you hang up?" she asks.

"I forgot what I was going to say."

"Oh."

As to be expected, an uncomfortable silence falls over the phone. I actually begin counting my breaths.

Finally, Rose comments. "So, have you been well? How is the pregnancy going?"

"It's going. Oh yeah, that's why I called. I'm having twins," I say nonchalantly.

"What! That's super."

"Super?" I laugh.

"Yeah, you know my grandmother was a twin. She had a twin brother."

"I never knew twins ran in our family."

"Well, her brother died before you were born and you know Nana died when you were five. After Mom's first divorce, I had to stay with Nana. She talked about her brother all the time. I still have a picture of the two of them when they were little. I'll send it to you."

"That will be nice," I say as I take a second and realize that I am actually enjoying my mother's voice.

"Um . . . Patricia is giving a baby shower-engagement party."

"Oh, my God, you're getting married too! What does the ring look like?"

"It's nice," I state.

"Two-carat nice or flawless three-carat nice?"

I remove the phone from my ear and give a dumbfounded stare at the receiver. I can hear Rose repeatedly call my name. Upon hesitation, I connect back to the earpiece. "Yes."

"You didn't answer me?" she says.

"I don't know how many carats. I don't really care about stuff like that."

"You get that from your father," she states.

"What's that supposed to mean?"

"Nothing. He's not a stickler for details. I'm the opposite. So when is the party? Am I invited?" she questions.

"I don't know, and I guess you can come if you want."

"Of course I want to come. Let me get Pat's number and I'll get all of the details."

I retrieve Pat's number from my book and give it to Rose. We talk a few more minutes about the babies and then hang up. Immediately, I regret inviting my mom. Totally conflicted, I don't know what possessed me to call in the first place. While contemplating, I place my hand on my stomach and scratch my stretching skin.

"Look here, Pharr babies, you will not have my emotions running amuck. I blame you for this."

I roll to my side and close my eyes. Within minutes, I am sound asleep.

That morning, I am sluggish. With intentions to divert my listless mood, I decide to go walking. The doctor said that it's good for the pregnancy, and I've gotten away from my routine over the last month. I figure today is a great day to start back. I set my sights on two miles, but one mile in, I begin cramping. The twinge grows and I have to stop. Within a block of my favorite coffee shop, I pause to massage my side. I feel the babies moving. The discomfort moves from the left side to the lower front and I bend forward in agony. There's nowhere to sit but the curb, so I slowly attempt to make it one more block. My ardent stride is now a hobble as I hold my stomach and apply slight pressure. Finally, I make it to the shop, walk in and sit at a booth. I try Rome on my cell, but there is no answer. Lia's phone goes directly to voice mail. I know Andre is at work and would love a reason to leave, but I will not be his excuse today. I lean against the table and the sharp pain hits again.

"Damn it!" I clench my teeth. I grab the phone and try Rome again, still no answer. I dial Omar's cell and he picks up on ring two. Before I can finish explaining, he is asking directions to the coffee shop. About ten minutes later, Omar is helping me to his car. Now, since the pain is mounting, I decide to go see my doctor. Omar insists on taking me. Though I am hesitant, I can't drive, so that's my only option. I notice Omar's nervous behavior. He continuously asks about the pain, as if he can diagnose the cause. Finally, I make small talk to calm him.

"I woke up early this morning. Guess what was on."

"Uptown Saturday Night," he responds.

Shocked, I look at him. Simultaneously, we speak. "I was going to call you."

"Why were you up?" I ask.

"I had just gotten home. Why were you up?"

"Couldn't sleep. Where were you at four in the morning?" I curiously ask.

Omar simply winks at me. Another sharp throb kicks in.

"Damn you." I scream just as Omar is pulling into the office parking lot. I grab my stomach and lean back in the seat. He screeches to a stop, gets out and helps me into the lobby.

"I'll grab your stuff. What's the doctor's name?"

"Pagota," I answer.

Omar parks and grabs my phone from the floor and my purse. As he heads back into the building, the phone rings again. It's Rome. Omar sees his name on the caller ID and answers.

"Hello."

Rome, shocked at the voice, stutters as he asks for me.

"Rome, it's O. She's at the doctor's office. I'll give you directions—"

"I know where it is. I'm on my way," he interrupts.

Omar goes into the office and waits in the lobby until Rome gets there.

I try to get comfortable on the bed with scratchy paper, but it's useless. The pain is dull again, but any position still brings discomfort. Dr. Pagota comes into the room and tries to soothe me.

"Why am I hurting?" I ask as soon as she walks in.

"This is what we are about to find out."

The doctor asks a series of questions as she pokes, prods and pushes. She hooks up the sonogram and studies.

"Your babies are turning around. It seems they both want a little camera time." She chuckles, but I am not amused.

"Everything else seems to be in order. Your blood pressure is slightly high, but that's not why you're having pain. I do want you to watch your diet and try exercising."

"That's what I was doing when these children started playing switcheroo. Are you sure everything is okay?"

"Yes. Because you're carrying twins, you may experience more discomfort when they are moving. Your organs have to shift to make room."

"Oh great. What next? Real contractions are going to send me right over the edge."

Dr. Pagota laughs. "You'll be fine. And guess what? We can see the sex of both babies now."

"Really?" I say, lifting my head. I look at the little white images. "I can't. Rome's not here. I promised." Just then, there's a knock. Dr. Pagota opens the door.

"Rome, you're here."

"I talked to Omar. Are you okay?" He walks over to my side and kisses my forehead.

"The babies are doing somersaults, my organs are shifting. Other than that, I'm fine."

"When I got your message, I . . . I . . . just—"

"It's okay now. I didn't mean to worry you. Oh, you want to know what we're having?"

Rome gives a confused look as I point to the sonogram. Dr. Pagota glows as she takes her little stick and begins to explicate the sonogram. "Here's your son's head, his back, his legs, and see right there"—Rome and I look closer—"this is how we know it's a boy."

Rome's eyes bug. His smile nearly leaps from his face.

"What about the other one?" I ask.

"Well, he's a little smaller than his brother."

"Two boys. We're having two boys!" Rome exclaims.

Squeezing my hand, he nearly shakes me off the reclined bed. Grabbing my shoulders, he yells, "Two boys!"

"I heard, I heard."

Dr. Pagota prints out the sonogram picture. Rome is beside himself. I give him a pleasing smile.

"I see you're happy," I comment.

"I'm beyond happy," he says.

My grin spills over to hearty laughter. "Two knuckleheads, poor me."

Dr. Pagota hands Rome the sonogram. He stares at the black-and-white print. "Congratulations. Gwen, watch your blood pressure. Here's a prescription for a mild painkiller. If you have any more problems, call. You can get dressed." She leaves as Rome continues to look at his sons' first picture.

While we get a bite to eat, Rome finally gets to the question that I was expecting the moment I saw him walk into the office.

"Why did you call Omar?"

"I didn't have anyone else to call. Neither you nor Lia answered your phones. Why didn't you answer your phone?"

"I was asleep. It was on vibrate," he responds.

"Oh," I answer.

"I don't like you hanging with him."

"Then be available when I need you."

The brazen statement silences him and there is no more discussion about Omar the rest of the day.

Everyone is overjoyed about the Pharr babies, which are now referred to as the Sutton boys, and Rome and I make plans to fly to New York to see my dad while I can still fit down the plane aisle. Since there are specials available, we decide to go this weekend. My pain completely subsides by the next day and the rest of the week goes quickly. We leave for New York on Thursday.

Marvin greets us at the airport, and he is so thrilled to see me, his eyes water with tears of bliss. We make four stops before getting to the house, just to visit several old neighborhood friends. Everyone makes a big fuss over the twins and has advice to give about raising boys. The last stop is by the funeral home. Once there, my godfather, Uncle Reggie, comes running out the front door. With his arms stretched, he nearly hugs the breath out of me. He looks frail, but apparently he's been taking his iron, 'cause I couldn't pry him loose. Reggie is a tiny man, standing only five-six, and at sixty-six years young, his head would be completely gray if he weren't still dying it jet black. His wife of twenty-six years died eight years ago, and he has been a swinging bachelor since. The women in the neighborhood all vie for Reggie's attention.

Rome extends his hand, but Reggie reaches out and gives him a tight hug. With a strong pat on Rome's back, Reggie says, "You're Patricia's boy. I remember you. Yeah, boy, your momma was some kind of fine back in the day. How's she doing?"

"She's fine," he responds.

"I bet she is, I bet she is," he counters with a slick grin.

We walk into the funeral home, and as soon as the sterile smell of embalming fluid hits my nose, I know I'm back home.

The next four days pass like four hours. Marvin coos over me, taking me from neighbor to neighbor, showing off the swollen belly that carries his future grandsons. Day three I actually get to rest while Rome and Marvin have a "boys day." I pray this day is peaceful and that Marvin doesn't grill Rome about the shotgun wedding. Though Rome doesn't discuss "boys day" conversation, I am positive Marvin got everything off his chest.

When we all sit down and have breakfast Sunday morning, I am filled with elation. I finally feel like part of my life is coming together in just the way it should. I'm sober, my dad seems to be proud of me and Rome can't keep his eyes off me.

"Thank God my life is good," I whisper just after the prayer. Marvin made waffles, my favorite. And as I sit down and partake of my beautiful breakfast, I look at the men in my life and I begin to slowly weep. First I try to hide the tears by extending my eyelids to refrain from blinking. But when Rome reaches and grazes my hand, it's too overwhelming. I blink and the first tear falls onto my plate. Quickly, I excuse myself and charge into the bathroom. Both men rush to my aid. They knock on the door repeatedly with a barrage of questions. I try to gather my emotions as I quietly answer from the inside. Within a minute, I open the door to see two very shocked men standing at the frame of the tiny bathroom.

"I'm fine. I promise. I'm just pregnant, I can't control my emotions."

Knowing this is a sentiment they will never understand, both men simply nod in unison.

"Let's finish eating. I'm okay," I reassure them as I walk to the table to continue eating. The men follow, but the remainder of brunch, both men keep glancing up from their plates to inconspicuously peer at me. My eyes remain on my plate until I finish. However, neither man is good at being subtle. Therefore, without looking up, I comment, "I'm okay, guys."

I know if I see my father's proud smile and Rome's adoring glances, back to the bathroom I'll go. It's best to just focus on the waffle and sausage. This way, no one will worry and the last day will pass just as gracefully as the others. We attend church service, and immediately after, Rome and I head to the airport. Thankfully, Marvin has to quickly leave for the funeral home. So there is no time for long good-byes, and I board the plane tear-free.

Exhausted from the visit, I close my eyes and rest the entire plane ride. I haven't said much since the breakfast breakdown and Rome's concerned, but he knows it's best to simply wait until I am ready to disclose. Therefore, he wraps his fingers within mine, kisses the top of my palm and lets me nap.

The evening at home is just as quiet as the flight. But at night, just before I fall asleep, I turn on my side, drape my arm around Rome and gently squeeze. He turns over and faces me. In a soft whisper, I speak.

"Thanks for not bugging me about today."

With a slight grin, he responds, "I'm learning."

I turn on my back and take several deeps sighs. Leaving Rome in suspense, I wait another ten minutes before I speak again.

"When I saw you and Dad today, it reminded me of when I was little. We used to always have breakfast together before church." Though I am not making eye contact, Rome can tell I am on the edge of another breakdown. He wants to hold me, but he hesitates. Amazingly, I can feel his apprehension, so I reach across the top of his bald head and softly rub his peach fuzz. I faintly whisper, "I want a family. I want to be happy . . . with my family. I've never had that."

Rome bends over and kisses my belly. "We are a family." I nod as I continue to stare toward the ceiling. He nestles just above my bosom and murmurs, "I love you, Ms. Gwendolyn Pharr, soon to be Mrs. Sutton." The muscles from my smile release a single tear, which falls on Rome's crown. It unveils my fragility. Rome wraps his arms around me and silently prays.

God, I know you don't hear from me like you should. But please help me with this. I want this—more important, she needs this—and I want to be here to give her everything she needs. But I'll mess it up if I do it alone. I have to step it up and I need you. I hope you're listening. Rome soon falls asleep, tightly cuddling me.

11

In three weeks, my stomach grows approximately sixteen more centimeters. In my words, I am "good and pregnant." My breasts hurt, my feet hurt and my appendages are swollen. The temperature is rising and my patience is getting shorter with every intensifying degree. At first, shopping was fun, but now if I see another embroidered blue onesie, I'm going to vomit. The big engagement/baby bash is in two days. Between gifts from Patricia and Lia, the house has no empty corners or closets. My space is rapidly becoming too small. Of course Rome continues to pressure me to permanently move in. He even turns his spare room into the boys' room, buying cribs and having a mural painted on the wall as an added incentive. With gifts stacked high in the boys' room, I reorganize them each night until I decide everything is perfect. This evening, I actually think about permanently moving in. The wedding date is not set, but once the twins arrive, there is no way I'll have the energy to do it on my own. I figure I best move while they are still in the womb, so I make plans to sublet my place until my lease runs out. Unlike usual, I don't dither. I can hardly believe it, but Rome is making the relationship effortless. From the evening bubble baths to the new housekeeper, he is truly taking care of me. Half of his energy is going toward making the relationship work, the other half is deep into his career. Both have grown by leaps and bounds. I actually have to sit awhile in order to come up with things to worry about.

I'm doing payroll today, so I go into the office early to retrieve the checks from our accountant. Rome has finally agreed to let an accounting firm take care of the bills. This makes my life easier. When I get to the club, Marie is already there. She's excited about a new idea to have an ole-school dance contest. We go to the office and discuss. However, once we close the door, we each take turns showing off our favorite dances from the past. She's a cool girl. I would love for her to hang out with Lia and me, but, like Rome, Lia hasn't been around much lately either. In the middle of our giggles, Rome comes into the office. Marie quiets and Rome stops in his tracks. I waddle to him and pinch his side.

"Rome, of course you know Marie. You haven't even seen her since she started working here," I say, smiling.

She walks up to him and gives him a hug. "Good to see you again."

Rome turns to Marie and speaks. "Can you help me get some boxes out of the car?"

"I can help," I say.

"No, you shouldn't lift. You can help, right?"

Marie nods and they leave.

I finish my books. It takes Marie and Rome twenty minutes to return. When she does, she grabs her things and says good-bye.

"Where are you going? Are you coming back?" I ask.

"Yeah, I have a doctor's appointment I forgot about. I have to hurry."

"Okay," I say with hesitation before she shuts the door.

Oddly, Rome leaves immediately after, saying that he had a bunch of errands to run and that he just came by to drop things off and say hello.

Rose is coming this evening, so I rush to the house after stopping by the liquor store to stock up on my mother's favorite. Though I am around alcohol at the club, the liquor store trip is more difficult than I thought. I pace each aisle, reminiscing about my favorite drinks and cheerful drunk moments. Finally, after twenty minutes of perusing, I grab the bottles I come to and hurry from the store.

I place the Stolichnaya and Kahlua in the cabinet and begin to clean the house. True, the housekeeper came just days ago, but I want it sparkling. Rose is staying at Rome's place, since I only have a one-bedroom. I won't admit my excitement, not even to myself, but there is an extra pep in today's step as I prepare for Rose's arrival. Just as I am placing the clean white sheets on her bed, the phone rings. Instinctively, I know it's Rose. Hesitating, I fear it's not good news. I pick up the receiver, but don't speak at first.

"Gwendolyn, are you there?"

"Yeah, what happened?" I say with disappointment.

"My manicurist went into labor and I had to wait for another girl, so I missed my flight. There isn't another one to Detroit until tomorrow morning, so I'll be on that one."

I say nothing. I sit with a blank stare, knowing my mom is not going to show up.

"I know you think I'm not coming," says Rose, interrupting my thoughts. "I'll be there at two tomorrow."

"The shower starts at three. If I pick you up, I'll be late and that would be rude."

"If you give me the address, I'll get there."

"How?" I ask.

"Taxi."

"Just call before you get on the plane, that is if you don't miss it tomorrow. I'll see if Rome can pick you up."

"I promise I'll be there," she vows.

"I have to go." I hang up and toss the uncovered pillow

across the bed. I walk into my living room, plop on the chair and flip on the television.

"She's so predictable," I whisper while lying down. Quickly, I fall asleep. When I awake, it's close to ten at night and Rome is lifting me from the couch.

"I've been trying to call. Where's Rose?"

"Missed her flight," I mumble.

Rome knows it's best to say nothing.

"I knew she wasn't coming," I observe before drifting off to sleep.

12

The day of the big event starts smoothly. I awake early, prepare breakfast and Rome and I eat a smorgasbord of omelets,
sausage and hash browns. I rise to take a shower and waddle
to the bathroom. Rome laughs as he follows behind, tickling
my side.

"Stop it."

"Why, you said you weren't ticklish."

"Stop it, I have to take a shower. Make yourself useful and
get my phone. It's probably Lia."

I rush into the bathroom and shut the door. Rome answers
the phone and is very glad to hear Rose's voice on the other
end. She was able to get on an earlier flight and is already at
the airport. Rome decides to surprise me.

"Gwen honey, I have to go home. I need to shave my head
and I don't have clippers here."

With nothing on but a pair of blue panties, I open the door.
"Okay, I have some running around to do, anyway. I'll see you
at the shower." Rome kisses me and walks from the room.
"Oh, who was on the phone?" I call out.

"Telemarketer," he says before walking out the door.

I shower and dress for my day. Lia picks me up and we go
to pick up a frame I had engraved for Patricia, as a thank-you

present for all her hard work. Around 1:00 P.M., I still haven't heard from Rose, and I make peace that my mom is still as unreliable as always.

I gear up my energy for the day with a medium chai tea from Cup of Joe's. Lia walks two stores down to a sandwich shop to grab a bite to eat. As I am walking from the door, I bump into Marie and nearly spill my hot drink on my new mango-colored dress.

"Gwen, what a surprise."

"Marie, yes, it is. What happened to you the other day?"

Seeming a little uneasy, she continues to walk away.

"Is everything okay? Are you coming to the shower today?" I ask.

"No, I don't think Rome would want me there."

"Did you two fall out? I don't understand."

"Look, you seem really nice. Personally, I think you deserve someone better than Rome, but oh well. You won't be seeing me anymore."

"Wait, Marie, what are you talking about?"

"If you want to know, talk to your cheating boyfriend." She continues to walk. "Ask him about Miami. Ask him about Ariel."

I halt and turn with a befuddled look. I then scurry back to the car and wait for Lia. Immediately, I grab my phone to call Rome, but before I can dial, the tears are streaming down my face. I toss the phone down and scream. There is no proof, she didn't even say anything, but my heart fears there's a big unfaithful lie just around the corner. My mind rapidly replays past conversations, looks and behavior. The more I think, the more I become upset. The last thing on my mind is the party, which starts in thirty minutes. I sit in the front seat staring at the bumper of the car parked in front. It bears one of those WWJD bumper stickers.

"Jesus would kick his butt," I shriek.

When Lia returns, I play it cool and we arrive at the party

fifteen minutes late. After sitting in the car for about another ten, I plaster my smile on and walk into the home of Patricia Sutton-Barnes. Before I get a few feet in, everyone rushes and pets everything from my ring to my twenty-eight-week swollen tummy. My toothy grin and wide-eyed expression are stuck as I nod my way through the crowded room of pastel-colored dresses. I am ushered to the corner chair, adorned with two big blue bows.

Everything in the room sounds like chicken chatter as one phrase rings in my head: *Did Rome cheat? Did Rome cheat?* The silly grin is slowly drying my mouth out and my lips stick to my teeth as I try to readjust my expression. Patricia moves in close and whispers, "I have a surprise for you."

Quickly, the grin is back as I am now trying to figure out the best escape route. Suddenly, I see Rome come from the back holding the hand of a tall, voluptuous woman sporting a cinnamon red bob.

"Oh shit," I whisper.

"My Gwendolyn," Rose says, dashing over to me. She wraps her arms around my neck and my scary smile morphs into a crooked, closed-lip grimace as my neck bends into Rose's bosom. The grip lifts me to my feet and Rose reaches in for a more embracing squeeze. As I look over my mother's shoulder, I catch Rome's eye. He smiles and I glare. The chuckling, the grins, the fondling over the baby clothing, are too much to bear. The entire party, I am one gasp away from choking.

Finally, I excuse myself, step outside and sit on the bottom step at the end of the porch. With my head against the wrought-iron rails, I close my eyes and breathe slow and deep. So lost in thought, I don't sense the body heat approaching, until I feel a kiss on my forehead.

"Gwenie."

Thankful to hear my friend's voice, I open my lids and immediately a tear falls down my cheek.

"What's wrong?"

I quietly nod back and forth. Lia sits close and takes me into her arms.

"Did somebody upset you? Want me to curse them out?"

I softly chuckle and lay my head on Lia. Rose comes out onto the porch.

"There you are. Everyone is looking for you."

"Gwen needs a moment, they are going to have to wait," Lia sasses.

"Well, it's rude. This is a party in her honor."

"And who are you?" Lia continues with attitude.

"I'm Rose, Gwen's mother."

"What!" Lia screams. She stands and quickly apologizes. "I'm sorry. I'm Lia, Gwen's best friend."

I still say nothing as I adjust my head back to the rail.

"Gwendolyn, are you coming in? Should I get Rome?" Lia asks.

"No!" I exclaim.

Rose walks to the first step, but Lia halts her. "Really, she needs a moment. Tell them she's fine." Rose hesitates and then retreats back into the house. As soon as the door closes, she bombards me with questions, but I answer none of them. Finally, Lia asks, "Do you want to be alone?" I shake my head and reach for Lia's hand. Lia sits and holds on to her disconcerted friend. At least ten minutes pass before I make my second appearance, but just as I walk in the door, I deliver one question to Lia.

"You remember Ariel?"

Lia shrugs her shoulder and walks back into the party with me.

I continue to thank the women for the dozens of baby gifts and gift certificates. I purposely avoid Rome most of the party and say few words to Rose. With Lia as a buffer, I sit behind the pyramid of blue presents, smile for the camera and speak only when spoken to. Finally, Rome slides in next to me, kisses my neck and whispers in my ear. "I love you."

I simply reply with a nod and he goes to refill my cup of water. Just then, Lia jumps up and claps her hands.

"That's the girl," she calls out.

I give a confused look.

"The girl in the club hallway that day. Remember, I was leaving with my sex list. The tall one, kinda Asian features."

"Marie?" I question.

"No, that's Ariel. I thought I recognized her, but I wasn't sure. She was the crazy girl that used to stalk Rome. Marie is your assistant, right? Where is she, I wanted to meet her. I thought she was coming."

Just then, Rome returns with my water.

I swiftly turn in his direction with a very angry look. He, completely confused and suddenly concerned, slowly responds, "What?"

"Remember your crazy ex Ariel?" Lia asks.

"Yeah, well, she really wasn't my girl." His tone is very low and deliberate as if he had been planning that response for a while. Only this scene has thrown him off, but his body language screams "guilty" as his neck tenses and left eye twitches. Rome folds his arms and continues to stare at Lia. At that second, Lia connects the dots. Knowing she has said too much, she darts across the room for a baby blue cupcake. Rome turns to me, but knows not what to say. My lips are shut so tightly, they form little wrinkles around the crevices. Rome instantly goes back to "Cheating Men 101" and remembers the first cardinal rule: play innocent until proven guilty.

"What was that about?" he asks. With a curt military turn, I walk away.

The shower is over and engagement party guests begin arriving and I have run out of places to hide. After spending fifteen minutes in the master bedroom, another thirty out back and an additional ten in the bathroom, I give up and take my place beside Rome and listen to his toast.

"I want everyone here to know, how lucky . . . no, blessed I am to have someone like Gwen in my life. We have been friends for over twenty-five years and now my friend is about to become my wife and I can't believe she chose me." I hear this toast as one big pile of hot bullshit. As he gives me a sincere smile, I begin to cry. Everyone in the room takes my weeping as delight from his endearment, but I am flustered, embittered, pissed and so discombobulated that tears are inevitable. However, I simply play along with the crowd of "oohs and aahs." An hour later, a migraine is starting, so I go to Patricia, thank her for everything, but kindly insist that I must leave. Next I go to Rose.

"I'm so glad you came. I'm surprised, but pleased. I have to go. Lia said she would bring you to the house."

"No, I'm leaving with you," Rose states.

"The party is just getting going. Look, there are drinks. Enjoy yourself. I have a headache, I have to go lie down," I insist.

"I didn't come to party, I came to see you."

"Fine. Come on to the house."

"I got a hotel. It's a very nice suite. Why don't we stay there tonight," she offers.

At first, I am about to reject the proposal, but I then figure it's the best place to hide out. By the morning, I'll be able to sensibly approach Rome. I inform Lia that we are leaving. She grabs her things. Rose says good-bye to Patricia and grabs her purse from the back room. I mingle next to Rome and tap his arm. "I'm leaving."

"What? No," he says.

"I have a migraine. I have to go."

"Well, let's go."

"No. Stay here and entertain. We'll talk in the morning."

"But—"

"Not now, Rome." I speak with an infuriated tone. Rome quickly backs off. He is aware that I may know the truth, and if I do, he needs the night to get his game plan together. Therefore, he pecks my lips and walks me to the front door. I don't even say good-bye as I exit with Rose. Rome leans against the door frame and watches us go down the street. Distress builds from his gut to his throat as he tries to keep up the pleasant expression that's quickly dwindling.

Lia drops Rose and me off at the hotel, and I immediately crash onto the bed and pull the pillow on top of my face. Rose, at a loss for words, sits on the corner of the bed and rubs my ankles. After minutes of ankle caressing, I lift the pillow and peer down at Rose, who has now added a soft hum to her circular motion.

"What are you doing?" I ask in a less than pleasant tone.

"Rubbing, keeps your ankles from swelling, that and elevating them. You're carrying twins, you have to be careful, blood circulation is very important."

I drop the pillow back onto my face. Rose continues to hum and rub for another fifteen minutes. Finally, she rises and begins her nightly regime. She removes her wig, her makeup and takes a shower. By the time she is done, I am asleep. However, when she gets into the bed, I awaken. I barely open my eyes, but once I take a glance at Rose, I damn near jump up from the bed.

"Oh, my God."

Rose quickly covers her partially bald head with her right hand and her chest with her left.

"Your hair? What . . . why did you . . . when . . . ?"

"I've been in chemo since last year. They removed my right breast in December. My left one is still holding strong though."

I sit up against the headboard and stare at my mom in awe.

"It's okay. I'm fine. They got it all."

"I just . . . Why didn't you say something? Why didn't you tell me?"

"Well, we really don't talk, and I didn't want to call you with my problems. I thought that would be selfish. It's not like you're a doctor."

"No, but I am your daughter."

"Oh, you're my daughter now, I thought I was more like an acquaintance."

I give my mother a pitiful look and gaze at her chest.

"See, I hate those looks. As soon as my chemo is over, I'm getting a new pair. I'll be back to a full C before you know it. Plus, my old ones were getting a little saggy."

"What if you had died?" I say, flabbergasted.

"I told Jack to call you if I got really sick. But it was just breast cancer. It's very common these days. I am fine. Now, what about you?"

I fall back onto the bed and let out an exasperated huff. Just then, my phone rings, but I don't answer it. Rose lifts to get the phone, but I motion to let it go. However, after three more consecutive calls, I answer. And, just as I suspect, it's Lia.

"I'm fine, Lia," I answer. "I'll explain tomorrow, and no, you didn't do anything wrong. Love you and good night." I hang up and toss the phone down on the bed.

"It's too early for trouble in paradise," Rose hints.

I roll over to my side before speaking. "I'm tired and going to sleep now. Do you have enough room?"

"I do," Rose comments before grabbing the decorative pillow and placing it underneath my feet. She lies down beside me, something she hadn't done in over twenty-five years, and retires for the evening.

I sleep until almost noon the next day. Rose awakes early, has a great continental breakfast and makes plans to go shopping with Patricia—all before I open my first eyelid. When I rise, I am still angry, as if no time passed. I make dinner plans with Rose and head to the house to change clothing. I knew I should have left some maternity clothes at my house. The entire ride home, I practice my argument with Rome. Like a lawyer, I have three opening statements prepped and ready to fire. Statement one leads with a question about Miami. Statement two is flat-out accusatory. Statement three is coy, asking him to give his definition of cheating. My mood when I see him will determine my lead-in.

I open the door of his home and toss my things on the counter. I notice the large pile of gifts sitting in the corner. Slowly, I tread into the bedroom and see Rome sitting on the edge of the bed with his head in between his palms. By his somber expression, I know there is no need for any of my planned statements. So I lead with the first thing that comes to mind.

"Why?"

Rome buries his head lower, almost covering his entire face with his massive hands. I walk over and pop him on the top of his head.

"Shit, Rome! I can't believe you."

He slowly lifts his face and stares at my sudden burst of tears.

"Baby, I didn't—"

"I know you did, so don't lie," I shout.

"I wasn't going to lie."

"Good, 'cause you fucked up."

I walk into the bathroom and slam the door. Rome continues to sit on the edge of the bed. Inside the bathroom, I pace the floor. My footsteps become heavier as my breathing augments. I wrap my hands around my neck and pull on my skin to soothe my itchy, dry throat. Suddenly, I rush from the bathroom to grab my inhaler. Rome darts to my aid, leaning his arm around my back. However, I continuously shrug my shoulder to ward off his attention. As soon as my breathing is regulated, I shriek, "Get off me!"

"Are you okay?" he asks.

"I said get off me." I rise and move away from Rome. He follows me back into the bedroom as I go to the dresser to remove my jewelry. Close on my heels, he follows me into the kitchen. I grab a spoon from the drawer, but bump into Rome when I turn toward the fridge. I thump him in the neck with the spoon.

"Ouch."

"Get out!" I yell.

"Will you let me explain?"

"No."

"Gwen, it's not what you think."

With the spoon jammed into the side of his throat, I back Rome into a corner.

"I think you just don't know how to keep your dick in your pants. I think I shouldn't have trusted you. I think you're self-ish and always will be. I think—"

"You're wrong. I wanted to do right. Please just listen."

Suddenly, my taut jaw and intense stare morph into a jit-tery frown with mawkish eyes. I can see the remorse in his gaze and feel his compunction when he touches the base of my chin. The combination of his voice, stare and touch is the triple-combo that may knock me out. Consequently, I look down at the ground as his thumbs softly circle my cheeks.

"I fucked up, I know. But I swear, I only want to be with you."

As I continue to look at the tiled floor, I speak. "Did you sleep with your ex in Miami?"

Rome is silent for a second before responding. "I didn't go to Miami expecting to see Ariel, and—"

I interrupt with a more braying tone. "Did you place your dick inside that girl?" I look up. Though it's difficult for me to face his truth, it's much harder for him to face my disap-pointment.

"I'm sorry," Rome says, lowering his hands as he looks away.

"I can't do this with you. I can't." I move from the corner and walk into the bedroom. "And this girl . . . Ariel, Marie? Whoever she is. She was all up in our business. I thought she was cool. She knew the whole time." I begin to break down. "When you saw her at the office, you still didn't tell me."

"I didn't want to upset you. Ariel is crazy. She thought I wanted her back."

I smack him in the chest. "Why did you do it, why?" I sob.

Rome continues to speak. "We're having babies."

I sniff up my few tears, face him and boldly respond, "I'm having babies . . . . You're fucking other women."

I plop down on the bed, still holding the spoon. Rome kneels by the bedside and lightly massages my calf, but I push him off with the other leg. "Stop touching me. I'm serious."

"I'm serious too. We are engaged. I still want you to be my wife."

"Why, Rome?"

"'Cause I love you."

"That's not a good enough reason." I slowly remove the ring from my finger and slide it into the palm of his hand. "You're not ready, and I'm not sure if you ever will be." I leave and go into the guest bedroom. I release a long sigh and spend an hour lying in bed, staring at the leafy trees outside my window.

That evening, I call Lia and invite her to join me for dinner with Rose. Of course Lia obliges. Never being the one to turn down a meal engagement, she promptly meets Rose and me at the Blue Pointe lobby at 7:00 P.M. Before we sit, I pull Lia aside and beg her not to mention Rome or the incident. Lia agrees, but tonight Rose is the one concerned about my well-being and the details of the pending wedding. Over the shrimp-and-pasta dish, Rose can't stop gabbing about the imminent nuptials. I just sit and silently listen, nodding in between the pauses. Lia joins in with plans for her ideal wedding, but my mind is across town and it's not until dessert that the two blabbering tongues realize that I am not a participating party.

Rose's tiramisu is down to its last crumb when she finally asks, "Why are you so quiet? Is everything okay?"

With a solemn expression, I look up from my key lime pie, bite my lip and shrug my shoulders.

"Well, what was that?" Rose questions.

"I don't have anything to say," I whisper.

Rose glances at Lia, who quickly looks across the restaurant.

"Let's finish this and leave," I say.

After seeing my demeanor, Rose decides it's best to stay with me. I know she simply wants to pry, but I don't have the energy to fight her. Therefore, once we get to the condo, I rapidly try to think of an excuse to keep from talking. I turn on the television and invite her to watch. Rose eagerly accepts.

I toss her an oversized shirt and a pair of sweats. "Get comfy," I state.

Rose and I sit on opposite ends of the couch as I flip to her favorite channel, AMC. *Brief Encounter* is just beginning. Rose's eyes light up as she speaks. "I love this movie."

"So do I," I retort as I look at my mom and smile.

We snuggle underneath the chenille cover and begin our movie night. However, just as Laura, the female lead, is about to start her voice-over about Alec, her romantic interest, I have an overwhelming desire to discuss my issues with Rose.

"What's wrong with me?" I question as I glance at Rose.

Though her attention stays forward, she quietly comments, "I won't judge you."

"What do you mean?" I ask.

With her face still forward, she continues to talk. "If you want to talk, I'll just listen, I won't say anything."

I am quiet as I continue to watch the movie for another fifteen minutes. Finally, my inner voice overrules my better judgment and I slowly begin to open up. I start in the middle. "I don't trust him. I wish I could, but he is who he is . . . a dog."

Rose turns toward me with an endearing expression. She doesn't move closer, but she invites more conversation. I, conflicted, want to shut up but can't. I need to let it out and my therapy appointment isn't for another two days. Yet, Rose is here, so I continue.

"I wasn't thinking. I should have never had sex with him. He's out of town working right now, probably cheating. I didn't want to be some man's baby momma. As common as it is, it still carries a stigma. And . . . I don't care about what people think, but I didn't want that for me. Not that marriages always last, so . . ." I fade into silent thoughts for another minute and then begin again, just as random as before. "I know he loves me. We love each other, but what's that mean. . . . I can't be with a man that is going to cheat on me every few months. Sometimes I wish I had stayed with Omar. But that was a mess too." By now, Rose has turned her body toward me as she tries to piece together these arbitrary links of my puzzling life. "We used to fight. It was passionate, but it wasn't right, not healthy. But I was the center of his life and that's what kept me in it. I was his top priority, but it was screwed up 'cause there was no balance. You know what I mean?" Rose nods intensely. "Oh God, I've messed everything up. Now, Omar's moved back and he wants us to get back together. Rome slept with his ex and now I can't be with him. I'm pregnant with twins and I don't know how I'm going to raise them on my own." This time, I take a long pause before continuing. "I wanted a drink tonight."

Rose leans over and reaches for me. She lightly tugs on my arms to pull me closer. I hesitate, shyly nod and motion that I'm fine. However, I desperately want the reassuring comfort of a hug. My leg begins to twitch. The anxiousness doesn't come from the intense conversation, but rather the overwhelming desire for consolation—more so, solace from Rose. Though I'm elated that my mom is here during this difficult time, it's a first and I don't know how to cope with this conflict of emotion. From the time my period started during a middle-school assembly to the time I entered rehab, Rose has never been there. But she's here now and seemingly concerned. I pray silently that this is not a trick, but that finally Rose is actually fulfilling her position as a caring mom. Simultaneously, I kick myself for desiring my mother's compassion. I feel the tears building, and instinctually, I attempt to rush to the bathroom, but my legs won't budge as I sit there trying to blink my tears back into my sockets. Rose can feel the pain and knows that if a move is to be made, she must make it. She slides closer and gently tugs me again, but I don't shift. Other than the leg jitter, I am frozen. Years of discord has both the mother and daughter scared to make the next move. Yet, we silently yearn for harmony. I don't trust Rose, and Rose doesn't trust herself. It's a stalemate. I eventually lean my shoulder in her direction. It's a diminutive shift in weight, but it's enough for Rose to move completely in. She takes me and cuddles me like a newborn. The cradling causes me to weep, and this moment marks a rebirth of our relationship. Nothing else is said that night as we take in the remainder of our favorite "chick flick," embraced in silence.

The next morning, over brunch, Rose surprises me when she tells me that she often wishes she had stayed with Marvin. Shocked, I nearly choke on my omelet.

Immediately, I say, "You should have never married him."

"How could you say that?" Rose responds. I simply laugh as Rose looks on with a bewildered face. "What? What's so funny?" she asks.

"How we can casually talk about something so serious like this is some after-movie conversation and all the characters are fictional. It's funny, that's all," I say.

"Well, it's long overdue. I love Marvin."

"You don't have to explain," I say, secretly wanting her to continue.

"But I want to." Rose rises and makes herself a Black Russian. Stirring the ice with her fingers, she sits and looks into my eyes. "Do you mind?" she asks, pointing to the drink.

"It's about twenty-five years late for that question," I sneer sarcastically.

Rose is not affected by the sarcasm as she takes her first sip before explaining, "This will be quick. I've practiced how I would explain this for years—"

"I practice conversations in my head too," I interrupt.

Rose chuckles and carries on. "I'm sorry. I'm sorry for not being able to deal with everything I brought on. I do love your father. He is a wonderful man. And he tried his best to make me happy, but it wasn't enough. When I met Marvin, I was going through a time where I just wanted someone to take care of me. I had just gotten out of an abusive relationship and he was my knight in shining armor. I was so pitiful when we met. I was a wreck, not caring if I lived or died. I was even on drugs." Rose takes a big gulp of her relaxation and I make another pot of coffee. I can hardly believe the words leaking from her mouth. "Marvin put me back together again. He was my wizard, I was the Scarecrow, and he gave me a heart."

"The Tin Man needed a heart, the Scarecrow needed a brain," I cut in.

"You know what I mean," Rose scoffs. "He helped me get clean—how could I not fall in love with him? When everything is so perfect, it's so easy to think that's where you belong. But it's an illusion. I didn't realize it at the time, but I used him to heal myself, when I should have just gone into a clinic. By the time I had you, my life was good, but I was so bored, I was slowly losing my mind. I abhor routine and that was my life. I felt immature for wanting to leave, but if I had stayed, I would have begun using again. I just know it. I felt like a quitter for leaving, but I had intentions of coming back. I didn't take you with me because Marvin was a much better parent than me. I didn't even know how to do your hair." I notice a squeaky tone in Rose's voice. I am cautious not to look up, just in case I begin to tear up. The conversation is deep enough, without the watery sentiment. "I met Jack a month after I left. I never cheated on Marvin, just so you know. Jack whisked me away from all my problems, or so I thought. The fact is, we stayed so busy, I didn't have to deal with my issues. I never wanted to, anyway, so this was perfect. Did Jack love me like Marvin? No. Your father adored me, Jack and I have . . . we have a partnership. But once I realized that, it was too late to come back. Plus, I knew that Marvin would never want to travel and do all these other things that I desired, so even if I did return, could I stay—"

I interrupt and make eye contact before questioning. "But what about me? Why wasn't I enough to make you want to come back?"

Rose doesn't answer as she looks down into her empty glass of ice.

"It's rhetorical, really. It's not like I don't have the answer," I comment.

Rose's face is still lowered. She starts her sentence with a moan, but eventually words form. "You were better off without me. I drank too much, I smoked too much and I lied too much. I didn't want those things to influence you."

"That's a lie!" I yell to Rose's surprise. "Just say you didn't want to be a mother. Just say you didn't want the responsibility of being someone's mom. That's the truth, so just say it."

"Fine." Rose retaliates with flailing arms and accidentally knocks the glass onto the floor. The shattered tumbler releases another outburst of emotion as Rose stands and yells, "Being a mother was too much responsibility!" She rushes to the bedroom and slams the door.

I stare at the broken glass for seconds before getting the broom to sweep the mess. Once the floor is clear of shards, I pace back and forth, and ultimately decide to go check on my mom. I knock on the door several times before Rose opens it. She looks into my empathetic eyes. This time, I know it's my turn to make the first move. I open my arms. Rose leans forward and places her head on my shoulder. However, she keeps her arms by her side.

She murmurs into my ear, "I'm sorry. Please forgive me." I squeeze tighter. Rose finally lifts her arms, completing the hug. "I do love you. I do," Rose assures me. This time, no tears are released, only a heap of anguish. It's amazing how long it's taken to have this conversation.

The first night together, Rose and I birthed a new relationship. The next morning, it accelerated through the awkwardness of puberty, and by the time I take Rose to the airport, two days later, we are each sending our baby off to college. Both proud at the accomplishments the other has made, and knowing that the separation is necessary for maturity.

I wave good-bye as my mom walks to the ticket counter. Suddenly, Rose jogs back to hug me one last time. "I'll be back when the babies are born." I give her a doubtful look; to which, Rose responds, "I'm serious. I'll call you, you'll see." I grin as my mom trots back to the counter to get her boarding pass. From the car, I watch her disappear into the crowd of travelers. With a euphoric spirit, I smile all the way back across town.

I arrive at the club, close to one o'clock. Thinking Rome is still out of town, I plan a few more stress-free days. Yet, when I open the office door, Rome is sitting at my desk, working on the computer. We look at each other, but say nothing. I walk in and take a seat at the other desk. Just then, Rome speaks. "Do you need the computer?"

"I'm fine," I retort.

I grab a stack of paperwork and start my workday. Forty minutes of silence pass. Finally, I burst into laughter.

"Oh, you think this is funny?" Rome asks.

"Yes, I do. It's immature and it's funny."

Rome doesn't know what to think. He's not sure if I have forgiven him, or if this is some ploy to get him to admit some other soiled deed. But there is no more foul play, so my attempt is in vain, at least in his mind. Therefore, he waits for my next move, which comes immediately.

I rise, walk over to Rome and kiss him on his lips. Rome tries to steal another kiss, but I move away.

"We can work this out, I know it," he says.

I slowly shake my head in despair. "I can't be with you if I don't trust you. Let's just have these babies and see what happens after that, okay?" I trot back to my desk, leaving Rome tattooed with confusion.

Underneath his breath, he whispers, "'Let's just have the babies and see what happens'? What in the hell are you talking about?"

I look up from the desk with a lighthearted smile. "We are having these children, there's nothing we can do about that. And I thought it would be great to marry you, but I don't know if I'm ready to handle someone like you. So let's take this one thing at a time. Now, are you going to be on my computer all day? If so, can you e-mail me the file in my documents that says 'ole-school love'? I'm working on sponsorship for the next one."

"I'm done," Rome says, rising from the desk. "I'm going to lunch."

I give him a casual wave as I walk to my computer. Rome gives me one last peer before shutting the door, but I pay him no attention as I open my file and begin working.

After a few days of this baffling behavior, Rome can't take it anymore. Andre offers up no good advice, he only tells Rome to be there for his children and that things will eventually turn around. With each passing day, Rome's confusion grows to resentment. Yes, he is the one who messed up and he apologized. But for me not to forgive him, and simply disregard him altogether, is unacceptable. He decides to play along with my game. If I can act like I don't care, so can he. Two more weeks pass and Rome goes out of his way to show that he is cool with being "just friends." He is determined to break this drama. Problem is, I'm not acting. I've accepted that I do care, but that right now is not the time to be in a relationship with Rome. Though I explained it twice, his pride blurs his understanding. To add insult to injury, Rome catches me coming back from lunch with Omar. He's been cool all this time, but on this day, he loses it. As soon as I get back into the office, he storms in, fussing and cursing.

"What is going on with you, Gwendolyn? First you give the ring back, and then you want to be friends, now you kicking it with O. Is this some sort of game to you?"

"What?" I innocently ask, turning away from my desk. By now, my belly is so big, I can't easily rise, but I get into position for face-to-face banter.

"I said I was fucking sorry! What do you want me to do?"

"I want you to stop yelling," I say calmly.

Rome lowers his tone, but he's still enraged. "We should be together. We love each other and you're running around here tripping."

"I'm tripping? My mind is on the fact that I am going to have two very large objects pulled out of my vagina in a couple months. I'm reading books on pregnancy and motherhood, I'm going to Lamaze, I'm practicing my breathing, I'm still working here and I'm scared. I don't have time to be tripping. You're tripping for thinking that I'm tripping. How 'bout that?"

"You seeing Omar now?"

I finally work my way out of the seat. "Omar and I went to lunch. He is my friend. I can have a decent conversation with him, without stress." I grab my books and place them in my bag. "I'm going home to work." I place my bag on my shoulder and head toward the office door.

Rome mumbles under his breath, "You'd rather be with someone that'll beat your ass instead of someone trying to do right."

"What the fuck did you say?" I snap.

Rome is silent as he walks to the file cabinet.

I waddle with fury and cramp Rome's personal space as I get an inch away from his face. "You think hurting my feelings is going to make me want to be with you? Yeah, we used to fight and it was messed up. But I'm not that woman anymore, and he's not that man. You want to know the difference between you and O? He doesn't think with his dick. I'd rather be with someone who makes me a priority than someone still trying to figure out what that means."

I whip around, leave the office and storm down the hall. I get in my car and drive off. Furious, I want to go back and give Rome another piece of my mind, but I know it will only stress me more. I plan to go home, but somehow my car ends up at Comatose. I sit outside in the parking lot for three minutes. When I realize that I must leave, I crank up the car, but it's too late. Omar is already rushing out the door toward the vehicle. He taps on the window, and I hesitantly lower it halfway.

"You okay?" I nod yes.

"You wanna come in?" I shake my head.

"You sure?"

"I am."

Omar stands beside the car and waits for me to say something else, but I simply stare at him.

He smiles and says, "You look so beautiful."

I quickly roll up the glass, put the car in drive and leave him, bewildered, in the parking lot.

I work from home over the next few days. Rome doesn't call and neither do I. It's Friday night, and I've had a week of little communication with the outside world. I call Lia up for some much-needed noise. I haven't seen her in two weeks. No Lia means there's got to be some new action in her world, and apparently, the action is so hot that Lia is still unavailable. Her phone is going straight to voice mail. I call repeatedly throughout the night, and leave a total of four messages.

"Maybe there's a little needy friend inside, after all," I whisper before falling asleep.

Bright and early the next morning, my cell phone starts ringing. Eager to speak with any human being, I answer quickly, but take a deep gasp when I hear Omar's voice. It's the voice I want to hear, but know I shouldn't listen to.

"I want to see you," he states.

"Yeah, we should talk."

"Want me to come over?"

"Yeah, but you shouldn't. So I'll meet you at the coffee shop."

"Give me an hour."

When we disconnect, I lift from the bed and rush as fast as I can into the bathroom. The load of an additional nine pounds of belly weight adds thirty minutes to my morning regime. However, I still get to the coffee shop within forty-five minutes. As I wait for Omar, Lia calls. We have a brief discussion and agree to meet later for dinner. I don't mention my whereabouts, for I know Lia will go into a tirade that I'm not prepared for, and Omar is approaching. Therefore, I get off the phone and rise to greet him. My protruding stomach makes front clutches difficult, so I hug him from the side. We sit on the patio in back and have drinks. I have tea and he has coffee. Before conversation starts, Omar is elated.

"Please stop smiling," I request. Omar instantly grimaces. "That's better." I sip my green tea, and we stare at one another over the brims of our cups.

"I enjoy you, Omar, I always have. I don't know what this is. I just wanted to see you. I wanted to see anyone, you just happen to be the one who called."

"I see, thanks."

"No, I don't mean it like that. I've just been locked up in the house this week and I was lonely for attention."

"Why didn't you call me?"

"'Cause you can't come to my rescue every time I need something."

"Why not? That's what friends are supposed to do."

"You and I are more than friends. It's a fine line we walk, and I have to make sure we don't cross it."

"I told you that I would respect whatever it is you and Rome are doing. What are you doing, by the way?"

I shrug my shoulders and Omar sees some qualms in this once-solid relationship. He reaches across the table and grazes the top of my hand.

"Babe, I'm here whenever you need me. In whatever way you need me." Omar makes his move. I remain silent and drink my tea. Other than a few rings on Omar's phone, talk is sparse. As I finish, Omar gives a sly grin. "I have a surprise for you."

"You do?" Omar nods as I look around the table. He leers at me and my curiosity grows. "What is it?" Omar simply holds up his finger. "I always hate when you do that. Tease me with a soon-to-come surprise. How many times have I said, don't foretell me about a bombshell, just let it blow me away when—" Just then, my bomb walks through the door and halts my reproach midsentence. "Tracy!" I shriek.

Tracy, healthy and happy, rushes over to the table. I struggle to wiggle up from the chair. "Look at you, you're huge!" He laughs.

"That's the first thing you have to say to me." Tracy squeezes me. "I've gotta go to the little girls' room. I need a better greeting when I return." I toddle into the coffeehouse.

Gwen leaves, Omar leans in and whispers, "I think Gwen wants us to get back together."

Tracy turns toward the shop and then looks back at his brother. "What about Rome?"

Omar shrugs his shoulders. "Probably messed up. I don't know. I don't care. I can make her happy."

"I guess."

"I'm telling you, man." Omar pauses and looks around at the beautiful landscaping around the environs. "It's different this time. We're different and timing is everything."

"But she's about to have babies, two babies."

"I've always wanted kids, twins."

Tracy tries to calm his overly anxious brother. "Just chill, don't push the issue. She's got a lot going on right now."

"I'm good. I'm following her lead. Here she comes."

Tracy rises and meets me with a huge smile. "You are a beauty, beyond words." With one hand underneath my stomach and the other on my hip, I smirk. "You're full of shit." Tracy lets out a chortle and kisses my forehead.

Omar goes inside, orders a few sandwiches and we spend another hour at the coffee shop catching up.

Tracy and I spend the day running around the city and eating junk food. By six, I am exhausted and gassy. Though I'm hungry, eating out with Lia is the last option. Once Lia hears this, she plans to come over and cook. As I suspect, Lia has added a new delightful dish to her epicurean feast of life. His name is Idris Pittman, and though his odd name fits her usual roundup of peculiars, his occupation doesn't. He's a student in divinity school, studying to soon take over his father's church. Lia has her normal first-month glow, but I don't give this one more than six weeks. I tell Lia that by the time I give birth, Idris will be history, but Lia disagrees. She can't say how long it will last, yet he has piqued her interest far beyond her normal six-week tendency. I only have one thing to say:

"It's going to be a very capricious period. Mark my words."

13

"She's slowly killing me, man," Rome says as he sits on the edge of his couch, talking to Andre. "She carries on like we're not in a relationship and we're not having twins."

"Yeah, well, you know Gwen. She's stubborn."

"So I messed up. Why can't she see the bigger picture?" Rome yells.

"Why are you yelling at me? I'm still your friend."

Rome clasps his hands, groans and mumbles inaudible slander.

Andre walks over and attempts to ease his friend. "It's going to be okay, man."

"No, no, it's not. I love her and I want to be with her, but more important, I'm not letting another man raise my children. How would you feel if Tonia was seeing another man and he was raising Zora?"

"Why do you think I'm working instead of doing my music? I want to keep my family together. If the woman of the house is not happy, then everything is messed up. Personally, I can't believe Ariel. She actually started working for Gwen? Where were you?"

"I've been out of town. See, when I told you she was crazy, you didn't want to believe me."

"Well, I believe you now. Man, if she'd showed up at the shower—"

"Don't even say it." Rome halts and seconds later continues. "I need to figure out what to do about Gwen. She's due in about eight weeks . . . and I just want us to be together. Maybe she'll listen to you."

Andre gives a reassuring nod, but deep inside he knows that convincing Gwen is not going to be easy.

Across town, Tracy, Omar and I are having dinner at Omar's place. As we laugh and kick it, I easily slip back into my old self. I allow Omar to pull me to the center of his living room and slow dance to The Commodores, his favorite group of all time. I open up to his embrace and his subtle touches. Other than the off-balance issues and occasional spurts of gas, I almost forget I'm pregnant. However, when Omar pulls me close and delivers a sensuous kiss, it snaps me back into reality. I quickly pull away.

"I can't do this," I say, rushing back to the kitchen to join Tracy's dishwashing frenzy. Omar comes behind me and softly grazes my neck. I feel myself weakening. He slowly pulls me out of the kitchen and into the bedroom.

"We should talk," says Omar. "I'm just going to come right out and say it. I want to be with you. I know you and Rome are going through things, but honestly, you were with me first. So what I'm saying is, why don't we try it again? I know you want to have a family. I want to be there for you and your sons."

Stunned by O's blatant request, my gaped expression goes blank. I can't speak, so I begin to blink rapidly as he moves closer. Omar kneels in between my legs as I sit on the edge of the chair.

"I will take care of you and your sons. We can be happy."

"This isn't right. Rome and I just split up a few weeks ago and these are his children. I just need some time, okay?"

Omar nods as we hold on to each other.

Late that evening, he prepares to leave for the club and I wait for Tracy to take me to my apartment. Continually, I tell him how glad I am to have him home. He assures me that he has his life together and that he is happy to work with Omar at Comatose. I chat away the entire ride home. I talk about the babies, the club and all the impending changes.

I beam and clutch Tracy's wrists as he walks me into my building. I invite him in and he obliges just for a minute before going to the club. Tracy looks around at all of the baby things and holds up several pairs of matching blue outfits.

"These are cute," he says.

"Everything in here is blue. Boys wear red and brown, but no, everyone at the shower bought blue."

I toss my things in the closet and rush to the bathroom. When I come out, Tracy is leaning against the fridge, eating a Popsicle. I lean against the frame of the door and watch him gobble the ice.

"Everyone laughs at the fact that I love Popsicles, but you guys always eat them when you come over." Tracy laughs and finishes the treat. I continue to stare at him. He is intrigued and asks, "What?"

"Thank you," I whisper, but he has no clue what I am speaking about, so I continue. "I never properly thanked you for, you know . . ."

"What are you talking about?" he finally asks.

"The accident."

Tracy leans his back against the stainless steel, lifts his hand and gives me the okay sign.

"You rescued me, you saved me. I wouldn't be here today. I'd be in jail, or I'd be dead."

Tracy—never one for mushy sentiment—merely walks over, gives me a hug and responds, "No problem." He then turns and leaves, but quickly opens the door again and comments, "If you need anything, call me, I'll have my phone on."

"Okay," I say before he shuts the door.

I retire to the bedroom and call Rose. We've spoken more times since she's left than we have in the past five years. Though still cautious, I am excited about the potential relationship brewing between us. I even open up to her about therapy. Rose, being an advocate of Ph.D help, encourages me to continue the sessions. Though with this current mess between Omar and me, I don't know if the sessions are helping. I am, however, writing in my journal now. Just jotting down little facts, things that are in my heart, or things I find difficult to say. Once I put them in the journal, it clears my thoughts for therapy.

Releasing has never been an easy thing for me. I've always found it more therapeutic to hold things in until they simply went away. That's what my family does, and that's the way I was raised. However, as I embark on a new generation, maybe it's time to change. So after my long, warm bath, I pull out my tapestry-covered book and begin writing. At first, I write fragments of random thoughts, but my main thought is about Tracy, so I figure it's time I speak about him and about the night he saved my life.

THE ACCIDENT CONTINUED/TRACY
Session Eight

After the crash, I sat on the glass-covered street, stared at Omar and prayed that he would move. Tracy made it to my side and leaned over to make sure I was okay. With tears streaming down my face, I motioned toward Omar's body. Softly, I whispered, "Did I kill him?" Slowly, we approached his body. Tracy kneeled and checked his pulse. "Where's your phone? We need to call 911." My tears flowed heavier and my body began to convulse. "Go get the phone!" I limped over to the truck and nearly passed out again. I fell against the door and held on to its edge as my body slid down the side of the fiberglass. Tracy rushed to me and tried to find the phone. "I felt a pulse, he's not dead. Help me look for the phone." I heard him speak, but I couldn't move.

"He looks dead! I'm going to jail, I killed him."

"He's not dead! He's not dead!" Tracy repeated.

I'm still frozen against the truck. Tracy continued to rush back and forth between the two of us until EMS arrived. They hurried to Omar and began CPR. Minutes later, two police cars pulled up and the officers began asking a million questions. Tracy calmly answered them as he held me close. Simultaneously, attendants took my blood pressure, poked and prodded to make sure that I was well. My heart began to pound as the officer pulled out his pad and asked the infamous question: "Tell me exactly what happened?" I opened my mouth to face the firing squad, but Tracy beat me to the punch as he explained.

"We were leaving a party at Doc Jay's up on Central Avenue. When we got to this intersection, another car came speeding through and kept going. It made us swerve out of control. We hit that phone pole and the truck bounced back into the street." My nerves were on edge as he described the incident. By now, they'd hauled Omar off into the ambulance and I just knew I was about to be hauled off to jail for manslaughter. "Omar was thrown from the car and—"

"Who was driving?" the officer interrupted. My stomach flipped and nearly made me pee on myself. I opened my mouth to speak, and then without a blink or a pause, Tracy answered, "I was."

"Have you been drinking?"

"Yes. I had two beers, but I'm not drunk."

The second officer went to the car to retrieve a Breath-alyzer. "Please continue," the other officer stated.

"Omar was asleep in the back, so when the pole hit the back passenger side, he was thrown through the window. She was pinned in the car, so I helped her out. Luckily, I wasn't hurt. That's it. We called 911 and waited here."

The officer quickly turned to me and delivered a guilty look as if he knew Tracy was lying. "Can you confirm his story?" he asked.

Still very frightened, I squeaked as I tried to answer. Finally, a very soft "yes" came out as I slowly nodded my head. The officer shoved the Breathalyzer in Tracy's mouth.

The other policeman pulled me away from him and spoke to me in private. "I need to get your name and information. Fill out as much of this as you can." She handed me a clipboard. My hand shook as I wrote, again the tears streamed down my face. Suddenly, another officer came to me and tapped my shoulder.

"Is this yours?" he said, handing me the diamond ring.

Before I could speak, I nodded no. "It belonged to Omar. I mean, it still belongs to him. Oh God, he's not dead, is he?"

The officer didn't answer, she simply placed it in a small Baggie and walked back to the accident scene. I glanced over at Tracy. They cuffed him and placed him in the back of the squad car.

"They're taking you? They can't!" Tracy tried to calm me down as I became hysterical.

"Ma'am . . . Ms. Pharr. You need to calm down."

"No!" I yell. "You can't take him! Can I have a second please," I begged. The officers looked at each other and gave me one minute to speak with Tracy.

He looked me in the eye and moved in close to whisper, "I'm fine. Go get yourself checked out."

"What about you?"

Tracy continued to speak. "I may do a couple of months for this, but, you need to go away and get it together. You are better than this. Don't worry, everything will be fine."

The officer slammed the door shut and drove off with Tracy crammed in the backseat. I finished the form and handed it back to the officer. She took me to the hospital. Fortunately, other than a bruised rib and a few cuts, I was fine. The nurses checked me out by the afternoon and I found Omar, who was in building C, the coma wing. Omar was unconscious and they were running scans to check brain damage. The doctors already detected some spinal cord damage, but they weren't sure how extensive the injuries were. Both his parents were deceased, so there was no one to call but Tracy and he was still locked up. I sat by Omar and stared at the EKG machine for hours. I found myself chipping at the tips of my nails, waiting for his little jagged line to go straight. I just knew he wasn't going to make it. The longer I sat there, the sharper my headache became. This was the absolute lowest point in my life. I was an alcoholic and drug user in an abusive relationship. My boyfriend might die because I was driving drunk, and all of this was making me want to drink some more. Tracy was right, I had to get my life together, because I was slowly killing myself. This was my warning. If I didn't go now, I was never going to go. Once he came out from the coma, I wouldn't be able to leave, and this was going to be my life.

"I don't want this to be my life," I remember whispering.

I sat for another hour and then headed back to Omar's apartment to gather my things. I called a bondsman and *gave him Tracy's name. But when he called to check on Tracy, I discovered that Tracy had already made bond. I went to the airport, changed my flight plans and flew directly into Virginia. My aunt Vivian, my father's sister, was the rock that we all called on for advice. She took me in and I enrolled in a clinic for alcoholism. My first week there, I got ahold of some aspirin and overdosed. At the time, I just wanted to sleep away all of my troubles. I only intended to take two, but I couldn't stop putting them in my mouth. I remembered thinking I could finish the bottle and just end all of my stress and personal disappointments. The pain hurt throughout my entire body—every nerve and every muscle ached—and I couldn't have liquor to soothe the pain. I thought the pills would do it. After the overdose, they moved me to the sanatorium. I was there for nine months and my aunt came to visit every day. She never told anyone in the family, who assumed I was working there. I owe her my life—she and Tracy, who ended up doing six months for probation violation. He still acts like his sacrifice wasn't a big deal.*

After I was released, I found Tracy and wanted to check on Omar, but he no longer wanted to speak to me. Tracy only had one request and that was for me to take care of myself. I promised I would and I didn't see him again until that night at the club ten months ago. When I told him I was sober, he had this expression of euphoria and peace.

Yes, he is a gun-toting thug, a hustler and a gambler. But God surely has to show him some mercy, because he is my angel and he sacrificed himself to save me.

Session Done

14

I lie on my back at my thirty-two-week appointment as Dr. Pagota checks my heartbeat and those of my two boys. So sick of being pregnant, I wish the doctor could just deliver the babies right now. I turn my head and look at Rome, sitting on the other side of the room. He's zeroed in on my stomach, purposely not making eye contact. I turn and look at the ceiling. We haven't said five words to each other. Dr. Pagota notices the tension but is careful not to say anything. She's dealt with many eight months pregnant women and it's no big deal for them not to be speaking with their mates at this time of the pregnancy.

As we are walking into the parking lot, Rome takes my hand and speaks. "Is this how it's going to be?"

I turn to Rome with a dismal expression, sigh and try to keep walking. He tightens up on his grip and pulls me into his side and gives me an unexpected, passionate lip-lock. As the suction loosens, he connects with my bottom lip, gently sucks on its fullness and weakens my knees. I slightly push him in the chest.

"Something wrong with me kissing you?"

I say nothing and keep walking.

"Damn it, talk to me."

"About what, Rome?"

"It's been one month, I know you're not still mad about Ariel."

"I'm not," I proclaim.

"Then what is it? You don't talk, you don't call unless it has something to do with the babies. This is some bullshit. We don't even act like friends anymore."

I move toward the car, but Rome is still holding my hand. "Can we do this in the car?" I ask.

"No. We will do this right here, right now. What is wrong with you?"

I look toward the sun and wrinkle my face. Rome forcefully tugs on my arm. The shake isn't hard enough to hurt, but enough to jar me into answering.

"You hurt me," I shout. "Look, I want to be your friend, but I don't have shit to say to you. Now let go of my arm." I jerk my hand away and trudge toward the car. Rome doesn't let me get too far ahead as he takes me by the shoulder and thwarts my movement. He moves to my front and stares into my face. With both hands on my shoulders, Rome speaks, very slow and clear.

"What do you want me to do? I've said I'm sorry fifty times. You know I love you—"

"How, Rome?" I interrupt. "How do I know you love me, when you run around sleeping with all these women?"

"What women!" he yells, overdramatically eyeing the parking lot for imaginary women.

I take hold of his chin and snap his face toward me. "Stop playing. You cheated on me when I was four months pregnant. Did you even think about what this would do to us, or did you just think I'd never find out? I don't even know if you used a condom."

"I thought about it, and I made a mistake. I didn't set out to cheat. The temptation . . . I just . . . she was . . . Look, I fucked up! I don't know how else to say it. But, my God, I won't do it again."

With my folded arms resting on top of my belly, I look down at the pavement. Finally, I speak. "Can we go now?"

Rome, exhausted and defeated, slowly opens the car door and helps me into the seat. He takes me back home. Of course we have nothing to say during the ride home. But as I exit, I comment, "I just need some more time. I don't trust you, Rome. I'm sorry." I shut the door and walk into my building.

Close to two in the morning, I wake up to a throbbing pain in my side. Immediately, I reach for the phone and call Lia, who answers on the second ring.

"Lia, I'm in pain, can you come over?"

"Baby, I'm in Chicago with Idris. He's speaking this evening at some church here. Where's Rome?"

"I don't know."

"Well, call him! He needs to come over there."

I rise and try to get comfortable. "I'm okay, it's starting to go away."

"I'm calling him."

"No! I'll do it." I pause and move to the edge of the bed. "Stay on the phone with me while I go to the bathroom."

"Okay. Someone should be staying with you. It's too close to labor time. Do you want me to come stay with you?"

"Maybe, we'll see."

"You are so hardheaded. You cannot be waddling around that place by yourself."

I finish in the bathroom and head back to the bed. "Where's your man? I hope you're not waking him up with all this talking."

"Girl, please, I have my own room. He's not sleeping in here with me. All we've done is kiss."

"And you're good with that?" I say.

"Believe it or not, I am. It's kind of sexy to imagine how good it's going to be," she responds.

"Okay, well, I'm back in the bed. Call me when you come back."

"Call Rome, he should come over."

"Good night, Lia."

I prop my pillow against my back as I hold the disconnected receiver in my hand. I begin to dial Rome's number, but dial Tracy's instead. He's still at Comatose, so he agrees to come over as soon as he gets the bar tended to. Forty minutes later, I am still awake as I watch reruns of *Law & Order.* Thirty minutes into the episode, I hear a knock and keys jiggling in the lock. I roll over in expectation of Tracy, but to my surprise, it's Omar. He insists that Tracy had somewhere else to go, so he volunteered to come. I hesitate to let him stay, but after he persists, I agree to let him sleep on the couch. I immediately go into the bedroom and close the door. A few minutes later, I hear a faint knock on the door.

"What do you want, O?" I ask with a hint of exasperation.

"I'm going to sleep, do you need anything? Are you still in pain?"

"No," I reply.

"Wake me up if you need anything."

"I will. Good night."

Omar lingers by the door and I can see his feet under the edge. After a couple of minutes, I ask him to come in. Omar does, but stands against the wall by the door frame. Like a shy kid, he holds his focus toward the ground and tilts from side to side as he speaks.

"I don't want to burden you, Gwen. I just want to lay next to you until you fall asleep."

We sit in silence as Omar softly massages the arch of my foot. Enjoying the caresses, I place both feet in his lap. Before long, I drift off to sleep.

Around seven that morning, I wake up, and to my surprise, Omar is asleep beside me, with his arm draped around my chest. As I rise, I also feel a light headache rearing. "I feel like shit," I say, traipsing across the living room toward the kitchen. Suddenly, I hear keys in the front door. Still in a daze, I question the identity of the morning visitor. When I hear Rome's voice, I almost go into labor. Holding the bottom of my stomach, I hastily respond, "Hold on." Rushing back to the bedroom, I think of a place to hide Omar. However, he's so groggy, he won't budge. As I scan a place to conceal my ex, I realize that there is no crevice large enough, and it would be worse if he were caught hiding. Quickly, I rush back to open the door, keeping the chain secured. I peep out.

"What are you doing here?"

"I got a message from Lia this morning saying that you were having pains. Why didn't you call me?"

"I'm fine, now."

"Let me in," Rome gently demands.

I bite my bottom lip and simply look at him through the opening fracture.

"What's wrong with you? Let me in here, I'm tired. I just got done with the shoot."

I shut the door, remove the chain, squeeze through and quickly shut the door behind my back. My explanation starts immediately. "Don't jump to conclusions. I called Tracy, but Omar—" Before I can get the next word out of my mouth, Rome smacks the door open and storms into the place to see Omar walking into the room wearing only his boxers.

Omar jumps to his and my defense. "I only came to check on her."

"I don't care what you came to do. You're not getting Gwen back," Rome yells. I cautiously step in between the two men. However, Omar is very calm as he takes a seat and begins to place on his jeans.

"Rome, stop yelling," I order. "I asked Tracy to come over and he sent Omar."

Rome points at Omar. "You're not raising my sons, know that."

I begin to push Rome back to the door.

"I'm not leaving. Tell that nigga to leave!" Rome shouts.

"You are out of control," I say, continuing to shove him toward the exit.

Finally, in the hallway, Rome calms. With heartbreak stretched across his face, Rome appeals to me. "Baby, what are you doing? Are you trying to hurt me, to get me back? You have . . . right now. What are you doing with him?"

"Nothing. I promise. O and I are not doing anything, I swear."

I realize his suffering and brush my head against his shoulders. He cups the back of my neck and kisses the top of my head. "I'm so sorry I hurt you," he whispers as I nuzzle into his neck.

"Rome, I just . . . I don't know."

"I know, baby, I know. But give me another chance."

I pull away from his body, look into his eyes and nod yes. Rome welcomes my hug. "But I'll call you later, please."

"No," he says, trying to go back into my place.

"I know you're not saying you don't trust me, are you?" I ask.

"I don't trust him," Rome comments with clenched teeth as he points to the door.

I kiss the corner of his lips and pull him away from the door and a few feet into the hallway.

"I will call you," I repeat. Rome gives me one last hug and walks away.

Inside my place, Omar patiently waits for me to return. He rises and takes me by the hand. "You okay?" he asks. I give a timid nod.

"Notice how I kept my temper," he says. "That's the way it should be. I can't have you all stressed out." Omar reaches for me. I allow the comfort for a moment, but eventually pull away.

"You have to go. I appreciate everything, but I have to shower now and you have to leave."

"But—"

"No." I turn around. "I can't do this, O. It's too nerve-racking. I appreciate you being calm just now, but this isn't going to work."

"So what's up with us?"

"What's up? We're friends." I continue to walk into the bedroom. "Lock the front door, please. I'll call you. I promise." I walk into the bathroom and close the door.

Omar stands in the bedroom, attempting to figure out what happened in the hallway. With hesitation, he starts to leave. But then, he decides to write a note. He sees a book on the nightstand, grabs it and begins to rip a paper from the back. He realizes it's my journal and begins to put it down, but the book opens to the page with "The Accident," and it catches his attention. He reads the first line and his intrigue will not let him close the book. Conflicted, Omar is frozen. Suddenly, he hears the shower water turn off, so he grabs his things and leaves with the journal in tow.

While I am getting dressed, I remember I have a therapy appointment later today. With my belly too large to fit behind the wheel, I wonder who will take me. At that moment, my cell phone rings. It's Tracy, and I am poised and ready to let him have it.

"If I call you, do not send your brother," I squeal without a hello.

"I'm sorry," he apologizes. "You okay?"

"No. But I'll tell you all about it, when you take me to therapy today. Can you?"

"Sure, what time?"

I give him the time as I continue to get dressed. I sit on the bed's edge and wiggle into my skirt. Out of breath, I reach for my inhaler as Tracy gives his explanation for not coming over. Just then, I notice my journal missing from the night-stand. I open the drawer and still don't see it. I halt Tracy mid-sentence.

"Hold it a minute," I say as I look around the bedroom. Rising from the bed, I look in the closet and in the bathroom.

"Gwen, you okay?" Tracy calls out.

"I don't think so. I can't find my journal." I continue to search the room. "I know it was in here." I try to bend to look under the bed, but I am too big. So I grab the broom and sweep under the edge of the bed, but no luck. "I think O took my journal. I had it last night and now it's gone."

"Why would he take your journal?" he asks.

"Oh shit! Oh shit! Oh shit!"

"What?" Tracy wonders on the other line.

"I wrote about the accident in the journal. If he has it, he knows. I gotta call him. No, you call him."

"What do you want me to say?"

"Something. Just see if he's different."

I hang up and continue to hunt around the room until Tracy calls back. He couldn't reach Omar, but he agrees to keep trying, until he picks me up at 1:00 P.M.

I am on pins and needles until Tracy arrives. Before I can get the car door shut, I reel off twenty questions. But Tracy gives no solid answer. He has no idea where his brother is and Omar's not answering his phone. The headache that started an hour ago is now pulsating through my eyes.

"I can't take this," I scream.

Tracy uses his calm, soft voice in an attempt to soothe me, but it only upsets me more as I insist he not patronize me with baby talk. With low curses and grumbles, I stress all the way to therapy and back home. Once there, Tracy tries Omar again, but no luck.

"He's not at the club, he's not home. I don't know where he is."

I pace my living-room floor. "What if he's at the police?"

"He wouldn't," Tracy states.

"He might . . . he could go there, show them the book. Could they come and arrest me?"

"Stop thinking like that. No one's coming to arrest you. I will go with you and tell them it's a lie."

Holding the bottom of my stomach, I make a distressed face. "I knew this would eventually happen. I knew someone would find out I was driving. I can't believe I wrote in that damn book. Out of all my issues, I decide to write that one. I'm so stupid."

Late that evening, I decide that I have no choice but to go to the police in order to beat Omar to the punch. Tracy attempts to convince me to wait a few days, but I sense I don't have that long. First thing tomorrow morning, I plan to go to the police, and so reluctantly, Tracy decides to go with me.

When Rome walks in the door that evening, I am a nervous wreck. My actions are jittery and I've eaten three Fudgsicles. With a half-ass smile, I greet Rome at the door, and he welcomes me with yellow and red tulips. As I take them and place them in some water, I fight back the tears. We leave and go to dinner.

"I've been thinking about names," he says while eating.

Puzzled, I give Rome a mystified look and then suddenly realize that he is speaking about our boys. "Yes, the names," I comment as if I hadn't missed a beat.

"What about Roger and Roland?" he asks.

"Who names their child 'Roger' these days? It's too old and too English."

I point to my purse, and Rome hands it to me. I pull out a piece of paper with names scrolled down the entire front and back. "I sat up the other night writing down different combinations."

Rome inspects the list. Between the head nods and face scrunches, he disagrees with the first twenty-two. Finally, I see a smile.

"Which one?" I ask.

"I like Jaxson Rome and Jalen Cole Sutton." I wrinkle my face and frown.

"That was my favorite at one time, but I don't know if I like it. What about Aidan and Ethan?" I respond.

"They sound like actors," Rome comments.

"Actors might not be bad."

"Unemployed actors."

"Oh, what about your name?" I inquire.

"I don't want either of them named Romulus or Earl. I like Jaxson Rome," he says.

"Look at the back side, see if you like another one."

The name conversation temporarily takes my mind from my pending dilemma; however, as soon as we get back to Rome's place, my worries continue. With plans to go to the authorities tomorrow, I must tell Rome tonight, but my current sexual craving overrides my appetite for honesty. I'm not sure how much I will enjoy the awkwardness of eighth-month-pregnancy sex, but I intend to have an orgasm before the sunrise. Feeling less than sexy, I sit on the edge of the bed and try to come up with my "come on" line, to attract his attention.

Replaying each of them in my head, I realize they all sound silly and now I feel overweight and ridiculous. Therefore, I sit quietly until I come up with a better solution. Finally, it hits me, just be frank.

"Hey," I call out to get his attention away from ESPN highlights. "I think you owe me an orgasm."

"Huh?" Rome questions me with a peculiar expression.

"I wanna have sex. But I'm big and pregnant and I don't want to do too much moving around. I just . . . I just want to have a really great orgasm."

Laughing, Rome moves to the chair and kisses me, first on

the lips and then on the stomach. Next he lifts my skirt and his head disappears underneath. As he pulls me to the edge, I lay my head back and enjoy the pleasure. A few moments later, still carrying a euphoric glow, I sit on the edge of my seat and think about how to tell Rome about the accident. Since candor seems to be working on my side, I decide to go with that approach. As Rome walks from the kitchen with a bottle of water for me, I just blurt it out.

"Tracy wasn't driving the night of the accident, I was."

Rome stops so quickly, he nearly falls forward. The sudden jolt makes him gasp and water trickles from his lip. He slowly hands me my bottle and stares in astonishment. I take a sip and place a pleasant grin upon my face, as if I hadn't just delivered a shocking blow. Rome kneels by my chair and continues to stare.

"Say something."

"Damn!" Rome sits on the floor by the chair and looks up at me. "What happened?"

In less than two minutes, I explain the entire incident to Rome. After a one-minute pause, I deliver my latest news bulletin. Suddenly, his manner goes from surprise to concern.

"You can't go to the police. Let me call my boy, he's a lawyer."

I grab the back of his shirt as he rises from the floor. "No," I shout. "I don't want anyone to know."

"You have to tell someone."

"I was driving drunk, I was high and I lied about an accident. I'm going to be in trouble."

"That's why you need a lawyer."

"So you're not mad or disappointed?" I ask.

"I'm shocked. I can't believe Tracy did that. I can't believe you let him—"

"Don't say that," I interrupt. "I feel bad enough. I'm the reason why Omar's paralyzed. Not a day passes that I don't think about it, and just when I was starting to get over it, he pops up."

Rome takes me by the hand and pulls me up from the chair. He holds me tight. "First of all, Omar wouldn't go to the police. Next, if you do go, I need to go with you. Don't go without me," Rome pleads.

"I just want to go to bed and pray that this is all over in the morning."

Rome escorts me into the bedroom. Now very alert, he sits by my side and watches me sleep. He softly circles my navel and snuggles his head in between my breasts and my belly. Thinking I am sound asleep, he slips out of bed and drives to Comatose. He leaves several messages for Omar with the staff. Prepared for any type of altercation, Rome makes sure he has his gun with him. Though he has no plans to use it, he's not sure of Omar's state of mind. For three hours, Rome waits for Omar to show, before heading back home.

Deciding to wait another day, I do everything possible to keep my mind occupied. I spend the day shopping online for the last bit of necessary baby things. With enough bottles, nursing pads, pacifiers and rattles to last five years, I decide to shop for postpregnancy clothing. Small sizes will keep me motivated to lose the weight, so I go to several of my favorite online boutiques and order skirts and dresses in size 8. After eating an entire Tombstone pizza, I call Lia for a bit of entertainment. She and Idris decide to stop by. I am pleasantly surprised, for Lia never brings her love interests around—unless she's falling for them. Actually, she and the dates rarely stay interested long enough for formal introductions. Therefore, I tidy the house, and an hour later, I meet Idris Pittman and the new and improved Lia McNair.

Surprisingly, Idris has an incredible sense of humor. Because he's a pastor, I thought he would be rigid and dry. But he is nothing of the sort. From the kitchen, I watch him and Lia interact. I notice how Lia stares at him when he talks. Maybe Idris is special. He's definitely cute in a quirky, nerdy way. A tall, thin man sporting black wire-rimmed glasses, he sits casually with his legs crossed, and tells his stories about growing up in the South.

He reminds me of a young Glynn Turman, I think approvingly. "I like him," I whisper as I walk by Lia and take a seat. Lia beams.

The remainder of the evening is extremely pleasant. We sit and talk about love, children and religion. Lia's actions are decorous, much less raucous than normal. It seems genuine, though. It's almost like he calms her spirit. He's good for her. I give my approval by giving a tiny wink as they leave.

I retire for the night. Though it's only nine, I am bushed. Just before I fall asleep, Tracy calls. He can't meet me at the police station in the morning. He has to leave town. He doesn't give any sort of explanation, he only says he must go. He tells me to reconsider, but I feel that it's best, so I decide to go without him. Omar is still a no-show, and the only person who has heard from him is Kain, the other manager at Comatose. Omar told him he had to leave town for a few days, but didn't say where he was going.

Close to nine the next morning, I am prepared to leave the house. Rome calls and says he's on the way. I walk downstairs to wait for him. I take a seat right outside the building and soak up some sunshine. Looking down the street, I notice Tracy approaching. I rise with excitement as I see him rushing toward me. With a skip-trot combination, Tracy hurries toward me and hugs me tight.

"I thought you weren't coming."

"I'm not," he replies. I notice an eerie look in his eyes.

"You okay?" I ask. "Have you heard from Omar?"

"He's not going to go to the police. Please don't do this."

"Where are you going?" I ask.

"To New York. I'll be back next month."

I know Tracy is in some kind of trouble, but as usual, he denies it. I give him another hug, this one extremely tight.

"Be careful," I say.

"Always," he says with a smile. "Keep those boys in there, until I get back," he says while rubbing my stomach. I let out a chuckle. Tracy turns back to me and comments, "You're my hero."

I smile and reply, "You're mine."

I watch as he walks back down the street to his car. It's a Wednesday morning, and traffic is minimal, so I have no idea what's taking Rome so long, but I continue to patiently wait. Just then, a sleek black Navigator pulls up to the building front. Thinking it's Rome, I rise, but it speeds past me down the street and then slows down.

"They must be lost," I comment softly.

Just then, I hear gunshots pop. I look in the truck's direction and suddenly my heart drops.

"Tracy!" I call out. I hear squealing tires. Trembling, I hurry in that direction. About five yards away, I can see Tracy's body lying on the pavement. My heart plummets to my stomach and immediately causes prickly pains to run across the front of my tummy. The pain settles in the lower side, near my kidney. I almost fall to my knees. I dig my nails into the brick wall of the building. With tears streaming down my face, I scream out for help. However, no one is on the desolate street. Using the wall as an aid, I move closer to Tracy, who seems to still be moving.

"Tracy!" I yell again. I reach in my purse and dial 911. Frantically, I give the street location as I gasp for air. Taking deep breaths from my inhaler, I take bigger strides to reach Tracy's side. I take hold of his arm and shake it vigorously.

"Damn it, Tracy! It's okay, you're okay." I look around and call hysterically for assistance. Tracy is bleeding profusely from the chest. His breathing is staggered as blood spews from his mouth. I see another truck coming down the street. I duck down behind Tracy's car, in fear it's the shooters. However, it stops up by my building. I realize it's Rome. I pop up and yell down the street. Torn between leaving Tracy and rushing to Rome, I bobble back and forth. Feverishly, I take a few more steps toward Rome and call out to him as he exits his truck. He looks up and peers down the street. I scream again, and he finally sees me. Like a tailback rushing for a touchdown, Rome takes off running.

"Did you call 911?"

My tears flow faster as I nervously nod.

"Calm down, man, you're going to be fine." Rome questions me. "What happened?"

"Some guys in a truck drove up and shot him. Where's the damn ambulance?" I scream. Suddenly, the pain in my stomach causes me to drop to a squat. Holding the bottom of my stomach, my eyes tightly shut as I let out a moan.

"What's wrong?" Rome's attention turns toward me.

"Nothing," I say, looking down the street as I hear sirens approaching.

"You're in pain. We got to get you to the hospital."

"I hear the ambulance." I try to move to the corner to get their attention. As I see them approach, I step to the corner and wave my hand. They approach hurriedly, scoop Tracy up onto the gurney and immediately go to work. As the EMS attendant asks me for details, I cringe in pain.

"We've got to get you to the hospital," shouts Rome. "Stay here." He rushes to get the truck.

I watch as they work on Tracy and lift him into the back of the ambulance.

"We're going to follow you," I tell them. Rome rushes to the curb, hops out and pulls me inside the truck. We take off behind the ambulance. By the time we get to the hospital, I fear something is wrong, for my pain is incessant. I can barely stand when Rome pulls up to emergency. They put me in a wheelchair and rush me down the hall. As I'm being wheeled away, I call out to Rome, "Find out about Tracy." However, he's stopped by a nurse and asked to fill out some paperwork. Rushing through the questions, Rome scribbles on the paper and hurries to join me. The traumatic event sent my body into premature labor. The nurses panic from my blood-soaked shirt, for fear I was injured. However, once they realize that it's not my blood, they take me down to the maternity ward.

In an adjoining wing, Tracy is rushed into surgery as well, with multiple gunshots to the chest. The doctors work madly to stop the bleeding and operate. Because his blood pressure is steadily dropping, they fear cardiac failure. They hook him up to the heart monitor and try to get to the main source of blood loss.

More worked up about Tracy than myself, my blood pressure is rising. My water breaks, but my cervix is not dilated. Inducing labor is an option, but with me only being 33 weeks, they worry that it will still take too long for me to have a vaginal birth. They opt to perform an emergency C-section. A nurse comes from the room to inform a very worried Rome, who is pacing outside the door. He wants to come in, but they can't allow it until the surgery is over. They send him to the waiting room and promise to update him as soon as possible.

In Tracy's room, the doctors are able to close up one of the aorta valves struck by the bullet. However, there is another bullet lodged in the top of the heart tissue. If they don't remove it, he will not make it. His bleeding is slowing down and the doctors have another tube feeding him more blood as they begin to operate. Yet, once they get to the bullet, they see it has fractured a third of the capillaries leading to the major organ. They will have to stop his heart to operate. They hook up his heart to the machine and bring his heartbeat to a complete halt. Within a minute, the surgeon has the vessels tied off and is removing the bullet. He sews up the fracture and loosens the blood vessels to restart the blood flow. Everything seems to be flowing fine and now it's safe to restart his heartbeat.

In room C-13, I am prepped and ready for surgery. Between my hysterical questions about Tracy and my excruciating pain, the doctors decide sedation is best. Now completely under, they open my stomach layers. The nearly mature babies are positioned well for the doctors to remove them easily from my womb. Baby one is lifted out of my stomach and placed on a tiny sterile table. Within two minutes, baby two is being taken out and placed on an adjoining table. The doctor carefully sews me back up as one nurse cleans the infants. Other than a little excess blood, the surgery is clean and effortless. It happens so quickly, it's amazing that two lives have just been brought into the world. Time of births: 12:29 and 12:31 P.M. I remain unconscious for another twenty minutes.

Tracy's heartbeat starts to slow, and the doctors are relieved. Restarting the organ is always the trickiest part of heart surgery. It beats four times, then stops. The doctors send the organ an electric jolt, but nothing. They try again, and the heart jiggles, but it doesn't beat. The monitor machine gives one last peak, then levels out flat. The surgeon looks up at the clock and speaks.

"Time of death is twelve thirty-two P.M." He removes his gloves, and another doctor begins to sew up Tracy's chest cavity.

When I come to, Rome is standing over me holding the bigger of the Sutton boys. With one child weighing five pounds, and the other weighing four pounds, two ounces, the nurses feel good about the babies' premature births. All organs are working properly and they have no issues. However, the smaller baby will have to remain in the hospital until he weighs at least five pounds. I blink several times and clearly see Rome holding my son. I give a tiny smile, but I'm still in some pain.

Before I can ask, he answers, "Both boys are fine. He's over there." Rome moves to the side so I can see my other son. The nurse comes into the room and speaks to me, checks my blood pressure and repositions my body. Rome hands me the baby. He then rolls the bed of the second boy over to my side.

"I don't want to pick him up, he's too small," he says.

"They're okay?" I ask for another confirmation.

The nurse substantiates Rome's previous response. With a sigh of relief, I cuddle one newborn as I look upon the other. I kiss my son's head and then inquire about Tracy. However, Rome has no idea of his condition. I give the nurse Tracy's name and ask her to check on him. When she leaves, Rome assures me that Tracy is fine. Moments later, the nurse calls Rome into the hallway. Asking the general questions about the next of kin, she inquires the whereabouts of Tracy Kirkland's family. Rome tells her about Omar, his deceased parents and then lies and says he's Tracy's uncle. She delivers the terrible news. Taken aback, Rome stays in the hallway to gather his composure before walking back into the room with me. When he walks in, I'm trying to nurse one of the babies, but having difficulty with him latching onto my breast. He walks over and holds his son's head still, while I place my nipple in his mouth. The baby turns his head away and begins crying. His crying sets off the other baby and I fretfully look to Rome for help. He searches the room for something to stop their crying. He finds one pacifier and places it in the smaller boy's mouth. Then, suddenly, the baby in my lap latches onto my nipple and begins nursing.

"Look, look," I call out to Rome.

He sits on the edge of my bedside and gazes at the wonder of breast-feeding. Excited, I stare at my son.

"We've got to name them. Jaxson, Jalen?" Rome says.

I give a halfhearted grin and respond, "Jalen, I love. Jaxson, not so sure about."

"What about Jordon or Jonah?" he proposes.

"Jalen and Jonah? No, that's not it." I pause for a second as the baby turns away from my nipple. I move him to my chest. "Are you full, Jalen?" I ask the baby before turning to Rome. "I really like Jalen, we just need a name for him." I pause again while repositioning baby Jalen. "Ooh, what about Tracy?"

Rome is silent at first and then comments on another name, as if I hadn't asked the question. "What about Jameel?"

I look over at my other son sleeping in his tiny bed. "Jameel," I say with a smile. "I like it. Jameel and Jalen. Yes! So this one's Jalen and the other is Jameel.

Now what about Tracy?" I ask again.

Rome walks over to his other son and rubs his back.

"Rome! What happened to Tracy?" Rome gives me a nondescript expression, but he still says nothing. I know it's not good. Immediately, the tears start flowing. Rome rushes to take Jalen from my arms.

"Did he . . ."

"I'm sorry, baby," Rome whispers.

My tears turn to a fluttering whimper. The sound resembles the noise of a wounded dog, and it grows louder as I can no longer control my emotions. I sink down in the bed, turn my face into the pillow and scream. Rome places Jalen in his bed and tries to console me. Still, I cry sporadically throughout the rest of the evening.

Rome calls Comatose and leaves several messages with Kain for Omar. Finally, Kain calls him back and says Omar is flying back from New York to take care of arrangements for Tracy.

Three days after delivering, I get to go home with Jalen, but I have to leave Jameel in the hospital for a few more days until he gets his weight up. This is the absolute worst for any mother and I don't take it well. Once I'm released, I sit in the

baby nursery until dark. Finally, Rome forces me to go home
and rest. We retire to his house, but resting is the last thing we
do, for Jalen cries all evening and throughout the night. By
morning, I am exhausted. I sleep for two hours, wake up and
I am ready to go to the hospital to see Jameel. Lia meets me
at Rome's house that morning to take me. I have to feed Jalen
in two hours, therefore he has to go as well. Rome plans to
meet us at the hospital later that afternoon, for he has to get a
few hours of sleep.

   I nurse Jameel when I arrive and the doctors think he
should be able to go home next week. I contact Kain, to get
the information on Tracy, but he has none. He has only
spoken to Omar once, and still hasn't seen him. The hospital
contacted Rome, since he listed himself as kin, but he can't
do anything until he hears from Omar. Right now, everything
is at a standstill and Tracy's body is still in the morgue. The
next day, when I return to the hospital, I go to see Tracy. Leaving the baby with Lia, I take a peaceful moment with my
friend. My warm tears fall upon his cold body as I tenderly
stroke his cheek. I stare upon his body in disbelief. Right after
murmuring a silent prayer, I tell him about the boys, officially
named, Jalen Rome and Jameel Tracy Sutton. Then, as the
coroner approaches, I kiss Tracy's cheek and say a final
farewell to this part of my past. Placing my hand over my
heart, I mash into my chest, as if I can stop the pain, and then
slowly walk back upstairs to my future.

   That evening, Rome reluctantly leaves town for two days
to shoot another music video. Rome had agreed to take time
off once the boys were born, but since the babies were born
early, this is a job he was already committed to. He still
agrees to turn it down, but I convince him to go. I promise
that I'll be fine with Lia, who took off this week.

   Kain finally calls with Tracy's memorial service, which is
tomorrow at 2:00 P.M. at Mason Williams Funeral Home. Lia,
Jalen and I arrive an hour early. Though I want to speak to

Omar about the accident, I desperately want to avoid him today. When I arrive, I speak to the funeral attendant and he directs me to the designated section. In the center of a tiny pulpit area, sitting on a podium, are Tracy's remains, sealed in a bronze urn. There are no flowers, only chairs. Lia takes Jalen and sits in the back while I walk to the front and stand in front of the urn. Constantly peeping over my shoulder, Lia keeps reminding me of the time as I silently pray. Thirty minutes later, I am ready to leave and Jalen is getting antsy. As we are leaving, a very petite young woman is walking into the funeral. As she passes by me, I smile and continue to walk. However, she quickly calls out to me a few feet away.

"Excuse me, aren't you Gwen?"

Lia hastily steps in front of me while questioning, "Who are you?"

"Marissa," she replies with a hopeful expression.

I move to the side and study the diminutive woman standing only about five feet. I finally answer, "Yes, I'm Gwen."

Eagerly, the woman walks closer to me and extends her hand. "Tracy always talked about you." I give Marissa an oblivious look. "Oh, Tracy and I were . . . well, I was his girlfriend."

I pose an even more confused look. "I didn't know Tracy had a girl. How long—"

"For almost a year," Marissa interrupts. "We broke up for a little while when he moved to Atlanta, but then we got back together."

"Wow, nice to meet you. This is Lia and this is Jalen," I say as Marissa plays with Jalen's cheeks.

"Tracy always went on and on about his sister, Gwen. He told me you were pregnant. He was all excited about being an uncle."

"I wasn't his real sister, you know," I say.

"I know, but as far as he was concerned, you were."

Marissa and I both share a somber moment of silence as

we reflect through our stares. Finally, Lia speaks. "Gwen, we have to leave . . . remember."

"Oh yeah, it was nice to meet you, Marissa. We have to go."

Just then, a navy blue Denali pulls up to the funeral home and parks directly behind Lia's car. Kain and Omar step out. I glance at my phone for the time. They're early. Lia grabs my arm and we abruptly end the conversation with Marissa. Lia hustles me to the car as if she is my bodyguard. However, Omar and I connect when we pass each other. This is a most uncomfortable close encounter. With a look of contempt on his face, he continues to stare at me as he stands on the front stoop of the funeral home. After I get Jalen in his car seat, we speed off. I can still feel Omar's eyes burning through me. That look stays with me the rest of the evening. Close to midnight, I decide I must talk to Omar. Therefore, I call him. Naturally, he doesn't answer, so I leave a long, baffling message that says absolutely nothing. I don't believe Omar will go to the police, but I don't trust his next move—whatever it may be.

Rome's plane arrives at 2:00 the next day and by 3:00 P.M., he is holding his baby boy in his arms. We go to the hospital and receive a pleasant surprise: Jameel can leave. Rome rushes home to retrieve the other baby seat. Elated, I quickly call my family to inform them of the good news. Marvin is thrilled, he wants to come see us and is trying to convince Reggie to take the ride with him from New York. Though Rome wants to send him a ticket, Marvin hasn't been on a plane since he was a teenager and would much rather drive.

We settle in Rome's abode and now the question in my head is: where will I finally decide to reside? I am leery about moving in with Rome, but don't want the headache of caring for two newborns on my own. Things will be simpler if I just stay here, but there's still the issue of us being in a relationship. I do not trust this man. I ponder this the rest of the

evening—it consumes me, so I barely speak. Rome is so enthralled in the twins, he doesn't mention my calm behavior.
It's not until both boys are asleep, and we lie on the couch for
a bit of shut-eye, that we speak in detail. Rome brings up
Omar and the journal.

"I saw him at Tracy's funeral, but he didn't say anything."

"I hate to say this, but I would have to kill Omar if he tried
to harm you guys."

I look at Rome and keep my mouth shut. Though it was six
years ago, it seems like yesterday, when we were all great
friends—now it's come to this.

"You let me handle Omar. I will let you know if I need you."

Rome takes the pillow and playfully tosses it over my face.
Pretending to struggle, I play along. This merry moment
leads to passionate kissing, which is quickly halted with my
comment: "You can't have any for another six weeks . . . at
least not with me." I'm jesting.

Rome doesn't find it funny, though. "I'm not sleeping with
anyone but you," he sternly states.

"Okay, I was joking," I say, even though my distrust is still
strong.

One hour into my sleep, Jameel starts crying. I groan
loudly as I turn over. Rome taps my shoulder.

"I got it, babe. Just rest until you have to nurse."

Rome rises and checks on Jameel. I watch him change his
Pamper and rock him back to sleep. With a peaceful smile on
my face, I drift back to sleep with a more solid decision to
sublease my apartment.

TRUST
Session Nine

*Even when I was little, I had trust issues. I was a
chubby kid, and it wasn't easy for me to make friends.
When I did, I usually found out it was because they*

wanted something from me. So the trust thing started young for me. I always felt like people had ulterior motives. I can honestly say that my dad and Lia are the only people I completely trust, and Lia is borderline. Not that I think everyone is out to get me, but people are flawed. They put themselves first; they lie, cheat and steal—if necessary. I go into every situation with that in mind. Since Rome and I go so far back, I do trust him with my friendship. He would never betray that. However, he has addictions—one in particular, women. I know this. Which is why it was so stupid for me to trust him with my heart. I really thought that his love for me as a friend would outweigh his cheating nature. Silly, I know, for men don't work like that. With them, love and sex are like the femur and humerus—both necessities on the body, but they work independently of one another. However, that doesn't just apply to men, because I know my mom loved us when she left, but her love didn't stop her from going away. I blame her for my trust issues. I'm always waiting for people to disappoint me. Once they do, I chalk it up to human nature. I never take blame in the fact that I might have pushed them away by not completely trusting in the first place. If I anticipate the pain, it's never as great. I did, however, step out on faith with Rome. Deep down, I wanted him to prove me wrong, even though I knew he was going to mess up. It's so hard for me to believe that people change. I think people make temporary adjustments in order to get what they want. But once they are comfortable, their old behavior will come out. It's inevitable. I used to be an alcoholic and I didn't change into a new person. She is still there, and every day is a struggle to keep my new disposition on life. If I get comfortable, I can slip up, therefore I stay on my guard. I can't even say that I trust myself, and those who doubt themselves are sure to doubt others. The land of distrust is never a good place to live, but here is where I reside and I'm not sure I'll ever relocate. I visit other places from time to time, but I always come back home. If it weren't for my twins, Rome wouldn't even have gotten a second chance. But it's important to break the cycle. My grandma left her husband, and my mom left my dad. I don't want my sons to think that this is how it should be. Therefore, my decision to live with him has less to do with love and more to do with self-improvement. I don't trust Rome has changed, but I trust he is making a great effort to do so, and if I don't learn to trust, I'm going to be very lonely— whether I'm in a relationship or not. I see that in my mom's eyes. The more I learn about our similarities, the more it scares me. Oh yeah, I do trust God—first and foremost—and I trust that God is going to hear my plea to transform my heart.

Session Done

15

The next morning, Omar calls. He wants to meet over lunch. I tell him Lia has to come along to help me with the boys, and we agree to meet at 1:00 P.M., at Goldengate Café.

Lia takes a seat near the front as I wait for Omar. He waltzes in with a pleasant expression. The first thing I notice is my journal in his right hand.

"Hi, Pop," he says with a small grin. As if we were a couple, he softly kisses my hand and strikes up conversation.

"How are you feeling?" he asks. I give a quick nod and we take a seat at a booth near the back. We sit in silence for a couple more minutes.

"I'm sorry," I quickly state.

Pausing, Omar sucks in a deep breath before responding. "Yeah . . . you and Tracy, I can't believe . . . you know what, I'm not ready to talk about it. I really want to just forget the whole thing." He slides the journal across the table.

"I didn't know what to think. I thought you would go to the police."

"It crossed my mind for a second. But then I thought about your children, and Tracy. I wouldn't put you through that . . . for what? I always wanted what was best for you," he says calmly.

"Thank you," I whisper.

"My brother is gone," he murmurs.

Before I realize it, I'm crying. Tracy is gone and Omar has no one. The tears continue to flow, for him and for me. Omar moves to my side of the booth and comforts me.

"I'm fine, " I say, sniffling. "You know what, I'm not really hungry. Can we skip this lunch?" I ask.

"I drank last night," Omar candidly confesses.

"What? No, Omar, don't do this."

He simply shrugs nonchalantly and rises.

"Call me sometime," he says before walking away. I stare at his arm. Riddled with guilt, my chest begins to ache. The pain quickly moves upward to my head, so I reach in my purse for a pain reliever and go over to Lia.

I settle into Rome's home and actually begin to unpack a few things. By week three, I am unpacked and am finally comfortable calling this my new home. The twins are growing rapidly, and though I don't have the 3:00 A.M. nursing routine quite down, I am getting into the swing of having two little ones completely dependent upon me. Rome is the biggest help. He is only taking jobs that will have him out of town for no more than two days. And when he's in town, I don't lift a finger. He even has a housekeeper come in during the week to help clean the four-bedroom house. Rome is making plans to sell the club, since his career is taking him out of town more each week. When he's in town, he wants to spend it with his family, not overseeing a bunch of clubbers. He realizes that season in his life is over. Plus, with the money he can make from selling the club, he can upgrade all of his video equipment. It's a win-win situation.

Things are progressing and seem to be great—all except my spirit. Not sure if it's postpartum depression or another condition, my mornings drag, my days creep by and all I want to do is sleep. Within the last week, I notice that I don't even want to tend to my five-week-old sons. I start asking the housekeeper, Carla, to do nanny duties. I used to rarely go two hours without washing my hands, but now I go three days without showering or bathing. Not that I don't have time, I just have no energy to put on clean clothing. Rome is so busy with the club, his burgeoning career and fatherhood, he doesn't notice his diminishing woman, who is falling further into a depression.

Having her calls unreturned in two weeks, Lia makes an unannounced visit. Dressed in a rust-colored suit and sporting patent leather maroon Louboutins, Lia forces her way into the house to visit. Immediately, Lia notices my hair. It has grown out of its posh, cute trim and is pushed back with a blue bandana. Not long enough for a ponytail, stray ends stick out from behind my ears.

"What have you been doing with yourself?" Lia asks as she canvasses the living room.

I simply shrug my shoulders and close the door. Immediately, Lia rushes to the babies, both in the center of the floor on top of a big plush comforter. By now, Jameel has outgrown Jalen, but both boys are identical as they lie there in their Pampers.

"Where are their clothes?"

"They don't need clothes. They aren't going anywhere."

Lia looks at me draped in a big furry robe and replies, "Where are your clothes?"

"I don't have any. My fat ass can't fit anything in the closet. The maternity stuff is too big; the old stuff is too little. This is all that fits, and so, this is all I wear." I open my robe exposing a pair of cutoff jogging pants and a stretched-out T-shirt.

"You look an absolute mess." Lia rushes to close my housecoat. Tears begin to form in my eyes. Lia panics.

"I'm sorry, I'm sorry. Please don't cry. I was joking."

"No, you weren't. I do look a mess. In fact, I am a mess."

Lia consoles me with a bear hug, which sways me from

side to side. "What's wrong with my friend? Why haven't I heard from you in two weeks? What have you been doing?"

I point to the boys, lying peacefully on the floor. Lia grins at her godsons as they kick at the ceiling. She kneels and tickles the boys. They coo and squirm.

"Jameel throws up when you tickle him. Turn him over, so he doesn't choke," I say very casually. Lia quickly picks up Jalen and turns him on his stomach.

"That's Jalen," I inform her.

"How can you tell?"

"Jalen has a mole on the heel of his right foot." Lia checks the heel and sees the mole. She kisses his foot and speaks to him.

"Little Jalen, you almost fooled me. Did you try to fool your auntie Lia on purpose?"

"Don't talk to him, talk to me," I urge.

"I miss them," Lia says, with her attention still on the babies.

"You don't miss me?" I ask.

Suddenly, Lia realizes that I am in dire need of some adult attention. Therefore, she picks up Jameel, places him on her lap and sits down by me. Caressing my face, Lia ogles my swollen bosoms. "Wow, look at your breasts."

I quickly close my robe. "They hurt, almost all day. Especially when it's time to nurse. Oh, and they leak, it's a pain in the ass."

"Well, you can't expect to get big breasts like that without paying some costs. But they are gorgeous. Let me see them again," Lia says with excitement.

"No. I wish I could give them to you."

"I already have great breasts. But you should figure how to keep those babies. Are they going to go away after you stop breast-feeding?"

"Probably."

"Well, stop now. Maybe you'll be able to keep some of the

fullness." Lia giggles, lightly tapping the side of my right breast. All of this is to encourage me, but it doesn't work. I just sit with a gloomy expression, staring straight through Lia's humor and girlish fondling.

"Let's go to the park. I'm done with work for the day and I have a change of clothing in the car," Lia says. But I don't respond until Lia physically shakes me from my stupor. "Did you hear me?"

"I don't want to go to the park."

"Too bad, we're going. Do the boys have clean clothing?" I nod.

"Okay, you go find some sweats, put on a baseball cap and I'll get them dressed." Lia forces me from the couch and pushes me in the direction of the bedroom. Just before I get out of ear's reach, Lia yells, "Oh, and brush your teeth. That might make you feel better. It will surely help me."

Lia places Jameel under one arm and tries to pick up Jalen, but she's having trouble carrying both boys. "How do I do this?" Lia mumbles. She places Jalen back down and positions him in the center of the comforter. "I'll be right back," she tells him. "Don't roll anywhere." Lia quickly rushes into the boys' room and grabs two tiny pants and long-sleeved shirts. She comes back into the living room and dresses them both. As she finishes, she calls out to me, but doesn't get an answer. With the boys dressed and lying back on the floor, Lia hurries to find me sitting on the edge of my bed, wearing only a pair of sweats. Lia stands at the door entrance and points. "Get dressed. You know I'm trying to stop cursing, but you are pushing my nerves today." I rise and turn around so that Lia can see how fitted the pair of sweats are.

"They look like thick leggings," I whine.

Lia bursts into laughter. "Maybe we should go to Target instead of the park."

"You think?" I say, and then a smile creeps over my face.

Suddenly, from nowhere, I chuckle. This quickly rolls into hearty laughter.

"Finally! You had me worried. Look, just put on one of those stretchy maternity skirts and a shirt, the boys are ready." Just then, one of the infants lets out a loud cry. I rush to the door, but Lia halts my steps. "I got them, go change so that we can go." Lia rushes back into the room to tend to a crying Jameel, who is screaming for some reason far beyond Lia's knowledge. It takes her a few minutes, but she eventually gets him to hush. Ten minutes later, I am dressed and we pack up and head to Target.

Though my mood is somber most of the day, Lia manages to make me smile a few times throughout the afternoon. However, the most important thing is that I find several new outfits to wear until I get my weight down. We never make it to the park, but the day is well spent. When we arrive home, the boys are asleep, so Lia and I actually get some quiet time to talk. Since most of the day was spent trying to cheer me up, Lia had no time to give me an update about her and Idris, who are doing very well.

"It's been two and a half months, and I think I love him."

I silently stare into Lia's eyes.

"What? Why are you looking at me like that?" Lia questions.

"'Cause you never say the word 'love'. Unless you're speaking about shoes, designer shoes at that," I mention.

"Well, he is couture, exclusive, only five pairs made. He's the perfect stiletto, with a high arch and no foot pain. I'm serious. It's just something about him. I can't put my finger on it, but whenever we are together, I can't help but think about spending years and years with him. I miss Idris when he's not around, and I just really, really, really like him."

"Wow, three 'reallys' in a row," I cynically comment.

"Yeah, that's got to be love, right?"

"I guess," I respond, shrugging my shoulders.

"You should know. You love Rome. Is that how you feel when he's around?"

"Not really, but it's different. We were friends already. I don't get that mushy feeling around him. But I do love him."

"Well, I'm calling it love. I'm happy and I don't think about being with anyone else."

"That's a first."

"That's what I'm trying to tell you. This is it." I rise and I giggle quietly underneath my breath. "I hear you. Stop laughing and be happy for me."

"I'm very happy for you. I've been waiting for this side of Lia to emerge. It's cute. If you want this to be it, then I hope it is."

"Thank you," Lia says, beaming.

I return with two bottles of water. Lia takes hers and leans softly on my shoulders as I flick on the television. We flip through a couple of stations, and then Lia speaks. "I don't want him to know about my past. This is the first time I've ever really cared what a man thought about me. When he looks at me, I feel so precious. I don't ever want him to stop looking at me like that." Lia turns up her water bottle and waits for me to jump in, but I don't. Finally, after a few more minutes, Lia questions, "Don't you have anything to say?"

I nod and look at my friend. "I guess you really, really, really do like him—"

"Love him," Lia interjects before turning back toward the television and leaning back in the chair.

She stays with me for another thirty minutes, but then prepares to leave and meet Idris for dinner. She gives me a tight hug around the neck and promises to come by later in the week to check on me. As soon as she leaves, I go into the kitchen and cook. This is the first night in a week that I've actually cooked. Normally, Rome calls and we decide what to eat for takeout. But tonight, I plan to surprise him with a home-cooked meal. Lia's visit, though unplanned, was necessary. I am in better spirits and I get the energy to fix my hair and put on a little makeup. Unfortunately, the fridge and cabinets don't have a great variety of food. Therefore, I settle on penne pasta with spicy chicken. Thankfully, the boys are still asleep, and I get most of the dinner prepared before they awake. Close to seven, I am done and decide to make fresh lemonade. Just as I pull the lemons out of the fridge, the doorbell rings. With an apron filled with lemons, I rush to the door.

"Who is it?" I call from inside, with no reply from the visitor. I look out the peephole and see Ariel Marie Collins.

Totally surprised by my presence, she stutters, trying to form a sentence. "Um . . . I'm looking for Rome."

"I know you did not show up at this house? Are you stupid? I'm not pregnant anymore, and I will beat your ass," I say furiously, opening up the door.

"Really, Gwen, violence is never the answer," she says with a cool attitude.

"You better step off this porch before I knock you off."

"Just give this to Rome." She hands me a letter, which I snatch from her hand.

"Good to see you again," she says while I'm closing the door in her face.

"She's got some nerve," I say, walking back into the kitchen.

I place the letter on the living-room table. But as I finish the lemonade, the letter seems to be calling my name. It becomes a constant distraction. I keep walking back and forth, staring at the white envelope, as if I can see through its thin paper. Finally, I can't take it anymore. I grab the envelope and sit on the chair. Just as I am about to open it, Jalen starts to cry. I hurriedly nurse my son. Pacing the floor with him attached to my nipple, I open the letter. With no shame, I tear into the envelope and read the first line aloud.

"First of all, I must say it is wonderful to have you back into my life."

I rise with anger. My face distorts and brows furrow. "'Back into my life?'" I continue to read aloud.

"I know you have your family, but you're not married. When we saw each other last week, I realized what we have. I have decided to relocate back to Detroit permanently. The agency you referred me to booked me two jobs. I'm really modeling now and I owe it all to you. How shall I pay you back? I can think of 69 or so ways . . . smile! Love Ariel."

"Last week? I'm going to kill him," I whisper.

I fume, and without hesitation, I clomp into the bedroom. With my son tucked between my right arm and my chest, I pull the suitcase from within the closet and randomly toss the boys' clothing into the bag. While mumbling obscenities under my breath, I pack the boys' things in a matter of minutes. I place Jalen down beside Jameel, just as he is starting to awake. I look down at both boys with my lips pressed tight.

"Your father is going to get it!" I express with fervor. I rush around the room, gathering up my necessities, while dialing Lia on my cell. Lia, being on her dinner date, doesn't answer.

"Lia, listen. I have to come to your place for a few days. I'll have the boys with me, and I'll explain later. I'll let myself in. Hope that's okay. I really need this." I write Rome a note, which I leave underneath a magnetized refrigerator frame of the twins. Adding insult to injury, I place Ariel's letter just below mine. Within the hour, the boys and I are settled into Lia's place.

Rome comes home close to 9:00 P.M. He places a phone call to me, but I don't answer. Concerned with my whereabouts, he dials Lia, to no avail. Rome eventually walks back into the kitchen to grab a bite to eat and sees the pots on the stove.

"That's what I'm talking about." He grins before fixing a plate. As he leans against the counter, waiting for the microwave to heat his supper, he glances at the letter on the stainless-steel refrigerator door. Peering at the ripped paper, he leans in closer and removes it from underneath the frame. Slowly, he begins reading.

I prepared dinner. There's also fresh lemonade. Ariel came by and left you a letter. Damn, Rome, why? I had no energy to argue, so I simply left. I'll call in a few days to let you know about the boys.

"Shit!" he shouts. Quickly, he begins reading Ariel's letter. The microwave buzzes at the start of her first sentence, but it's pointless, his appetite is ruined. Nearly tripping over his feet, Rome rushes to his cell and nervously dials my number. No answer. Next he calls Lia, but still, no answer.

"Fuck!"

He stands in the center of the living room and rapidly repeats the obscenity. He tries to call me for a fourth time. Rome then calls Ariel, who picks up on the first ring.

"Hey, baby," she answers.

"Don't fucking 'hey, baby' me. You came to my house tonight?"

"Yeah. I wanted to thank you for the referral. Plus, when I saw you the other day, you made it seem okay to come by."

"I saw you at a video shoot. I gave you a card of an agent. How did this seem . . . Why the fuck did you come to my house? What did you say to Gwen?"

"Nothing. I gave her the letter to give to you," she peacefully states.

"That is my girl, the mother of my children. I'm placing a restraining order on your ass."

Ariel laughs.

"We are not going to be together. I am marrying Gwen," Rome yells.

"Really, Rome? Then why were you inside of me not so long ago? Even the other day, you looked like you wanted to lay me down right there on the set."

"Stay the fuck away from my family." He hangs up the phone.

Rome tosses his cell on the couch and his tense body follows suit. Grabbing his head, he moans in misery.

"Gwen, please call me!" he agonizes. But there is nothing

but silence after his voice finishes its last echo. Finally, his phone rings.

"I can't believe you," Lia screams from the other end.

"Hold up! I didn't do anything."

"Then why is your girlfriend at my house crying, and why did some ho show up on your doorstep like the postman?"

"Let me speak to Gwen."

"Gwen doesn't want to talk to you. Why do you keep messing up?"

"Oh, my God, Lia. I promise. I haven't slept with Ariel. I saw her at a video shoot and gave her a business card of an agent, that's it. I have to speak to Gwen," Rome begs in a quavering voice.

After a deep sigh, Lia lowers her tone, and calmly asks, "What do you want me to do? Gwen is not going to believe you."

"I know, but you have to make her," he insists.

"I'll do what I can."

Lia hangs up the phone and Rome continues to gaze at the ceiling. He lies on the couch for close to an hour and his frustration gets the best of him, until he can't take anymore.

"This is some bullshit. I have done nothing wrong and I'm going to straighten this out before the morning."

Rome grabs his keys and heads to Lia's home. On the phone with Andre the entire ride, Rome gets advice from his sensible friend, who pleads that Rome remain calm and see things from my perspective. Rome promises to stay composed, explain his side and beg his family to come home. But things don't go as easily as he had planned.

Idris opens Lia's door, steps outside and speaks to Rome.

"I'm sorry, brother, but the ladies sent me out here to talk to you."

"I don't want to talk to you, I just came here to get my girl and my sons."

"Gwen's not coming home with you tonight."

"Bullshit!"

"Watch your language," says Idris.

"Look, I mean no disrespect. But she cannot leave, take my sons away and expect me to be okay with that. I've done nothing wrong. That girl who came to the house is crazy. I haven't been messing with her."

"Yes, that is the story I heard," Idris says calmly. "Honestly your mess is none of my business. But this whole situation has my girl disturbed, and that is my business. What I cannot allow you to do is come in this house and upset the order to a greater degree. So I'm sorry, you have to leave. I will deliver a message to sister Gwen, but right now she does not want to lay eyes on you and she made that point very clear."

The two men stand eye to eye, and though Rome has nearly forty pounds on Idris, this man of God has a stance one hundred times as strong. It is evident that Rome is not going to break the entrance of Lia's home on this evening. So, with a stiff upper lip, Rome clears his throat and gives his message.

"Tell Gwen, I'll be waiting out here when she's ready to talk." Rome turns around and walks to the car. Idris watches him get in, and then goes back in the house. With my ear pressed against the wood, I nearly fall forward when he opens the door. With wide, curious eyes, I stare at Idris, waiting for him to repeat what I couldn't hear through the thick maple wood.

"He said he would be outside when you were ready to talk."

Lia quickly jumps in. "Outside, where? In the car?"

"I guess," Idris responds.

Lia cracks the door, peers out and quickly shuts it. "He's just sitting out there. What now?"

I press my lips together and scratch my forehead in thought. After a few seconds, I reply, "He'll leave in a minute." I walk back into the living room and tend to my sons.

Close to 2:00 A.M., I toss in my slumber. Both boys are asleep, Lia is passed out in the bedroom and Idris is on the pullout sofa. I tiptoe to the door, peek out and see Rome's car still sitting at the curbside. Hastily, I shut the door and lean my body against the wood. It would be a lie to say I didn't want to talk, but it would also be untrue to say that I'm ready to hear what I think could be another lie. Therefore, I trot back to the bedroom and attempt to sleep. It doesn't work. I toss another four hours and soon, Jalen wakes up first for his morning feeding. While I'm nursing, Lia creeps in the room and whispers, "He's still out there."

"Are you serious?" I question.

"Yes. You have to talk to him. My neighbors are going to call the police. Plus, I think he's innocent this time. Ariel is really crazy. She knew you would read the letter. She was trying to start something."

I groan, loosen Jalen from my nipple and hand him to Lia. I put a jacket over my sweats and walk to Rome's car. Feeling my presence, he opens his eyes and turns toward me. He clears his throat and unlocks the door. With my jacket clutched tightly, I plop down in the passenger seat and keep my focus on the yellow house four doors down.

"I'm not fooling around with Ariel."

With my lips tightly puckered, I circle the inside of my right cheek with my tongue, a nervous habit I've had since I was a child.

"I would not lie to you—"

"Anymore," I add to his sentence.

"Anymore," he mutters.

Rome stares at me as I continue to concentrate on the bright-colored abode. After seconds of cold silence, Rome pleads for me to speak.

"You wouldn't have come out here, if you didn't want to talk."

Slowly, I turn my head while keeping my body positioned forward and rigid. I barely open my mouth to utter the words. "Trust is a big thing with me. I took a chance on you, and you . . . you . . . continue to lie to me. Why?"

"Oh, my God, baby. I'm not lying. You have to believe me."

"Why didn't you tell me you saw her?" I express in a soft but firm tone.

"It wasn't a big deal. It was on a set. Ariel is crazy. She makes up situations in her head."

"Why did this woman think it was acceptable to come to your house at night?"

"I keep telling you that she's crazy. I'm placing a restraining order on her."

Rome reaches over and lightly caresses my arm. I allow his contact, but show no emotion. "I can't help what other people do. I only know that I did nothing wrong. She's a video chick. I will probably run into her again. You can't get jealous over these girls."

"Jealous? You slept with her, Rome. Don't act like I'm being unreasonable."

We silently sit in the car for another three or four minutes. Finally, I speak to my downhearted boyfriend. "You should go home." Without a second of eye contact, I reach for the door and step out. Rome's eyes follow me to the door, and then he leaves.

The next morning, Rome is sharing his issues with Andre. The entire time Rome is explaining, Andre is nodding his head. Rome finally tires of his friend's bobblehead-doll ways and asks him to comment, and he does quite bluntly.

"It's your fault," Andre says.

"What! You've got to be joking."

"I know you, Rome," Andre explains. "You like to charm women, or as you put it, 'help women.' You know Ariel is crazy and you did just sleep with her some months back. Why talk to her at all?"

"What's wrong with me helping people see their potential?"

"Nothing, if they aren't going to try to thank you sixty-nine ways when you have a wife and children."

"Gwen is not my wife, and if she doesn't learn to trust me, she never will be. I don't want a wife who doesn't have my back." Rome huffs while puffing out his broad chest.

"You think you have some say-so in this? Gwen is holding all the cards, and if you don't get it together, she's not going to become your wife, and you will be writing her a nice-ass check every month."

Rome quickly quiets his manner. "Well, I've apologized over and over. I'm not doing it anymore. I told her nothing happened and she's going to have to believe me or . . ."

"Or what?" Andre questions.

"Or she can just stay mad and find somewhere else to live."

"You don't mean that."

"I'm not going to spend the rest of my life tipping around Gwen's insecurities."

"You cheated, bro. You cheated while she was pregnant. You've got at least four years of tipping before you are completely forgiven. That's the rules."

"Fuck that. I'm a good man and a good father, and she knows that. She'll come around." Rome grabs his coat.

Andre restarts his nodding. This time, he adds a Mafia-like exaggerated frown where his entire face looks contorted.

"Just keep apologizing," he says.

"Why? So she can think it's okay to run all over me, like Tonia runs your ass!"

"What did you say to me?" Andre says with anger.

"Man, you let Tonia dictate your life."

"Wrong, I do what's best for my family. I put them first. Just because I'm not selfish and I listen to my wife doesn't mean she runs me." Andre starts to walk away, but Rome quickly catches up.

"I'm sorry, man. Gwen has got me tripping. I know you handle your business."

"Damn right I handle my business. And part of that is letting Tonia think she runs things. But trust me . . ."

"I know. You wear the pants," Rome adds with a smile.

Andre simply shakes his head. "Women, with them, they slowly kill you, but without them, you go a lot faster. I'll talk to her."

Rome grabs his jacket and heads to the door. Just as he is leaving, Andre delivers his bit of sunshine underneath the cloud.

"Hey, Tonia's pregnant again."

Rome chuckles, and congratulates Andre. "I don't know how you do it."

"Why do you think I'm so good at silent nodding?" Andre laughs loudly.

Four days pass before Lia realizes that I am not going home. Yes, she loves me, but her house and lifestyle are not infant-friendly. Therefore, Lia decides something must be said, so she sends Idris, the family's new mediator, to talk with me. However, after I explain that I simply don't trust Rome, Idris disagrees with Lia and tells me that I should spend some time away from him. Though I partially believe that Rome did end things with Ariel, I am not sure he is completely innocent. Furthermore, I don't want to be that girl-friend who feels compelled to open her man's mail or sniff his shirts for traces of perfume. I hate that he brings out that trait.

"He alters my personality and that's not good," I confess.

In his normal composed manner, Idris sheds light on my comment. "You allow him to alter it. I don't doubt you love Rome, but is it a healthy love?"

"Yes," I am quick to retort, and then retract, "I think so . . . Why can't he just act right? We have children."

"Would you say that Rome has changed?"

"Kind of. He's definitely more settled, but he still flirts and looks at women. I feel like he's just waiting to replace me."

"Well, Rome could be completely faithful and you'd still feel like that."

"But I wouldn't. I honestly don't feel that he can be faithful. That's my problem. I know him all too well. I've seen the women he's run through. He played them all. I refuse to let him play me," I state.

"If you feel that way, why did you start seeing him in the first place?"

I poke out my bottom lip and mumble gibberish that resembles the words "I don't know."

"Well, other than the fact that he's the father of your sons, you need to come up with other reasons," Idris says.

I sandwich my head between my palms and groan. Idris rises, taps my shoulder and leaves. I am left to make the "why do I want to be with Rome" list and the decision to stay or leave. Surprisingly, it only takes one minute to come up with the first 10 reasons. Proud, I sit back and review my answers:

1. *He has a good heart.*
2. *He is the father of my children.*
3. *I want my children to grow up with both parents in the same house.*
4. *He is trying to change his ways.*
5. *He pampers me.*
6. *He loves me the best way he knows how.*
7. *He's a really good father.*
8. *We have great conversation.*
9. *We're friends.*
10. *I love him.*

If I didn't love Rome, I would have walked a long time ago, and I would have never had his babies. There is a reason why I never got pregnant by Omar or any other man. I didn't want to get stuck with them. But with Rome, I let my guard down. In truth, we're so close, my life wouldn't be the same without him in it.

After another day of contemplation, I decide to stay. In the long run, moving out will only complicate our relationship, which currently has no title. Though I am in the house, it's not the same. We just walk around the space barely saying a full sentence to one another. Most of the time, I sleep in the other bedroom. With our nonexistent sex life, Rome makes a few attempts at spending a romantic evening with me. However, after the kids fall asleep, I soon follow.

An indecisive relationship is already a mental warfare, add two eight-week-old boys to the mix and it's downright exhausting. When the boys are asleep during the day, I'm still at the club, and though Rome is speaking to some people about selling the three-thousand-square-foot venue, no paperwork has been done. Rome is always out of town, so I'm practically raising these boys on my own.

On one evening that I'm truly about to have a nervous breakdown, my mom calls and delivers interesting news. She is coming to visit. She hasn't seen her grandchildren and she can hear exhaustion in my voice. Normally, I would be concerned about my mother's sleeping arrangements and the length of the visit, but after hearing this, I only have a one-word question: "When?"

"This weekend," Rose replies.

I collapse on my bed. "Thank God!"

On the other end, Rose gives a hearty laugh. Inside, she is bubbling over that I am excited. Finally, her chance to be there for me, an opportunity she's been waiting for.

16

Two days into Rose's visit and it's already a huge difference in my attitude. My weary, swollen lids are starting to be repaired and I am actually able to get out of the house before early afternoon. Rose doesn't realize it, but she is quickly making up for all those missed years.

When Rome returns from his commercial shoot in Canada, he comes to the house to see his new extended family. And though Rose has cooked enough dinner for the weekend, she suggests the two "not so" lovebirds go out on a date. Excited, I am dressed and ready to go before Rome can say okay. Though my eagerness is attributed to a simple evening out with an adult, Rome assumes my anxiousness is about him. Before we get to the restaurant, he mentions his delight about my excitement to see him. At first mention, I am about to burst his bubble, but then I place my palm on top of his and smile. "This night will be very good for us," I say.

Dinner is superb, but it's my after-dinner mood that comes as a surprise. While riding around the city looking for a place with chocolate cheesecake, I make an interesting suggestion.

"Let's go to a hotel."

Giving me no time to retract my proposal, Rome makes a beeline straight to the Hilton. As if this were prom night, he nervously ushers me out of the car and escorts me straight to the room. I sit on the edge of the bed and watch Rome remove his shoes and pants. We haven't done it but once since the big argument. I know he's excited, but is this going to solve anything? I finally speak.

"Just 'cause I said 'let's go to a hotel' doesn't mean I am trying to have sex."

Now down to his boxers, socks and T-shirt, Rome gives me a perplexed look.

"You don't want to do it?" he asks, sounding like an anxious sixteen-year old about to do it for the first time.

"I didn't say that. But you just assumed that that's all I wanted when I could have just wanted to chill."

"Oh," Rome says with apparent disappointment as he goes to the bathroom.

I continue to sit on the bed's edge and listen to him urinate through the open door. I begin to chuckle. When he exits, he can't help but ask the source of my amusement.

"What's so funny, Gwendolyn?"

"You are, Romulus."

He sighs, reaches for his pants and slowly begins to place them on. "So what do you want to do?" he asks.

"Oh, I don't know . . . have sex, maybe."

"Why are you playing with me?"

"I'm not," I respond. "I never said I didn't want to have sex, I simply said that you assumed that I did, and you shouldn't have made that assumption. You know, women hate when—"

Before I can make my proclamation clear, Rome silences me with a kiss. Supporting his weight with his left hand, he lifts my skirt with his right. Finally, the night's games are over and we are making love. Afterward, I lie beside Rome and stare at the ceiling. My first words are "Maybe we shouldn't have done this."

His response, "Women."

We both let out a disgruntled sigh, and the intense conversation we've avoided all night begins.

"Don't lump me in the category with all women, you know I hate that. I don't act like the women you hang around," I fuss.

"You are right now. You suggested we have sex, and as soon as we do, you say we shouldn't have done it. You know that's crazy, right?"

"I was horny, and when you're horny, it's easy to confuse that with wanting someone. I just don't want to confuse anything."

"You are the only one confused. We don't have to have a title to have sex," Rome replies.

"See, that's what I'm saying."

"Exactly what are you saying?" Rome questions.

"If it's up to you, we can just keep doing it, without any clarity as to where we stand. But I can't."

"Fine, let's stop tripping, get married and raise our family."

"We can't," I state.

Rome rises and reaches for his underwear. "Your ass is crazy. I've already apologized and told you that I don't want to be with anyone but you. If you can't handle us sleeping together without a title, then don't suggest it." Rome continues to get dressed while he talks. "I'm not playing these games with you, Gwendolyn. If you want me to just be here for the boys, then that's what I'll do."

Interrupting, I ask, "You're not going to take a shower?"

"No, I'm going home."

"What if I'm not ready to go back?"

"Then stay."

With an overexaggerated frown, I slump from the bed and walk into the bathroom. Rome is fully dressed when I walk back into the bedroom. His keys are in his hand and he is ready.

"You ready?" he asks, walking toward the door.

"I guess so."

I follow him to the parking garage and hop in the car; however, I place my hand on top of his to prevent him from turning the ignition. I have to apologize. "I'm sorry."

Rome says nothing and turns the ignition. He pulls onto the street and then pulls over. "I don't know what to do about you anymore. I fucked up! I'm trying very hard to be faithful to you, but damn . . . you make it difficult. If you don't want us to be together, for real, let me know. That way, you can move on and so can I, and we'll figure out how to raise the boys."

I absorb every word, but don't know how to respond. I'm not ready to let go, but I'm not ready to completely give in and trust either. Yet, a decision must be made. I give a simple response. "Okay."

Confused by my answer, he makes a face and mutters, "What?"

"Give me this week. I'm sorry I'm so confusing. I'm a woman—what do you expect?" I smile, hoping to get some resemblance of a grin from Rome. After a couple of sighs, I succeed.

He smirks, tousles my hair and delivers a rhetorical reply. "What am I going to do about you?"

We ride back across town to relieve my mom from granny duty. Rose is sprawled across the bed and the boys are asleep. The house is clean and she even made a pie. I hate to admit it, but it's really good to have my mom here.

Marvin is visiting in two days. He made Rome promise not to tell, and he even put aside his lifelong aversion to flying. However, Rome keeps his own secret from Marvin, who has no idea that Rose is also here vacationing. So it's going to be an interesting stay once Marvin gets to town.

Rome meets my dad at the airport and takes him to the house. When they arrive, Rome walks in first and finds both of us in the bathroom bathing the boys. Marvin walks in and takes a seat in the living room. Rome tells me I have a visi-

tor in the living room. At first, I'm upset with Rome for inviting someone over without me knowing. However, once I see
my dad sitting nervously at the edge of the black leather
couch, I yelp with joy. I'm truly a daddy's girl. I leap into his
arms and hold him tight. Overjoyed, I continue to squeeze,
relishing the moment. Rose rushes into the room, holding
both boys under each arm.

"What is the commotion?" she asks before placing eyes on
her ex-husband.

"Marvin?"

"Rose?"

They stare at one another. With my arm still wrapped
within my father's, I speak. "Wow, this is awkward."

But Rose instantly turns on the charisma. "Nonsense.
Marvin, you look good. Come give me a hug." Rome takes
the boys, I slowly let go and he moves toward his ex with
open arms. The two embrace.

Marvin's face lights up like a Vegas billboard when he approaches his grandsons. He takes Jameel in his arms, Rose
moves in and cuddles Jalen, and both grandparents sit on the
couch and cosset their grandsons. I cheerfully lean against the
wall and watch a sight I never thought I would witness. Rome
softly massages my shoulder as we both continue to look on.

"Can you believe this?" I whisper. Just as he nods, I smack
his arm. "Why didn't you tell me Dad was coming?"

"He made me promise not to—he wanted to surprise you,"
answers Rome.

"It was a great surprise. Thank you."

"You mean I finally did something right?" he jokes. I
wiggle my nose and squint my face.

Rome's face glows as he stares at me. "The boys look like
you when you make that face."

"Please, they are the spitting image of their father," I
respond.

The rest of the weekend, the three generations laugh, bond

and renew our family. It's amazing what babies can do. They have single-handedly put my family back together again.

Monday, I go into the office at Ole School. With Mom and Dad both at the house, I know the boys are well taken care of. I spend most of the day at the club checking inventory, paying bills and ordering stock. It will make the rest of the workweek much lighter. Also, I finally have time to meet with Marissa to get information on Tracy's case. Marissa took the police a wealth of information from Tracy's computer. Now they have leads on his murder. It seems that the Cubans in Atlanta came after Tracy once more before he left. An altercation erupted and Tracy beat one of the Cuban compadres to a pulp. He and Jason had been communicating about the incident. Now the authorities have all of the correspondence. They should be able to make arrests soon. In a way, I always knew Tracy's street antics would get him hurt. I wish I could have been there for him more. However, after listening to Marissa, who constantly warned him, I see it wouldn't have made a difference. He had already paved out his life. Tracy, in his own way, was very intelligent, as most criminals are. I only wish he had used his skills for good. I miss him a lot. Marissa and I plan to meet again next week for lunch and I'm sure there is more to come involving this story.

Rose, the socialite, has invited the whole gang over for dinner, and though I would rather have an evening alone with my mom and dad, Rose insists she and Marvin get to know the people influencing her grandsons. Therefore, I hurry home to help prepare. With two bundles of pink tea roses under my arm, I come into the house ready to set the mood. However, when I step into the home, there is an unfamiliar silence. I pause, wondering the whereabouts of the family, until I hear another very alien noise. A horrid expression smashes onto my face as I suddenly hear a rhythmic moan and syncopated knocking. With tense neck muscles, I tiptoe into the living room and place the tea roses on the table. The high-pitched whimpers grow louder and my stomach uproars. I move closer to my mom's bedroom until two words stop me dead in my tracks.

"Oh, Marvin!"

As though my feet are soaked in superglue, I am stuck. I heave as my lunch rises up to my esophagus. "Oh God," I mutter. Suddenly, I hear a whimper from the boys' room, so I whip in that direction, but then hear rumbling in Rose's room and don't want to get caught eavesdropping on my parents doing the nasty. Therefore, I grab the flowers and run back out to the garage. Peeping through the cracked door, I see Rose, barely wrapped in a robe, run from her room into the twins' room. Marvin follows seconds later in his shorts.

"This is so disgusting." I moan. I continue to lean against the garage wall until the coast is clear. Still shaken, I walk back into the house and pretend as though I know nothing.

"Oh, hi, dear," Rose says as she walks from the room, holding Jalen.

"Hi, Mom," I respond with a shaky voice. I place the tea roses on the table and reach for my son. "I got him. Were you resting?" I mention while motioning toward her robe.

"Yes. I have to take a nap when they take one. I'm sure you understand," she answers.

"I do," I say with a smirk.

Marvin bursts from the room, now dressed in slacks and an undershirt. Carrying his grandson, he nonchalantly walks up to me and kisses my cheek. I study their interaction from underneath my lowered brow.

"Oh, they're good," I whisper to Jalen, "but I'm onto them."

Dinner is set for 7:00 P.M. and by 7:10 P.M. everyone is in place, and Idris is saying grace. Marvin sits at one end of the table and Rome at the other. A plethora of food is stretched across the rectangular dark wood. Tonia, Andre and Rose sit on the right side, and Idris, Lia and I sit on the left. The whole gang is present, and during the meal, there are at least five concurrent conversations. Jalen is quiet the entire dinner; however, Rose has to bounce Jameel on her knee while she eats. Though I offer to coddle him, Rose refuses. The dinner party is an overall success. However, while I'm placing whip cream on the cheesecake slices, I can't hold my peace.

I spill the beans to Lia. "When I came in today, I heard Rose and Marvin doing it." She lets out an indistinguishable sound of repulsion.

"What's wrong with you?" Rome asks as he enters the kitchen.

"Gwen saw her parents doing it."

"I heard them, not saw them," I quickly correct.

"When?" Rome asks.

"Today."

"How do you know?" he questions.

Just then, Rose enters the kitchen to help. "Know what?"

Like three puzzled amigos, we begin our dance of ignorance. Between the nods and shrugs, Rose is sure something is amiss. However, she doesn't have time to pry—there is cheesecake to eat and she will not have her dinner guests wait. "Let's get the dessert on the table."

Rose grabs two slices and we grab the remainder. After a few cocktails and jokes, the house is quiet by 10:30 P.M. Rome is at his computer, and Marvin and the twins are asleep. Rose and I are resting on the couch. I move to the end of the sofa and massage my mom's feet. Yet, as soon as I try to relax my mom, I get the third degree.

"What was that kitchen conversation about? I saw those looks. You guys were talking about something."

"We were?" I say, knowing that I should quickly come up with a better reply.

"So . . . you're going to make me ask again?"

"You don't want to know," I respond, hoping she will just drop it. But she doesn't. Therefore, after three more questions, I simply blurt out, "I heard you and Dad in the bedroom."

Rose keeps her composure and snickers. "You heard us tending to the boys." Amazed at my mother's brazen averting tactic, I clarify her statement. "I heard you tending to each other."

Suddenly, Rose clears her throat and rises from the chair. "Want coffee?" she offers.

Chuckling, I respond, "Hell nah, I don't want coffee. I want answers."

Rose continues into the kitchen and pours a cup of black liquid caffeine. I remain on the couch to give my mom a few moments to get her story together. With an arrogant smirk on my face, I wait for Rose to return. Before Rose gets to the couch, she asserts, "We are adults . . . and we were married."

"*Were* married, *not are* married," I say. "What about Jack?"

"What about him?" Rose hastily responds to my guilt trip. "If you must know, Jack and I are separated."

Suddenly, my looks of shame turn to those of concern. As I rub my mom's legs, I respond, "Are you okay?"

"At first, no, but now, I'm good."

"How long has it been?" I ask.

"Months."

"Why didn't you tell me?"

"You have enough going on. How are you and Rome?"

"Quit changing the subject. Why are you sleeping with my daddy?"

"It just happened. Now refill my coffee, and add some Stoli."

I walk into the kitchen and refill my mother's cup. When I return, I ask one more time, but after Rose's blunt response— "Your father is good in bed, it's been a long time and I needed it"—there is no more sex conversation. The imagery is too much to bear. After a few minutes, I speak. "Are you up to something?"

"No, Gwen. I'm a good person, maybe a little selfish, but I know I have a good heart."

Just then, Marvin steps from the bedroom and asks to see Rose. She excuses herself and they retire to her room. The thought of hearing them again makes me quickly go to my bedroom, close the door and bury my head in the pillow.

The rest of Marvin's visit is extremely pleasant. When he leaves the following Thursday, he drags his feet getting to the airport. This time, it has nothing to do with his fear of flying; he simply doesn't want to leave his family. I pull into the Delta baggage claim area, hop from the car and tightly squeeze my dad.

"I promise to bring the boys to New York soon. So sad I had to have two babies to get you to Detroit, but I'm so glad you came," I say with a huge smile.

"I will be back, I promise."

"You better, and call me when you get back."

We hug once more and I nearly tear up as I watch my dad walk into the airport. Though I am sure Rose and Marvin did it one more time before he left, I never let on. Marvin embarrasses much easier than Rose, and I can't have my daddy ashamed to face his baby girl.

However, Mom doesn't get off as easy. I continue to interrogate her about the escapade after Marvin leaves. I still believe my dad is too good for her—yet and still, deep in a place where I hate to admit it, I wish they had never separated.

It's Monday morning, and I am on my way to the club when my phone rings. It's Marissa. With sighs and long pauses, she explains to me that Omar is not doing well. He fell into a deep depression about three weeks ago. He's constantly drinking again and has fired Kain, the only manager at Comatose who would listen to him. By the time Marissa finishes her talk, I have redirected my car and it's headed toward Comatose. I walk in the deserted club and find Omar in his office, which reeks of imported liquor. With no pity, I walk in with guns ablazing.

"If you drink up your orders, the club is going to be short," I loudly exclaim.

Omar, obviously tipsy, reaches up his arm and grins from ear to ear. "Pop! I miss you, girl. Come give me a hug."

I slowly approach and lean over into Omar's embrace.

"Why are you drinking?" I ask.

"Why not?"

"Because you stopped, we both stopped, remember?"

"Well, you're not around, so I started back," he answers.

I take a seat. Of course I want to fuss, but I know it's a delicate situation. So, instead, I try a softer approach.

"You were doing so well. What happened?"

"Everyone leaves me . . . my mom, my dad, you, Tracy, everybody. The club is in debt, and I only got it so that my brother and I could have a business. Now he's gone and everything is going to shit." Omar reaches in his bottom desk drawer and pulls out a bottle of Grey Goose. "I would offer you some, but you don't drink." He bursts into laugher as I look on in distress.

"Omar, stop this. It's not what you want."

"How do you know what I want?" he shouts. "This is all your fault." Immediately, I rise, but he quickly switches his demeanor. "I'm sorry, Pop, I didn't mean that."

"That's not fair," I utter.

"I know. Just sit with me a minute," he begs.

I slowly sit, fixating my eyes on his actions. Omar pours the vodka into a paper cup on the table.

"Don't drink that," I request.

Omar pauses. "Kiss me."

"I'm not kissing you, O."

"If you don't kiss me, I'm going to drink." He places the cup to his lips and peers at me.

"Fine," I shout. "One kiss, on the cheek. But you cannot do

this to me, or you." I lean over and kiss his cheek. Omar slides the paper cup over to me. I go to the office restroom and pour it out.

"You know, I must love you to let you waste good vodka."

"O, what happened?" I yell, walking back into the office. "You are doing your thing. Look at this place. And why did you fire Kain?"

"I miss you, Gwen. How are your children?" He seems lost.

"They're fine, but I didn't come to discuss my life. I came to see about you."

"Why?" he asks.

"'Cause I care about you," I respond.

"Nah, you don't."

I snatch the bottle of vodka from his grips. "Yes, I do. I don't want you living like this, O. You've got so much potential—this club and your business. Are you seeing someone?"

"Look at me. Women don't exactly go for the handicapped type."

I look down at his arm. I am frozen for at least a minute. Omar slams his hand on the desk to get my attention.

"Gwen?"

"Lots of women would talk to you, but not like this. You are no good to any woman, if you start drinking again, and—"

"How are you and Rome?" Omar interrupts.

"Fine," I say, looking away.

"I smell something. What happened?" Omar pries.

"Look. Let's go get some food. I know you haven't eaten. And we need something to soak up this liquor."

We go to lunch and I spend the day attempting to coach Omar into sobriety. Before I return home, I've promised to go to AA meetings with him once a week and see him through this period. That night, I discuss my day's dealings with Rose, who totally disagrees with me going to AA meetings. So much so, that she offers to go with him instead. I understand my mom's concerns; however, it doesn't matter. I am determined to help him through this crisis—especially since I still feel responsible. My only dilemma is the wrath of Rome when I tell him my decision.

I wait until after I've attended the first meeting before telling him. As expected, he loses it. He argues that Omar is still dependent on me and that going with him to Alcoholics Anonymous is only going to make it worse. This point I have already contemplated, and it's not going to change my assessment. However, the stubbornness in my tone makes Rome more determined to seal this relationship. He gives me an ultimatum.

"You have to decide. Are we going to be together or not?"

"We are living together and taking it slow. This is good."

"Good for you," he mumbles. "I gave you your ring back, but you don't even wear it." He leaves the house.

I know he's serious. I simply have to try to trust him, or move on.

After the second AA meeting, I am quickly falling back into Omar's world. We talk every day and have had three lunch dates. Omar seems to be out of his depression. I don't know if it's my involvement, or if he was exaggerating to get me back into his life. However, I like to see the spark back in my friend, and want to take a little credit for it. By the third week at AA, Omar makes his move on me as we are leaving the meeting. Standing at the car, Omar wraps his arm around my waist, and pulls me into his side. Omar feels like this might be his last chance to let me know how he feels. He's been beating around the bush, but enough time has been wasted and he wants me back—and he knows just what to say.

"Gwen, you know I love you, right?"

I nod yes, wondering what his next line is going to be.

"I've cleaned up my act. I'm not the same Omar."

"I know—" I say, and then he silences me with a small peck.

"Listen. I need to talk right now. I have to get this out." Omar leans against the car and stares into my eyes.

"I never stopped loving you. I tried to respect this whole Rome thing. But I know it's not working out. You don't look happy. But I can change all that. I know what you need, security. You will never have to worry about me cheating or leaving."

I don't want to hear what he's saying, because I know it's completely true. Omar would never leave. He's not that type of guy. I want to be in a relationship, one filled with love and trust. With Omar, I can have both; with Rome, I can have one. Yes, Rome is the father of my kids, but is that enough to make the relationship last? All of these thoughts flurry in my head as Omar continues to speak.

"I wanted to marry you all those years ago, and I still do. In order to be the best husband for you, I will do whatever it is I have to do. You know I would be a great father. I would make amends with Rome. I just want you in my life. Do you still love me?"

I soak in each of his words. I'm so lost in thought, I can't immediately respond.

Omar continues. "I know I sound like a punk. I don't care anymore. All you can say is, you don't feel the same way. But fuck it, I'm tired of pretending like I don't care if we are together or not."

"I do still care about—" Before I can completely finish the last word, he kisses me. The kiss is electric. I want to deny the sparks, but I can't rebuff the natural body reactions happening underneath my clothing. Neither can Omar as I feel his growing reaction. He quickly backs away from my hips.

"I'm sorry," he apologizes. "It's been a while."

"So I have nothing to do with it?" I flirt.

Omar laughs. "You have plenty to do with it. It's been a while, 'cause I only want to be with you."

"You're full of it, but I will accept that answer for now."

Omar's eyes light up as he shows his surprise. "I have something to show you."

"What?" I question.

Omar moves away and speaks. "Okay, look at my right hand." Omar slowly moves his index and middle finger.

I stare intently and immediately tear as I try to talk. "When? How long? What does this mean? Are you going to recover?"

"Calm down. We don't know yet, but it's a good sign. I have to do my exercises, and we'll see."

"Oh, my God, I've been praying so hard for this. I asked Idris to do a special prayer, and this is wonderful." I tightly embrace Omar. Beaming, I ogle him from top to bottom. Suddenly, my phone rings, and I instantly remember my dinner date with Rome.

"That's Rome." I look at my watch. "I should be pulling up at the restaurant about now." I rustle through my purse and grab my phone on the last ring.

"I'm on the way. I got held up."

"How long before you get here?" he asks.

"Fifteen minutes. I'll see you, bye." I quickly hang up before he can ask my whereabouts. "Omar, I have to go."

"I understand," he says peacefully.

"I promise I will think about everything you said. I'll call you tomorrow." I get in the car and crank up the engine. I pull away, leaving him standing in the parking lot.

Before I get onto the main street, I call Lia.

"Omar just poured his heart out. He says he loves me and wants us to be together."

"Blah-blah, what's new? Omar has always loved you, but he is troubled. So if you don't mind taking care of someone forever, go ahead and be with him."

"Well, aren't you clear-cut this evening?" I say.

"Gwen, we've been down this bridge. You have two men vying for your love. You need to decide before both of them realize you're insane and leave. Weigh the odds."

"I have. Rome is fun and sexy. We have lots in common, but he is a womanizer."

"People change, Gwen. You used to be an alcoholic, but not now."

"I still have the tendency. I think about it more than you know," I admit.

"But you resist the temptation because you've decided it's not worth it. It's the same thing with him. Just because he thinks about it, doesn't mean he'll act on it."

"Okay, well, it's not him, it's me. Guess what I did?" Lia is quiet as I confess. "I went through his phone to check his calls. I'm not that girl, but this is what I've been reduced to. I don't want a relationship like that, always wondering if he's with another woman."

"Then there's your answer. If you can't get over that, then you can't be with him. Is that what you want to hear?" Lia says with frustration.

"I just want you to understand where I'm coming from."

"I do. A girl must have her list of 'dos and don'ts,' and she can't compromise. I can get over trust, because hell, I used to be a ho. I'm still recovering, I found myself having daydream sex with this guy I saw at the gas station, but that's another story. Anyway, I can't tolerate a man that abuses and one that smokes weed. It's a deal breaker. If trust is a big issue with you, you may never get over Rome's infidelity. But that doesn't mean you should be with Omar."

"But Omar would never leave me, and he forgave me for everything. I almost killed him and then lied about it. That, right there, is a testimony of his love."

"I guess," she says.

"Things are different this time. Oh, and he's got some

movement in his hand. Though I would be with him, whether he is paralyzed or not. It would be nice if he weren't."

"Where are you headed, home?" Lia asks.

"No, I'm meeting Rome for dinner. He wants me to tell him my decision tonight. He's probably got someone waiting in the wings."

Lia asks, "Are you ready to be his babies' momma?"

"Don't say that."

"But that's what you'll be. You and Rome are cool now, but as soon as you get with Omar, things are going to change. You will be his babies' mother. You will have to deal with custody and you can't avoid it." I am silent as Lia continues. "Rome does love you. He has called me a million times about you. I know he is sorry, but you're the one who has to be convinced. I don't know what else to say."

"I know."

"Just don't get with Omar because you feel guilty. If you decide to be with him, let it be real," Lia asserts.

We are silent for a second as I travel to my destination of ultimate decision making. Just before she and I disconnect, Lia speaks.

"I went down on Idris last night. I couldn't help it. The slut spirit hit me while he was in the shower. As soon as I heard the water stop, I went in there and dropped to my knees."

"Okay . . . ," I respond with a trembling voice. "And so—"

"So we aren't supposed to have sex. I've been trying, Gwenie, but it's killing me. Between the no cursing and no orgasms, I'm flipping out. And you think you have problems."

"Have you talked to him?" I ask.

"Yes. He says it's hard on him, but that he wants to abstain until he gets married or at least engaged."

"Oh."

"What am I supposed to do?" Lia questions.

"Wait, I guess. This is the man you love. What did he do last night?"

"He tried to stop me at first, but then he just stood there and took his blow job like a man—a man who hadn't had a blow job in a very long time. I was hoping he would return the favor, but no."

"What did he say?"

"Wow," Lia responds. "Afterward, he just looked at me, kissed my forehead and said, 'Baby, I know it's hard, but we have to wait.' He could have said that after he hooked me up. Shit, Gwen, I'm horny as hell."

I softly giggle on the phone as I'm pulling into the restaurant. I attempt to wrap up the conversation. "Baby, I understand, but a woman that can't wait may be *his* deal breaker."

"But he tells me all these stories about what he used to do with different women. Idris is a freak; I just know it. I don't want to wait," Lia whines.

"Then tell him, and if he says good-bye, accept it." Lia huffs on the other line. "Baby, I'm here at the restaurant. I have to go. I promise I'll call you tonight."

I walk in the restaurant and we are seated within ten minutes and the first few are extremely formal. A few comments about the boys, their day and their plans for the week are the main topics. However, right after we order, I start.

"I know you want to talk about our relationship, but—"

"Actually, I don't want to discuss us. I just want to have a nice dinner," Rome interrupts. "I've never been able to make you rush. But that doesn't mean I'm waiting on you. I'm going to date other people. You should too; then I guess we'll see what happens."

I, shocked by his candor, simply lower my head toward the drink menu and grit my teeth. After moments of me silently perusing the cocktail list, Rome pushes it down to the table.

"You okay?"

"I am," I blurt out before going back to me menu.

"You don't drink. What are you doing?"

"I like to look at the funny names," I say.

Dinner is pleasant but filled with awkward silent moments as we both ponder each statement before speaking. As if I'm sitting across the table from a stranger, I don't recognize any of his tactics. Is this his defense mechanism, or has he found someone else?

This verbiage sounds too insecure, so instead I ask, "Are you over me?"

"Nope," he quickly replies.

Silence again befalls the table. I finish my last bit of food and contemplate dessert.

"You want dessert?" he asks.

"I don't think so," I respond.

Rome scans the short menu and also decides to decline.

He picks up the check and we walk to the car. We part and meet at the house. Still a little taken aback, I don't call anyone on the ride home. When I walk in the door, Omar rings my phone, but I don't pick up. I place my things down and we go into the room and peek in on the twins. They are both asleep. My phone rings again.

"Someone is really trying to reach you," he insinuates. I don't comment. I turn off my phone and toss it in my purse. While bringing his beer into the living room, I begin my talk.

"So how long have you been thinking about this dating thing? Don't get me wrong, I think it's a good idea. I was just wondering."

Rome takes a sip of his beer and replies, "Not long. Personally, I don't know how we will date and live under the same roof, but I figure since you aren't trying to forgive me, I have to move on. I'm the father of your kids, but I can't keep kissing your ass."

"I don't want you to kiss my ass," I comment.

"Well, that's how you're acting."

I walk back into the kitchen and stare into the refrigerator. Not that I'm hungry, it's the aimless wandering that occurs when I don't know what else to do. Rome walks in behind me and takes me by the waist.

"Maybe we aren't supposed to be together. I know you're thinking it, so you can't be mad."

"I'm not angry, and for the record, I do forgive you. I just have some issues I need to work out," I reply softly as we embrace.

Rose comes from the room and sees us. She immediately smiles and tiptoes back into her room. However, Rome notices and calls out. He walks from the kitchen and finishes his beer in the bedroom. Rose puts on some tea and saunters into the living room behind me.

"So, did you two have a nice dinner?"

I nod silently.

"So . . . ," she hints.

I only respond with a soft sigh.

"And what does that huff of hot air mean?"

"Nothing," I utter.

"Why don't you and Rome cut all this pride aside and be together?"

"It's not about pride. I don't trust him right now, and he's tired of waiting on me."

"Oh, so it's about timing. I can understand that. Sometimes it takes years to appreciate what you had."

I give my mom a peculiar look. "Are we still talking about me?"

"Of course," Rose says as she dances around to the couch and takes a seat. "I like Rome, but you have to like him."

"I do. I love him."

"Baby, love is simple, but forever is tricky."

"I hear that."

We sit back and mold our bodies into the soft leather. After a few minutes of silence, Rose speaks. "It's going to be hell raising the boys alone." I quietly nod as she continues.

"I don't want you to have to go through that. Do you really think this is best?"

"You know, I wouldn't have all these trust issues if you'd never left me."

"Yes, blame me for your craziness," Rose says with a sarcastic grumble. "Where's your aspirin? My head is—"

"I threw them all out."

"Why?"

"I have addictive tendencies. When I notice the signs, I take all precautions."

"Oh," Rose mumbles. "I just want you to be happy. I support you no matter what you do." Rose walks into the bedroom, but just before she closes the door, she announces, "I'll be going to see your father next week, hope you can do without me for a few days." I spring up just quick enough to see Rose close the door.

"Hey," I holler before I realize that my scream might wake the babies. As I pass Rose's room, I jiggle the door, but she has locked the room, asserting her power as Mom. All I can do is laugh.

Before seven the next morning, there is an overzealous knock on the door, followed by three doorbell rings. Rose is in the kitchen brewing coffee, but she quickly tosses her things down and rushes to answer the door.

"What's all the pandemonium?" she says, flinging open the heavy cherry wood.

On the other side is Lia, with her eyes nearly bugging from her cranium as she makes quick, tiny, repetitive jumps.

Thinking someone is after Lia, Rose grabs her arm, pulls her inside and closes the door. Before Rose can ask a question, Lia jams her left hand in the center of Rose's face. Though the sparkling princess-cut diamond is only a half-inch from the bridge of Rose's nose, she knows her jewelry.

"Is that a two-carat Asscher cut, with a 1.10 or higher ratio?"

"Hell yeah!" Lia yelps.

Rose takes her hand and studies the gem. "Good clarity, nice table, no cutlet . . . this is good." Rose holds Lia's diamond up to the light and checks out the reflection. "Very good symmetry grade. I think this might be a VS1."

"A VH1?" Lia questions.

"VS1, my dear. Very slightly included or flawed, that's the type of clarity. Of course you can't tell without magnification."

"But I wanted a flawless diamond," Lia whines.

"And I wanted a flawless man, but hey . . . ," Rose adds.

I drag myself from the bedroom and Lia runs and jumps in my face. "Look!"

I wipe the sleep from my eyes and focus on the sparkling stone. "So I guess you're getting married."

"Aren't you excited?" she asks.

I plaster a huge grin on my face.

"That's not real excitement, Gwenie!"

"It is," I say, barely acknowledging the ring and moseying into the kitchen. Rose follows close behind me and whispers in my ear, "Be happy for your friend."

"I am," I reply. "So when is the wedding?"

"We didn't get that far, he just asked me last night," Lia answers, walking in behind Rose.

With a very sincere smile, I say, "I am very excited about my friend finding a life mate. I wish you all the happiness in the world."

"Thank you." We hug as Lia extends her left hand from the embrace and holds it up to the light.

"It has a flaw, but only under a magnifying glass."

"It's okay that your diamond is not perfect, Idris is, and that's all that counts," I respond.

"I know." Lia beams.

17

The club finally gets a serious potential investment group—three Greek brothers who are interested in the space for a fraternal hall and event facility. They are willing to pay a little more than the asking price if Rome pays this year's taxes on the space and he can be out of there in a month. He agrees, and so now we wait on the paperwork. It looks like the deal is going to go through. Rome and I begin saying our good-byes to an era. Since our dinner a month ago, he has made no advances on me. I have officially moved into the other bedroom, and he is casually dating another young woman. Though he doesn't bring her to the house, I have my spies. The woman's name is Caitlan Kiel. She's an assistant to some big record executive. Her father's German and her mother is Senegalese. She's extremely attractive—the "trophy wife" type—right up Rome's alley. Surprisingly, I thought I would be more upset, but I'm not. It hurts each time someone calls me and says that he just saw Rome with some other girl, but I was always waiting for that call, even when we were together. So, really, it's never too shocking. There are days that I miss him terribly. Then there are days I figure we were meant to be friends. Those days normally happen when I spend time with Omar. I ration my time with him, though.

Besides, I don't have that much time, considering I am getting the club ready to be purchased and still raising my boys. Now that Rose has returned home for a while, the task of rearing my sons is challenging, and until I can get a handle on that, rekindling a relationship with Omar holds a distant second.

Lia is eagerly planning the wedding that will take place at Idris's church uptown and be officiated by his father. It's in eight months and I feel the entire courtship has been rushed, but wouldn't dare taint a second of Lia's happiness. It must be real, for Lia has been completely faithful. She doesn't even see Jasmine when she comes back to Detroit to visit. Even Jasmine, knowing the old Lia, tries to tempt her with a little afternoon delight, a dessert Lia has never been able to resist. However, after seven years, she no longer has a taste for that treat. We're all surprised.

In Lia's mind, she never quite deserved a man like Idris, but his goodness is slowly starting to make her feel good about the woman she is. Lia McNair is making a stab at the "forever thing," something she never thought she would do. Ironically, I, the friend who's always wanted a commitment, am feeling like forever is impossible. The tables have turned, and I hate to admit it, but I am a bit salty. Thankfully, the bitterness is sweetened by Lia's bliss. I am actually enjoying helping Lia shop for a wedding dress, which is a very demanding task. Lia changes her mind on the design every two days. If I can hold out until the end of the month, Rose will be back. Then I can start house hunting. There is no way Rome and I can continue to live together.

The planning for the big party bidding a final farewell to Ole Skool is well under way. Doug E. Fresh, Slick Rick and Big Daddy Kane are performing, and the radio ad is complete and will start airing this week. Placing the club's final liquor orders, I pause and accept the sentimental moment overwhelming me. This club holds so many memories for me. I remember the opening like it was yesterday, though it was eight years ago, a long time in nightclub years. Our goal was to make Ole Skool the largest adult nightspot in Detroit, and it was for years. However, change is inevitable. When Rome, Omar and I started the club, we were in our twenties, with nothing on our agenda but how to have the next great party. Things are poles apart now. As much as I will miss the club, I'm ready to do something new. Exactly what that is, I'm not sure, but it will not have anything to do with nightly activities. I want to be home with my boys, that is my main priority. I open the bottom drawer, pull out a stack of folders and place them in a cardboard box. I glance in the drawer and see the corner of a wooden frame. Staring at a photograph of me, Lia, Rome and Omar, a tiny smile creeps across my face. I rub my hand across my friends. I am so engrossed in the snapshot, I don't see Rome standing at the entrance of the door.

"Knock, knock," he says while tapping the door frame. I look up and give Rome a girlish giggle. I hold up the frame and motion for him to come closer. He takes it from my hand and laughs.

"Wow, look how everyone has changed. We don't even look like this anymore."

"I know," I concur. "Things are set for next weekend. Everyone is confirmed and all the food and drink orders are filled."

Rome pulls up a chair and scoots close. He places his hand in my lap and speaks. "Thank you, thank you for everything."

"This is my job," I say curtly.

Rome turns my chair around and caresses my forearm, bringing my brusque tone down one notch. "I mean thank you for everything. I appreciate you putting up with my new career and me. You are a great mother and I just . . . I love you."

I place another stack of papers in the box. "I love you too," I casually reply. Rome can see the protective armor surrounding my body, and he hasn't the energy to attempt penetration. He simply rises and leaves the office. I stare at the door minutes after he leaves. It's something about Rome that makes me weak, and each time he leaves a tiny portion of me follows.

"What is it about this man?" I whisper aloud. This question lingers throughout the day.

Later that week, Lia and I have a sleepover evening, some-thing we used to do often. We sit up and watch old movies while eating popcorn and chocolate. I get Jalen asleep by nine, and Jameel sits underneath Lia, as if he's her date. Halfway through the first movie, Lia starts talking, normal ritual for Lia. She never makes it through a movie without some sort of counseling session. Tonight's therapy topic is should she, or should she not, tell Idris about her sexual his-tory. However, before she can finish the sentence, I have a ready response.

"Hell no. Are you crazy?"

"But . . ."

"But nothing. I know you mean well, but when I saw how many partners you had, I looked at you sideways. Just imag-ine how your man is going to look. It's a bad idea," I warn her.

"I want to be honest, though."

"Has he asked you?"

"No," Lia replies.

"He doesn't want to know. Don't go volunteering extra in-formation. He might say he doesn't care, but trust me, he doesn't want to hear that the love of his life has had one hun-dred partners."

"Ninety-six," she corrects.

"Whatever, too damn many."

Lia is quiet for a few seconds as she contemplates my wise words. Then she asks, "What if he asks me?"

"He won't," I assure her.

"But he might."

"Idris knows you fooled around. If he didn't ask before he gave you the ring, I'm sure he's not going to ask after. But if he does, you better come up with a nice number under forty and remember it, just in case he asks you ten years later."

Lia takes a mental note and then speaks. "Maybe you are right. I won't say anything." Lia sits quietly, focusing on the tube. Jameel finally falls asleep and I take him into the bedroom. As soon as I walk back into the room, Lia starts up once more.

"So what are you going to do?"

"About what?"

"About your situation. You're in Rome's house, you still drive his car and you're not even with him anymore."

"I know. I'm going to start looking as soon as Mom gets here. I could get another lease, mine ended last month. But I do need more space."

"You and Rome will work it out. I feel it."

"Hush and watch the movie."

Lia grins, turns around and watches *The Bridges of Madison County.* However, Lia can't be quiet for too long. "You know what I think?"

"No, but I'm sure you're going to tell me."

"I think you love Omar, but you are in love with Rome. Omar's your safety net. If you get with him, it's only because you know he'll be there. That's not love, that's practicality."

I slowly turn to Lia, lower my tone and speak in a profound manner. "Everyone is not a risk taker, and that's okay. That doesn't mean they can't be happy." In the same mode, I return my focus toward the movie, and Lia is unbelievably quiet the remainder of the 135-minute feature.

Friday, before the big event at Ole Skool, Rose arrives in town. With babies in tow, I am circling the airport terminal.

Finally, I see the red bob popping in and out of the crowd of travelers. A surge of excitement rushes through my body when I catch my mom's eye. My therapist is right—the reconnection with Rose has been healing. Though I don't deny it, I certainly can't give Rose total credit for my attitude adjustment. Deep down, I still haven't gotten comfortable with Rose being around, for I'm always waiting for her next disappearing act. Unfortunately, the damage done may take years to repair, but these frequent visits are continuing to make a wonderful start. Rose tosses her things in the back of the BMW and hops in the front seat. She kisses me on the forehead and turns to the back to make googly faces at her four-month-old grandsons. I prepare to pull away from the curb, and then Rose halts me immediately.

"We have to wait for your father."

With an astonished look, I shriek, "What?" The shrill frightens Jalen and he begins to cry. "See what you did, you made me scare Jalen." Rose comforts him as I pull back over to the curb.

"I wasn't sure he was coming until yesterday. Won't this be nice?" Rose says with a big smile plastered across her freshly painted face.

With my eyes squinted and brows lowered, I stare. "What is going on?"

Innocently, Rose responds, "Your father wanted to come see you."

"We couldn't get Dad on a plane in over thirty years and now he just hops on a plane at a whim's notice 'cause he wants to come see me? You can do better than that."

"It's different when you have grandchildren. As elders, we don't have that long on earth. So we have to cherish every moment in our life."

"You are so full of it," I shout. "You and Daddy are having a fling!"

Blushing slightly, Rose runs her fingers through her bob and looks out the window.

I motion toward her hair fidgeting. "I also play with my hair when I want to avoid questioning."

Before I can finish, Rose hops from the car and scurries toward the airport doors. My eyes follow my mom's black low-heeled Mary Janes until they halt at a pair of brown suede Hush Puppies. My eyes slowly move up the embraced couple and I see Mom wrapped all over Dad. They both seem happy, but this hug gives me a bit of uneasiness.

"Oh God, he's wearing that stupid cap," I whisper.

When I was younger, Marvin used to wear this old black fedora whenever he would go out on dates. He would tilt it to the left and pull it down just over his left eyebrow. Today it is at full tilt, which makes me very nervous.

When we arrive at the house, Marvin conveniently leaves his bags in Rose's room. I say nothing, but notice everything. His step has more pep and his grins are long-lasting. If my love life weren't so jacked up, I would have plenty to say, but I am in no position to give love advice. However, these Detroit rendezvous will not continue without some explanation.

Rose prepares dinner and I realize how much I have missed my mom over the last few weeks. Though I offer to help, Rose insists that I rest and prepare for the party tomorrow night. I do just that. I pull out my new dress and search through my closet to find the perfect pair of shoes. It's then that I realize the perfect pair is still at the store. I rush to the phone, call Lia and ask her to go shopping tomorrow morning. Lia obliges and picks me up at nine, Saturday morning.

I arrive at Ole Skool an hour before the club is scheduled to open and there are already people mingling in the parking lot. "It is going to be a busy night," I whisper. Before I can get a foot in the door, half the staff is calling my name. Marcus, one of the bar backs, is taking cases from the back and pulling them closer to the bar, and Michelle is preparing the greenroom for the artists. Bartenders are cutting lemons and limes, filling ice bins and placing all the liquor bottles on the shelf. From nowhere, Rome appears and pulls me to the back office. He closes the door and stares at me.

"What's wrong?" I question.

Rome continues to look with an awkward half smile, half frown, and replies, "This is the last night."

"And we are going out with a bang," I say with a huge grin. Rome's face fills with lament.

"What if this is a mistake? The club has been my bread and butter. What if this video stuff doesn't work out?"

"What are you talking about? It is working. Ole Skool has had its run. We need a change. You can always open another club if you want." Rome doesn't respond and so I continue. "This is a great idea. Look at the money you will get at the closing. You're going to buy more equipment. Why are you tripping?"

"'Cause I've always been in the nightclub business. I feel crazy giving it up."

"How many careers have you had?" I ask.

"Doesn't matter, I've always had a club to fall back on. Now with the kids, this may be a mistake."

Vulnerability is a rare thing for Rome, but it is written all over his face tonight. I only know one way to respond. I stretch my arms out, grasp his shoulders and pull him into my chest. I hold tight. "We'll be more than fine—wonderful, in fact," I whisper, and then quickly hear my own words and wonder why I said "we." I release and look at Rome, whose smile still has a bit of a grimace. I lower my head, lift my eyes to his and wink. Just like that, his scowl disappears.

"It's gonna be hot tonight, right?" he says.

"That's what I'm trying to tell you," I respond.

Rome nods and smiles brighter.

"That's what I'm talking about, stop this sulking."

Rome leans over and kisses my cheek. "Sam should be here with Doug E. Fresh and Rick by ten P.M. I need to get to the front."

"Who's running cash tonight?" I ask.

"Moo Moo," Rome answers.

"Okay, I'll be back and forth, posted near bar 2."

"Good. Long as we watch the show together."

I nod and Rome leaves. I check the change in the safe and call Moo Moo on the walkie-talkie. We discuss the money runs from the front cash box to the safe. I grab my keys and leave the office. Before I can get to bar 2, Lia calls my cell. She and Idris are at the back door, so I let them in. As soon as the parking-lot minglers see the back door open, they rush to the steel exit.

"The line is in the front," I yell. And though a partygoer offers me an extra $50 to avoid the line, I simply close the door as soon as Idris steps in.

"Idris? I didn't think you were coming."

"Preaching the Gospel has nothing to do with Big Daddy Kane. Are you kidding?" Idris bursts into a few lines of "Smooth Operator." Lia and I snigger at his cute, but very corny, demeanor.

"Do you need me to do anything?" Lia asks.

"No, the doors are just opening, go enjoy yourself. Tonia and Andre are inside somewhere."

Idris and Lia walk toward the front and I continue making my rounds.

By 10:00 P.M., Ole Skool is wall-to-wall packed. Around the stage, people are clamoring, and the show is about to begin. All three artists are chilling in the greenroom, along with me, Lia and Idris. The host, a local disc jockey, announces Slick Rick and the bodyguard escorts him to the stage. Instantly, the club time-warps back to 1988. He starts the show with "Mona Lisa" and amps the crowd. Though

Rome and I are supposed to watch the show together, I can't find him in the crowd of people. However, as Slick ends "Children's Story," Omar gently wraps his arm around my waist. Shocked to see him here, I freeze before gently warming up to his embrace. I want to ask him why he's here, but I know why. He is a huge Doug E. Fresh fan and half of Detroit is in the place tonight. It's too loud to talk, so I stand by his side and continue to watch the show. An hour later, Doug E. Fresh is in the middle of his infamous call-and-response segment and the audience level is almost unbearable. His stage performance has everyone in the club feeling sixteen again. Lost in the moment, I notice the time and rush to the door to meet Moo Moo. Quickly, we make the cash run to the back and place the envelope in the safe. Minutes later, I am back in the front, enjoying the show. With my arm draped around Omar's shoulder, we laugh and sing along. And then I notice a beer in his hand. Just as I am about to ask about the drinking, I see Rome at the bar staring at me. Though the club is packed, there is a direct beeline from my eyes to his. Almost as though his X-ray vision is parting the crowd, I feel his pensive stare. Though I'm doing nothing wrong, I instantly feel guilty. I move a few inches from Omar and turn toward the stage. A few seconds later, Rome is not there. Readjusting my position, I try to see through the dense audience, but I don't see him.

Omar notices my distraction and questions my uneasiness. I point to his beer. With a nonchalant expression, he whispers in my ear, "It's just a beer." I frown and shake my head in disapproval. He finishes the last drop, leans in and whispers again, "That was my only one. No more." I glare harder. Omar gives a boyish grin and kisses my cheek. "I'm good," he promises.

I focus my attention back to the stage and spot Idris a few feet ahead; I move forward. Omar follows, but somehow he loses me in the crowd. I meet Marissa by the stage just before

Big Daddy Kane opens his show. Immediately, Marissa tightly wraps her arms around me. She tells me that they've arrested two guys suspected of Tracy's murder. We share a moment of liberation before I grace the stage to dedicate tonight's event to Tracy. Afterward, I find Tonia and Andre in the crowd. I stay with them the remainder of the show.

After 1:00 A.M., the show ends and it was phenomenal. The crowd chants, "Encore!" As I make my way back toward the greenroom, I run into Rome. He smiles, but I see underneath the veneer. However, I'm not about to apologize for doing nothing—especially since he's been running all over town with God knows whom. Therefore, I immediately jump into business.

"The drivers are around back. They have directions to the hotel, right?"

"They do," he answers.

"Where are the guys?" I ask.

Rome points out front and then I hear a melody of freestyle rhymes coming through the walls.

"The show was incredible."

"It was," Rome curtly responds.

I look at my watch. "I have to meet Moo Moo." Just then, Rome grabs my arm and spins me around. He passionately presses his lips against mine. The rousing kiss catches me off my guard. When our lips disconnect, I am light-headed. Without a word, I leave the office and do my cash run with Moo Moo.

Around 2:30 A.M., the crowd dissipates to around one hundred people. Tonia and Andre left a while ago and Lia and Idris are leaving now. Rome goes with the artists to the hotel and I am doing my normal club rounds. I check with each of the bartenders to make sure they are putting up the liquor, which stops serving in one minute and then I run into Omar at bar 3. He sits alone drinking another beer. I, the constant caretaker, go to his side. I take the beer from his hand.

"What is this, O?"

He snickers, but doesn't answer.

"Are you drunk?"

Again he doesn't respond. I feel myself getting angry. I walk behind the bar and dump the remainder in the sink. When I pass by him, he grabs my arm.

"Stop it, Omar."

"Come on. I just want to dance," he insists.

"Whom did you come here with? How are you getting home?"

"Marissa is around here somewhere. Unless you want to take me home," he suggests.

"No. I can't believe you're drinking again."

"This is why I need you, Gwen. You keep me straight."

"Me? My hands are full keeping me together." Then I finally say what I should have said long ago: "Omar, I am not responsible for you."

"No, but you are responsible for this," he says, pointing to his paralyzed arm.

My eyes water. "Why are you being unfair?"

"Me? What's not fair is the fact that I used to have you. What's not fair is that I used to have this hot-ass career. What's not fair is that I used to be able to give hugs. I can see women look at me and smile. But as soon as they see I can't move my arm, they walk the other way. That's not fair. This whole club shit was my idea! Do you remember that? I told Rome we should do this shit! He has taken my whole fucking life." Omar's voice grows louder and people are starting to look. From my peripherals, I see Tina, the bartender, leave and walk toward the front. About fifteen seconds later, Moo Moo is rounding the corner. I take Omar by the hand.

"You are out of control. I can't believe you sat up here and got drunk." Moo Moo follows close behind. I take Omar to the greenroom and shut the door. Moo Moo knocks on the door.

"Gwen, you okay?" he asks.

"I'm good."

Omar plops down in the seat. He is a mess. I kneel by his side. My temper lowers as I try to reason with him.

"I don't know why life deals us blows. But you still have so much more to be thankful for. You have a sports bar, and you are getting feeling back in your arm."

Omar lays his head on my shoulder and slurs, "I just miss you so much. You make me want to do right."

"I know, baby," I whisper, and give in to his need. I slightly rub the nape of his neck and comfort him. He's like my baby, always has been. Ironically, this feeds my innate nurturing quality. It's comfortable, but it's also detrimental.

"We should just get married," Omar mutters.

At that moment, I realize that I could marry Omar tomorrow and probably be with him forever. At the same time, I remember why I walked away four years ago. This is not the kind of relationship I want.

"So what's up?" he says.

My smile disappears. "I can't marry you. In theory, you and I seem great. But this relationship is not good for me. I'm sorry, it just isn't."

Omar grabs my wrist. "But—"

"As much as I care about you, I'm not that person anymore. I'm sorry, but I don't owe you. I have to go."

Omar stands and speaks. "So you just gon' leave me?"

I slowly walk toward the door as Omar's voice grows louder. "Huh, Pop! You gon' walk out on me?" He rushes behind me and raises his hand to strike me. I tightly grab his wrist and give him the most evil glare he's ever witnessed. He quickly catches himself, and is suddenly aware of his behavior. "I'm sorry. I'm sorry, please don't go," he begs.

I continue out of the room and shut the door, leaving Omar's yells echoing. "You gon' leave me!" As I step a few feet from the door, I feel the tears forming in the corners of my eyes. I hasten to the office, and as soon as the door shuts,

I break down. I release a river of emotion for ten minutes. Then as quickly as it started, it's over. I wipe my face, pull it together and walk back into the club. I walk up to Moo Moo and ask him to check on Omar in the greenroom. Moments later, he returns with news that Omar is not there. I quickly canvass the club, but then give up. Omar is an adult and I have to let go in order to move on. I finally get it.

Ten minutes before close, Rome gets back. Moo Moo and his crew escort the few patrons out and Ole Skool closes its doors for the last time. I am exhausted. I go into the office and begin counting the money. But before I can finish, my eyes are dozing, and a minute later, I'm asleep. Thirty minutes pass before Rome opens the office door and sees me napping. He carefully lifts my body from the desk chair and walks me to the couch. Just as he places me down, my eyes pop open.

"What time is it?" I ask.

"Almost five," he replies. "I'm done here. How are you getting home?"

"I'm driving," I say.

"You okay to drive?"

"I am," I answer.

Rome looks at the half-counted money and says, "I'll finish up, you go home, and call me when you get there."

Without hesitation, I go to the closet and grab my things. As I'm leaving, Rome adds, "Tonight wouldn't have happened without you."

With classic Gwen sarcasm, I respond, "Sure it would have, but it would have been a mess." I leave, but on the ride home, I still worry about Omar. Tons of questions seep in and out of my mind. Did he get home okay? How long is he going to stay angry? Is he going to heal? Does he forgive me? Why isn't love enough?

Once home, it takes me two hours to nod off to sleep. The only thing that brings me comfort is that I am able to release some of the remorse. I begin thinking about my sons, our well-being and my crazy parents. Finally, sleep brushes across my lids and I fade out. Just before the slumber takes full control, I smile while thinking how proud Dr. Bourceau is going to be. My appointment is Monday morning and I can't wait to give her progress. Forgiveness has never been a big winner with me. Once I'm burned, that's pretty much it. It's especially hard to pardon the ones I love. But tonight I forgive the person I love most, me. I know this one act is going to start the chain reaction of many more acts of clemency.

"This is big," I whisper during my drifting off. Within seconds, I am asleep.

FORGIVENESS
Session Ten

Ever since I was little, I've had a problem with forgiving people, just like trusting. The two go hand in hand. I remember when my friend Tamika stole a pair of my Barbie doll's shoes. We used to spend every day after school together, but after that day, I never spoke to her again. My dad would encourage me to go over there, but I just couldn't, even after she gave the shoes back. As I got older, it got worse. If someone did me wrong, that was it. I give new meaning to the phrase "Fool me once . . ."

After my mom left, it was a wrap. I would imagine people doing me wrong, and then push them away before they actually did anything. It soon became paranoia. I thought the whole world was against me, always prepped to hurt me. After my mom left, it took me an extremely long time to get close to anyone. Which is why I'm so surprised that I've let her back in so easily. I sometimes stare at her from across the room and imagine myself hurling large porcelain saucers in her direction, just to watch her dodge them. *I don't want to cause her bodily harm; I just want her to know how it feels to always be on guard. I haven't forgiven her, but I'm happy she's around. It's hard to explain. But there's not a second that she's in my presence that I don't think about that last hug she gave me when I was twelve. Every time she touches me, I think it might be another fifteen or twenty years before I see her again. So no, I haven't forgiven her and I'm not sure if I want to. She did what she did and it was messed up, that's that.*

When it comes to Rome, I don't know how to feel. He messes up 'cause it's part of his character, not because he's trying to be spiteful. I'm an adult now, and I can understand it a little better. But it doesn't make me feel better about it. The worst blows are the ones to the heart. It's shitty when you hand someone your heart, and they caress it, kiss it and make it beat to a better rhythm, only to turn around and place tiny paper cuts in its side. Paper cuts aren't visible, but the unbearable pain stings for days. As for the heart, it's years. Imagine someone slicing across the bridge of your heart—could you forgive him or her? Well, I can't. So back to Rome, I vowed never to be one of his kills—and yet, I fell into the trap. I'm finding it impossible to forgive myself for falling for him. I set myself up for the pain, so who's to blame? I want to blame Rome, but I can't. He would never do anything to hurt me on purpose. He's been taking care of me since I was eight.

Which brings me to Omar. I've finally forgiven myself for what I did to him. It was a mistake and people make mistakes. Forgiving myself helps me understand this phrase much better. Omar is still struggling with his addiction, but that's not my responsibility. I did all I could do, and I have to accept that. He still has the bar. Moo Moo's the manager. Although I pass it often, I haven't stopped by. I think distance is best, at least for now.

Finally, if I want to stop pushing people out of my life,

I have to learn how to forgive. I've lost so many associates and friends, people who were good to me, good for me. I felt I was better off without them, but I was wrong. I know I'm not better off without Rome. I just don't know how to start over. Rose being here is the start of it, though, the beginning of me wanting to forgive, or excuse. My sons are the biggest reason. They are bound to hurt me over the years, but I can't exclude them if they do. That would be insane. Yes, the desire is definitely there, which is big. But I must now put my longing into practice.

Session Done

18

Monday afternoon when I return from my appointment, I see Rome's truck in the driveway. I walk into the house to see him sitting on the floor playing with his sons. Rose waltzes from the kitchen, eating a Popsicle.

"I never used to eat these things, but since I've been here, I really like them."

"That better not be my last one," I state.

"Hush your pot and, come on, let's get ready to go."

"Where are we going?"

"To eat, but we have to make a stop first."

Rose nods toward Rome and then walks in the bedroom.

"Was she acting weird to you?" I ask.

"I have to tell you something," says Rome.

I perk up and take notice of his grave tone.

"Your mom and your dad are back in love."

"What?"

"For some reason, they thought you would take the news better from me. They're getting married."

"Who is?" I question with a curt tone.

"Rose and Marvin."

I squint at Rome and then release a loud chortle.

"Ain't nobody getting married."

"No, for real," he comments.

I immediately rise and bang on my mother's bedroom door. Rose flings the door open and faces me.

"Why are you messing with my dad?"

"I'm not messing with your father, as you put it. I love him and we have decided that we want to be together again."

"Well, I don't think that's a good idea," I say.

"Lucky for us, we don't need your approval," Rose says as she wraps her gold Pashmina around her neck and walks into the kitchen. I continue to banter with my mother.

"Why didn't you just say something? Why bring Rome into this?"

"He's part of the family," states Rose.

Just then, Marvin walks into the home. I quickly shift my attention toward him.

"Dad! What are you doing?" I ask.

Rome grabs Jameel and Jalen and takes them into their room.

"We have to talk, you can't marry her." I push my dad into the bedroom and shut the door. "What is going on? It's one thing for you guys to be fooling around, but married?"

Marvin takes a seat on the edge of the bed and tries to calm my frantic behavior. "Have a seat, baby doll." With my arms folded, I continue to pace the floor, but Marvin takes me by the hand and stills me. "I thought you and your mother were getting along?" he inquires.

"We get along fine, but you don't need to marry her. She's unstable. She just got divorced. How do you know she really loves you? What if she leaves again?"

"Gwendolyn, calm yourself. I think I can make my own decisions, so just calm yourself," he repeats.

I take a seat beside my father and place my head on his shoulder. I whisper, "I worry about you. I don't want you to get hurt."

"Baby doll, I will be fine. I could marry your mom and she

could leave this earth three days after. I can't worry about that. Nothing is guaranteed. What I do know is, right now, she is the woman I want in my life. And at fifty-eight, right now is all that counts."

"But—"

"Life is too short to spend years wondering what could happen. That doesn't mean go out and make stupid decisions, but you have to trust yourself sometimes. Trust that you know what's best for you. Now, I've prayed about this, and if this is okay with me and God, you're going to have to get over it." Marvin grabs his tie from the edge of the dresser. I sit on the bed, staring at the baby blue wall. "Your mom has a good heart."

"She does, but she's crazy," I respond.

"Where do you think you get it from?" Marvin says, looking over his shoulder and giving me a wink. I walk up behind him and straighten his tie. With my chin propped on his shoulder, we stare at each other in the mirror. His deep voice lowers another octave when he speaks. "Everyone deserves a second chance, Gwendolyn."

I poke out my bottom lip and squint my eyes.

"Don't you think so?" he asks.

Slowly, I nod my head, kiss his temple and we leave the bedroom hand in hand. Rose and Rome sit in the living room, quietly waiting. When I walk out, I walk directly up to Rose.

Only my left brow rises when I speak. "You better take care of him. I mean it, lady. I know how to get to New York."

"New York? We're moving in here with you," Rose states with a serious tone.

"What!" I yelp.

Rose nudges past me and hugs Marvin. "I'm joking, honey. Can we go get married now?" Rome and I grab the boys and we head downtown to the courthouse.

"Hell, I guess black *is* the new white." I chuckle softly.

During the ceremony, I continually think about my dad's

words, and every time I glance at Rome, he is staring at me. As though he is reading my thoughts, his eyes are asking for another chance. I try to avoid his random glimpses, but even when I'm not looking, I can feel his ogling. It continues throughout dinner and into the evening. Rose and Marvin go to Rochester and stay at the Royal Park Hotel, a newlywed present from Rome. This way, the remarried couple can have a few days of privacy, enjoy the golf course and the spa. Plus, I couldn't bear to stay in the house and listen to their sex sounds bouncing off the walls. However, this leaves Rome and me alone. By 7:00 P.M., I feel the tension mounting. I have things to say, he has things to say, but neither one of us knows how to begin. Therefore, we walk around each other for at least two hours as we play with our boys and watch television. Finally, when the twins are asleep, there are no more distractions to keep us busy. We sit on opposite ends of the couch and watch a comedy on HBO. Though it's not a bit funny, we keep our focus forward and watch intently. Thirty minutes of silence pass, and I know that if anyone is to speak first, it has to be me. Rome has said all he is going to say, and I must make the first move. With my body curled up in the seat, I bite my bottom lip and take in a deep breath.

At last, I speak. "I don't want to move out."

Rome takes a few seconds before responding, but when he does, he takes the same approach. He keeps his focus on the television screen and replies, "Does that mean you trust me?"

"It means I want to," I say, taking a glance in his direction. Rome is quiet. "I miss my friend," I continue. He walks to the opposite end of the sofa and kneels in between my legs. Rome lays his head in my lap and whispers, "If you let me, I promise to take care of your heart."

He wraps his arms around my waist. I gently scratch the back of his freshly shaven head and he snuggles closer between my legs. The harder he squeezes, the more I fear. How-

ever, I'm not running this time. I am going to take a chance.
Rome takes my hand and motions toward my bedroom.

"I'll be in there in a minute," I mutter. I walk into the boys'
room and cover each of them with blankets. I kiss Jalen, and
whisper, "You look just like your daddy."

I begin to beam, flip off the light and grab a Popsicle from
the fridge. I lean against the counter, taking licks from the last
banana Pop in the house.

Silently, I pray, *Okay, God, I'm stepping out on faith. If I'm
going to be with this man, I need you to make him act right.*

Just then, Rome calls from the bedroom. "Gwen, what are
you doing?"

I walk out of the kitchen and retort softly, "I'm talking to
God about your crazy behind, I said I'd be there in a minute."
I sit on the couch, cross my legs and finish my treat. *See, God,
that's what I'm talking about. He thinks he's going to boss me
around, and that's not going to work.* Just then, Rome comes
from the bedroom. Wearing only boxers. He struts across the
living room and snatches me up from the couch. I playfully
slap his back.

"Put me down, you bully."

Rome says nothing as he carries me into the bedroom.

"Put me down, I'm not done talking to God."

"Don't worry, you're about to scream his name over and
over again. I promise."

"Romulus Sutton, don't play with the Lord. He doesn't like
that. I'm serious."

He places me down on the other side of the bedroom
threshold. Softly holding my face within his hands, he kisses
each cheek. "One day at a time," he whispers.

"Yes, and hopefully—" I comment.

"3,520 days later—" Rome interjects.

"I won't have killed you?" I interrupt.

Rome chuckles. "No. We'll still be taking it one day at a
time."

"Yeah, yeah, same thing." I respond with a grin.

Rome kisses me and pulls me into the bedroom, and 284 days later, Jameel and Jalen welcome their baby sister, Saidah Rose Sutton. Rome and I still aren't married, but an elopement could be in the near future. Rome did, however, add another diamond to my ring. It's gorgeous, but completely flawed— just like our relationship. But who cares? Flawed diamonds still last forever. So that means there's hope for us yet.